Always in September

SEASONS OF INTRIGUE

BOOK ONE

Always in September

Doris Elaine Fell

CROSSWAY BOOKS

A DIVISION OF GOOD NEWS PUBLISHERS

WHEATON, ILLINOIS • NOTTINGHAM, ENGLAND

Cover illustration: Chuck Gillies

First printing 1994

First British Edition 1994

ISBN 1-85684-093-X

Production and Printing in the United States of America for
CROSSWAY BOOKS
Norton Street, Nottingham, England NG7 3HR

Library of Congress Cataloging-in-Publication Data
Fell, Doris Elaine.
   Always in September / Doris Elaine Fell.
      p.   cm.
     1. Women journalists—France—Paris—Fiction. 2. Terrorism—
France—Paris—Fiction. 3. Americans—France—Paris—Fiction.
4. Terrorists—Canada—Fiction. I. Title.
PS3556.E4716A49 1994   813'.54—dc20   93-11682
ISBN 0-89107-760-X

02		01		00		99		98		97		96		95		94
15	14	13	12	11	10	9	8	7	6	5	4	3	2	1

Dedicated to
Mom's friends and mine.
These friendships meant even more to us
than beautiful, mountain-rimmed Harrison Lake.
Wilma Buzzard and her kids:
Suzanne & Lynda
Gene & Gary
and to
Sheila & Ron Cragg
Carole & Bill Page
And especially Carol & George Pappas
who shared the final hours
of Mom's journey with me.
. . . . .
And in memory of Mom
Edith C. Lavett
(January 19, 1898–February 16, 1990)
and my friend
Helen C. Crawford
(June 18, 1897–January 23, 1993)

Prologue

Porter Deven fought chest pain as he took the steps two at a time to his office in the Parisian high-rise. Reaching the empty corridor on the fifth floor, he vowed again to shake the thirty-five pounds that made his ruddy face pudgy and his thick neck bulge.

Satisfied that he was alone, he moved stealthily down the hall, his squeaky left shoe breaking the silence. He inserted his passkey in the door marked DEVENSHIRE CORPORATION and entered. Once inside, he locked the door and glanced at the wall clock. Five minutes to go. He had cut it close. Drew Gregory's call would come through at seven. Gregory was punctual.

Porter sucked in his breath as he opened the blinds and stared out on the city he had come to love—bleak this morning in the January winds. Other than Paris and his floppy-eared basset hound, Porter loved nothing—not even his job as Station Chief with American intelligence. Below him unending traffic sped insanely along the boulevard. Ongoing construction threatened his view of the heart of Paris. Still, in the distance he could distinguish familiar century-old spires, turrets, red mansard rooftops, and the bright awnings of sidewalk cafes. Central to these, the tranquil Seine took a winding path between the Right and Left Banks of the city. Off to one side, the glare of a hazy sun reflected off the Eiffel Tower; its iron girders looked to

Porter like a steel pagoda constructed from a kid's giant Erector set—much like the one he had built as a boy, the one his father had toppled with the toe of his boot.

The blare of the phone splintered his moment of reflection. He spun around, loosening his collar as he slumped into his worn leather chair, the only comfortable piece of furniture in the room. He caught the phone on the second ring.

His thick moustache twitched as he said, "Deven speaking."

"You sound winded, Porter. It better be important to get us both up this early on a Sunday." Drew Gregory's monotone voice came across the wires from London, a no-nonsense kind of man without even a trickle of laughter.

"Initiate secure key," Porter ordered. He flicked on the scrambler and said brusquely, "Ebsworth's back in town."

"Ryan Ebsworth?" Drew asked. "You're certain?"

"In from Canada. Checked into the Hotel de Crillon this morning."

"That sounds like his usual good taste."

"But he's too close to the American embassy for comfort, Drew."

"Then you're expecting trouble?"

Porter grunted, his anger rising. "Every time Ebsworth's in town, something major happens. The last time it was a bombing."

"But no way to tie it to him?"

"None," Porter admitted. "But with these recent threats of terrorism against the European Community, Ebsworth's timing worries me."

"How's security at the embassy?" Drew asked.

"Heavy since that second bomb threat in Madrid. We've advised our embassy personnel here to keep a low profile." Porter shifted, drumming his fingers against the desktop. "These relaxed border crossings may be good for a United Europe, but they're a menace to us. It makes it too easy to target Americans."

"Ebsworth still needs a Canadian passport."

"Not if he's carrying false identification. With his fluent French and German, he could pass for a European easily."

"Maybe you're attaching too much importance to him, Porter."

"He's my link to something bigger. It's who Ryan Ebsworth knows that's important. I'm convinced his contact is here in Paris right under our noses." Porter didn't risk adding that intelligence reports indicated a continual flow of illegal weapons to the Middle East. Ebsworth might be the courier.

"Have you notified French Security or the Canadian embassy?"

"No, Drew, but we've stepped up our own watch on Ebsworth."

"That's good, but what about Sherman Prescott—that young American who lost his wife? If Ebsworth is back in Paris, Sherm Prescott won't be far behind him."

"Yes, we've checked with Prescott's secretary. She said he's flying out of San Antonio on a business trip to Europe this week."

Drew pierced Porter's ear with a quick, low whistle. "Then he is heading our way."

"That's what disturbs me. Mr. Prescott is like a bloodhound tracking Ebsworth."

"Can you blame him?" asked Drew.

"Amateurs like Prescott make our work harder. If something major is building over here, the man could be endangering his own life. The more Prescott knows about Ryan Ebsworth, the more we risk him uncovering our whole operation."

"If we told Prescott the truth about his wife, he'd back off."

"And break international security?"

"Porter, be reasonable. The man's wife was murdered."

"And if he knew the truth, he'd go for Ebsworth's jugular. The record on Melody Prescott stands: death by drowning."

"According to Mr. Prescott, Olympic swimmers don't drown. He won't rest until he clears up his questions."

"We want answers, too," Porter reminded Drew. "And Ebsworth is our man. We can place him twice in Paris when something major blew. Once in Angola. And back in Canada when those classified documents were passed." Porter couldn't keep the bitterness from his voice. "*You* blew the Canadian operation, Drew, but I still want the Parisian who received those documents. Ryan Ebsworth knows who that man was. And he knows whether Prescott's wife was involved."

"Not involved, Porter. An innocent victim."

"I don't know that for certain."

"But I do," Drew shot back.

Ignoring Drew's irritation, Porter continued, "Do I need to remind you that we can place Sherman Prescott in Canada and Paris at the same times? And if he's enroute here now with threats of terrorism erupting, we won't be able to protect him."

"You'd waste him?"

Porter could picture the crow's-feet lines around Drew's eyes drawn taut, the piercing gray-blue gaze suddenly cold and cynical, his patience rubbed raw. But Drew's tone was controlled when he spoke. "So that's it. All this time you've thought the Prescotts were involved."

"Only his wife."

"We both know differently, Porter."

"Drew, I need you here to make certain that Mr. Prescott doesn't ruin things for us."

"I thought I was over the hill now, Porter—too old for anything but a desk job here in London. Find someone else to do your footwork."

As Drew's venom seeped over the phone wires, Porter curbed his own anger. "I'm ordering you back into action, Drew."

Drew paused—a momentary delay. "I can tidy things up here in London by the end of the week. Is that soon enough?"

"Sooner if you can."

"And Ryan Ebsworth in the meantime?" Drew scoffed.

"Under twenty-four-hour surveillance."

"Make it twenty-six and you won't lose him this time."
With that the phone went dead.

Porter swiveled his chair and stared out on Paris again, his anger slowly subsiding. Ever since Porter had made Station Chief, a shock to both of them, Drew had put distance between them. Porter at forty-seven had youth to his advantage, but Drew Gregory had the better service record—no shadowy clouds like the ones that haunted Porter. Drew was the straight-shooter; he was gutsy, but he was honest and fair.

Now they were at odds. Drew's belligerence was evident whenever he took Porter's orders. They had their different strategies. They had fought their separate wars—Porter as an intelligence officer still living the bitter memories of Vietnam, Drew as a frightened seventeen-year-old in the thick of the Normandy Invasion.

Porter snatched an emery board from his vest pocket and jabbed at his thumbnail, brooding. He and Drew were both guarded, enigmatic men. But it was Drew's binding cord of integrity, an unbending rod of steel, that would one day be Drew's downfall. Or worse, ruin Porter himself. Right now he needed Drew Gregory, but he despised the man.

Chapter 1

The jaws of the massive iron gate clamped shut behind Andrea York as she accelerated her second-hand Porsche. Breaking the five-mile speed limit in the underground garage, she roared into her empty parking space. In the deathly stillness, she glanced around and then let herself into the building. Alone, late at night, she felt skittish in the darkened building with its creaky elevator.

She ran up the stairs instead. As she hurried down the corridor, the muffled voices of her neighbors broke the silence—people she still didn't know. Stepping into the solitude of her own apartment, she bolted the door and kicked off her shoes. One shoe flew into the air and landed toe-up against its mate. Her ankle ached as it always did after a long day at *Style Magazine*.

Andrea went straight to her bedroom, flipping on lights along the way. Well-lit rooms comforted her—dispersing the shadows and lessening the intense isolation she felt this evening. For a week now, she had kept late nights at her office in Beverly Hills, purposefully keeping her desk cleared, her fashion articles and designs on target. She didn't want to be overwhelmed with the work load when she got back from her trip abroad. But was Paris worth this exhaustion? She smiled faintly. Paris was worth it.

Lately she had thought of little else. In five days she would escape the patchy smog that clung to Los Angeles and wing her way toward the Champs-Élysées. She had the coveted assignment to the "City of Light"—three weeks studying French fashion and browsing in the haute-couture boutiques. Her family saw Paris as a feather in Andrea's cap; to Andrea it was another rung higher on the corporate ladder, another mile closer to her personal goals. All of it expense-free, thanks to Rand Jordan, publisher at *Style Magazine*.

The lonely apartment lost its feeling of entrapment as she whirled around in her stocking feet and pirouetted across imaginary clouds. Finally, she stopped dancing, her ankle pain suddenly unbearable. She slipped off her jeweled watch and jade ring and hung them on the jewelry rack. Then she stripped, scattered her clothes across the bed, and headed for the sunken tub and whirlpool.

Walking into her dressing room was like stepping into a delicately scented garden. She loved the lingering fragrance of her Yves Saint-Laurent perfume, the dusting powders and bath gels and the scented oils and lotions with their Lancome labels. Even the basket of silk flowers on the wall smelled faintly of the damask rose petals her grandmother had put there.

Andrea crossed the room barefoot to the pullman counter, her manicured toes curling on the cold pink tiles. She flipped on the radio for the eleven o'clock news, her mind steeled against any reminders of drive-by shootings in Los Angeles or of unrest and terrorism in Europe. She hoped to hear tomorrow's weather report, Stefan Edberg's latest tennis scores, and perhaps a human-interest story.

"This is Todd Owen," the radio voice said, "filling in tonight for . . . "

Someone was always filling in for her favorite commentator. Owen's voice droned on. "Desert life is returning to normal after last night's 6.4 quake . . . "

The telephone rang. Andrea turned on the brass faucets over the tub and allowed the water to drown out the ringing. Her answering machine would pick up the call. She was back at her counter, staring at herself in the gold-gilt mirror.

She cleansed her face, wiping away the makeup, uncov-

ering tired circles under her eyes and a faint wash of freckles across her cheeks.

Andrea leaned forward and glared at the freckles. She
didn't look like a stunning, ambitious fashion journalist in
her mirror. Instead, she saw a hint of that freckled-faced kid
she so despised, the one who made her look younger than
her twenty-six years. With the makeup facade gone, she felt
vulnerable, her soul naked and exposed as her body was
now.

Andrea gently applied a minty cream facial and slipped
into the whirlpool bubbles of the tub. As the steamy water
washed over her, taking the pressures of the long day with
it, she placed slices of cucumber over her eyelids and
relaxed. The minutes ticked away. Slowly, even the pain in
her left leg and ankle eased.

She dropped the cucumber slices on the tub ledge, her
eyes refreshed and tingling now. She had been born a
footling breech with an injured ankle. "Born backwards,"
her dad always said. "Vying for attention from your birth.
But nothing kept you from walking!"

Her oval tub was situated in full view of the mirrors that
spread across the dressing room. She stared at herself again,
the self that showed above the bubbles scudding across the
scented water. Her eyes traced the strawberry-red birthmark that cut from her right shoulder across one breast.
She hated its ugliness, its reminder that her beauty—the
price tag in the fashion world—was flawed.

Her grandmother's self-portrait stared down at her as she
bathed. Katrina had taught Andrea to walk without braces,
without even a limp, saying, "A weak ankle and a birthmark
are not hindrances, Andrea, only stepping stones."

Katrina's picture resembled a French Impressionist
painting—bright blotches of color, part of it faint sketches,
but the piquant face clearly Katrina in her youth, single
and attractive. The lips were a fiery fuchsia, the thick-
lashed blue eyes expectant. She wore a daring off-the-shoul-
der gown with a wide band brooch at her neck and a hat of
the thirties tight against her forehead; three gray-blue
feathers protruded from it. Gloved hands clutched a bou-

quet of flowers—her grandmother before marriage, before widowhood.

The phone rang again. Andrea ignored it and allowed herself the continued luxury of soaking, time forgotten. The ringing stopped.

Todd Owen caught her attention. "This late-breaking story just in from London," he said, his voice tense. "A powerful explosion ripped through the financial district of London leaving dead and wounded in its wake."

Andrea sat up; the water splashed over the edge of the tub.

Owen's voice broke through her fears. "The bomb left a fourteen-foot crater . . . sprayed jagged glass . . . the Irish Republican Army acknowledges responsibility."

The phone rang for the third time. At this hour it would be her mother calling from Index, Washington—calling to discuss this latest act of terrorism in Europe. Andrea didn't want to argue with her. She was going to Paris, no matter what.

Owen's further comments drowned out the sound of her mother's ring, " . . . last week's bomb threats in Madrid . . ." Stepping from the tub, Andrea wrapped herself snugly in a pink bath towel, but she couldn't stop trembling. She snapped off the radio—angry at Todd Owen, angry at another bombing in Europe.

"More terrorism," she muttered to herself. "Bombings in Madrid and London, but not in Paris—not in glittering, glamorous Paris."

۞ ۞ ۞

At dawn a persistent ring split the silence. The sound awakened Andrea—shattering her dream images. She grabbed blindly for the phone, irritated.

"Hello," she grumbled.

"Andrea, this is your mother."

"Where are you?"

Winifred laughed. "In Index, Washington. Where else?"

"Mother, it isn't even six o'clock yet."

"I know, honey, but I tried to reach you last evening."

Andrea cringed against the subtle reprimand. "I told you I'd call home before I left for Paris."

"We need to talk now. Something's come up, dear."

Andrea braced herself for her mother's news report. "Is Dad all right?"

"Your father's fine, but we want you to come home."

"I can't. I'm going to—" She bit off the words to avoid another argument. "I can't come," she repeated. "You know I have other plans."

"Couldn't you change them for Katrina? Your grand-mother is gravely ill. She has had multiple cerebral strokes."

"Strokes?" Andrea gasped. "Is she in the hospital?"

"Not now. She's in the Bethann Nursing Home."

"You . . . you know she never wanted to go there."

"It was your father's decision. It's *his* mother."

Andrea fought for control. "You never said she was that sick, Mother. You've mentioned headaches and flu and—"

"We didn't want to alarm you. But if you had only come home at Christmas like you promised, you would have real-ized that she can't take care of herself any longer nor remember anything."

"But Katrina will get better—won't she, Mother?"

"At eighty-one? What's happening to her is irreversible."

"But, Mother, she's not old to me."

Wini mellowed. "Maybe not, but she can't be young forever."

Outside, dark shapeless clouds tumbled across the sky in shifting surrealistic patterns, slowly propelling the sprawl-ing metropolis into a smog alert. Andrea sat motionless on the edge of her bed, a lump in her throat. Katrina faded in and out of her thoughts—illusive at first. Then her features came alive—a snappy, vital woman with a delicately sculp-tured face and dancing sapphire eyes.

As far back as she could remember, her grandmother had lived with the family. Her grandmother had been the one who took Andrea's leg brace off and forced her to stand. Katrina had paid for ballet and modern dance lessons to strengthen Andrea's ankle. It was Katrina who met her when she came home from school, who taught her the old Swedish songs at the piano. Katrina spent her pension checks on pretty clothes and missionaries, left soap on the dishes when she rinsed them, and often over-watered Wini's African violets.

"Andrea, dear, say something," Wini urged.

"I'm thinking about the things I did with Katrina."

"Like trout fishing when she almost drowned?"

"Oh, Mother, she just lost her balance in the river trying to put a worm on her line. But she was great at berry picking. And poring over fashion magazines or checking out my boyfriends."

Andrea's voice caught as she thought about Neal Bennett and Katrina's wise counsel when that relationship ended, "Let him go, Andrea. Let Neal go."

Aloud she said, "Mother, do you remember when Grandma and I baked cookies to surprise you when you came home from work?"

"You surprised me, all right—with a flour-strewn kitchen. You two were a couple of conspirators, always hobnobbing together or whispering on the back pew at church. Or sorting through your grandfather's war mementos. You'll have wonderful memories—"

"She can't die, Mom," Andrea whispered.

"Honey, if she has another major stroke, we may lose her."

"I'll come home, Mom. Somehow I'll get there."

When her crying subsided, Andrea bathed and carefully applied her makeup to cover the tear streaks. Then she slipped into a royal blue suit and a blouse high enough to cover her strawberry blotch. She draped a silk scarf artistically around her neck, dabbed perfume under each ear, and left for work, the floral scent filling the Porsche.

On her drive to Beverly Hills, she rehearsed her excuses to Rand Jordan. What would he say when she asked for time off? Would he give the Parisian assignment to someone else? Finally, she settled on, "Mr. Jordan, I need to be gone from the office for a few days. I have urgent business matters to settle before going to Europe." But she wouldn't mention illness or close family ties.

Behind her the driver in the BMW tailgated, turning with her on Wilshire. Both of them were trapped in the bumper-to-bumper traffic snaking up the wide boulevard. After three years in L. A., she loathed the traffic and oppressive smog and the charred cinders left by civil unrest. Still she loved this marvelous complex city with its synthetic glitter, marbled skyscrapers, and streets winding through ethnic neighborhoods.

The tailgater stayed with her as she maneuvered up Rodeo Drive past the prestigious shops and boutiques in Beverly Hills. She lost him as she turned her Porsche into a private parking lot.

Moments later Andrea pushed her way through the revolving doors of the pink-faced building on the corner. Chic stores lined each side of the spacious lobby. Rand Jordan's millinery display filled the first glass-encased shop with extravagant splashes of color. Floppy straw hats with exotic peacock feathers sat atop rustic shelves. A picturesque rose toque vied for attention with a chartreuse cartwheel embellished with maroon bows and ribbons. A wide-brim felt hat overshadowed an old-fashioned Dolly Varden. The Regal Queen with its touch of royalty reigned over them all, a frivolous creation like her grandmother had worn forty years ago.

Rand Jordan's plush suite was on the second floor. Andrea found him there, sipping coffee, a portfolio of sketches spread on his desk. She considered him handsome. He wore his forty-two years as well as his expensive steel gray suit, neatly over broad shoulders and narrow hips. He thrived on fashion, exemplified this morning in his plum tab-collared shirt, artsy silk tie, and cap-toed Italian shoes.

He beckoned her in, his expression arrogant, demanding. Light brown hair covered the tips of his ears and swooped low over his thick left eyebrow, drawing attention to the sea—green eyes that scrutinized her with cynical intensity.

He nodded toward the chair across from his desk. "You're

early this morning," he said. "Having second thoughts about Paris? Or more concerns about terrorism after last night's bombing?"

Those eyes brightened as she came toward him, his gaze saying, *Miss York, you're beguiling.*

She turned crimson. "No, Mr. Jordan. Paris is still on."

"Then you want to discuss your new designs, the ones for the February issue?" He nodded to a portfolio upright on the floor, his glance not missing her shapely legs.

"No." She hesitated, bracing against the threat of his anger. "I need . . . I need time off."

His attempt to smile furrowed his shiny forehead. "That's impossible, Andrea. You leave for Europe this weekend, and we have a magazine issue to plan before that."

"My grandmother is ill," she said softly.

"And we're to stop production until she's better?"

She raised her voice. "Katrina is my best friend."

His lips tightened. For a moment he stared beyond her. Then he said, "How much time are we talking about, Miss York?"

She hated being at his mercy. "Three or four days. I could leave today—"

He seemed to be considering. "Did she have a heart attack?"

"No, Rand, multiple cerebral strokes."

His gaze remained unsympathetic. "Then there's nothing you can do even if you rush home."

"There's one thing. I can still tell Katrina I love her."

His apathy splintered, but his manner stayed brusque. "We have deadlines to meet. Why didn't you mention her sooner?"

"I just found out this morning."

He flipped through a file on his desk. "What about your article on Italian ready-to-wear?"

"I'll finish it on my way to Seattle and fax it to you."

She fought for control as he looked skeptically her way. "Please, Rand. My grandmother is all alone in a nursing home."

"So? You see that as San Quentin?"

"Worse," she whispered.

"Visiting her won't solve anything. Won't she put up a fuss when you run off to Paris?"

"Not if I go to Normandy—to the military cemetery where my grandfather is buried." To Rand's arched brow, she added, "My grandfather died in the Normandy Invasion."

"That was decades ago," he said, standing.

"Yes, but I *promised* to take Grandmother there someday."

"A sentimental journey to view war memorials?" he mocked.

"Something like that," she admitted. "When I was little, my grandmother told me there was a traitor in Grandfather's unit." Her composure shattered. "Sounds silly, doesn't it? But as a child I was certain that Katrina and I could solve the mystery of who it was."

"If only you could get to Normandy?"

"Something like that."

Jordan walked around the desk and brushed a strand of hair from her face, his eyes gleaming. She eased away from him.

"Andrea, you still want this Parisian assignment, don't you?"

"More than anything, Mr. Jordan."

"But you want Normandy, too?" He rubbed his jaw, thoughtfully. "I've booked you at the InterContinental in Paris. A friend will drive you there. As long as you get your articles in as planned, the rest of the time is yours."

He kept rubbing his jaw. "I'll have my secretary arrange a rental car for you at Orly Airport, say two weeks from Friday. From Orly it's an easy drive to Normandy. Take a few days there, but if you value your job," he warned, "be back from your grandmother's on time. It's too late to replace you. I'd have to go to Paris myself. As you know, I would never have given you this assignment—"

"If Pam Eden hadn't broken her leg in *your* office that night a few weeks ago."

He looked embarrassed, ruffled for the moment. His voice deepened, "Then we understand each other, Miss York?"

"Yes, I'm Pam Eden's substitute."

"Precisely. Nothing is to interfere with your Parisian assignment." He gave her a twisted grin, his mood vacillating with his words. "You're ambitious, Andrea. Competitive. Don't put your promising career on the line for your family."

She stood, careful not to brush against him.

"Should my secretary make your reservation for Seattle?"

"No, I booked one before I came to work."

"*You what?*" he asked, his voice turning harsh again.

"I'm sorry, Rand. I didn't mean to be presumptuous."

He ignored her apology, his thick brows still arched.

"*Style Magazine* has invested *heavily* in you, Andrea. Don't forget it. I've arranged a personal interview for you with Yves Saint-Laurent. You'll be the envy of all my competitors in Paris."

"I know, Rand. I'm grateful. I can handle it."

"Good." This time his smile turned sympathetic. "Perhaps your grandmother will not be as ill as you fear. It's important to both of us. Have a safe trip home, Andrea. We'll talk again before your flight to Paris."

Jordan watched her walk across the room, an attractive woman with a chimerical personality and flecks of red in her sun-golden hair—the clicking of her heels silenced by the thick coral carpeting. She was stunning as always, even from the back, in the suit she had styled herself. Yves Saint-Laurent would find her as charming and desirable as he did.

At the door she turned and faced him, a sadness in her eyes. Her gentle expression contrasted with the boldness she usually evidenced in the weekly magazine-planning sessions. This sudden vulnerability—the unsullied freshness in her smile—made her even more attractive to him. Rand winked to reassure her.

"I'll be back on time," she promised.

The door closed softly behind her, the scent of her perfume still invading his office. He longed to travel to Europe with her to show her the glittering night lights of Paris, but she had long ago brushed off his interest. The romance of Paris would be lost on Andrea York, but not the beauty of the city. She would add to this. His gaze stayed riveted on the door where she had swept gracefully from the room—the gifted, talented Miss York, an asset to Rand and his publication. But he knew that her goals were always on future achievements, on a job and a promotion beyond *Style Magazine*.

He leaned against his desk and pressed the intercom button.

"Cindy, book me a tentative flight to Paris for Saturday. I may have to take the Yves Saint Laurent interview myself."

"Will you be traveling with Miss York?" she asked.

"No, alone if I go."

"The same airline?"

"You know I hate flying. Book me on the Concorde out of New York. That'll give me fewer hours in the air."

Chapter 2

As Andrea stepped from the car, the tantalizing fragrance of snappy mountain air greeted her. She forced herself to look at her grandmother's new home, loathing the shingled one-story building that held Katrina captive. The grounds were well kept, but the front of Bethann Manor needed a fresh coat of paint, and the drain spout needed repair.

She skirted the rain puddles and made her way through the double glass doors. Her eyes focused briefly on the oil painting of children fishing on a river bank. Their future lay ahead of them, a mockery here in this place.

She urged herself forward, her heels echoing down the tiled corridor. Pine-Sol fumes burned her eyes, but they could not hide that faint smell of urine as listless men and women maneuvered their wheelchairs aimlessly around her.

A tottery man balanced precariously in front of her. "Get out," he warned, prodding her with his cane, "or they'll keep you. Don't matter if you done nothin'. No way out once you're in."

She patted his gnarled hand. "I'm looking for my grandmother."

Disappointment fogged his eyes like cataracts. "For a hair's length, I thought you might be looking for me."

Andrea weaved her way among the others, fighting tears, slowing long enough to ask for directions to Katrina's room.

Rounding the corner to 209, Andrea almost stumbled over a wheelchair. She barely recognized her grandmother's thin, tired face. Katrina looked neglected. Her hair was brushed straight back, her breasts flat beneath the blue-checkered hospital gown, her belly restrained with a tight web belt. A shawl, intended for warmth and modesty, lay crumpled on the floor.

Andrea knelt beside her grandmother and tucked the lap robe around the bare legs, restoring dignity with the gesture.

"Oh, Grandma," she cried. "Grandma, it's me. Andrea."

Katrina stared back with vacant blue eyes, the sapphire glow gone. She smiled a pleasant, childlike smile, no recognition in her gaze. Her thin hand trembled beneath Andrea's.

Andrea grabbed the nurse passing by. "My grandmother doesn't even know me," she said, her voice frantic.

The nurse nodded. "She only asks for Conrad and Andrea."

"*I am Andrea*, but why is she here all alone and not out there with the others?"

"Mrs. York cries when she's there. It disturbs them."

As the nurse hurried away, Andrea put her head on Katrina's lap and wept. Then she heard her grandmother's soothing whisper, "Don't cry, child. It will be all right. Conrad will be here soon."

As Andrea drove through Sultan and neared the forested foothills of the Cascade Mountains, she felt that old excitement of going home. Strange. She was always anxious to get away, yet equally joyful to come back again. She pulled to a stop at the narrow, single-lane bridge into town and waited impatiently for her turn to cross.

Seconds later she roared into the center of Index. She almost passed Sabrina Jensen, blonde and attractive as ever, pedaling her bike past the Pickett Museum. Sabrina skidded to a stop in front of the General Store that specialized in everything from friendship to deli sandwiches and axle grease.

Andrea leaned out the car window. "Hi, Sabrina."

"Well, the wanderer is finally home," Sabrina said as they clasped palms, their grins broadening.

"Just long enough to see Katrina."

"Not the rest of us? Not Neal? This is your old home town."

"Yes, Index and Skykomish Valley have been home to the Yorks for four generations."

"You should be proud of your roots, Andrea."

Andrea felt an unwanted rush of color to her cheeks. She pulled her grasp from her friend's hand. "I am proud. It's just that I've always wanted something more."

"Ever since third grade you've been telling me there's adventure for you beyond our rugged mountain peaks. What's it going to be this time, Andrea?"

"Three exciting weeks in Paris."

"Paris? After that, maybe you'll come home to stay?"

Andrea glanced toward the craggy Cascades. "Maybe. Someday."

"You belong here, Andrea. The town's in your blood."

"I don't want it to be. I hate going to the annual July 4th hoopla. And I'm tired of hearing the old-timers reminisce about Index at the turn of the century."

"You used to enjoy it," Sabrina scolded softly.

"So what if Amos and Persis Gunn ran the post office and the first York in town laid the last rail for the Great Northern? I've seen snapshots of my great granddad standing at Maloney's Siding waving the first train through. It may have been a boom town back in Sam York's day, Sabrina, but I don't care about those things now."

"You care."

Andrea's cheeks flushed scarlet again. "Dad keeps telling me that the ore mines played out, the quarries shut down, the logging camps folded, the boom towns dwindled, *but Index went on.*"

She looked away. The faces of the jagged granite peaks stared back at her. The mountains and the unparalleled beauty of the valley had been in the Yorks' blood for generations, but only Paris stirred an ambitious dream within Andrea.

She glanced back at her friend. "Sabrina, my grandmother is dying."

"I'm sorry, Andrea. The whole town feels badly. Sunday brunch at the Country Inn isn't the same without her."

"Index won't be the same when Grandma's gone. I won't want to come back. I don't want the old-timers to reminisce about Amos and Persis Gunn and Katrina all in the same breath."

"Andrea, let's jog in the morning and talk some more. But we'll need to run early. I have to be at the schoolhouse before my students arrive."

"Could we run the old trails?"

"Sure. Stay longer and we'll rock climb the Town Wall or I'll introduce you to Bungee jumping. It's exhilarating. Total freedom."

Andrea shuddered. "Total *risk*. See you tomorrow."

She gave a wistful glance toward the Bush House as she drove by. Coming back to Index was always a nostalgic journey. Her grandparents had honeymooned at the Bush Country Inn, too poor to even leave town for a proper exotic honeymoon.

On rare occasions when Andrea thought about marrying, she dreamed of a wedding in the tiny Wayside Chapel a mile from Sultan where only the family and Sabrina could crowd in. She wanted to spend her honeymoon at the Bush House, up the narrow, creaking stairs, down the hall to room 7. It was the end room with a four-poster bed and marvelous antique furnishings where her grandparents had honeymooned. But when would she meet anyone that special?

Odd, she thought. *Neal was never part of that dream.*

She turned at the corner and pulled into the driveway of the turn-of-the-century homestead, a double-story frame house with blue-shuttered windows and a latticed dormer in the attic.

"Mother, where are you?" she called as she banged into the house and dropped her suitcase in the hallway.

The answer came from the dining room. "In here, dear."

She hurried into the room smiling. "Well, Mom, I'm home."

"I'm glad." Winifred, a slender woman in her early fifties, went on pampering her African violets. She patted the soil in place and then glanced up, her eye shadow a perfect match to the light blue top she was wearing. "Honey, you should have called us. Dad and I would have met you gladly."

"I know, Mom, but it was just as easy to rent a car and drop by to see Katrina on the way home."

"The nurse told me you were there when I checked on Katrina."

Andrea's cheerfulness wavered. "Why, Mother? Why did you put Katrina in a nursing home?"

"I work, Andrea. I drive all the way into Everett and back every day. In another three years I can retire."

"Is a pension and a thirty-year pin more important than Grandma?"

Wini wiped the dirt from her hands, her face troubled. Particles of sand spread across the newspaper, dotting the picture of the IRA bombing in London. Their eyes locked.

"We need my income, Andrea, more than ever since your father's heart trouble. It was stressful trying to take care of Katrina and work. She kept falling—down the staircase once. It was more than we could handle, short of hiring someone to come into the home."

"Mom, I would have helped with the expenses. Hired help would have been better than throwing Katrina out of the house."

"No one threw Mother out," Will York said from the doorway.

Andrea's father was looking at them with eyes shaded by bushy gray brows. A tremor tugged at his flabby jowls; an expanding midline pushed against his shirt buttons. His hair had grayed since he took an early retirement from the

Loth Lumber Company in Gold Bar after an almost fatal heart attack.

As she ran toward him, Andrea noted with panic that his face looked ashen, his lips blue. "Dad, are you okay?"

"I'm just worried," he said, yanking off his silver-rimmed glasses and rubbing the corner of one eye. "Mother calls me Conrad now. She doesn't even know that I'm her son."

"She didn't know me either," Andrea whispered.

"I prayed that Mother would die rather than have you see her this way." His voice sounded infinitely sad. "I'm like Katrina, gathering up my memories. I understand about her shoe box of mementos now. That's all she had left of my father, a handful of memories."

"Will, your mother had a good life. You saw to that."

"She never got to see the cemetery where my father was buried, the one thing she always wanted to do."

"Dad, I'll go there for her while I'm in France."

Wini stared incredulously. "You're still going to Europe with your grandmother so ill? With London being bombed?"

"I have no choice, Mother. *My job is at stake.*"

Will tipped Andrea's chin until their eyes met. "We won't stand in your way, Andrea. We love you too much for that."

He leaned down and whispered, "Your mother will be cleaning Katrina's room while you're gone. Perhaps you'd like to rescue your grandfather's Normandy treasures before you go away."

She squeezed his hand. "I'd like that, Dad."

As she climbed the stairs, she heard her mother's angry words, "Will, why did you give in to her? You wanted her to stay home as much as I did. What if Katrina dies while she's gone?"

His voice sounded bone-weary. "I can't ask Andrea to choose between her family and career. This trip means too much to her."

"Once, not long ago, her grandmother meant more."

As Andrea slammed the door to her grandmother's bedroom, the vibration jarred Katrina's music box. Strands of "Stardust" permeated the room with a sense of Katrina's presence. Andrea's eyes traveled slowly from the empty rocker to the antique dresser cluttered with perfume bottles. Katrina's open Bible lay on the bedside table, her bifocals and the York cameo necklace on top.

A framed picture of Conrad York, striking in his captain's uniform, rested against the lamp. She studied the finely chiseled features—strong cheekbones, the firm York jaw line, the cleft chin. Thick sandy brows crested the wide-set blue eyes, his gaze unflinching. As Katrina often said, Andrea looked like Conrad in the blueness of her eyes, the stubborn chin, the side profile, the reddish-blonde hair.

From the closet, she pulled down the shoe boxes with Conrad's treasures, *hers now*, and spread the contents on the canopy bed. Useless trinkets. Treasured memories. Gingerly, she fingered her grandfather's wide gold wedding band, his dogtags, and his Elgin wristwatch. She scanned a news clipping, "Normandy Revisited," and traced his name on the pocket-sized Bible. Her hands trembled as she held it. Psalm 23 was underlined and dated June 3rd, 1944, three days before he died on the beach at Normandy. She felt as though she were invading her grandparents' private world as she stared down at the tightly-wrapped packets of Conrad's dog-eared letters; they were censored letters, frayed pink ribbons holding them together. She could not bring herself to open them.

The hands of Conrad's Elgin watch still rested at ten. *Was that the hour he fell?* she wondered. *Or did time tick on after his death?* His initials CWY were engraved on the back— Conrad William York—her father's name, too. She decided to have the old Elgin repaired for her father's fifty-fourth birthday. He would like that.

She picked up the faded snapshots of the men in army uniforms; the same face was circled in each snapshot. On the back Conrad York had written "My men: Drew Gregory, Vincent Giovetti, Smitty, Wendall Salisbury, Weinberger." Names of the men in her grandfather's command. Some may have even died with him in Normandy. Names from the past. The name, perhaps, of a traitor. But had the man betrayed his country or only her grandfather's friendship?

Chapter 3

Porter Deven munched a continental breakfast, his eyes on Drew Gregory cutting across the crowded street. Drew seemed invincible, side-stepping speeding cars, his stride swift and deliberate. If he saw Porter in the cafe window, Drew gave no indication. He entered the room, slid into the seat across from Porter, and gave a curt nod as he thumped his hands on the table top, rattling Porter's coffee cup.

"Nothing's sacred any more," Drew said gloomily. "Some far-out faction has just threatened the national cemetery in Normandy."

"In Colleville? That's hardly the place for terrorists, Drew. Maybe it's more anti-American sentiment on the rise."

"Anti-dead. I have some old war buddies buried there. York and Weinberger." Drew leaned back, his handsome face troubled.

To Porter, Drew looked more like a history professor than a man with thirty-plus years with the Agency. He had stayed physically trim, his gaze serious, his silvery-dark hair parted on the side. His quick sprint and firm, coppery skin made him look much younger than a man in his sixties.

"You're looking fit, Drew," Porter said. "Have some coffee."

"Nothing. I've had breakfast."

"Thanks for coming to Paris earlier than I expected."

"You give the orders, Porter."

Porter bit the end of a croissant and chewed vigorously, warding off the need to apologize again. Drew Gregory was an action man. He belonged in the thick of things, not behind the desk where Porter had sent him.

The minutes ticked away. Porter had an irritating way of ignoring people as he ate, his dour expression as hang-dogged as his moustache. Drew stared hard at the stocky, balding man across the table, probing beneath the stern features. Had this man deliberately betrayed him?

Porter came in complex layers. He was shrewd, skillful, bordering on genius. A moody antacid type, he stayed tight-lipped about his past, yet was opinionated on diplomatic issues. He had a strange affinity for Eastern religions, a vague, passing involvement ever since being rescued by Taoist monks in the jungles of Vietnam. Porter was single, had always been, as far as Drew knew.

They had been friends once, but even before Porter's promotion to Station Chief, their friendship had turned sour in a debate on the secret wars in Laos. Porter had spent four years in Indochina—two with the marines, two with the C.I.A.. He came out of Saigon, his fierce anger directed at the White House for stopping a war they could have won. Drew considered Vietnam a political fiasco. It had left men like Porter disillusioned.

In his bitterness, Porter had become a man obsessed with power. He ran the Agency like a military campaign, some of his strategies brilliant, some inscrutable. Porter wasted good men when they threatened his leadership. Drew saw himself as one of Porter's victims. Drew's code name "Crisscross" had been compromised, his covert activities split wide open by a clerical blunder that left Drew with no hope for promotion.

With his cover blown, Drew barely came out of Croatia with his life. An Agency crisis followed—internal upheaval in the organization, a public opinion uproar at home over any American involvement, and the threatened compromise of other agents behind the lines. Drew submitted a request for severance from the Company. The paperwork stopped on Porter's desk; he had been quick to arrange Drew's reassignment as diplomatic attaché, State Department, London. A desk jockey demotion as far as Drew was concerned.

۞۞۞

Porter broke their silence. "How's Robyn, Drew?"

Pain shadowed Drew's eyes. "She's beautiful. Successful. Doing well without me. But we're not here to talk about my daughter. So tell me, Porter, why didn't you get someone else to handle this latest problem with Ebsworth and Prescott?"

"You've been on the case all along. You know about both men."

"So my reprieve is only temporary?"

"Let's see how you handle this one."

Drew scowled. "Any word on Sherman Prescott?"

"Nothing yet. Kippen Investments in Paris are close-mouthed about his schedule. But we're checking all flights out of Dallas and Houston. So far Prescott hasn't shown."

"While we're waiting for him, what have we got on Ebsworth?"

"He's staying clean, but things happen when he's in town. Bombings. Key witnesses dead. A sale of warheads."

"Conjecture," Drew said, baiting Porter. "Maybe he just likes Paris. It's the city he frequents the most."

Porter gulped his cold coffee. "His main contact is here. I know it. I'm just missing some little clue. Ryan Ebsworth follows the same routine. He takes his meals at the Cafe Amitie near the embassy. In the few days he's been here, he's hit all the art museums. The Louvre for one. And the Impressionist paintings at the Jeu de Paume Museum. He spends a couple of hours a day with his easel, acting the part of a true Bohemian."

"Sounds like my ex-wife. She's into art. But there's nothing Bohemian about Miriam. She goes for the old Dutch masters. She'd find Ryan Ebsworth's art work unimpressive. So what about his mealtimes at the cafe? Any particular hour?"

"It varies. He arrives alone. Eats alone. Flirts with the waitresses, one in particular named Collette Rheims."

Drew was thoughtful. "He makes no other contacts?"

"He speaks openly with the maitre d', Jacques Marseilles."

"I assume you've checked this Jacques out?"

Porter bristled. "His uncle owns the restaurant, but Jacques runs the business. He saw this country ravaged during World War II and fought back with the French Resistance under the Marie-Madeleine Fourcade network."

A sly, unguarded smile cut across Drew's face. "Old Hedgehog? The legendary slippery lady herself?"

"That's the one, Drew. The Gestapo picked her up back in '44 for coding messages to London. And right under their noses, naked as a jaybird, she slipped through her cell window, her dress and her money clenched in her teeth."

"Gutsy lady, Porter. She also smuggled out a map on the Nazi defenses to Eisenhower before D-Day. We kept hoping we'd meet up with her when we marched from Normandy to Paris."

"Too bad you missed her. She was quite a beauty."

"So this Jacques worked with Fourcade?" Drew asked, serious again.

"Says he did. He could have been one of her three thousand agents passing secrets to Britain. Madame Fourcade bit the dust back in the summer of '89, but there are still several groups of Resistance survivors around. Marseilles might belong to one of them."

"What do we know about the man, Porter?"

"He spends most of his time at the cafe. He keeps to himself outside of that. Goes to the opera sometimes. Nothing else. Except for the uncle, his family was wiped out in the war. Jacques never married, but he has a mistress. Nominal Catholic. Few close friends."

"With the embassies so close, there must be a lot of international traffic through the Amitie."

"Yes, Drew, I eat there myself often."

"People are talkative when they wine and dine. Perhaps Ebsworth is listening, gaining information and passing it on. Maybe this Jacques Marseilles is Ebsworth's contact."

Porter jabbed his thumb with the emery board, splitting his nail. "I'm telling you, Drew, we've already checked the man's records. They're legitimate. He's a smooth talker. Well respected."

"So was Gorbachev back in his day."

"Come on, Drew. Don't put old Russian labels on everything."

"No labels. I just want to consider the man's politics. If this Jacques served in the French Resistance, he'd have the ability to listen, to pass on information."

"Drew, that was decades ago."

"Then update me. Where does this Jacques stand in relation to the new European Community and the economic chaos in Russia?" Drew lowered his voice. "What about the old eastern bloc countries? The shaky unity in Germany? What does Jacques say about the dust particles at the Berlin Wall? The burrs at NATO or that civil war that tore through Yugoslavia? Did Marseilles provide a haven for any of the Stasi agents still striking deals with the West?"

"I don't discuss politics with the man, Drew."

"You rarely discuss politics, Porter. I want to meet with this Jacques Marseilles and his uncle. Perhaps we could have lunch at their cafe tomorrow. If our man Ryan Ebsworth is there, I'll size up his friendship with Jacques for myself."

Porter shoved back his chair. "The uncle is never there, but the last time I saw Ebsworth and Jacques together, they argued Yeltsin politics, nothing more. Ebsworth is an intelligent man. He speaks several languages fluently. He's well read."

"I don't judge a man's intelligence by what he reads."

"How then?" Porter asked.

"By the way he lives."

⚙⚙⚙

Ryan Ebsworth, a spindly, raw-boned man, left the Hotel de Crillon and strolled a short block to the cafe, arriving late for his noon meal. The name Cafe Amitie was deceptive, a thought that amused Ryan. In the beginning, it had been little more than a sidewalk coffee shop patronizing its philosophical summer crowd. Even after the expansion into an elegant restaurant for the elite of Paris, the Marseille family maintained the original name.

Sauntering into the lobby, Ryan spotted Collette. She smiled expectantly when she saw him. He went to her and caressed her, kissing her on both cheeks, and whispered in French, "I'm at the de Crillon. Come by when you get off."

She blushed in answer, but he knew she would call.

He nodded to the maitre d', a well-groomed man with thinning gray hair and darting dark eyes. The stress lines around Jacques Marseilles's mouth deepened as Ryan reached him.

"So you're back again," Jacques said bitterly, a slight quiver to his closely cropped moustache. "You're dining alone?"

"Yes. And, Jacques, I'm expecting a phone call."

Marseilles stiffened. "It would be best—"

"We like your help, Jacques. You will let me know when my call comes through? And, Jacques, for the next few days, I'll be in the Montmartre district painting. My usual corner."

Ryan kept his voice low. "If someone wants to get in touch with me, anyone, let me know. Send Collette Rheims." He nodded toward her. "She'll know where to find me."

The maitre d' snapped his fingers, his beady eyes like sooty coals. A black-tie waiter appeared immediately. "Monsieur Ebsworth would like his usual corner table," Jacques told him.

Ryan followed the waiter, thinking, *Jacques worries for nothing. What are a few phone contacts from his private office? In-coming calls mostly. Nothing that will dirty Jacques's hands or ruin his uncle's thriving business.*

The restaurant offered anonymity for Ryan, a perfect place to gather information or pass it. Other guests rarely noticed him. He ordered immediately—frog legs, a salad, and a bottle of Dubonnet. As he waited, he watched the diners—tourists puzzling over the menu, diplomats boasting too loudly, Americans hurrying through their meals, the true Frenchmen savoring each morsel and sipping wine, unhurriedly.

The atmosphere fed into Ryan's artistic nature—dazzling chandeliers, bronzed statues in the entryway, and a spiral stairwell in the lobby that led to romantic dining in the balcony. Colorful flecked Impressionist paintings hung on the walls, a Degas and a Monet and one of his favorites by Renoir.

At twenty-four Ryan had come a long way since his days as a bellhop, his rise coming quickly, illegally. He had nerves of steel. He liked the fast pace, the risk, the daring. He would do it over again.

As he finished his salad, he suddenly noticed Porter Deven at a table across the room. *Coincidental?* he wondered, tensing. He long ago had pegged Deven as an intelligence operative, someone too interested in what he was doing. But what of the stranger with Deven, a tad of familiarity in his stoic expression?

Ryan's photographic memory snapped a picture sealing the profile, the build of the man in his mind. Ryan guessed him to be six foot or more. If the stranger knew Porter Deven, he'd be a man to watch, perhaps to avoid.

Ryan sipped an after-dinner drink, a wine of delicate flavor, his gaze shifting to the maitre d'. Jacques made his way among the tables, nodding to one guest, smiling at another, his pace slow and discreet. When he reached Ryan, he forced a smile. "I'm sorry about the *menu change*, Monsieur," he said.

Contact.

Ryan's adrenalin raced. The adventure never ceased to thrill him. He extended his open-palmed hands to his empty plate. "The frog legs proved tasty nonetheless."

"You can take the call in my office."

"When?" Ryan asked, glancing toward Porter Deven.

"Twelve minutes."

Ryan let the minutes tick away. Four. Five. Six. His excitement skyrocketed. He stood slowly, dropped his napkin on the plate, and made his way to the main lobby. As soon as he reached the spiral staircase, he ducked behind it, waiting.

Deven and his guest came seconds behind him, the stranger's stride fast-paced. Ryan judged him to be in his early sixties; the man's profile tapped at Ryan's memory again. *The American agent Crisscross*, Ryan mused. *Could he still be alive?* Rumors had him dead in Croatia months ago.

Ryan's mouth twisted into a triumphant smile as Porter Deven and *Crisscross* raced out the cafe door and stopped short, their expressions impassive. Ryan had foiled Deven's efforts again. Deven glanced up and down the street, tossed his cigarette to the sidewalk, and stomped off in the direction of the embassy.

As he reached Jacques's office, Ryan heard the phone ringing. He slipped inside, a cold shiver running the length of his spine as he answered.

A familiar voice broke over the wires. "Monsieur Ebsworth, we have a *menu change* for you." The caller spoke French clearly, a harsh quality fragmenting his speech, a few syllables only, but enough for Ryan to know that the man was not a native speaker. "Monsieur, your flight to *old Babylon* is cancelled. But we've arranged diversionary activity for you. We'll be in touch."

Old Babylon—Baghdad. Diversionary activity? A bombing? An assassination? But no part in the arms-sale negotiations in Baghdad. Ryan broke into a cold sweat. His usefulness was running out.

Chapter 4

Sherman Franklin Prescott jogged steadily into the snappy January wind. He had rugged Alpine features: strong, well-chiseled facial bones, deep-set dark eyes, muscular shoulders, powerful lanky legs. He exuded strength when he ran or skied and showed equal skill and discipline as an executive with worldwide Kippen Investments.

But inside, life held little meaning for Sherm. He still missed his wife, longed for her. Sometimes her features seemed distant now, undefined. He kept her photograph by his bedside and looked at it often—yearning to bring her eyes and smile back into focus. At unexpected moments he thought about her running into his arms at the airport or slipping her hand into his at church. He missed sharing his life and dreams with her, missed hearing her voice cheering him on when he needed it. All the cold showers in the last twenty-eight months couldn't blot out his desire to hold Melody once more, to love her.

He hit the four-mile mark, pounding the trail around the lake, his heart thumping rapidly, sweat glistening on his bronzed skin. He side-stepped the scrub oaks and cut back across the lawn toward the condominium, barging into his house, his chest heaving rhythmically.

There was still an hour of daylight left before Buzz Kippen, his father-in-law, came by for steaks, salad, and an evening of paperwork. Sherm pulled off his sweat top and tossed it in the corner of his study. Dirty clothes on the floor had always been a sore spot with Melody. But he lived alone now, was accountable to no one. His twice-weekly maid, a matronly, hard-working Latino, would be in tomorrow.

He was heading for the shower when the phone rang.

"Prescott," he said picking up the receiver.

"Sherm, Jack Sedgwick. I've been trying to get you for hours. Your father-in-law said you left work early."

"I'm getting ready for a trip abroad."

"Business or pleasure?" Jack asked.

"Business with some skiing in Switzerland if I'm lucky."

He sank into his leather chair, forming a pleasant mental image of his friend in Canada. Jack was also in his mid-thirties, a good-natured, solidly-built banker.

"You were just in Europe a few weeks ago, Sherm."

"I'm watchdog for our overseas offices, all of them. Munich. London. Geneva. Paris. And a new office in Brussels."

"Paris? Ebsworth is at the de Crillon in Paris right now."

Sherm's pleasure faded. "Ryan Ebsworth? Why?"

"His aunt didn't say, but she's worried about him."

"Jack, the man's involved in my wife's death–maybe only as a witness. But I'm stymied. The last time I tried to contact Ebsworth, an American intelligence agent stopped me cold. Said I had no authority, no reason—"

"You do now. That's why I called. Last Sunday Tina and I had dinner with Ebsworth's aunt at the Harrison Hotel. She told us that Ryan definitely knew your wife when he was a bellhop."

Jack cleared his throat, the sound grating in Sherm's ear. "According to Ryan's aunt, bellhops weren't supposed to swim in the guest pool. She admits now that Ryan bragged about swimming with Melody every morning."

Rage surged through Sherm. "Maybe they swam in the same pool, but they did not swim together."

"Look, ole chap, I'm just telling you what I heard."

"What you've heard goes against the laundry maid's testimony that held up in court. The maid said Ryan was afraid of water— he never even got his feet wet. He just sat on the pool's edge annoying Melody, enamored with her."

"What held up in court was Kathryn Culvert swearing that her nephew never showed up for work that morning. You have to understand, Sherm, Kathryn is an honest, devout woman. Until the other day, she really believed Ryan."

Sherm asked stiffly, "What changed her mind?"

"She found a newspaper photo of your wife in Ryan's wallet when he was packing for Paris." To Sherm's deathly silence, Jack said, "I asked a Royal Mountie friend of mine to open the case again and check on Ryan's whereabouts the day of Melody's death. He told me the file on Melody is sealed."

Pressure crushed Sherm's temples. "Why seal the RCMP file on a drowning?"

"The order came from higher up than RCMP."

"A coverup? Ebsworth must know something about Melody's death. That leaves me no alternative. I'll have to risk contacting him again, Jack. I'll push my trip ahead a few days and fly direct to Paris. The Hotel de Crillon, you said?"

"When will you be our way again, Sherm?"

"In September."

Sherm hung up and headed for the bedroom. He flipped his briefcase on the bed and emptied out the contents. Still rankled, he took a manila envelope from the file cabinet and thumbed through it—photos and news clippings of Melody's death, posthumous tributes on the Olympic gold medalist who had drowned in shallow water, and the reports that he had been gathering on Ryan Ebsworth. Tiny fragments of truth that might someday unravel the mystery of Melody's dying.

Did Ryan Ebsworth really meet her that morning? he asked himself as he placed the envelope in the attache case. *Did he lure her from the indoor pool to the lake?*

Sherm's mind went back to that time a year ago in the Harrison Hotel when a casual remark had made him suspicious of Ebsworth. Sherm had been talking to one of the receptionists when she said, "That poor bellhop who found your wife was so upset that he resigned immediately."

That bellhop who found your wife.

Sherm had found Melody himself and carried her limp body back to the hotel. "What bellhop, Henny?" he had demanded.

Henny hesitated, flustered. "Mr. Prescott, I know what I'm saying. I was on duty that day. Ryan Ebsworth came running in and said your wife was face down in the water."

"The police records say he wasn't working that morning."

"I don't know about that, Mr. Prescott, but Ryan was here that day. And he was scared."

"Henny, you should have told us this before—"

"I never thought it was important. I—I always thought he was just rushing in ahead of you to tell us what happened." She trembled when she added, "He's living in Paris now."

Sherm had flown to Paris immediately, but Porter Deven intercepted him. He could still hear Deven saying, "Ryan Ebsworth and your wife may have been involved in something illegal, Mr. Prescott."

As Sherm raged, Deven had picked up a folder and studied it meticulously. "According to this, your wife drowned. In the interest of national security, Mr. Prescott, I would let it go at that. Forget Ryan Ebsworth."

Never, Sherm thought as he locked his attache case and stared at Melody's empty side of the bed. *Never. Not until I know the truth. I promise you that, Melody.*

After work the next day, Sherm caught the airporter to Houston. Once inside the air terminal, he walked briskly. His strapping six-foot-three frame towered above the other passengers as he wove his way toward the Air France boarding gate. He traveled light—one compact garment bag and his Hartmann attache case, his American passport locked inside.

He had wanted to shower and shave before the flight, but it had been too late. He felt the stubble of a beard, but even more he felt the onset of another throbbing headache. He had grown accustomed to them and the numbness that often controlled his mind since his wife's death, lingering like some incurable disease.

He ran the last few steps, his body responding mechanically in a desperate attempt to catch the plane. Two flight attendants greeted him as he ducked to enter the cabin. The brunette tapped her wristwatch, her smile pixieish. The older woman took his travel bag. He nodded gratefully, his brow furrowing as the pain tore at his neck muscles, gyrating down between his shoulder blades. When he reached his seat in first class, he dropped his Hartmann to the floor and toed it into place. Then he loosened his tie, grabbed a pillow and eased his lanky body into the window seat moments before the pilot taxied the 727 down the runway.

It was like a jackhammer inside his head now, pounding relentlessly, the pressure building. His eyes felt bruised to the touch, the sockets like dead weights.

As the plane leveled off at 38,000 feet, the younger flight attendant came to him, her elf-like grin gone, and asked, "Are you all right, sir? Are you ill?"

"It's just a migraine," Sherm mumbled.

"Can I get you something? A drink maybe?"

"No, I don't drink. But coffee later. Nothing now."

"We'll eat soon. I'll save your tray until later."

He forced a smile.

She was back within moments. "Sir, here's something for your eyes." She dropped a cold terry cloth into his open palm. It slapped gently over his wide gold wedding band.

As they winged toward Paris, he stirred frequently, stretching his legs to ease the cramps that came after hours of inactivity. At last he dozed, a fitful sleep with the clatter of silverware and trays behind him and the familiar sound of Melody's voice faintly in his consciousness.

Somewhere between deep sleep and wakefulness, he dreamt. In his dreams he saw Melody in her wedding gown, her beautiful oval-shaped face shadowed behind the lace-fringed veil. He heard himself repeating the wedding vows they had written together.

"Melody, I take you as a God-given trust . . . to love you, to keep you from all harm."

He had broken that promise.

He reached for her, but she slipped from his grasp. He fought against wakefulness, wanting to stay with her, images of her cascading over the edges of memory. She was swimming free-style toward him, laughing at him. They were at the swim meet, Melody cutting the water with swift, even strokes, ahead of her competition—Melody going for the gold, Melody winning, the crowd cheering as she balanced on the edge of the pool. She whipped off her swim cap and gave her grandstand smile, but the kiss that she blew from the tips of her fingers was for him only.

Outstripping the winds, his dreams sucked him into a kaleidoscopic whirlpool—a maelstrom of lake water swirling relentlessly, spraying sun-glinted blues around him. Faster. Faster. Narrowing. Drawing him into a darkened eddy. Then she was lying alone, face down in the waters of Harrison Lake, the strap of her Body-Glove swimsuit caught on a rotted tree trunk.

Sherm woke with a start, his headache dull, the pulsation gone. An empty void gnawed inside him, that unending longing for Melody, now gone even from his dreams. Semi-darkness shrouded the interior of the aircraft. Even in the shadows, the pixie attendant caught his eye. She came at once with a cup of coffee and a croissant. As she handed the tray across to him, she whispered, "Cream or sugar?"

"No. Black, thank you."

It was bitter-tasting against the morning coating in his mouth. He gulped the steaming coffee and signaled for a refill.

As she poured it, she said, "Your dinner's a cold, soggy mess. But we'll be serving breakfast in a couple of hours."

As she walked away, he thought back to that first bitter September after Melody's death. He had flown to the Harrison and dropped a dozen red roses on the lake waters, grappling for answers as he watched the flowers drift from shore. It was then he allowed himself to accept the fact of her death. But he could not accept that she had drowned.

It was always there in the back of his mind, some word, some phrase that he could not remember, something that Melody had said that last day. She did her morning laps in the hotel pools, never in the lake in the chill of September, and never, never alone.

Outside his plane window, it was still inky blackness, the wing of the plane a shadowy outline with only a flickering light on the tip. Soon dawn split the sky. In seconds an intense, red fireball cut across the horizon. Behind Sherm, salmon and tea-rose streamers trailed the plane. The torched colors subsided, leaving in their wake delicate pink sun rays reflecting off the fuselage and invading the rippled, unbroken clouds beneath them. Far below, out of view, lay the ocean and beyond that, Charles de Gaulle International.

Sherm grabbed his briefcase and headed for the bathroom. Twenty minutes later, he returned to his seat, the cramps in his legs gone. He felt refreshed in a clean winter blue dress shirt and silk Jacquard tie, his face smelling of after-shave, and the pleasant taste of mint on his breath.

As soon as he checked into his hotel, he would confront Ryan Ebsworth. This time Sherm had the edge on Porter Deven. Deven and his Agency had no way of knowing that he was en route to Europe. But once Sherm located Ebsworth, it wouldn't take Deven long to find him.

Chapter 5

A ndrea lingered at the front door facing her mother, the keys to the Hertz rental dangling on one finger. "You've been crying, Mom," Andrea said gently.

"It's an old habit of mine. I never get used to you going away, especially now with Katrina so ill." She dabbed her eyes. "You're sure you don't want me to go to the nursing home with you? I could get the day off."

"I'd rather go alone. You don't mind, do you, Mom?"

"I don't. You know that. But I really hate to see you traveling to Paris by yourself. It's just not safe these days."

"I'll be all right. I'm twenty-six."

"I worry anyway," Wini admitted. "I don't take threats of terrorism lightly. And I'm worried about AIDS in the fashion industry."

"There's one bright spot, Mother," Andrea said softly. "Investors are opening the field to women designers now."

"That's all that matters to you? You're indifferent—"

"Not indifferent. Just practical. We lost a young man at *Style Magazine* last month. He died of AIDS. We didn't know he was—that ill."

"And Rand Jordan? What about him?"

"Don't worry about Rand. He has two loves—success in his career and beautiful women."

"Then I have reason to be concerned." She cupped Andrea's chin. "Honey, when you get back from Paris, why don't you start a fashion shop here in Index or Sultan? It's so lonely without you. Come home. Marry. Your Dad and I want some grandbabies to fuss over."

Andrea thought of Neal Bennett and recoiled. "I'm too busy."

"To even meet someone? Where will your world of design end?"

"In a fashion collection of my own, Mother."

"We have your grandmother to thank for that ambitious dream. She's the one who filled your mind with fashion shows."

"Katrina liked pretty clothes, but she spent just as much money on missionaries and youth camps."

"I have to grant her that. Now go before I cry again."

Andrea's father cut across the yard to the car with her, carrying her overnighter. To break their painful silence, she said, "Dad, I'm sorry I won't be here for your birthday."

"At my age a birthday forgotten is best."

"I'll mail your present."

His eyes teased as he tossed her suitcase into the back seat. "You do remember my neck size?"

"It's something really special this time."

"I love you, Andrea. You know that, don't you?"

"I've never doubted it." She buttoned his topcoat.

"Mother and I pray for you often."

"I'm okay, Dad," she said too hastily.

"Just okay?" Then he backed off, saying, "The nursing home was my decision, not your mother's. If there had been another way—"

"Dad, is there any way I can get in touch with the men from Grandpa's army unit?"

His bushy gray brows arched above the rim of his glasses. "Whatever for? They may all be dead, except for Wendall Salisbury. He still sends Christmas cards. He lives in some farming community south of Des Moines. Summersville? Wintersville?" Irritation crept into his voice. "Andrea, you know your mother throws out the Christmas cards the day after New Year's. So why this sudden interest?"

"Grandma kept a news clipping on some veterans going back to Normandy on D-Day, forty-four years after they first landed. I wondered if any of them were friends of Grandpa's."

"I don't know. I wasn't there, sweetheart." He forced a smile as she slid into the driver's seat. "Be careful in Paris."

"I'll be busy, Dad. There'll be no time for trouble."

"Katrina used to say that trouble found you."

She squeezed his hand. "Keep her alive until I get back."

"We'll do our best. Call us collect, every day if you have time. If you get to Normandy—"

"I'll get there." Her gaze met her dad's. "Katrina always said I look just like Conrad."

His shoulders squared. "You're a York, all right."

"Dad, maybe you'll get to Normandy when Mother retires."

"Not likely. Your mother will never walk among war memorials for a vacation." He stepped back from the car.

"Will we see you this Easter, Andrea?"

"If I can get some time off."

"Try, won't you?" he asked, his breath frosty in the January chill.

"I will. Maybe Katrina could come home for a few days then?"

He glanced wistfully toward the house. "Perhaps."

As she backed the car out of the driveway, he waved frantically. "Andrea," he called. "I remember. Wendall Salisbury lives in *Winterset*, Iowa."

"Good thinking. Thanks, Dad. I'll try and call him."

At Bethann Manor Andrea found her grandmother slumped against her pillows, one trembling hand resting in the mush bowl, her eyes staring blankly at apricot walls.

"Hi, Grandma."

Katrina squinted half-mast, a puzzled expression twisting the corners of her mouth. "Do I know you?"

"I'm Andrea. Your granddaughter. I've come to feed you this morning," she said, lifting a spoon.

Katrina clamped her mouth shut.

"It's okay, Katrina," Andrea said gently. "You never were into uncooked eggs and lumpy cereal. But I'm going to do your hair today and make you pretty again."

Katrina watched intently as Andrea unpacked the shampoo and placed the threadbare Bible and Conrad's picture on the night stand. When she fastened the cameo necklace around Katrina's neck, a faint sapphire glow sparked in her grandmother's eyes.

"Oooh, Conrad gave me that the day we were married."

By late afternoon, Katrina lay in her bed dozing, a halo of gray-streaked curls framing her face. The smell of perm solution saturated her pillows. She looked old and fragile lying there, her beloved Conrad—forever a young man—in the photo beside her.

Andrea laced her fingers around Katrina's vein-riddled hands—hands that had once held brushes and painted landscapes. She shuddered at the thought of Katrina dying while she was away in Paris. Andrea gazed at her grandmother's wrinkled face. She tried to picture her young and vibrant—meeting Conrad for the first time. They had met on a train—Conrad a handsome, shy young man; Katrina a budding artist. Weeks later Katrina had followed him to Index and married him. She had shelved her love of art—for the joys of marriage and motherhood—to be picked up again someday.

When Conrad died in Normandy, Katrina had stayed in Index, in the town where she had promised to wait forever for Conrad. She kept the York homestead by taking in laundry and ironing and working part time in the General Store. Only now and then did she find time to get back to her easel. *Now* the death of a loved one was stalking Andrea, her own career weighing in the balance.

But, Grandma, Andrea said softly. *You sacrificed your whole art career by staying in Index.*

Katrina stirred, awakening with a smile on her lips. She looked around, bewildered for a moment. The smile faded as her gaze settled on Andrea. "I thought Conrad was here," she said. "Have you seen him? He promised to come back to me."

"He's in Normandy, Grandma. Remember?"

Katrina focused on the picture of Conrad, a flash of yesterday coming alive for her. "Oh, yes. He's hunting for a traitor in his unit. He's a captain in the army, you know."

"Yes, we're all very proud of him," Andrea whispered.

"But they never found the traitor."

"I know, Katrina." Andrea caressed her grandmother's hand.

"You seem to like me, young woman."

"Very much so. But I must go away in a few minutes."

"Don't go. You bring me so much joy when you come."

"I'm going to Paris and Normandy. I'm going to the cemetery for you—to see Conrad." Andrea choked on the words.

"Oh, no. No, child. Something will happen to you there."

"I'll be all right. I'll be back again in three weeks."

Katrina plucked at the sheets. "Conrad didn't come back."

"But I will. I'll come to see you at Easter or sooner if I can."

"Maybe I'll be home again by then. My granddaughter and I like company on the holidays. I'll tell her you're coming."

"*I am your granddaughter. I am Andrea.*"

Katrina turned suddenly fretful. "Can you get me a ticket to Normandy before you go? Conrad is waiting for me."

Andrea leaned over her grandmother, washing Katrina's face with her tears. "Yes, he's been waiting for you for a long time by a pure river, crystal clear."

As she placed her cheek against Katrina's, the cameo necklace snapped free and dropped on the bed between them. "I'll look for Conrad for you. You just get well, Grandma."

Katrina clutched the necklace in her fingers and pressed it into Andrea's hand. "Give this to my granddaughter for me," she murmured. "I want her to have it."

"*I am your granddaughter.*"

"Yes, I know, Andrea," Katrina answered, a flicker of recognition momentarily lighting the tired sea-blue eyes.

❦❦❦

The day before her trip to Paris, Andrea hurried to the Denby Jewelers in Westwood. Repairing the watch for her dad's birthday was her way of saying, "Dad, I'm sorry for choosing Paris over my grandmother, my own career over a family crisis."

Andrea tried to brush off her guilt as she entered the jewelry shop. She waved at the owner, a gangly man bent over his work bench, a jeweler's loupe clipped to his glasses, his skin an indoor white.

"Good morning, Mr. Denby."

He peered at her over the loupe and smiled. "Ah, Miss York, are you looking for another jade ring?"

"Nothing new, but can you repair an old watch for me?"

"That's my business."

His back stayed hunched as he stood and grasped the Elgin with his tapered fingers. "That's an old-timer. They don't make them like that nowadays."

"It belonged to my grandfather. I'm hoping you can make it run again for my dad's birthday present."

"It's been done before," he said, prying the back open.

Bushy brows arced as he lifted out a tissue-thin film with a pair of tweezers. His pleasantries vanished.

"What do you think, Mr. Denby? Can you do a rush job?"

He didn't hear her. "There's a screw or two missing in the watch, probably to make room for *this*."

"Can't you replace the screws?"

"That's not the problem." He twisted the tiny film against the light, his manner incriminating. "Must have been important for him to hide this in the old Elgin."

He had her attention now. "What is it, Mr. Denby?"

"Cryptic film of some sort." His eyes darkened as they met hers. "Was your grandfather military intelligence?"

"Infantry, I think. An army captain. Why?"

"Then you'd best tell him what he left hidden in the watch."

"Sir, my grandfather died fifty years ago."

"World War II," Denby mused. "Thought so. That's my war. Looks like the kind of coded message we used back then. I guess you never opened the watch before, did you?"

"No reason to."

"That's why the film's intact. It's been air-tight. It makes no difference now. Whatever message he was trying to send is of no use to anyone today."

Denby's unspoken words shouted, *Traitor. Traitor.* Had her grandfather's answer lain dormant in his watch all these years, she wondered, or had Katrina hidden the truth on purpose?

"Miss York, about this watch, might run you sixty to seventy dollars to get it running again. Take about ten days."

She frowned, but not at the price. She had expected it to be even more. "You can't do a rush job?"

"A week at the earliest."

She trembled, her fears centering on the tissuelike film Denby held in his hand again. Her grandfather's secrets dangled at the end of the tweezers, the jeweler's gaze impugning her grandfather's integrity. She wanted to snatch the tainted Elgin from Denby's hands and flee.

"I guess the watch repair will have to wait until I get back from my trip to Paris, Mr. Denby."

"Paris, eh? You're adventuresome. I thought the White House was discouraging travel abroad these days."

"They are," Andrea admitted. "But this is a business trip."

Denby replaced the message and snapped the case shut. He patted her hand gently. "Was your grandfather killed in action?"

"Yes, the Normandy Invasion."

"Then whatever debt he owed has been paid." He handed the Elgin to her. "Normandy was *my* battle. A bloody mess. If you ever get this code deciphered, let me know."

She didn't answer him. Her feet were walking, but inside she was running, running from her grandmother's words: *There was a traitor in your grandfather's unit.*

Back at the apartment, away from Denby's accusing gaze, she sorted through her grandfather's possessions again—his well-read Bible, the dogtags he had once worn, the snapshots of his friends. She looked at the names her grandfather had scrawled on the back: Drew Gregory, upstate New York; Vince Giovetti, St. Petersburg; Smitty, Brooklyn; Weinberger, San Francisco; and Wendall Salisbury from Iowa—the one who sent Christmas cards. A war had brought them together. A war had torn them apart.

She wondered what these men had wanted to be before the war took a chunk out of their lives. What caused one of them to betray his country? For her grandfather's sake—for her own—she longed to know the answer.

◉◉◉

It was late, one o'clock in the morning in Winterset, Iowa. She'd be calling a stranger out of bed. She dialed anyway.

Several Salisburys were listed, the operator told her; five began with W—a Wilbur, a Wade, and three W. Salisburys. She jotted down the last three numbers.

Wesley Salisbury's wife was irate at being awakened. "Prankster," she said, slamming the phone in Andrea's ear.

Andrea's second call went better. "If that's you, Spence," a sleepy voice said, "call back in the morning. If it ain't you and it's important, hang on."

She hung on. When he spoke again, she said, "I'm trying to locate a Wendall Salisbury, a friend of my grandfather's."

"It's the right name, but the wrong hour."

She apologized, but the man said, "Never mind. I don't sleep all that well anyway. So who's your grandfather?"

"Conrad York."

He sucked in his breath before he repeated, "Y-O-R-K?"

"Yes, he was a captain in the army."

"Captain York?" Again there was a gurgling in his throat, annoyance in his voice, "The York I knew died a long time ago."

"In Normandy? Omaha Beach?" she asked.

"Yep. I was one of his men. His granddaughter, you say?"

"Yes. I'm going to France—to Normandy."

"My Missus and I did that awhile back. Forty-four years

after the boys and I hit the beachhead. A whole plane load of us, mostly veterans and their wives."

"And did it help going back?"

"Cried like a baby," he admitted. "It's peaceful there now, not like the day we landed. But it all came back. We saw the captain's grave. He was a good man. Spent his spare time reading his Bible or bragging about his wife and kid."

"That kid was my dad."

"Figured that. Captain had so many plans for that boy." He sounded short-winded again, like a man who smoked two packs a day.

"Mr. Salisbury," she said softly, "I'd like to trace some of the men who served with my grandfather."

"Anyone in particular?" he asked.

"Vince Giovetti. Weinberger. Drew Gregory."

"Corporal Weinberger got *his* back there with your grandfather. Only they never found his body."

Andrea felt sadness for another young man who didn't come home. "What about the others?"

"Gregory was a tall, skinny kid who didn't say much until we were on the ship heading to Normandy."

Andrea heard a woman's scolding voice in the background, but Wendall Salisbury went right on musing.

"Most of us on the landing craft were seasick and barfing into our helmets, and I hear this kid telling Captain York that he hadn't turned seventeen yet. The kid's face was a mustard green like our uniforms. I figured he just wanted to get out of what lay ahead. Turned out he was telling the truth."

"Seventeen?" Andrea repeated. "How'd he get in the army?"

"Lied about his age. By the time the army caught up with his birth date, the kid was old enough to wear the uniform. He ended up decorated for bravery. Worked for the government ever since. Went back to Europe after his divorce."

"Where?" she asked eagerly.

"In London, the last time we heard. Why don't you send a cable or telex to the embassy there?"

But I won't have time to fly to London, she thought.

Aloud she asked, "Do you remember any of the other men?"

"Not really. You lose touch after all these years."

"What about Smitty?"

"Harland C. Smith? I forgot about him. Shouldn't have. He and Drew Gregory were always at odds. Fist fights and all. Smith lives in Paris. Owns some kind of corporation on the Champs-Élysées. Always said he wasn't going back to the streets of Brooklyn."

"I'd love to talk with him."

Salisbury gave a low chuckle. "We tried that on our Normandy reunion. Smith wouldn't even have dinner with us."

Salisbury kept reminiscing as the phone bill ran higher. "Of course, Miss York, if I remember correctly, we didn't take too well to Smitty. He was cocky and street tough. Always taking chances. He came to our unit on transfer in those final days of preparation for Normandy. He replaced one of our men injured in training. We were a tightly knit group, leery of newcomers."

The line was silent except for Salisbury's labored breathing. Finally, he continued, "Smitty said he worked for Eisenhower. I guess his bragging about the general just didn't sit right with us."

"But the G.I.s respected Eisenhower."

"You can respect a man, but it doesn't make you eager to risk your life for him. Some of the men didn't make it."

"I know. My grandfather was one of them." Her voice faltered, "Sir, were you with my grandfather when he died?"

"Not me, Miss York. Couldn't even tell you who was beside me running that bloody beachhead. But Smitty might have been there with the captain."

"Then how can I get in touch with him?"

Salisbury hesitated. "He's not a friendly man, Miss York. Not where your grandfather is concerned. But if you insist, let me ask my wife. She might remember how to reach him."

The minutes ticked away. Then he was back chuckling.

"Em says the company name was PLASTEC. Kinda' think she's right. Old Harland is into plastics—maybe computer parts or medical supplies. Whatever it is, you can bet it's profitable."

Chapter 6

Harland C. Smith, a sagacious opportunist, spent Saturday alone at his office on the Champs-Élysées monitoring the latest explosive situation in the Middle East. Periodic embargoes on food and medical supplies always made shipments to Baghdad difficult. Sending the arms through Southern Yemen or the Persian Gulf was impossible, through Iran unlikely. Turkey and Jordan were both dubious routes. A recent shipment through the Mediterranean had been intercepted by patrol boats, causing another international ruckus. This time he would suggest going direct to Libya or Syria under the guise of humanitarianism.

As he worked out the details mentally, he switched on his computer for a code memo. The screen indicated a telex message in the system. He punched the button and moments later stared at a printout of the message from Andrea York:

> *You served in Normandy with my grandfather, Conrad York. Request interview. Arriving Sunday, Charles de Gaulle International. Registered three weeks Interontinental Hotel.*

Her time of arrival and hotel phone number glared up at him. He didn't need Captain York's granddaughter stirring up bitter memories of his miserable years as a mud-caked

G.I.; he had put those days into a neat compartmental file labeled FORGET.

He had been transferred to the infantry unit, edged out as a courier to Eisenhower without an explanation. There had been no time to pass the microfilm to the German agent at the London pub. From the moment of transfer, he was at odds with the men in the unit, his freedom gone. His days were consumed by intense training sessions—scaling steep English cliffs in preparation for the second front in Europe, sea cliffs with death written all over them.

Planting the microfilm in the captain's watch had been a piece of luck. May of 1944 had come and gone, and June had washed in on them in torrential rains. Then Captain York rushed in and told them that D-Day was on. York was holding his watch to his ear.

"Trouble, Captain?" Harland had asked. "Let me fix it for you."

He had tampered with it, hiding the microfilm in the watch.

Now, as he thought about York's granddaughter, a headache stirred at the base of his neck and crept painfully across his forehead. He pushed his thick glasses up, his eyes narrowing as he pressed his fingers against the bridge of his crooked nose. His nagging concern persisted into a gastric attack. What if Andrea York were like the captain, bold and persistent?

At noon, Paris time, Harland shoved her telex into his pocket. He called the Cafe Amitie and left a message with the Maitre d', a *menu change* for the Canadian artist. Harland saw Ryan Ebsworth as a casual, flippant young man with a veneer of boyish innocence—a man without a conscience. Ryan would ask few questions, yet he possessed an artistic charm that women adored.

Harland's control of the Amitie was an added bonus. Jacques Marseilles, a weak, cowardly man, paid to keep his past hidden; Harland disliked him. But in some ways Harland saw himself in Ryan Ebsworth—clever and capable, crafty and double-minded. Ebsworth liked the good life—plush hotels, rich foods, first-class air travel. He was

without political convictions. Harland imagined that
Ebsworth could kill with a smile. He'd order Ebsworth to
arrange a casual meeting with Miss York, keep her under
surveillance during her three weeks in Paris, and, *if necessary, eliminate her.*

⊛⊛⊛

Early in the afternoon, Harland's wife called to tell him
that she and the boys had returned from their holiday on
the Normandy coast. He missed Monique when she was
gone, always fighting the fear that she would go one day
and not come back.

The boys were the sons of his middle years; it was a
source of constant aggravation to be mistaken for their
grandfather. Anzel and Giles knew that their father was
American, but they knew little about his country. More
than anything, they were French. They were the result of
Monique's unguarded moments. She had wanted children.
Now as Harland grew older, Giles and Anzel represented a
powerful part of himself, his ongoing link with life.

Harland did not share Monique's love of Normandy. For
him it held black memories. He allowed himself to remember the blurred images: a ghostly fleet of warships crossing
the English Channel in the dead of night; B-26 Marauders
sweeping low over Omaha Beach; yellow-orange explosions
ripping men apart, lighting up the hellhole that awaited
them; landing craft pouring out men and equipment on the
bloody white sands; men dying before they could dig in.

Even now Harland felt the pounding of his own heart as
he had felt it that June morning in 1944 while he waited to
go ashore. His fear of battle and his hatred of Captain York
screamed into the pre-dawn hours. He despised York's
power to order him from the landing craft into battle. He
watched York shake his wrist watch, then lift it to his ear.
When their gaze met, it was as though York had stared
through Harland's nakedness to his very soul. But York had
no proof that Harland had tried to pass classified documents, to sell out to the Germans, anything to stop this inva-

sion. Winning or losing meant nothing to Harland. Living did.

As the ramp of their LST went down, they waded ashore, scrambling over fallen comrades and plodding toward hidden pillboxes where Germans waited to fragment their lives. Captain York crouched in front of Harland, racing a zigzagged line toward the cliffs. *Harland had to retrieve the captain's watch.* At the other end of that bloody beachhead the Germans waited. If he could reach them, the microfilm would be his ticket out of this hellish nightmare.

In blind rage at York and war, Harland lifted his M1 Garand rifle and fired his first two shots, making certain that Captain York was one of the battle casualties on the beaches of Normandy.

York fell face forward, his field jacket soaking in blood, his olive green steel helmet dropping beside him. Harland belly-crawled to the captain, recoiling at the moans of the dying man as he tried to tear York's watch from him. But Drew Gregory was there. And then a medic dragged York behind a grounded jeep.

Harland had crawled on without the microfilm.

Days later Harland pounced into the same foxhole with Drew Gregory, aiming for his jugular. Drew spun on his boots; the butt of his M1 splintered the bones in Harland's face, flattening his nose. Drew's self-defense injury put Harland out of the march to Paris.

After his medical discharge, Harland vowed to rise above the poverty of his boyhood and to rescue his mother from it. She chose to stay in the Brooklyn neighborhood and die there. He chose Paris.

So France had been his home for four decades, America all but forgotten. He rarely allowed himself the luxury of reminiscing. What was there to remember? His childhood was a painful blur, his mother cowering at his father's drunkenness. Then came the draft of World War II—his escape route from the noisy neighborhood into hell itself.

The only good memory from his boyhood was spending time in his uncle's watch repair shop learning the intricacies of the trade. Harland's gaze went automatically to his jeweled watch. He eased his finger under the band and adjusted it on his wrist. A watch—the first symbol of power and greed he had ever experienced.

Harland had clawed his way to respectability as the owner of the Plastec Corporation of Paris. A facade, of course, but, by whatever means, he maintained his affluent lifestyle. His numbered bank accounts came from negotiating the sale of armaments to the highest bidder, mostly to Third World countries. The Plastec Corporation remained the cover for these illegal transactions, the unsullied, silent partner. What these other countries did with military weapons beyond the purchase date was of little concern to him.

🌑🌑🌑

Leaving his plush office on the Champs-Élysées, Harland walked to his apartment, a honey-colored stone complex that overlooked the Seine. The apartment was tastefully decorated, uncluttered, the ceilings low, the hardwood flooring highly polished, the seventeenth-century furnishings charming in their antiquity. He went at once to their bedroom that faced the private garden where Monique spent so many of her hours.

Four-year-old Giles looked up as Harland entered, his enormous brown eyes and long lashes like Monique's. The boy sat on their bed, his chubby bare legs crossed, his shoes still on. Giles made no effort to come to him.

His greeting when it came was a question, "Papa, you are home?"

It was an awkward moment. He wanted the boy to run to him. At times, like now, he longed for that paternal contact with his sons, particularly Giles. He adored the child, more because he was like Monique than for any other reason. As he passed Giles, he patted the boy's head.

Monique sat at her dressing table in a sheer lace gown, her back to him, watching him through the gilt-edged mirror. Harland went to her and stood behind her, his hands resting on her shoulders.

"I missed you," he said.

She caressed his hand. "You didn't have to come home early."

He studied them both in the mirror through his thick-rimmed glasses. His black penetrating eyes took in her beauty—the shiny dark hair, her curious brown eyes, the ivory skin, and wide, sensual lips, the graceful hands.

He placed his cheek to hers. "I love you, Monique."

She smiled. "I know," she said.

He had been captivated by her from the moment he had first seen her in Normandy, that day when he forced himself to view the war memorials. She walked carefree, a barefoot peasant girl leading a stray cow back to the farm. He was forty-eight then, single, uncommitted, his desire for her intense.

She was barely eighteen. He bought her with promises of the good life, the luxury of Paris—no questions asked about his background or his business—in exchange for her utter devotion and faithfulness. They kept their agreements.

Monique reminded him of what his mother might have been in her youth—a woman of beauty before poverty and despair dug ugly ridges into her features. Harland vowed that this would never happen to Monique. He lavished beautiful gifts on her, even choosing her wardrobe from the best haute-coutures in Paris.

"You look tired, Harland," she said. "Did something go wrong?"

He tried to blot out the memory of Andrea York's telex. "Nothing that I can't work out," he said. "But I need you, Monique."

She lifted her face, and he kissed her warmly. She was gentle, accepting. But he saw, as he gazed back in the mirror, what she must see all the time—their vast age difference.

Monique at thirty-seven was almost half his age. No matter how straight he carried himself nor how trim he remained, his sixty-eight years were clearly visible in sagging facial features, dark circles beneath his eyes, his hair streaked with gray.

"What you need, Harland, is a good meal and a drink. We'll eat early, as soon as Anzel gets home."

"Where is he?"

"He ran off to be with his friends the moment we got home."

"To avoid me?"

"Perhaps," she said softly. "Come, my dear, I'll get you that drink." She slipped her hand in his.

Harland smiled enticingly. "Why don't we ask the *bonne* to take Giles for a walk in the park—for an hour perhaps?"

She seemed amused, compliant as she sent Giles away. He slid from the bed and ran from the room, calling happily for the maid.

Harland faced Monique again, his longing mounting as he touched her. She loosened his tie as he slipped his suit coat off, her gaze settling on the telex crushed in his pocket.

"Business?" she asked, her voice troubled.

"Yes, but nothing for you to worry about," he answered.

Chapter 7

At dawn that same morning, Ryan Ebsworth split the sheets and tumbled out of his bed at the Hotel de Crillon, his bronzed body shivering as he stood.

"Collette," he called. "Where are you?"

The room was silent, empty. She was gone. He moved barefoot into the bathroom and glared at her note taped to the shower door. "Who is this Kathryn that you speak of in your sleep?"

He uttered a wry little laugh. If she only knew!

Kathryn was his godly aunt. She was against wars, repulsed by terrorism, and an advocate of marriage and the family. For more than two years as he had pursued his subversive political activities, he had steeled himself against her prayers.

He swore as he stepped into the shower, cursing Collette for her beauty and availability, his aunt for her prayers, his new assignment even more. Anger had roiled inside him ever since Wednesday's phone contact at the Cafe Amitie. His latest orders: *diversionary activity*. For Ryan the meaning was implicit. A bombing or an assassination. A blind stratagem to divert the enemy's attention from the major target. He knew that those who served the diversionary detail were often being tested for loyalty or targeted for death.

This time he was not to be trusted with the exchange of information nor with the role of a gentleman negotiator.

Why? he wondered. He was skillful at obtaining large sums for minimal arms, the money safely deposited to Swiss accounts. Why this new assignment, this risk to his own life? Where had he failed?

He left the hotel an hour later, balancing his art case, and walked the quaysides of the Seine, his thick beige sweater and leather jacket warding off the chill.

He considered going to the Louvre to work indoors, but found himself on the metro speeding to the hilly Montmartre district with its lingering Bohemian influence. Many sidewalk artists went elsewhere these days, refusing to risk the effects of cold weather on their canvas. But Ryan found satisfaction painting in the shadow of the whitewashed domes of the Basilica Sacré-Coeur, its stones growing whiter with the passage of time.

He went inside once, not for spiritual comfort, but out of curiosity. The broad nave and vaulted ceiling gave a hollow sound to the chanting at the altar. The vastness muted the steady pilgrimage down the aisles. Some came to worship; some came with cameras flashing.

He found no counsel staring up at the cathedral this morning either. His spirit still rankled, his mood black with despair as he set up his easel in the sheltered doorway of a tiny bistro. Someone was playing games with him, testing him. Someone was controlling his life, a father-figure as absent in face and name as his own father had been.

Ever since the death of Melody Prescott, Ryan had done exactly as he had been told, traveling in and out of Europe, brazenly arranging the sale of arms and documents one moment, painting the next. He recoiled now at the thought of shedding blood in an act of terrorism, of risking his own life.

Reaching for his palette, he dabbed at the Nile blue paint with the tip of his brush. Moments later his first strokes changed the bland of the canvas to blue, nothingness to sky. If he could only reproduce what he saw—the majestic cathedral before him or the tranquil, frothy clouds he had seen at dawn. Paris not quite awake, not quite in motion for the day. These were his most peaceful moments, paintbrush in hand.

In this brittle moment of peace, he had to admit that his lifeless efforts could never match the genius of his father's paintings. He could never finish a work of art that met the standards of Robert L. Ebsworth.

Ryan steadied his hand against the palette. Painting was his dream, a dream as elusive as his early boyhood in Quebec, Canada.

🌀🌀🌀

Six-year-old Ryan had sat squeezed between his parents in the old truck, his torn teddy bear clutched in both hands. "Daddy, I don't want to go away from Quebec," he cried.

"I know," his mother said, patting his bony, bruised knee.

"Don't upset the boy, Kori. He'll be fine."

"Without us, Bob? So far from home. He's only six."

"Your sister Kathryn will give him a good home."

"We don't know that for certain."

He had glanced sharply her way, his eyes off the road for a second. "Kori, you called your sister, didn't you?"

Kori cried then. "I thought you'd change your mind."

Ryan watched the needle on the speedometer swing ahead. He couldn't read two-digit numbers yet, but he could feel that they were going faster, too fast. His mother's hand gripped his, the teddy falling to the floorboard.

"Please, Daddy, I want to go back home. I'll be good."

His father's hands tightened on the steering wheel. "You're not bad, son. It's just when I'm painting you get in the way."

"But, Bob, you spank him so hard when you're drinking."

His father shrugged. "I'm no good with kids. I'm struggling to make a go of my art, Kori. Ryan's just one more mouth to feed."

"He's our son, Bob. You could get a job."

"As a hired hand on your sister's farm? I'm an artist, Kori."

Quebec was far behind them now. His father kept driving

hard across the prairie toward Harrison Lake. They had
stayed at cheap hotels and stopped only at petrol stations for
gas or to grab sandwiches and beer at greasy spoons along
the way. They had reached Kathryn and Ben Culvert's farm
in British Columbia late Wednesday.

His aunt and uncle came to the door together. Kathryn
looked down at Ryan and smiled. She was pretty even then,
her blue blouse and sweater reflecting what Ryan would
later realize were sky blue eyes. Ben looked older than his
wife, a stern-faced man with weather wrinkles on his skin.
He studied Ryan's parents coolly. Ryan shrank back from
Ben, but Kathryn smiled warmly again.

Ryan remembered their differences now—from the van-
tage point of adulthood. The Culverts had been dignified,
well-dressed; Kathryn's French was flawless. In compari-
son, his parents were shabbily clothed—his mother, thin,
nervous; his dad, slipshod in worn jodhpurs and scuffed
boots, a pack of cigarettes in his shirt pocket, a can of beer
in his hand.

Ryan's father tilted the beer can and emptied it. He wiped
his lips dry, saying, "All we want is a good home for the boy."

Ryan's uncle argued heatedly. Kathryn tried to calm him.

His dad said, "What we're doing is best for the boy, Ben."

Kathryn turned to her younger sister. "Kori, you can't
run out on this child. He's only a boy. He's much too little."

Kori pulled her sweater tightly around her. "We can
barely keep ourselves on the money Bob makes, let alone
keep a child."

"Then let Bob forget that paintbrush and get a decent job.
He could even work here at the farm with Ben."

Ryan's dad glared at Kathryn. "Never. Painting is my
life."

Ben's anger exploded. "Your son should be."

"Please," Kori had begged. "As soon as Bob sells some of
his paintings, we'll come back for the boy." Her eyes swept
over the Culvert luxury. "You've got to help us, Kathryn."

Kathryn glanced at Ben and then said, "We'll want a
signed release. A legal document. Ben can arrange it with
our lawyer."

"Anything," Bob snapped. "Just mail it. I'll sign it."

"If we don't hear from you," Ben said, "we'll take you to court for deserting Ryan." He stalked to the doorway and then turned back. "It won't be your painting that will matter then, Robert. It will be your inability to function as a parent."

Ryan's dad crushed the empty beer can and shook his fist at Ben's retreating form.

Whimpering, Ryan said, "Daddy, I don't want to stay here."

"Yes, you do, son. They've got lots of animals."

"Cows," Kathryn corrected.

"Let's go, Bob," Kori whispered, her hands wrapping over his doubled fist. On the porch, she called back, "Take good care of my son, Kathryn. I love him." Without a good-bye for Ryan, she ran to catch up with Bob.

Ryan tried to race after them, his arms outstretched, his fingers clawing at space. His screams followed his parents as they climbed into their truck and drove away. He didn't even remember them looking back.

"Come, Ryan," Kathryn had said in French, "let's go inside."

He ran from her, tearing across the yard, his short legs barely touching the ground. He hesitated at the barn, repulsed by the smell of cows, dozens of them mooing and stirring in their own manure. Then he scooted past the swishing tails, up the ladder to the hayloft and buried his face in the hay, drenching it with tears. His gut gnawed from hunger. He longed for a bathroom, but it didn't matter. He'd waited too long.

His aunt kept vigil that night at the foot of the loft. Between his sobs, he heard her humming hymns. The next morning he stumbled down the ladder, falling reluctantly into her open arms. She said nothing about his wet trousers. Instead, she kept her arm around him and led him to the house, up the stairs to the bedroom that would be his, and into the adjoining bath. He didn't fight her as she stripped off his clothes and helped him into the tub.

She scrubbed him down and shampooed his hair, rubbing his damp curls with such vigor that he was certain he would be bald like Uncle Ben when he glanced in the mirror again.

She pointed to his bed. "Put those clothes on, Ryan," she said. "And we'll go shopping and buy you outfits of your own. And maybe a bedspread and curtains to make this truly a boy's room."

"After this," Ben said from the doorway, "he'll take his own bath. He's not a baby, Kathryn. He's six. Remember that."

"Oh, Ben," she had laughed, "six isn't very old. I haven't corrupted him. But you're right. After this we will trust Ry to take his own bath and pick up his own room."

She scooped up Ryan's dirty clothes. Speaking in French, she said, "Now, I'm going to get breakfast for both of you."

"Good," Ben answered. "And, Kathryn, we'll speak no more of yesterday, *ever*. And from now on, you will use English when speaking to the boy in this house."

His uncle's words sounded sharp, but the blue-gray eyes that searched Ryan's were kind and caring.

His aunt smiled patiently. "Ry," she said, "outside from time to time we will speak French so you won't forget it. But in the house, for Ben's sake, we'll always speak English."

Ryan kept his distance from Ben, fearful that another father-figure might desert him. He did his chores, intrigued by the farm machinery, the milking, and the birthing that took place periodically.

When Ryan was nine, Ben turned over the responsibility of one of the calves to him. Ryan named it Moots for want of a better name. Besides Moots, he didn't risk making friends. But if he loved anyone, it was his Aunt Kathryn.

Whenever the chores were done, Ryan climbed back to the loft to draw. He advanced from crayons to acrylic paints by the time he was ten. Ryan wanted to paint more than anything else. He wanted to be better than his father, better than Robert L. Ebsworth, but his paintings were mediocre at best.

They heard from his parents five years later—and only then to be notified that his mother was dead from a drug overdose. Kathryn wept openly for her sister. Ryan never shed a tear.

The Culverts took him to an art museum in Vancouver on his fifteenth birthday. As Ryan wandered from room to room, he came to a landscape painting of Quebec that stirred childhood memories. The picture with its blend of azure blues, Kendal green, and corals was a masterpiece. Then he saw the artist's name in the corner: ROBERT L. EBSWORTH. It glared out at him, reminding him that he could never match his father's artistry.

"My father?" he asked bitterly.

Kathryn slipped her arm in his. "We think so. Ben is checking with the gallery owner."

"My father promised to come back for me when he succeeded."

"I know, Ry," she said.

The curator spoke pleasantly of Robert's popularity even in Europe. "There's a kind of madness to some of his work," he said as they stood before a third painting. "Drug-related, I'm sure. But he'd be one of the greats if he didn't dabble with cocaine."

Two years later Ryan's uncle died—leaving Kathryn well-off financially. In time, Ryan would be heir to a farm and hard sun-up to sun-down labor. But he told Kathryn that he wanted none of it. He'd look for a way to make money without milking a herd of cattle.

He repeatedly rejected her offers of agricultural training, enrollment at the university to develop his language skills, the immediate management of the Culvert ranch, or art school to feed into his artistic nature. Only travel satisfied his wanderlust. Though Ryan traveled often to Europe, he never looked for his father. Robert L. Ebsworth remained a faceless man.

The sun in Paris was high overhead now, beating down on Ryan. It took the coldness from the tip of his ears, warming him enough to unzip his jacket. He stepped back from his canvas and studied it critically. The frothy, almost mythical clouds were perfect, the Parisian sky the right shade of blue. But the dome on his cathedral was out of proportion, and one branch of the weeping willow tree lacked luster.

He lifted his paintbrush intending to wipe out the whole scene with two bold black stripes. Instead, in mockery he wrote ROBERT L. EBSWORTH in the corner of his own canvas.

A crowd of tourists leaving the bistro glanced curiously at Ryan. One wiry young man lingered by the easel, studying Ryan's canvas with brooding dark eyes. He was intent, olive-skinned. *Syrian, perhaps,* Ryan thought.

The stranger touched the picture, his smile scornful. "Your tree weeps," he said, his accent clearly Middle Eastern. "It shows the sadness of its artist."

He bowed curtly, turned, and disappeared into the crowd.

Ryan saw her then, Collette from the Cafe Amitie sashaying toward him, her cheeks flushed from hurrying. She was crazily dressed—her coat wide open, her jade blouse low-cut, her skirt short, her legs bare, her hands jammed into the coat pockets.

She nodded after the stranger. "I see Kusa found you, Ryan," she said. "When he came by the Amitie looking for you, he said you'd be working together. Is he from Canada?"

Kusa? de Kusa, the explosives expert? He was younger than Ryan had expected.

Ryan's eyes narrowed as he turned back to Collette, but he touched her rosy cheek gently. "I'm sure you didn't come here to talk to me about this Kusa."

"No," she admitted, smiling up at him. "Jacques sent me. He wants you to come at once. Something about a *menu change.*"

Chapter 8

Andrea York stepped briskly into the marvelous insanity at Charles de Gaulle International. It was a frenzy of activity and stepped-up security, of bright, dazzling lights and distorted sounds muffled by the roar of the jets. Above her vivid, billboards advertised French perfumes, wines, and the exotic fashions of seductive men and women with windblown hair.

Multiple languages bombarded her ears—the harsh, guttural sounds of German; the staccato speech of the French; the rapid-paced Italian; and the nasal twang of Cantonese as a Chinese man cut across her path, bowed imploringly, and excused himself.

Her patience frayed trying to find Rand Jordan's driver in the noisy chaos. She decided to forget about Francois Deborde and taxi to the hotel alone.

Ahead of her, beyond the currency exchange, a baggage carousel squeaked on its mechanical pathway. Leashed canines sniffed at the unattended luggage, their glistening bodies tugging against their restraints. As Andrea grabbed cautiously for her suitcase, she found herself face to face with a bundle of feathers clutched in the hands of a Hindu. The feathers dusted her face, tickled her nose, aimed for her eyes. She pulled back in alarm, her thoughts on terrorism and poison darts.

She inched her way toward the exit, putting distance between herself and the man with the feathery plumes. A placid gendarme waved her on out of the terminal. Within seconds she joined the curbside line at the taxi stand. As she stood there, she felt disgruntled, off-balance like her pullman suitcase, lopsided against its damaged wheel.

The air was stagnant with motor fumes, sweat, and heavy perfume. Taxis squealed to a halt, their drivers barking orders as they loaded their fares and screeched off. Still there was a semblance of order as people waited their turns, nonchalantly blowing smoke rings in Andrea's face.

Behind the smoke haze, she saw a stocky, middle-aged man with a shadowed beard and a triple chin, his dark visor cap shoved back on his balding head. A placard rested against his shoulder. Miss Y-U-R-k, it read.

"I'm Miss York," she cried.

He spat the stub of a cigarette from his mouth and grinned.

"I'm late," he said, his English clipped but clear.

He trashed his placard in the nearest bin, swooped up her luggage and was guiding her between taxis when she remembered to ask, "You're Francois Deborde, aren't you?"

He urged her into the taxi. She collapsed on the seat, bracing for a wild ride, uneasy because he hadn't answered. She repeated her question as he adjusted the rearview mirror.

"No," he admitted. "I'm his father. I'm Pierre Deborde."

The taxi zoomed forward and swept under the freeway sign pointing toward Paris. As they careened in and out of the traffic lanes, Pierre volunteered, "This is my son's taxi. Don't worry, Mademoiselle. You'll be at your hotel in thirty minutes. But first when we reach Paris, a drive down Champs-Élysées, compliments of Mr. Jordan."

As they neared the city, the Parisian skyline spread out before them. The Eiffel Tower stood high above the double-pitched mansard rooftops. Among the ornate buildings and the medieval cathedrals, Andrea spotted the flying buttresses of Notre Dame and the gentle flowing Seine.

Pierre sped up the tree-lined Champs-Élysées. Haute-couture boutiques branched to Andrea's left and right. At the far end of the boulevard stood the Arc de Triomphe. People milled under its arch; the French flag snapped above it. Pierre circled and drove the mile-long avenue once more, past the same fancy restaurants and fashionable shops.

"Oh, Pierre, your city is beautiful, breathtaking."

He smiled. "You are not like the others, Miss York."

"The others?"

"Monsieur Jordan's other women are caught up in their own glamour. But *you* see Paris." He blew her a kiss through the mirror. "All that is France, all that is French is here in Paris."

Andrea leaned forward as Pierre jerked to a stop in front of the InterContinental. It was Rand Jordan's kind of hotel, first-class, high-style perfection. A bright yellow awning shaded the hotel entry; flags fluttered on each side. A row of high arches ran along the face of the building and lantern-styled lights hung beneath each arch. A uniformed doorman smiled warmly as he helped her from the taxi.

From within the cab, Pierre called, "It takes a lifetime to know Paris. You must come back."

"I'll be here three weeks."

"Not long enough." He smiled pleasantly. "Your ride to the Dior fashion show tomorrow is already arranged."

"Will you be driving me, Pierre?"

His eyes twinkled. "My son Francois will, once I tell him how lovely the mademoiselle is."

She waved as he left and then followed a bellboy into the soft elegance of the lobby. Its nineteenth-century grandeur and crystal lamps impressed her as she walked across the thick oriental rugs to the guest relations desk. The concierge looked impeccable in his dark suit; his silk tie matched his silvery hair.

Another hotel guest reached the concierge ahead of Andrea. His fingers drummed impatiently on the marble-top counter. He was thirtyish, Andrea decided, tall and attractive, with raven black hair trimmed evenly across the back of his head.

"Mr. Bodinat, my name is Sherm Prescott," he said. "Is there a message for me?"

"No, Mr. Prescott."

As she stood beside the man, Andrea caught the alluring scent of his Lagerfeld after-shave, and she sensed his anger rising. She noted his strong profile, the determined jaw tightening. She wondered about the color of his eyes, whether he could smile. His voice was deep and resonant, clearly American with a slight southern drawl, polite, with a hint of sadness. He was sharply dressed in a rich taupe worsted-wool suit, a light blue-striped shirt, an expressive silk tie, and cap-toed leather shoes—not casual enough for a GQ model, but rather a picture of urban sophistication.

A businessman, she concluded, in Paris to defend the rights of his American corporation in a united European Community. He glanced at her unexpectedly. She looked away embarrassed, but not before she caught his fleeting smile, the look of pain, not anger, in his deep-set almond eyes.

She listened, intrigued as he asked, "You're certain there's been no message for me from the Hotel de Crillon?"

"Nothing at all, Mr. Prescott," Bodinat said.

Her sympathy for the dark stranger mounted.

Bodinat glanced at Andrea for the third time. Even the American gave her an apologetic glance, his eyes kind as he focused on her. "I'm sorry for taking so long," he said.

Immediately, Claud Bodinat snapped his fingers and beckoned to a blonde receptionist. "Micheline, come."

Speaking to Prescott again, Bodinat said, "You do have a guest, sir. Your friend, Mr. Porter Deven, asked to go directly to your room. We refused. Hotel policy, you know."

"Where is he then?"

"In the bar with a friend. You're to join them. He said it was urgent that he talk with you."

"Then I'll find him. Thank you, Mr. Bodinat."

Andrea didn't hear the rest. Micheline was welcoming her in perfect English. Andrea smiled, picked up her pen, and registered.

Moments later the elevator doors closed, blocking out her view of the American and the elegant lobby. She found herself comparing the stranger with Neal Bennett. Neal was a Don Juan, an amorist with windblown hair and a casual, indifferent manner. This stranger seemed confident, mature —a man with a purpose. In her jet-lag weariness, she thought of the Bush House back in Index and of her Mother wanting her to settle down and marry.

Andrea could still hear the deep, rich quality of the stranger's voice. In those fleeting glances at the reception desk, she thought his eyes were almond. Or were they hazel?

With a pang of homesickness, halfway between tears and laughter, she thought of Katrina. She'd call home before tumbling into bed and sleeping through her first day in Paris.

Ryan Ebsworth lowered his newspaper discreetly as Sherman Prescott strode across the lobby toward the lounge. He folded the *Le Monde* and tossed it on the end table. He didn't like it—Sherm Prescott and Andrea York registered at the same hotel.

Ryan had waited in the InterContinental all morning for a glimpse of Andrea York. He had wandered from the lobby to the terrace restaurant for a late breakfast. In the brief time since his phone contact at the Cafe Amitie, more information had been faxed to him. He knew that she was American, a fashion journalist with *Style Magazine*, employed by Rand Jordan, and that she was petite, poised, attractive.

Ryan had not expected her to be so shapely—so tantalizing. He noted her face—the classic features, the flawless, radiant complexion—and the shiny blonde hair that sparkled with red tints. As he watched her move toward the reception desk, he saw nothing in that curvy figure or rhythmic swing of the hips to suggest anything but physical intrigue.

So why was he to shadow her for three weeks? And to eliminate her if she proved troublesome?

He strolled to the desk. "*Bonjour*," he said pleasantly.

Micheline greeted him, flushing under his gaze.

He poured on his charm, speaking in French, saying, "I'm expecting a friend from America, Andrea York."

"You just missed her. She just went up to her room."

"She didn't ask for me?" He tried successfully to sound like a flustered beau, a Frenchman longing for his American lover. "She didn't say she was expecting me?"

Micheline shifted uneasily as if she had failed in her job. "No, Miss York was anxious to rest. She didn't mention anyone. Should I call her for you?"

"No, I'll come back for lunch with a bouquet of flowers."

Her cheeks flushed like uneven dabs of rouge as she said, "But Miss York plans to rest and have her meals in her room."

"She's not planning to lunch with that American gentleman?"

"Mr. Prescott? Oh, no. I'm certain of that."

"Good, I don't like competition, especially with Americans."

The rougelike blotches on Micheline's cheeks glowed brighter. "Should I tell her you'll be back in the morning?"

"No, let me surprise her." He managed to show disappointment with a helpless shrug, a forced droop to his smile. "I've waited so long," he said, his French flawless. "What are a few more hours? I'll be back in the morning."

"Don't forget the flowers," Micheline reminded him.

"For one so lovely? Never."

🌀🌀🌀

Drew Gregory twirled his tumbler impatiently as he watched Porter Deven. Porter was pouring another glass of wine, his eyes inflamed and fiery. But his hand was steady as he lifted his glass and toasted Drew.

"Are you sure you don't want some, Drew?"

"No. Why don't we order some coffee? You could use it."

"I'm fine," Porter argued. "You've just never grown accustomed to fine wines and French cuisine."

Obviously, Porter had grown used to both. He was an expert in his own kitchen, a connoisseur of French delicacies. But his culinary skills were wasted on his old basset hound, Jedburgh, his best friend.

"Why don't we call it quits for the evening, Porter? Forget about Sherm Prescott until morning. We could—"

He stopped, surprised to see Prescott hesitating in the lounge entryway. "I think that's your man, Porter."

Porter kept drinking. "He'll find us," he said.

Prescott glanced around the smoky room and then barreled toward them. Close up, Drew saw that Prescott had a couple of inches on him and an intense probing gaze much like his own.

"Mr. Prescott, I'm Drew Gregory," he said half rising and offering his hand. "A friend of Porter's."

Prescott responded, his grip firm, but his gaze turned back to Porter. "I got your message, Deven."

"Good. Sit down, relax, have a drink."

"I don't drink, Deven."

"You can still sit down. Have some Evian with Drew."

Prescott slid into the booth beside Drew and then glared across the table at Porter. "Deven, how did you know I was here?"

"We have a vested interest in the same person."

"Ryan Ebsworth?"

"We understand you've been trying to reach him at the de Crillon. He's off-limits to you, Mr. Prescott."

Prescott's eyes narrowed. "That's not your decision."

The man's voice was deep, his jaw line taut. *A handsome face,* Drew thought, *still marred by grief.* He noticed Sherm's wedding band and remembered with a nostalgic sting how long he had worn his own ring after his divorce. For Drew it had been a little circular bond with the woman he had once loved. Still loved. He felt Sherm Prescott's pain in a new way.

"Look, Deven," Prescott said, "I'm here on business with Kippen Investments. What I do with my spare time is my—"

"It's your business with Ebsworth that interests us."

"Us?" Sherm mocked. "Intelligence? National security again? Isn't that what you called it the last time we spoke?"

Porter lifted the wine flask. "So I did. But we're with Devenshire Corporation, remember?"

"It smacks of C.I.A. to me."

"It's my brother's export-import company."

"A good cover for you, Deven, with everything legitimate."

"Yes, we're well established like Kippen Investments. I told you before, we hold government contracts. We've had dealings with Ebsworth. Some major problems, too. Let us handle it. He's our competition in a way. In exports himself."

Nice touch, Drew thought. *He's exporting warheads to the highest bidder. And Prescott isn't buying any of this.*

"Once before, you accused my wife of something illegal."

The contempt in Porter's voice sliced the smoke haze in the lounge. "Our company lost some highly classified material about the time of your wife's death. Ryan Ebsworth and your wife may have passed it to a Parisian."

"You're wrong. And I'll prove it or die trying."

"Back off, Prescott. Give our Agency at least six more months to deal with Ryan Ebsworth."

"And if I don't, Deven?"

"You'll be forced to leave Paris permanently, Mr. Prescott."

"Does your brother's corporation have that kind of power?"

"Paris is on terrorist alert these days, Prescott. One call to the U.S. ambassador questioning your loyalties—"

"So your company wants six months? You've forgotten, Deven, that someone didn't even give my wife six seconds."

"That has nothing to do with Ryan Ebsworth."

"Wrong. Ebsworth may have murdered my wife."

"Murdered?" Porter mocked. "Are you forgetting that your wife drowned? *Six months,*" he repeated.

"I won't give you three months. I'll confront him in Canada on his own turf, away from your jurisdiction."

This time Drew signaled Porter to back off, but the wine had loosened Porter's tongue. He seemed spiteful, as though he could wipe the Agency's slate clean by transferring the guilt of Melody Prescott's death back on the man who loved her. A religious man, Porter had dubbed Prescott. *And what about you, Porter?* Drew wondered. *Are you more like I am—without belief in anything spiritual? Or are you still locked into your mystical Eastern religion?*

Prescott said, "I'm here on official business, Deven. What I do with my free time or on behalf of my dead wife does not concern you. Nor does it concern American intelligence or your brother's Devenshire Corporation."

Porter gave one final jab. "You're a religious man, Prescott. Faith, God, all of that. You know better than the rest of us that we all have to wrap it up sometime. Your wife just died sooner than you expected. Twenty-eight months ago, wasn't it? It's time you let her go."

Prescott got to his feet and stormed from the lounge.

"Was all that necessary, Porter?" Drew asked. "He has every right to be in Paris, every right to speak to Ebsworth. Don't try to break Sherm Prescott down with your threats."

Porter Deven slid out of the booth and thumped Drew's chest. "You blew this situation back in Canada when you involved Prescott's wife for whatever reason. You had your fingers on that Parisian and you let him escape with highly classified documents."

"Canadian intelligence was in charge, Porter. Remember?"

"I'm in charge here. And I'm not going to be this close to Ebsworth's Parisian contact and let some widower ruin it."

Drew slammed his empty water glass down. The crystal shattered as it hit the table. "You're wrong about Canada."

"Am I, Drew?"

Porter's speech was slurred now. It was futile to argue with him. They both knew that Drew was not responsible for the blunders in Canada, not completely. He and his Canadian counterpart had had everything under control. Then someone in the Agency or Canadian intelligence had blown the whistle, had knowingly or unknowingly alerted the Parisian. Melody Prescott had been caught in the cross-fire. *That is the blot of iniquity on the agency's records,* Drew thought. *Beautiful, innocent Melody Prescott.*

"We won't win with Prescott," Drew warned.

"Why, Drew?" Porter wiped his mouth with the back of his hand. "Do you think his prayers will defeat us?"

"Perhaps they will, Porter."

Chapter 9

Sherman Prescott stood barefoot at his hotel window, his dark hair unruly, his robe tied loosely around him. He stared out at the rain clouds, darker now than when he had first awakened. Hazy sun rays jabbed futilely at them, painting Paris in uneven shades of gray. Winter lashed at his window panes—the winds of winter outside, the chill of winter inside him.

But it was always fall, always September in his mind—the September Melody died. The Septembers without her. He had met her in September and married her that same month between swim meets. Seven anniversaries later, childless years, Melody died. Autumn with its glorious burst of colors died with her.

September had outdistanced him, blinding him to the seasonal changes that would turn this dismal wintery day into spring, summer, and fall again. He wondered if the autumn leaves would ever glow again with those golden browns, cardinal reds, and saffron yellows that Melody had loved.

Even now his faith drifted like the wind-tossed clouds outside. Since Melody's death, he had struggled for constancy and lost it on every turn. He wondered if his deep communion with God had been too wrapped up in his wife. His faith and Melody weren't supposed to die at the same time.

Sherm still buried himself in twelve-hour work days as

20-percent stockholder in Kippen Investments—Melody's
20 percent, his by right of inheritance. Her brothers, Tracy
and Paul, were disgruntled by his partnership, but not her
dad. Buzz Kippen—hitting seventy, giant-sized, stubborn,
square-jawed—had urged Sherm to stay on, at least until he
came to terms with Melody's death.

Sherm was unaware of anyone in his hotel suite until a
uniformed steward pressed a steaming cup of charcoal coffee into his hand. The intruder was a rawboned man with
a black bow tie and stark white Rockport walking shoes. His
thick upper lip curled as he eye-balled Sherm, a morose
expression plastered on his face.

"Monsieur," he said, pointing to the food cart by the
phone, "I've brought your breakfast."

Sherm nodded and sipped the coffee, scalding his throat
as he swallowed. "There's a tip on the dresser," he said in
French.

Giving a sardonic grin, the steward scooped up some
coins.

Alone again, Sherm ignored the silver tureens of food, his
thoughts on last evening's confrontation with Porter Deven.
For hours he had brooded, void of a game plan until an idea
came to him, straight from Porter's own suggestion.

"One call to the U.S. ambassador," Porter had said.

Sherm wanted an appointment with the ambassador—a
chance to explain that his efforts, *a personal matter*, were
being impeded by a representative of the U.S. government.

At midnight Sherm had placed a call to his father-in-law
in Texas. Buzz Kippen, politically oriented and powerful,
counted senators in Washington among his close ties. Buzz
promised to push the right buttons and get Sherm access to
the ambassador.

Sherm sipped a second cup of coffee as rain drops pelted
his window. His thoughts were as bleak as the smoky-gray
clouds. Porter Deven had crept under his skin, his words
cutting even deeper. Deven was right; it was long past time
to let Melody go. At the gut level, Sherm begged for God's
guidance; but pride egged him on. He wanted to defy Deven

and pursue Ebsworth. Deven's concern about terrorism remained distant, out of reach, like Melody.

The ringing phone jolted him. His father-in-law? He straightened and glanced down at the rain-splattered sidewalk below. The sight of Ryan Ebsworth startled him even more than the persistent jangling of the phone. Ebsworth sprinted toward the InterContinental in an unbuttoned raincoat, his blue sweater clashing with an olive green shoulder bag. He turned into the hotel entryway.

The phone rang again. By now Buzz would be cursing, his square jaw jutted forward. Sherm took quick strides, grabbed the phone and said, "Sherm Prescott speaking."

"About time, Sherm. It's your father-in-law."

"Thought so. What have you got for me? The ambassador's unlisted number? Great. That number again? Got it . . . No, Buzz. No trouble . . . So the ambassador and senator are old fraternity brothers?"

Sherm grinned, his prickly whiskers puckering his skin. "Thank the senator for me. It's in my best interest that the ambassador owes the senator a favor, don't you—"

Sherm stared at the receiver. Kippen had cut him off midsentence. That was Melody's dad—state his case, no wasted words, no squandering of time. But it was clear that Buzz Kippen was worried about him. If Buzz had been a praying man, he'd be on his knees now.

Sherm turned around and lifted the lid of the silver tureen. The eggs lay cold, lifeless, the grease forming a white coating on the platter. He dropped the lid in place and headed for the shower. He'd shave and dress and take a quick breakfast in La Terrasse Fleurie before he called the ambassador. It would give Sherm time to look around for Ryan Ebsworth, maybe even question the concierge regarding Ebsworth's presence at the InterContinental.

Andrea enjoyed the leisure of breakfast alone. Her table overlooked the terrace, potted palm fronds obscuring her view of the reflecting pool. A few tables from her, an attractive young man stood in the cafe entrance, a flower bouquet in his hand. His gaze followed the waiter's, settling on Andrea.

My driver, she decided. *But why the flowers?*

She had expected Francois Deborde to be stocky and dark like his father, but the lanky man who approached was a towhead with beige sun-kissed skin; his v-neck sweater matched the blue in his eyes. He gave her a pleasant boyish grin, laugh lines catching at the corners of his mouth.

"You don't mind if I join you?" he asked, stuffing the bouquet in an empty glass. "There's no other chair." He was apologetic, persuasive, ignoring the unoccupied tables nearby. "Besides, Miss York, the roses are for you."

She tensed, reminded at once of Neal Bennett's impulsive, charming ways, his endless pleasantries.

The stranger pulled back the wicker chair and sat beside her, waving off the breakfast menu the waiter offered.

"Are you Francois Deborde?" Andrea asked.

"Your driver? No, I'm his friend Ryan Ebsworth. Deborde has a habit of being late. But I plan to take care of you."

"You'd be busy. I'm here for the haute-couture shows."

"I know. You're here for three weeks representing *Style Magazine* and your publisher Rand Jordan. It's your first trip to Paris. You're single. You probably designed that lovely suit you're wearing. You like flowers, especially roses." He nodded at the tumbler. "I know all about you, that is, except for your beauty. I didn't know how beautiful you would be."

She turned crimson. "You're well informed." She blushed again. "About my background, I mean. Did you talk with Rand?"

"Not recently," he said, stalling.

She lowered her guard, studying him, seeing beyond Neal Bennett. She realized now how angular the young man's face was, how thick the eyebrows, how deep-set his eyes, their azure hues changing with his expressions. He wasn't handsome, but was most attractive with his Nordic features.

"I really must go," she insisted.

"But I'd be helpful. I know Paris. I speak French."

"You're Parisian?"

"I'm Canadian born, but I frequent Paris."

"On business?"

His thick lashes flickered. "I'm a street artist. My aunt encourages me to winter here to pursue my art career."

Andrea dabbed her mouth with a napkin, her eyes on Ryan. His skin was smooth, his nails even and well-trimmed with not a hint of paint embedded under them. She felt flustered under his gaze, annoyed that he knew so much about her.

"You're unsure of me," he said, his smile enchanting.

"I don't know you." *But I know what Neal Bennett is like,* she thought. *Brazen, indifferent, another unsettled dreamer.*

"We'll get acquainted over dinner, Miss York. A tourist on her own is an easy target for terrorists. I'll protect you."

Terrorists. Even the word made her shudder. Above the brim of her cup, she said, "I can take care of myself."

"I like the fire in your eyes, Andrea. Have dinner with me? We could dine at the de Crillon where I'm staying."

"Don't street artists stay in youth hostels?"

"I have a rich benefactor. I live well, eat well. Please?"

"Dinner is impossible. I'll be busy."

"Then I'll go to the fashion shows with you. Deborde's father is a member of the Chambre Syndicale, the designers' association. He can get me in." He nodded toward the lobby. "There. That's Francois Deborde near the door."

Andrea stood. "Then I must go, really."

"Not without your flowers." Ryan scooped them out of the glass and wrapped her fingers around them.

She laughed. "You're impossible." *Like Neal,* she thought, *but not quite like Neal.* Aloud she said softly, "Please tell Francois that I'm putting my roses in water. I'll be right down."

As Andrea left him, Ryan confronted Francois Deborde in the hotel lobby. "Francois, Miss York will be right back. While you wait, call your father. I need an invitation to the fashion show with Miss York. Tell Pierre I'll be there around three."

Deborde gazed anxiously toward the elevator.

"I'll be at the Amitie this morning, Francois."

"With the maitre d'?"

"With Kusa."

An involuntary tic pulsated at the corner of Francois's mouth. "Kusa," he whispered. "The bomb expert?"

"Proficient, adept with all explosives," Ryan answered.

Deborde's dark skin blanched.

"Deborde, we'll need you and your taxi next week."

Francois shot another furtive glance toward the elevator. "I can't risk it. I'm a French citizen," he said.

"And what will you do? Report us to French Security?"

"It isn't safe," Deborde protested. "Security is heavy around the embassies and the major government buildings."

"Then we'll strike where they least expect us. We need your help again. We pay well, remember?"

"My father—"

"Helping us protects him. Refuse, and you'll never drive another taxi in Paris or in all of France. And as honorable as your father is, his position would be compromised. We'd ruin you both. You do understand?"

As Deborde slouched toward the phones, Andrea stepped from the elevator, umbrella in hand, and made her way toward Ryan. She reminded him of Pierre Auguste Renoir's garden painting—delicate, gentle, elusive—someone who needed his protection.

He started to smile, but he spotted Sherm Prescott a few steps behind her. Without waiting to say good-bye, Ryan turned and left the hotel, striding briskly toward the Amitie, his thoughts pleasantly engaged on the intriguing young woman in the lobby.

Sherm Prescott swung his Hartmann attache case onto the concierge's marble-top desk. "Good morning, Claud," he said pleasantly. "Any messages for me today?"

Bodinat shuffled the papers in front of him.

"Claud," Sherm repeated, "are there any messages for me?"

The concierge forced a smile, an uneasy glint in his eyes. "Nothing, Mr. Prescott."

"No word from the gentleman at the de Crillon?"

"Ryan Ebsworth? No, Monsieur, nothing at all."

"What about Porter Deven? No message from him either?"

Bodinat's attention strayed nervously across the lobby to a casually dressed stranger in white athletic shoes.

"He's here at the hotel to protect you," Claud said.

Porter's watchdog, Sherm thought. *Is Ryan Ebsworth that important? Important to both of us,* he thought bitterly.

He keyed in the code on his locked briefcase and snapped it open. Melody's photo stared up at him. He set it aside, grabbed the snapshot of Ryan Ebsworth, and thrust it at Claud.

"Twenty minutes ago I saw this man enter the hotel."

The concierge studied the picture, weighing, Sherm was certain, the wisdom of responding, the safety of denial.

"Please, Monsieur Bodinat," Sherm urged, "did you see him?"

Claud ballooned out a sigh. "Is this your Mr. Ebsworth?"

"Yes."

"But you're not friends?"

Sherm's neck muscles tightened like rope cords, blurring his vision, threatening him with a left-sided migraine.

"He may have *murdered* my wife." He slid Melody's photo across the counter top. "My wife was young, Mr. Bodinat. Too young to die, too beautiful to be *murdered.*"

Claud traced the features of Melody's face, indecision written on his own. He shot a glance across the lobby to Deven's man. "Mr. Prescott, this is a matter for the police. We do not want a confrontation here in our hotel."

"There won't be," Sherm promised.

Claud handed both photographs back to Sherm. "Mr. Deven is from the American embassy, I believe. So this—this problem regarding your wife is more than *murder.*"

Sherm's silence seemed to awaken Claud's sense of justice. "Your breakfast steward, he is not employed by the hotel."

"Porter Deven's man?" Sherm asked.

He shifted and scrutinized Deven's watchdog again. The steward out of uniform? The same man minus a bow tie! He had steered the food cart to the bedside table and lingered there for a moment. Sherm turned back to Claud. "That man may have bugged my phone."

Claud flashed a conspiratorial grin. "My office phone perhaps."

"You'd let me use that?"

Claud nodded. "Your Mr. Ebsworth was here this morning. He wasn't looking for you. I'm certain of that. He had breakfast with the young woman sitting over there."

Sherm recognized her from the golden hair, the thinly arched brows. She was stunning in a tweed suit—her shoes, purse, and earrings all matching. One shapely leg swayed impatiently.

"She's waiting for her driver," Claud volunteered.

"Is she a Canadian like Ebsworth?"

"No, an American," Claud told him. "From Los Angeles."

"But they know each other?"

"Well enough for him to give her roses at breakfast. Important enough for her to take them to her room. But," Claud shrugged, "not well enough for him to wait for her."

"Who is she then?"

"Andrea York, an American journalist covering the fashion shows for her magazine. You met her here yesterday."

"Yes, I remember. But she's a friend of Ebsworth?"

"Perhaps. Why don't you ask her?"

The bitterness Sherm constantly fought bull-whipped him. *Friends with Ebsworth.* And why not? It was right in character. Ebsworth had good taste in hotels, in restaurants, and in women.

Drew Gregory arrived at the Amitie at seven that morning. He put his odds on some hidden relationship between Ryan Ebsworth and the maitre d'. Something linked the two men, something perhaps in Jacques Marseilles's past.

The cafe catered to the few patrons trickling in for an early breakfast or a cup of espresso and French pastries. Before being seated, Drew wandered down the hallway toward the cloakrooms to survey the exit routes Ebsworth might use.

He passed the door marked Maitre d'. The back entry to the building had to be beyond that, around the end corridor, but a hawk-nosed waiter appeared to redirect Drew to the dining area.

Drew chose a chair along the back wall with a good view of Ebsworth's corner table. It was occupied this morning by a swarthy young man with a strong, bony forehead that sheltered brooding eyes.

As Drew ordered a light breakfast with extra coffee, he asked the waiter a question or two about the maitre d'. The waiter returned with a sterling coffee pot steaming at the spout. Between the coffee and the research papers spread out in front of him, Drew could linger for hours, undisturbed.

Sometime later the maitre d' stood at his side. "Is something wrong, Monsieur? My waiter said you're curious about me."

"Yes, I am. You were with the French Resistance?"

"That's part of my distinguished career."

Drew pointed to the empty chair. "Join me," he offered. He signaled the waiter for two fresh cups of creamed espresso.

"That was it?" Jacques asked. "You just want to talk to me?"

"Yes. I'm researching British history."

"You're a writer?" Jacques asked.

"More a historian. Mostly World War II."

Jacques flicked a nervous smile. "The Resistance was hardly some noble British cause. We were Frenchmen fighting for France."

"Didn't de Gaulle start the Resistance from England."

"He fled there." Jacques's eyes glazed over, hardened, embittered. "Do you have any idea, sir, what it was like to have the Nazi swastika flying over the Arc de Triomphe? And de Gaulle fleeing to England?" His jaw jutted forward. "We could have won the bloody war without him."

"With him or without him, your Resistance fighters paved the way for the Normandy Invasion."

"And England and America took the credit."

"It was costly for us, too. I was in the invasion."

"As another Ernie Pyle?" Jacques asked.

"No. Infantry. What about you, Jacques? What part did you play?" *And what part are you still playing?* Drew wondered.

There was no answer. A waiter came by and whispered discreetly in Jacques's ear. Jacques stood, nodding politely to Drew as he brushed the espresso from his moustache.

"Good day, sir. I have other guests to greet."

Jacques took purposeful steps, offering brief and pleasant nods to his guests as he passed them and disappeared down the corridor toward his office, his countenance ashen, desolate.

Drew gave it another half-hour—waiting for the maitre d' to reappear, waiting for Ebsworth's arrival. Finally, reluctantly, Drew slipped into his damp trench coat, gathered up his papers, and left for his morning appointment with Porter at the embassy.

🌀🌀🌀

Ryan Ebsworth reached the Cafe Amitie determined to keep his phone report simple: *Andrea York identified, under close observation, presently at the Dior fashion show.*

As he entered the cafe, Ryan slipped by Kusa unnoticed and went directly to Jacques's office. A stranger sat at the desk; the maitre d' slouched despondently in the chair across from him.

"Are you looking for me?" the stranger asked, his ebony eyes cold behind thick lenses.

Ryan considered the man's question, his memory razor-sharp. The man's voice was familiar, his speech pattern clearly that of his phone contact here at the Amitie. They had met in Canada. *You didn't tip me when I lugged your suitcases to your room at the Harrison. But you paid me well to carry documents across the lake to the Jordanian for you.*

Cold sweat dampened Ryan's palms. *You're the last one who saw Melody Prescott alive.*

Calmly the man repeated, "Were you looking for me?"

"No, for the maitre d'."

"This is a private meeting," Jacques mumbled.

"Of course. My apologies, Jacques."

With another glance at the man behind Jacques's desk, Ryan left the office. As he wove through the dining room toward Kusa, he intercepted Collette with a tray full of food.

"Collette, the man with Jacques Marseilles—who is it?"

She glanced around, puzzled. "What man?"

"Back in the office with him. Tall, businesslike. Black hair. Black eyes. Thick glasses. A pugilist's nose."

"A pugilist's nose?"

"A fighter's nose. Broad. Wide-spread across his face."

She shifted the tray. "He's an American businessman."

Ryan gripped her arm. "The American, does he speak French?"

"Fluently. Ryan, let go of my arm."

"What kind of business is the man in?"

She considered the question, brows arched. "He owns the Plastec Corporation on the Champs-Élysées."

Ryan's spirit soared. "Doing what?" he asked.

"They make plastics for medical use and computers."

He added mentally, *And bullets and bombs probably. But not on the Champs-Élysées. The industrial segments would be on the outskirts of Paris. Or even in another country.*

"His name?" Ryan urged.

"What does it matter? He is well known. He eats here often with his wife and sons, Anzel and Giles. Sometimes he comes with President Mitterand or the American ambassador."

"The man's name?" Ryan insisted.

"Harland C. Smith," she snapped, trying to pull free.

Ryan released his grip and smiled. But his smile was not for Collette.

Chapter 10

Chic in her Italian tweed suit, Andrea York stepped into the Dior showroom and merged with countless foreign journalists. She felt their excitement, saw it in their bright faces and rapid movements. They were eager, as she was, to review the summer collection and photograph what the moneyed women of the world would be wearing in another six months. She recognized some of the affluent Europeans in the guest seats near the runway, ostentatious in their minks and diamonds and wide-brimmed hats.

Pierre Deborde hurried to her and grasped her hands. He was fashionably dressed, his body slimmed down by a tailored dark suit. But his sagging jaws bulged, almost hiding the nick in his treble chin.

"Lovely. Lovely, Mademoiselle," he said, still holding her hands. "You should be one of our models."

"Would the designers' association approve of me?"

"Perhaps," he answered optimistically. "With a growing European Community, fashion is taking a new direction and stretching far beyond Parisian borders."

"That's wrong?" she asked.

"Paris and fashion are one. Should we dilute what has always been purely French?" He shrugged, patting her hand to exonerate her. "But that is not your problem, is it, Miss York? Come. Mr. Jordan would never forgive me if you didn't have a choice seat. Allow me."

He took her elbow and cleared a pathway, using his stocky frame for leverage. Close to the runway he spoke sharply to two French journalists. One gave in, blasé, with a polite detachment as he vacated his seat. The other man scowled belligerently at Andrea. Deborde waved him off and then spent several moments identifying designers in the audience for Andrea—Lagerfeld, Gaultier, Gigli. Names that her grandmother would have recognized at once.

Andrea's thoughts wandered as Pierre's words droned in her ear. He could open doors for her, introduce her to some of the distinguished guests by the runway. She scanned the crowd, glad for the opportunity to brush shoulders with the publishing elite and the fashionably rich—contacts that would enhance her own career.

She recognized the designer across the room with the angular face and bony cheeks. The younger man beside him had crinkly smile lines around his eyes and expressive brows that arched as he spoke. His hands kept tempo with his speech. That could be Christian Lacroix, Andrea decided. As far as her grandmother was concerned, Lacroix had put zing back into fashion; Andrea agreed with Katrina.

But today belonged to the well-known, heavy-set Italian hovering in the background, a gifted, confident man with a wiry beard and glasses. Snapping his fingers, he called out last-minute instructions. The showroom filled with pulsating music and the blinding flash of camera bulbs exploding against a panache of elegance.

Deborde cupped his hands expectantly as the first gorgeous model wafted down the runway, sashaying in a $20,000 evening gown—kicking off the glittering haute-couture season to the strands of an Italian opera. She moved gracefully, her gown glove-tight, the skirt gently shaping with her body.

Applause erupted. The accolades barely faded before another model came down the ramp in a sleek body suit. Andrea sat spellbound. Each entry had its own sense of style: radical, exotic cuts; daring waistlines; soft, sexy gowns; lavish bursts of color. Katrina would have loved it. One after the other they came, the elegance of models momentarily possessing the treasures of fashion that would be worn by only the wealthy.

Andrea jotted notes and reloaded her camera. Mentally she ticked off the busy schedule that lay ahead—her trip to Normandy for Katrina's sake, the gala fashion luncheon on Thursday at the Imperial Salon in the InterContinental, and Friday's interview with Yves Saint-Laurent that would benefit her own career.

Before she left Paris, she would visit other fashion houses—Chanel, Hermes, Givenchy, and the Saint-Laurent Rive Gauche shops. She would study the sensational designs of Karl Lagerfeld, the provocative bare midriffs of Gaultier, the striking afternoon wear by Lacroix, and the shimmering magnificence of Romeo Gigli's capes.

Suddenly, for a moment the fashion show seemed fleeting, transitory. In hours it would slip through her fingers as quickly as life was ebbing away from Katrina. She felt an indescribable fear that her grandmother might die while she was gone.

For years Katrina had encouraged Andrea's dream—to design a fashion collection of her own. As Andrea strove toward her goal, she constantly squeezed out those simple traditions that Katrina clung to so tenaciously: the love of family and friends, the church, God. It struck Andrea as the orchestra music grew louder that in her climb toward the top, she had drifted to the fringe—frowning at believing in God, at following Him.

Pierre's nudge broke into her painful musings.

"There's Princess Anne," he said smiling.

Andrea followed his gaze as the British royalty took her seat among the other distinguished guests. Compared to the wild blasts of color all around her, Anne was modestly attired, her pigskin-gloved hands folded discreetly. She seemed shy and reticent, yet gracious as she returned Pierre's smile.

Loud applause drew Andrea's attention to the model in an outlandish evening gown with a high Victorian collar and a fatuous sunflower hat. The brunette turned directly in front of Andrea, their eyes meeting. In the Parisian's perfect expression—in the bold creation she wore—Andrea caught a glimpse of her own facade.

The model swayed past her again. Andrea's telescopic lens zoomed in on the girl's unruffled features, her ivory complexion, her bleak look, partially hidden behind thick eyelashes. The girl's face was a mirrored image of Andrea's own emptiness.

She glanced at the scribblings in her notebook. "Stunning," she had written. "Incredible. Sensational. Pizzazz. Dazzling." Empty, momentary words. A world of make believe, her mother would say.

〰〰〰

At the Amitie Ryan Ebsworth managed a calm expression as he studied Kusa across the table from him. He judged Kusa to be thirtyish, 140 pounds at the most, wiry. At the Montmartre district where he first had seen Kusa, Ryan had him pegged as Syrian. But once he recognized the name, he knew that Kusa was an Iraqi.

His features, like the American faces at Mt. Rushmore, were stoic, motionless. His cheekbones were high, his nostrils wide, his eyes piercing. Tiny pockmarks and a scar marred his lower jaw. Ryan knew the man's reputation. He was an anarchist, willing to die for what he believed in. Ryan had no intention of dying with him.

"We'll eat first," Ryan insisted.

He ordered *Supremes De Volaille Rossini* for both of them with wine to sedate his own uneasiness at the three metal briefcases leaning against the wall beside them.

"You worry too much, Eeebsworth," Kusa said. "The timing devices won't be set until we reach the airport."

Ryan's eyes strayed back to the metal cases.

Kusa snapped his fingers. "A slight twist only."

Yes, Ryan knew that one twist would activate the minute plastic switch, barely discernible by the lock. But how many minutes would he have beyond that?

When the meal arrived, Kusa glared with disdain at the breast of chicken with its goose livers swimming in Madeira sauce. He pushed the platter aside. Finally, he picked up a hard roll and gnawed hungrily at it. Between bites he stated their mission. He spoke of bombing Charles de Gaulle Airport as calmly as he might discuss remodeling the Eiffel Tower.

"Why an American airliner?" Ryan asked.

"You have forgotten the Gulf War. We have not."

As Kusa continued the detailed plans, the maitre d' made his way to their table. When he reached them, Jacques forced his public smile, his eyes black with anger.

"Here," he said, shoving a thick packet into Ryan's hand. "I was asked to give you these."

Ryan glanced inside the envelope, his spine rigid. He saw an American passport with a Keith Arlington I.D. and an airline reservation to New York, *authentic ticketing one way.*

He sat, speechless for a moment.

Jacques nodded toward the exit, his eyes shifting to the metal cases. "Please," he said, "get those out of here." He lowered his voice even more. "Leave immediately before their contents make shambles of my uncle's restaurant."

Kusa bit defiantly into another hard unbuttered roll. He tossed the rest onto his plate, splattering the goose livers and sauce. "No more, Eeebsworth," he said. "We go now."

They left through the delivery entry of the Cafe Amitie, carrying the explosives with them. Ryan held out his hand for the car keys; Kusa took the passenger side of the Renault rental without argument. They rode to the airport in silence except for the swish of the windshield wipers. Ryan kept to the speed limits, his mind repulsed at what lay ahead.

When they reached the airport, Kusa popped the hood of the Renault and deftly wired a timing device near the battery. He left the hood ajar, wiped his hands, and tossed the cloth to Ryan.

"The steering wheel, Eeebsworth," he said.

Ryan recoiled, expecting the car to blow momentarily.

"It will be awhile," Kusa said. "We'll be safely away from the airport by then. You know your flight number."

As Ryan leaned down to pick up one of the metal cases, Kusa held his hand in check. "We part here. We'll find our separate ways back to Paris." He grinned, an eerie, devilish smile, as he flicked the timing device.

"How many minutes?" Ryan asked, staring at the case.

"Forty," Kusa answered.

Forty minutes. Ryan started toward the terminal. The forged passport and plane ticket were tucked in his pocket. He picked up speed, putting distance between himself and Kusa, his knuckles white as he gripped the case. He was tempted to drop it anywhere and disappear into the crowd. But Kusa would be watching.

Ryan stepped into the nearest men's room. As he came out, he wondered whether Kusa was still in the terminal. Or had he put his cases down and fled?

Forty minutes. Ryan checked the television monitor. His departure gate was down a long corridor. He rehearsed Kusa's instructions as he picked his way gingerly through the congestion. He clutched the case against his body, trying to shield it from unnecessary jolts.

He had the security checkpoint in focus now. He stopped, his legs trembling. Sweat soaked his shirt and dampened his trousers. He was afraid to move, afraid to look around for Kusa. His thoughts were a mocking chant. *Forty minutes. Forty minutes. A one-way ticket to New York. A one-way ticket for Ryan Ebsworth.* Was it possible for the plastic device to go unnoticed by the x-ray?

Ryan did a mental replay of the steps ahead. Board the plane. Stow his briefcase on the rack above his reserved seat. Ease down. Stand suddenly, push through the boarding passengers to the flight attendant with a harried explanation, "My wallet! My passport. I must have left them in the men's room."

Too unbelievable with security so heavy. What if they stopped him from leaving the plane? What if they insisted on sending someone to the restroom with him?

Harland C. Smith had set him up. Andrea York was a lodestar, an excuse to occupy his time until he was sent to his own deathtrap here at Charles de Gaulle International. Ryan whirled around and faced the oncoming travelers. The metal case hit hard against his chest. Security guards paced everywhere. Signs nearby warned him: DON'T LEAVE YOUR LUGGAGE UNATTENDED.

A group of flight attendants came toward him. United? Unlikely, but Americans hurrying to board their airliner, each one dragging a luggage cart behind her.

"Mademoiselles," he cried in French. "Could you help me?"

The brunette nearest him stopped. He judged her to be thirty, friendly, nameless, someone's wife and mother. He was about to send her into fragmented pieces. As he struggled for words, her face blurred, giving her a Melody Prescott appearance. He blinked against the shattering image.

"Is something wrong, sir?" the American asked in French.

He asked for unnecessary directions. The flight attendant pointed him back toward the terminal exit. He nodded and bumped her deliberately as he turned. Her shoulder bag fell to the floor. As she bent to retrieve it, he wedged his metal case in with her luggage.

He took her hand to steady her and mumbled his apologies. She pulled away from him, uncertain, frightened. He watched her racing to reach her colleagues, his metal case balanced precariously on her luggage cart. He gave one parting glance as she slipped through security with a quick wave at a friendly guard.

Ryan turned and fled. He wanted to get as far away from Charles de Gaulle International as he could before the bomb exploded. Minutes later as his taxi merged with the traffic on the rain-swept freeway, an explosion rumbled behind them.

The driver swerved. "What was that?" he asked.

"A jet hitting the sound barrier," Ryan said calmly.

At the Dior fashion show, Pierre Deborde patted Andrea York's hand, excusing himself as he slipped past her.

"It's almost three," he said. "I'm expecting a guest, a friend of my son Francois."

"But he's not your friend?" she whispered back.

Pierre shook his head, his kind expression fading. "My son doesn't make wise choices."

Twenty minutes later, a young man squeezed past Andrea and took Pierre's chair. "That seat is taken—," she began.

Her words died midsentence. Her breakfast companion with the sky-blue eyes was sitting beside her. She tried to remember his name. It was gone. She tried to revive her irritation. It had vanished completely. She found herself amused at his presence.

He smiled broadly, a carefree, relaxed grin, as though he hadn't a concern in the world. The tempo of the music softened just long enough for her to hear him say, "Remember me, Miss York? I'm Ryan Ebsworth."

"Yes, the man with the breakfast roses," she said.

He lifted her hand to his lips and kissed it. His blue eyes danced as the orchestra music crescendoed and the next glamorous Parisian model floated gracefully down the runway in a smashing evening dress.

Chapter 11

Drew Gregory let himself into the Neuilly office and frowned at the sight of Porter Deven. Porter paced, vaulting back and forth across the room. One hand ran nervously through his hair; deep worry lines tugged at the corners of his mouth.

"Porter, what's wrong?"

Porter snapped to attention, his oversized moustache twitching as he said, "There's been a bombing at Charles de Gaulle International. It's a war zone out there."

"Casualties?"

"Several. Four confirmed dead. A flight attendant and three passengers. It damaged an American airliner and made shambles of the boarding area."

He worked his jaw soundlessly for a moment. "In the last hour there have been six bomb threats throughout the city. The calls could be pranks, but we have to take them seriously." He looked helplessly at Drew. "We've been expecting trouble, but it's hell when it comes. They've canceled all flights except those on the runway committed for takeoff. They're rerouting incoming flights. Evacuating the airport."

"Known terrorists?" Drew asked.

Porter shrugged. "Another Abul Abbas? Abu Nidal? Carlos? de Kusa? It's too soon for anyone to take credit yet. But it would have been worse if *that* plane had been airborne."

"Perhaps the timing device was off," Drew suggested.

"Most of the crew were on board, but the senior flight attendant never made it. She was just going down the ramp, pre-boarding pulling her carry-on, when the blast went off. They're certain she carried the bomb. God knows how she got through security."

"Have they questioned her?"

"How? She blew with her luggage."

"You said there were other casualties."

Porter nodded. "Cuts and bruises on the rest of the crew. Structural damage to the cockpit. Most of the explosion blew into the terminal. That's where the damage is greatest. The three passengers were killed there."

"Do we have any background on them?"

"Not yet. But the flight attendant was Francine Mixen. She's flown with the company for years. Midthirties. Married. One kid. Good reputation. Her friends are shocked."

"Maybe someone switched luggage on her."

"How, Drew? There are warnings against leaving your luggage unattended these days. Mixen would know that."

"What do we know then?" Drew asked.

"The crew arrived at de Gaulle in a company van straight from their hotel. They were heading for the boarding area when someone called to Mixen. She stopped. The others went on."

"So she knew the person?"

"Negative, Drew. Her colleagues insist that the man was a stranger. He spoke French. Tall. Fair-haired. Nondescript, except they thought him Nordic, attractive."

"Ryan Ebsworth perhaps?" Drew asked.

"Can't be. I have a man on Ebsworth twenty-four hours a day."

"Ebsworth is as slippery as a wet bar of soap."

"My men are good." Doubt dented Porter's defenses. "Mixen's colleagues swear that she didn't know the man."

"She would have been too smart to take anything on board for him, even if he were a friend. So how—"

"That's what the ambassador wants to know. He'll get the flak. No one will wait to see what really happened." Porter rubbed the back of his neck. "Mixen's family won't even be

notified properly. A camera crew at de Gaulle was inter-
viewing an incoming Japanese diplomat. They just turned
their cameras on the mess."

"Any precautions on the other bomb threats?"

For a minute Porter looked perplexed, exhausted. "They've
cancelled the opera this evening. Officials at the racetrack
were notified—they have a trotting event scheduled. You
can't shut down all of Paris, but they're advising any event
drawing large crowds to cancel."

"How can I help, Porter? Do you want me to head out to
the airport and see what I can unravel?"

"Yes. The ambassador asked me to send someone."

Drew was on his feet. "Should I take one of the cars?"

"Better take a taxi. French Security is swarming all
over the terminal. We've got two men out there working
airline security, Tony Brackmeyer and Lou Gleason. Work
with Gleason. See if you can identify the Americans.
Check the passenger list. The ambassador is pushing for
answers."

"To save his own skin?" Drew asked.

"He's a good man, an old friend, but Mac is worried.
There's going to be a lot of speculation—C.I.A. for one.
Some general or politician may have been scheduled for
that plane. We need to know whether it affects the
Agency."

Drew spread his hands on the desktop and leaned forward. "Maybe it was just a random flight with Francine
Mixen in the wrong place at the wrong time. I'll see what I
can find out."

۞ ۞ ۞

When news of the bombing reached the fashion show,
the ceremony and pulsating music came to an abrupt halt.
Pierre Deborde made a quick decision. He grabbed the
microphone and spoke rapidly in French. Stunned, hundreds of journalists folded their notebooks. The model waft-
ing down the runway almost stumbled on her $15,000
velvet gown. She caught herself, tried to regain her compo-

sure, then turned, and ran from the audience into the arms of the world-renowned designer standing in the alcove.

"What happened, Ryan?" Andrea whispered.

He took her hand. "There's been a bombing at the airport—"

"Terrorists? My parents will be frantic when they hear."

"You're trembling," he said. "Come, Andrea. We're to disband, go back to our hotel rooms, and stay there."

"Francois Deborde won't be back for me until—"

"I'll escort you to your hotel. Don't worry, Andrea. Tomorrow security will be better. It will be safer then."

"How can you be so sure?"

"Trust me, Andrea. The fashion show is not the target."

The crowd filed out in a muffled stillness. As Ryan and Andrea passed Deborde, he stopped them.

"Ryan, where is my son?" Pierre asked.

"Francois? At the airport perhaps, eh?"

Deborde's chin quivered. "If you hear from him—" He looked imploringly at Andrea. "My son—"

"Francois will be all right," she said.

"But these are such frightening times."

"They are only frightening when your political views are wrong," Ryan countered. "As you and your son well know."

"My son has no political convictions—at least none loyal to France." He sighed. "I share those of our President and the European Community. We seek peace, Ryan. World peace."

"Perhaps the terrorists do as well," Ryan challenged.

"By bombing the airport?"

"There's only minimal damage, Monsieur Deborde."

"You think like my son—without reason or humanity. What are a few lives lost? What does it matter that people died in the bombing? They are worthless to you."

Andrea felt Ryan's hand prodding her toward the exit. Outside she asked, "Why were you so harsh with Pierre?"

"Was I?"

"Yes. You were rude, Ryan. He's afraid of you. Why?"

"Forget Deborde. He's at odds with his son. That's all."

She sensed the chill in Ryan's tone, but he smiled. "Now,

let's have dinner together? You are hungry, aren't you, Andrea?"

"We're not to go outside. You heard what Mr. Deborde told us."

"We'll dine at your hotel in the Imperial Salon. It's elegant."

"We can't afford to eat there."

"I've told you, Miss York, I have a wealthy benefactor."

"Your aunt?"

"Andrea, my aunt would find you charming. *Trust me.*"

As he said the words again, she felt less inclined to heed them. But it was too late to back out, too late to form excuses. Right now she needed his company. She was afraid of being alone tonight, alone in the city of Paris.

۞۞۞

In his mind, Drew Gregory was still sorting through the rubble and carnage at the airport when he joined Porter Deven and another agent at the Amitie for a late dinner. Victor Wilson looked up from his meal long enough to give Drew a tongue-in-cheek smirk. It distorted his angular features.

"Porter tells me you need help rounding up Prescott and Ebsworth," Vic said. His smug grin stayed plastered on his face. "I met Prescott this morning. He tipped me for a cup of coffee."

Drew took a seat and grinned back. "I heard about that fete. Welcome on board. What took you so long to get here?"

"A long weekend in the English countryside."

"With a pretty girl, no doubt."

"Very pretty." Vic's crooked smile was back. "Porter cut my holiday short. He thinks Ryan Ebsworth is more important."

Drew surveyed the crowded restaurant. Ryan was not there, but the maitre d' was still on duty, kowtowing to his midnight guests.

"Ebsworth was here most of the day," Porter said.

"Not at the airport?" Drew asked.

Wilson's smirk broadened. "According to Porter's boys, Ryan entered the Amitie early and came out hours later."

Drew ridged the tablecloth with a fork. "There's a back entry."

"Drew could be right, Porter," Wilson said.

Good, thought Drew. *Wilson's my ally this time.*

They often worked together, surprisingly well with their opposing views and age difference. Drew remained old-school, the Office of Strategic Services still molding him. He half expected communism to erupt again or Kim Philbys to infiltrate the ranks. Wilson, with his brusque outer crust, found spydom a game more than a career. To him the cold war had been nothing but a passing Russian season; he welcomed the Boris Yeltsin Russia.

Vic Wilson boasted a bullet scar or six to prove that he had survived some nasty experiences for the Company. He had exchanged bachelorhood for two brief marriages—one to a Georgia belle, one to an English debutante. If he had children, he never mentioned them.

Vic showed little interest in the study of history—Drew's bag—except in making it. He counted danger as a personal friend. Still Drew found Victor Wilson a safe man to serve with. Besides, he played a tough game of tennis at the embassy gym and had set Drew to running every morning, a habit that had lightened Drew's weight and flattened his girth.

Drew focused on Porter again after placing his order.

"Do we have any more on Jacques Marseilles?" he asked.

Porter pushed back his empty plate. "What's important is not the maitre d', but what happened out at de Gaulle."

"There's a connection," Drew insisted. "The Amitie is a meeting place for more than diners and diplomats."

"Drew, Ebsworth was here during the hours that counted."

"But, Porter, three flight attendants agree that the man who talked to Mixen was attractive, blond, and spoke French. Two recalled his Nordic appearance. One spoke of his cobalt blue eyes."

"Significant?" Wilson asked.

"Yes, Vic. He's attractive to women. They like his blue eyes."

"You keep forgetting something, Drew," Porter said. "My men place him here at the Amitie."

"Were your men inside or outside?" Drew asked.

"One in the lobby. One across the street. The whole time."

"No one covering in the back?"

"Restaurant guests don't ordinarily use the back entry."

"Porter, Ebsworth is no ordinary guest."

Their eyes locked, Porter's dark and angry. "Chase your missiles, Drew. Prove the maitre d' is Ryan's point of contact. But right now I want to know what happened out at de Gaulle."

Drew moved his arms so the waitress could serve his meal. She was young and pretty, but the luster of innocence was gone. "That's Ebsworth's girl," he said as she left.

Vic glanced at the palm of his hand. "Her name's Collette Rheims," he offered. "She gets off duty in a few minutes."

"If she's Ebsworth's girl, be careful."

"She could be useful to us."

Annoyed, Drew snapped, "And, Wilson, you could be dead."

Porter slid back into the conversation with a question. "What did you line up at de Gaulle, Drew?"

Drew patted the miniature camera in his pocket. "Film."

"Anything else on the injured or dead?"

"The dead passengers were college kids on holiday from Yale. There's nothing more on Mixen other than what we had. But Gleason managed to photocopy the passenger list for me."

Porter held out his hand and took the list.

"I circled a few of the passengers, Porter. A senator from Virginia traveling with his family and two American servicemen flying commercial—one on furlough, one going home for discharge. A French diplomat returning to his post in Washington. A gentleman from Saudi Arabia, purpose of trip unknown; he was whisked away without rebooking."

Porter added circles of his own. "We'll run checks on all of them. What about the flight crew?"

"Good service records, particularly the pilots and Mixen."

Porter tucked the list into his pocket. "Did you see Tony?"

"Brackmeyer? Yes. He assisted passengers and family members into a private room. He'll get back to you if he learns anything."

"That's it then," Porter said. "I'll be going by the ambassador's on my way home. He'd appreciate a full report."

"Tell Mac that the carnage was worse than what he saw on television. A bloody mess. The bomb squad defused a bomb in the men's room. A second one detonated in a car rental in the parking lot."

"You'll have to file a report with Langley."

"I can do that as soon as I leave here, Porter."

Wilson shrugged. "Another all-nighter at the Neuilly office?"

"Yes, Vic, and you can develop the film for us. I'll join you both there after seeing the ambassador."

As the others stood, Drew pushed back his half-finished plate. "I'll linger over coffee. I'd like to talk to Jacques again and get a line on the uncle who owns this place."

Wilson pointed to the small print on the menu.

"Here, Drew, read this. 'Stephan Marseilles, proprietor. Serving exquisite French cuisine, a fifty-year family tradition on the Place de la Concorde.'"

"Thanks." Drew's neck muscles relaxed as he handed the film to Wilson. "On your way out, Vic, tell the maitre d' to join me for a cup of coffee. We can talk over old times."

"You're that interested in the Amitie traditions?"

"I'm trying to decide whether he's a hero or has something to hide. Jacques served with the Resistance network back in World War II. My war, Vic. But rumor suggests that he collaborated with the enemy."

"You're chasing missiles again, Drew," Porter warned.

Wilson was more considerate. "Or running on intuition."

"Give me something else to run on and I will."

Drew's suspicions persisted as he watched Jacques Marseilles make his way toward him, a flicker of indecision on the man's swarthy face. His steps seemed reluctant, like someone concerned about survival, not with discussing his past.

Chapter 12

When Andrea awakened, she found that security in Paris had tightened overnight. Yet nothing diminished the uniqueness of the city and its people. The Parisians seemed determined that their lives and business would go on as usual. Andrea admired their strength and polite detachment as they defied the terrorists to break their inner spirit.

For the next ten days, Ryan gave Andrea a personal tour of the *City of Light*. Between haute-couture showings, it was Paris on the run—a night at the neo-Baroque Opera House, spellbound; standing awed at the Notre Dame Cathedral with its rose windows and its ornate carvings of kings and apostles; strolling together along the Champs-Élysées; running through the Tuileries Gardens in the rain; browsing in the vendors' second-hand bookstores on the quaysides of the Seine; riding the Metro line, thundering full-speed beneath the city.

Early Thursday before her luncheon at the Imperial Salon, they viewed Paris from the dizzying heights of the Eiffel Tower. She rode to the top of the metal masterpiece with her eyes closed, her stomach at ground level. January winds blew the sky clear, giving them forty-mile visibility and plainly exposing the profile of the man who seemed to be following them—a dark, bony young man.

Ryan snapped Andrea's picture with all of Paris for a background, a whole roll of film at the top of the tower and another as she stood in the shadows of the equestrian statue of Henry the IV. Even there an older man stood nearby watching them, his coat collar turned up, his eyes shaded by tinted glasses.

Toward the end of the first week, Andrea sat by a cafe window sipping black coffee. In the sheltered alcove, Ryan played the role of a Bohemian street artist. His bold strokes of color left a vague impression of the Parisian way of life on his canvas, but Ryan was not an up-and-coming Van Gogh. Why then, she wondered, had his aunt indulged him in a winter in Paris?

She felt sorry for Ryan, more sorrow than she had ever felt for her grandmother's broken dream. Katrina had a definite artistic talent. Ryan had only a dream. Katrina's paintings, still packed in the dark recesses of her closet, had so much more skill than the dabs of paint on Ryan's canvas.

Andrea glanced at her watch, put down her empty cup, and left the bistro. Ryan looked up as she came toward him. He waved his paintbrush playfully, the tip almost touching her nose.

"You're not staying, Andrea? I'll only be another hour."

"I can't stay. I have my interview this afternoon."

"With the man of fashion, eh?"

"You don't like him, do you?"

A scowl cut across his brow. "I don't like anyone, anything that takes you away from me."

A dry, troubled laugh stuck in the back of her throat.

"I'm painting a picture for you, Andrea, but it isn't turning out very well."

"I won't have room for it in my suitcase."

"Nor on the walls of your apartment?" he asked.

She had to be honest with him. "My apartment is decorated just the way I like it."

"With no extra room on your walls or in your life?"

She felt color rise in her cheeks, a burning sensation that blended its shades with her birthmark.

"Will I see you tonight, Andrea?"

"I think not. I have plans with fellow journalists."

His scowl deepened. "I'll wait in the lobby until you get back. We can talk then."

"No, don't. I'll be late, Ryan."

"Tomorrow then?"

She nodded reluctantly. "Tomorrow if I find time. When I get back from shopping perhaps."

"I'll go with you."

He was annoying her now, harder to shake than a winter cold. A wind stirred, blowing against his canvas, sending a chill along her spine. His anger lashed out against the wind, against her. He began to pack up his easel.

She touched the blotch of paint on the back of his hand and said, "I must go, Ryan."

He refused to look at her. "Go then."

She went, determined to find her way back to the hotel. Ryan had walked into her life uninvited in the same way that Neal Bennett had. At times, like now as the Metro roared its way through the underground tunnel, she felt exposed, vulnerable to Neal's memory. It was still too soon—even these three weeks in Paris—to be involved with anyone, particularly with someone as possessive as Neal had been.

The next morning when she went down for breakfast, Ryan sprang to his feet, smiling, his spirits as bouncy as his steps. He held out his arms and flexed his muscles.

"I brought two good arms to carry your parcels," he said. "And I know the most expensive stores in town."

She felt herself smiling back at him. "You're impossible."

"That's what my aunt tells me." He took her elbow and guided her toward *Le Café Tuileries.* "They're holding a table for us, Andrea, under the palm fronds."

Their shopping madness took place near the Opera House at the Galeries Lafayette with its glass-domed atrium and elite fashion displays. She spent lavishly, selecting a purse and scarf for her mother and an extravagant gown and perfume for Katrina.

Balancing the parcels, Ryan joshed, "Who's your benefactor?"

"My pay check." She sprayed a floral scented perfume his way. "Get your aunt something, Ryan."

He ducked, rattling off his address. "Buy it. My wallet's in my pocket. Take it, eh."

As she paid his bill, she saw the newspaper clipping of a beautiful woman in the folds of his wallet.

"Who's this, Ryan? The girl back home?"

Vertical scowl lines deepened between his eyebrows. As she slipped the wallet back into his jacket, an involuntary tic threaded along his jaw line.

"Someone better will come along some day," she said.

His eyes sought hers. "Perhaps she already has, eh?"

"I don't think so," she said kindly. "You barely know me."

🏺🏺🏺

On Saturday they dined in elegance at Maxim's. As they ate, Ryan's eyes fastened on Andrea's cameo necklace.

"Why do you always wear that, Andrea?"

She touched it. "It belonged to my grandmother."

"She's dead?"

"No, dying."

"Really important to you, eh?"

"My best friend. We've had worlds of fun together."

"I never had a grandparent. Just parents who ran out on me."

Now it was Andrea's turn to ask, "Did they die?"

"My mother did. My father should have."

"What about your Aunt Kathryn?"

"I guess she's as close as anyone until I met you."

She steered his thoughts back to Kathryn. "What's she like?"

"Like no one else I know. Considerate. Warmhearted. She took me in when nobody wanted me. She's been good to me, but she's a bit old-fashioned."

"Old-fashioned? How?"

"Believing in God is really important to Kathryn."

"That's nothing to be ashamed of, Ryan."

"But it's where I disappoint my aunt the most."

When the waitress brought their dessert, she handed a message to Ryan. As he read it, the harshness she had sometimes seen in his many-sided personality returned to his eyes. He scrutinized everyone in close proximity.

Andrea shivered involuntarily. "What's wrong, Ryan?"

"I'm okay. But I need to get you back to your hotel."

"Is something wrong? Is it safe for us to leave?"

"For you? Yes." He helped her with her coat, caressing her shoulder. "I'll have to send you by taxi—alone."

Back at the hotel, settled comfortably in the pink-cushioned chair in her elegantly furnished *chambre*, she rationalized her friendship with Ryan. He had walked into her life unannounced. He was attentive, companionable, well-versed in art and the history of Paris. He was charming and cunning, intriguing and frightening. But what did it matter? It was better than touring the ancient and beautiful city alone.

On Sunday she buried her nagging concerns and went to the Louvre Museum with him. As they wandered among the art treasures, he told her about the lives of the artists as though he had known them personally. He mellowed as he pointed out Leonardo da Vinci's painting of the Mona Lisa— the gentle facial expression, the shiny shoulder-length tresses, the hint of a playful smile.

Ryan seemed most at home at the Jeu de Paume Museum walking among the Impressionists' paintings. Andrea felt certain that these musty, gilded paintings by Degas and Van Gogh were Ryan's only reality; his dreams and failures were wrapped up in them.

His mood plunged from enthusiasm to despair as he spoke of Impressionist artists who had lost themselves in alcohol and committed suicide. "Why, Andrea?" he asked. "They had so much to give."

She said softly, "I like the works of Monet."

"Then I'll take you to the gardens at Giverny where Monet lived and painted. It's off season, but I know the caretaker. We'll go on Tuesday, Andrea," he promised. Seconds crept by, his expression clouding. "No, we'll have to go on Wednesday."

🌀🌀🌀

By the time Ryan picked her up for the trip to Giverny, Paris had experienced another bombing. As she slipped into the car beside him, she said, "Ryan, did you hear about the bombing at the Eiffel Tower yesterday?"

His neck muscles tightened. "The Tower's intact," he said. "Be glad nothing happened when we were there."

"Ryan, the people in the observation deck were terrified. They said the Tower swayed as though an earthquake had split the ground beneath them."

"Forget it, Andrea. No one was injured seriously."

He remained aloof, taciturn, until they reached Giverny. As they walked the pebbled pathways and crossed the Japanese footbridge, Andrea tried to envision the grounds covered with dahlias and yellow verbascum, the arbors billowing with summer roses, water lilies on the pond, and patches of blue in the sky. Even winter could not dim the tranquility of Claude Monet's private world nor its peaceful effect on Ryan.

Standing in front of Monet's pink stucco studio, isolated even from the caretaker, Ryan spoke with reverence for the dead painter as though a revolutionary with a paintbrush was Ryan's only inspiration, his only hope.

As she tried to imagine Ryan in a setting like Monet's, in solitude, shutting out the world and whatever had wounded him, her disquiet grew.

🌀🌀🌀

When they arrived back at the InterContinental, she said, "I'll be away this weekend, Ryan. I'm picking up a rental car at the Orly Airport on Friday for my trip to Normandy and Clecy."

The tic along his jaw line intensified. "Why Normandy?"

"It's a private matter."

"And that excludes me? At least let me drive you to Orly and see you off safely."

She yielded on this point. "That would give me more time to polish off my article on Yves Saint-Laurent. I want to fax it to *Style Magazine* before I fly home."

She weighed telling Ryan about her grandfather, saw no reason not to. "I have to see Normandy alone, Ryan. My grandfather is buried there."

He seemed relieved. "You should have told me."

"I tried to tell an army buddy of his here in Paris, but Mr. Smith never returned my calls. His secretary said he was out of town, but his son Anzel said his father would be home for dinner. I guess Mr. Smith has forgotten my grandfather."

"But hardly about Normandy," Ryan answered. "I'll map out the route for you from the Orly Airport. They're good roads. You'll be safe. Keep the gas tank filled and air in the tires."

She patted his hand. "I'll see you Friday," she said.

For Ryan, the name Anzel Smith clicked. Anzel Smith, the thirteen-year-old son of Harland C. Smith. Collette at the Cafe Amitie had been adamant about that. Harland and his French wife had two sons, Giles and Anzel.

But why Smith's aversion to meeting the granddaughter of an army buddy? Why the threat, *if necessary, eliminate her?*

Reluctantly, Ryan made his way to the Amitie for his phone report on Andrea. If he could keep her alive for a few more days, she would be safely out of France. But the thought of her leaving him forever troubled him.

"You are late," the maitre d' said when Ryan arrived. "But another call will come before midnight. Wait in my office."

Ryan sat in Jacques's office, the lights off. Two hours later Collette came into the room, the light from the hall marking a path for her. She put a food tray in front of him and then searched his face in the semidarkness for answers, the usual merriment in her eyes gone.

Ryan had no answers to give her. He needed Collette to

warm his bed, to comfort him. But he did not want her beyond those moments. For all of her beauty and warmth, he loved someone else. But he remembered the coming weekend alone.

He caught Collette's hand. "I won't be busy this weekend."

"Then I'll come by," she promised.

He had eaten by the time the phone rang. He grabbed it, swearing as he untangled the cord. "Cafe Amitie," he said.

"Mr. Ebsworth," Smith said crossly, "you were late."

"Yes, sir." Time stretched to forty seconds.

"I expect you to make your reports on time. I have work for you and Kusa. High stakes—transportation and art—"

Ryan dreaded bombing the Metro or destroying the Louvre. He interrupted. "Miss York is leaving for Normandy on Friday."

"Someone must go with her."

"Sir, she insists on going alone. A private matter."

"And if you followed her, she would recognize you?"

Ryan risked the truth, "Yes, sir."

"Then *I'll go*. I'll join my family in Normandy for a holiday." Smith paused, then asked, "Is she driving?"

"She's picking up a Renault rental at Orly at ten Friday morning. I'll be taking her there," Ryan admitted.

"Then I'll see you at the Renault desk."

"How will I know you, sir? How will you recognize Miss—"

"I can identify you, Mr. Ebsworth."

Ryan disconnected. "And I can identify you, too, sir," he said into the empty room, "as the owner of the Plastec Corporation on the Champs-Élysées."

At Orly as the attendant behind the Renault counter scrutinized Andrea's passport, Ryan's gaze swept the concourse. Smith stood on the walkway outside the terminal, gripping an umbrella like a walking stick. Even behind his tinted glasses, he seemed to be giving them both a cursory inspection.

"Ryan, that well-dressed gentleman out there—who is

he?" Andrea asked. "I've seen him before. Maybe he's following us."

"So many people. What man?"

"There—" Color blotched her cheeks as the stranger turned and walked briskly toward the parking lot.

"Your passport, Mademoiselle," the attendant said.

Ryan reached out and took it.

"That man was watching us," Andrea insisted.

Ryan touched her cheek with the tips of his fingers. "Of course. You are beautiful, Andrea. Men notice you."

She pulled away. "You knew him. Was it your father?"

"My father? I wouldn't know him if I saw him."

Ryan picked up her luggage and escorted her to the shiny Renault at the curbside. "It'll hold the road well," he told her.

She smiled, no longer angry, as he opened the car door and let her slide in. He handed her a folded map.

"I've marked out the route to Normandy," he said, his voice strained. "It'll take you through Caen and Bayeux and on into Omaha Beach. An easy drive."

She pored over his markings with him.

"Andrea, the red dot is the turn off to Clecy."

"Good. I'll be staying there for three nights on the way back. I won't reach Paris until Tuesday, Ryan."

"That's a lifetime." He stepped back. "You'll want to top the tank at the nearest petrol station."

"Yes, the attendant told me. I must go, Ryan."

"But be careful, Andrea," he warned as she drove off.

By noon, Ryan was back in Paris walking into the swank offices of the Plastec Corporation on the Champs-Élysées. Harland Smith had class—carpets thick enough to sink in and exclusive furnishings that spelled power and prestige. His impeccable secretary sat at the desk, her brown hair brushed smartly away from her face. She waited motionless, unsmiling like an exquisite, life-sized mannequin.

"May I help you?" she asked, her voice subdued like the decor.

"My sister—please help her," he said, pointing toward the hall.

Her hand moved toward the phone.

"No need to phone. My sister fell in the bathroom."

The secretary showed signs of life—streaks of color in her cheeks, impatience in her gaze. "I'm here alone."

"Please, just help her," Ryan begged.

Concern cracked her rigid expression. She stood and hurried toward the hallway. "You wait here," she said.

He shut the door behind her, locked it, and moved swiftly into Harland's suite, a spacious, handsomely furnished room. He snatched up the portrait from Harland's desk. Monique was beautiful, Harland stony-faced beside her. Their sons looked like Monique, more French than anything.

Ryan twirled the address file and jotted down their Isigny address and phone number, the Paris home number beneath it. He forced the desk drawer open and scanned the corporation ledgers. Everything looked legal and in order.

The secretary pounded frantically on the outside door. Ignoring her, he pressed the dictaphone and ran it back and forth, listening to Smith's voice inflections. Ryan identified the same slurring of French words that he had heard so often in his phone contacts at the Amitie. There was no question in his mind. Now he could bargain Andrea's safety for Monique's, or better yet, for her sons'.

As he unlocked the door, the secretary's outraged screams echoed in the empty corridor. He shoved past her, knocking her against the wall, and fled to the boulevard.

Chapter 13

Andrea's grip on the steering wheel tightened. A cream-colored Peugeot followed her around the curve of the highway, tracking her since she had left Orly. She accelerated, racing ahead of a semi-truck. The Peugeot caught her within seconds. She hit the floorboard and shot past several cars. The Peugeot driver lagged a few cars behind her. She bypassed the lunch stop in Caen and the visit to the Bayeux tapestry.

Just outside of Bayeux, she risked a U-turn and circled back to a petrol station. As she skidded on the off-shoulder gravel, a transport truck with its horn blaring shielded her from her pursuer. The Peugeot sped on. She waited warily for its return. Nothing. A coke and a candy bar later, she continued her journey to Normandy.

She swung off on the country road that led to the military cemetery at Colleville. Ten minutes later, she stood alone on the bluff overlooking Omaha Beach. Blue-gray waters slapped brutally at the sandy beach where men once stumbled out of barges, dying before they reached the shore—a blood bath that included Conrad York.

She pictured that bloody shoreline with its hundreds of ships and barges, the thousands of men. She could almost smell the stench of death, hear men crying. She blinked against the imagery. There was no sign of war here now except the cemetery, the ruins of a chateau, and a concrete

German pillbox on the coast, its guns still positioned against the Allied landing.

A lone figure ran along the beach. "Don't run there," she whispered. "Not where my grandfather died."

She turned and faced the stark whiteness of the chapel and the endless rows of crosses. Row upon row of Carrara marble crosses, more than nine thousand of them keeping her grandfather company. Her eyes settled briefly on the Garden of the Missing where Corporal Richard Weinberger's name was engraved in stone.

The dismal gray of the sky and the chill of the winds that whipped her could not diminish her sense of serenity and solitude. Instinctively, she knew that this was not the burying ground for a traitor. Whoever he was, wherever he was, he was not buried here with her grandfather. Sombered, Andrea went the remaining few yards to her grandfather's grave. His inscription was simple:

CONRAD W. YORK
Captain Army Inf. Div.
Washington June 6, 1944

She knelt by the cross. "I'm Andrea, your granddaughter. Katrina was too sick to come, but she never stopped loving you, Grandfather. It won't be long now until you see her again."

Andrea was speaking audibly, softly. "I'm sorry you never got to come home. But Katrina wouldn't let them ship your body back to Index in a box. She said it was more honorable to leave you here where you fought and died." She swallowed hard. "I know you're not here, Conrad. But, if it helps, we're proud of you."

She touched her chin, smiling through her tears. "I have your stubborn jaw. And I've got your sandy-red hair." She shrugged apologetically. "I'm your only grandchild. I'm a fashion journalist. I'm good, too, Conrad. I'm designing a York collection of my own. That's the only way we'll be able to carry on the family name."

Footsteps on the path beside her startled her. She looked up into the cold, penetrating gaze of a man in his sixties, a man in tinted glasses. He gripped a black umbrella, his deformed left thumb resting on its handle. It was the man who had kept pace with her on her drive from Orly to Normandy. He took menacing steps toward her.

She stumbled to her feet. "Who are you?"

As she turned to flee, she accidently bumped into a heavy-set woman walking down the path. The woman stepped back and uttered an exclamation of surprise. Andrea grabbed her hand. "I'm Andrea York. My grandfather is buried here. Please, please help me."

The woman's gaze strayed to the grave, then back to Andrea. She patted Andrea's shoulder. "It's all right. Don't be alarmed. I'm Renee Lambeye." She beckoned to her family. "My husband Jean-Louis and our son Maurice will help you."

Jean-Louis pushed his cap back with a work-worn hand. He pointed to the stranger retreating toward the chapel. "That man with the umbrella, was he with you?"

"No. He must have followed me here."

Jean-Louis spoke to his son, a muscular young man. Maurice set out on a run a few yards behind the stranger.

Andrea spent the night in the safety of the Lambeye farmhouse, a stone building with ivy-covered walls. They sat around the table on bentwood chairs, sipping coffee and soaking hard bread in Renee's steaming homemade soup. As she sipped the soup, Andrea glanced around. A solid cast-iron range stood in one corner of the blue-tiled kitchen; utensils and pots hung on nail pegs close to it. It was a functional room, a simple way of life. As they ate, Renee told Andrea about the years of German occupation and the Normandy Invasion. Jean-Louis sat beside her, nodding with sleep.

"We've never forgotten that invasion," Renee said. "When we saw those ships, we knew that the liberation of France had begun."

Maurice joined them an hour later. "I followed the man to Isigny. He won't be back. Friends of mine and I will make certain of that. We want no more troublemakers in the cemetery."

He grinned and helped his mother to her feet so she could lead Andrea up the narrow wooden steps to the Lambeyes' bedroom.

"Yours for tonight," Renee told her.

An old enamel bathtub with claw feet stood in one corner and a bidet by the sink. The water closet was at the end of the hall. Andrea dropped exhaustedly on the bed and snuggled under Renee's eiderdown. She was still worrying about where the Lambeyes would sleep when she fell into a deep slumber.

It was one o'clock the next day when they reached the cemetery at Colleville. The mist-shrouded cliffs were buffeted by wind and a savage wintery sea; an eerie swirling fog hung just above the crosses. They walked in silence to Conrad's grave as the first drops of a heavy rain pelted them. Andrea had come to say good-bye for herself and for Katrina. Yesterday she had wondered why he had died. Today she understood. He had died for people like the Lambeyes.

She pressed her hand against the cross. "I love you, Grandpa."

Turning, she gave the Lambeyes a tearful smile.

Jean-Louis twirled his tweed cap in his hands, his weather-wrinkled face serious. Rain dripped down his nose. "It was a day like this when your grandfather and his men waded ashore," he said.

Renee pointed to the date on the white marble marker. "We will put flowers on your grandfather's grave on the sixth of June," she promised. "When we can no longer come, our son Maurice will."

"Thank you," Andrea whispered.

Andrea linked arms with Renee as they went back to the car. She kept her good-bye brief, light. With a quick wave, she left them. As she drove out of the cemetery and nosed the Renault toward Clecy, she looked back. The fog had engulfed the Lambeyes.

On Sunday Drew Gregory took the road between Chartres and Tours, turning southwest just beyond Vendome to the sixteenth-century village where the Marseilles had lived for generations. A steep lane near the cathedral wound up to Stephan Marseilles's hilltop chateau, a magnificent edifice with white stone walls and a slanting gray-blue roof.

On closer inspection, Drew found crumbling corners on the west wall; the chateau's grandeur was deteriorating from neglect. On the barren lawn, six old men braved the elements—engaged in a game of *boules* with not even a nod in Drew's direction. Five of the men looked as if they had been produced in the same mold—they had too many pounds, double chins, baggy trousers, and visor caps. The sixth man, older and more stately than the others, stooped to toss the leaden ball.

"Monsieur Marseilles," Drew said. "I'm Drew Gregory. I spoke with you by phone this morning."

The man straightened and scrutinized him. "The American G.I. who landed at Normandy? You wanted to see me about my nephew?" he said, his concentration back on the game.

"More about his part in that war."

One of the *boules* thumped on the ground and missed its target. Six proud men turned coolly, guardedly toward Drew.

"Why ask us?" Stephan Marseilles said. "Speak to Jacques."

"I did, sir. We spoke briefly about the French Resistance and the Normandy Invasion. But Jacques is a reluctant hero."

"There are few true heroes in war," Stephan said.

"And comparably fewer traitors."

Marseilles's lip trembled. "You accost me on my own property? Did you come to speak of patriotism or survival, Monsieur? You Americans and Brits," he scoffed, "we owe you a debt for the Normandy Invasion. But it was our

Resistance movement that gave the Frenchman back his pride and France back to the French."

His square jaw jutted forward as he said, "We know the price of freedom, Mr. Gregory. General de Gaulle lived in exile in London, but he rallied Frenchmen to resist the Germans long before the Normandy Invasion. We French were willing to die to see the swastikas torn from the flagpoles of our cities."

He kept his voice steady as he spoke of the fall of Paris and his utter contempt for Marshal Petain's puppet government in Vichy and *all French collaboration.*

Drew silenced him, saying, "Does that include your nephew?"

"How dare you condemn a Frenchman, Mr. Gregory."

"Not condemn," Drew said evenly. "I'm concerned that your nephew is still in trouble because of his collaboration."

"Impossible. That was fifty years ago."

Again Stephan's five aging friends moved closer, their rage turned on Drew. Marseilles waved them off, saying savagely, "Any collaboration on the part of my nephew ended years ago with the rape of his sister. So what do you want, Mr. Gregory?"

"I want the truth. Recent acts of terrorism in Paris may have been channeled through the Cafe Amitie."

"My nephew?" The old man's eyes blazed. "You have proof?"

"Surveillance photographs of Jacques with known terrorists."

Stephan turned abruptly and went into the chateau. Drew followed him into the kitchen and took a wooden chair across from Marseilles.

"Two coffees," Stephan called to an aproned servant.

The coffee was black and bitter, as bitter as Stephan's voice when he said, "Jacques has suffered years of isolation and shame. He would not betray his country again."

"Not willingly," Drew countered. "Tell me what you can about his past. Perhaps I can still help him."

"So you can write it up in some tabloid?"

"No, sir," Drew promised. "Nothing in print."

Marseilles gripped his coffee cup. He spoke reluctantly. "Jacques was thirteen in the spring of 1940 when the German *blitzkrieg* rolled into Paris. The streets of our city were deserted, the windows shuttered. The motorcycles with the side-cars came first. Then the Panzer divisions, tank after tank."

He shuddered, his upper torso convulsing for a second. "Paris fell without resisting. The Germans took over this chateau, too, making it impossible for me to return home. I escaped to the mountains until the Resistance began. That left Jacques responsible for the whole family."

His hands lifted apologetically. "Our people were starving. At first Jacques got by with stealing food from the Germans. When the S.S. guards caught him, they threatened to cut off his hands unless he betrayed the villagers who were resisting them."

"Inform on his own neighbors?" Drew asked.

"Yes. Jacques served the Germans for more than two years that way, keeping my wife and sister and the children in food. But he went home early one day and caught two soldiers brutally raping his younger sister. He killed them."

Stephan's voice faded. "Jacques escaped. My wife, my sister, and my children were executed in retaliation for the soldiers. Jacques went from one Resistance group to another trying to find me to beg my forgiveness."

"And did you forgive him?" Drew asked.

"I pitied him. A scrawny boy fighting as violently against the Germans as he had once served them for scraps of food. No matter what he did for the Resistance—hit-and-run raids against the German transportation lines, bridges and railroads destroyed, smuggling British fliers out of France—no one trusted him."

Marseilles seemed relieved to unburden his memories, to whisper his doubts. But as he leaned forward, his face filled with contempt for Drew. "You had traitors among your boys, too. The day Jacques's sister was raped, he was carrying Allied documents from an American G.I. to the German High Command, the initial plans for the invasion into France."

He paused. "Jacques never delivered them. The Germans scrounged the hills hunting for him, knowing that he was carrying those papers. When they couldn't find him, they spread word about his collaboration. They told the villagers that he betrayed his own mother and aunt—that he raped his own sister."

"And no one defended him?"

"Not until after the liberation of Paris. Unlike your country, Monsieur Gregory, we purged out the collaborators. Jacques was marked for execution. If it had not been for me, he would have faced a death squad at seventeen."

Marseilles drained his cup. "I couldn't let that happen. He kept my family alive for two years. Out of respect for my position in the village, Jacques was released to my custody. When I rebuilt the Amitie after the war, I put him to work there. We rarely see each other; that was part of the agreement."

Drew sat reflective for a moment before he asked, "Sir, did anyone else try to pass information through Jacques?"

The beady eyes darkened. "Once—right after the Normandy Invasion began. It was another American G.I., a boy not much older than Jacques. He begged my nephew to take him to the Germans. He claimed he worked with General Eisenhower."

"Sounds crazy," Drew said. "What did Jacques do?"

"Ran from that G.I. like a wounded animal. Wouldn't you?" the old man asked. "Even now, decades later, Jacques still feels the stigma of being a traitor."

"That may be why someone is using Jacques and the cafe."

Stephan's expression withered. "In recent years there have been rumors, but—I'm too old to fight another war."

"Then let me help you, sir. Give me permission to put surveillance equipment at the cafe in your nephew's office."

"Can you promise me that you'll protect my family honor?"

"Even if Jacques is directly involved in acts of terrorism?"

Marseilles blinked against the horror. "If he is betraying his country again, we Frenchmen will discipline him. Your word, sir?" He stood. "The men you met when you arrived, we worked together in the Resistance. As a committee, we will decide Jacques's fate. Your word, sir?"

"I can't make promises. But I'll try," Drew assured him.

Their eyes locked. "You are a hard man, Monsieur Gregory, a strange historian. But I won't ask who you really are."

They went outside, passing through another portion of the chateau. In its glory days it must have been magnificent.

"It's still a splendid old place, is it not?" Stephan asked.

"It's been in our family for generations. Now Jacques and I are the only ones left. Jacques has no heirs, nor do I."

He gave a curt nod to Drew and walked off, ramrod-straight, toward the five friends who waited for him.

❦❦❦

Late Tuesday Andrea arrived back at her hotel. Ryan Ebsworth met her in the lobby. He smiled as she reached him.

"I'm glad you're back. I was worried about you, Andrea. Did everything go well?"

She started to mention the man who had followed her, but she changed her mind. "I stayed with a lovely French family in Colleville and in a quaint hotel in Clecy."

"No trouble with the car?" he persisted, his voice thin.

Only with someone following it, she thought. She gave Ryan a sharp appraisal, not liking the question that settled in her mind. His blue eyes looked guileless, unblinking.

Uneasy, she fingered her cameo necklace. "Everything went fine, Ryan. Better than I expected."

"And you had a good trip back, eh?"

She had been jittery the whole way. She had glanced into the mirror until her neck ached, half expecting trouble. Now her fear turned to rage. Had Ryan had her followed? He was the only one who knew her Normandy schedule. She swallowed her anger and said, "I've lost my passport."

"Lost it? You had it at the Renault desk at Orly. I gave it back to you just before you left for Normandy. Remember?"

"No, I don't remember. I've looked everywhere."

"You can't leave France without a passport."

"I'm leaving Sunday."

"Please don't. Stay here with me forever."

She put her fingers to his lips. "Don't, Ryan."

"But I care about you, Andrea. I want to be more than just friends," he said.

His strange composite of tenderness and cunning, of shyness and daring, of sensitivity and secrecy troubled her. In Ryan she saw the artist who would never succeed, a young boy that would never grow old, an old man who would never be young. He hung in limbo, ageless at twenty-four.

"I'm sorry. We're just friends," she said gently.

"At least have dinner with me at eight."

She pushed the elevator button. "Make it breakfast."

He frowned. "I can't. I'm busy in the morning."

"A quick supper then," she agreed as the elevator closed.

She was back in the lobby before eight feeling surprisingly hungry. She sat down in a red-cushioned chair, one leg swinging impatiently as she waited for Ryan. As she watched the hotel guests, she recognized the ruggedly handsome Mr. Prescott cutting across the lobby. He strode briskly in her direction, an unruly hint of a wave to his jet black hair. He was sharply tailored. The subtly striped tweed suit, Londonish, emphasized his broad shoulders and narrow hips. His pensive gaze met hers. She noted again his strong profile, his powerful jaw line, the facial strength that Ryan did not have. She watched until he entered the Café Tuileries.

Just then Ryan arrived and leaned down to kiss her. She turned away so that his lips barely brushed her cheek. He took her hand instead and helped her stand.

"I'm sorry I'm late. Let's just eat in the Café Tuileries."

His suggestion appealed to her more than she dared admit. When they reached the cafe entrance, Ryan stalled, his eyes on Prescott. "Andrea, there's a nice cafe around the corner—"

"Ryan, no. I'm tired and hungry and we're here. Besides, I don't have my passport. I've told you that already."

🏵🏵🏵

He gripped her arm and guided her past Sherm Prescott, his mood at low ebb. The sight of the man filled Ryan's mind with images of Melody Prescott—the beautiful face, the bitter truth. He tried to focus on Andrea, but failed.

"Are you all right, Ryan?" she asked. "You look ill."

"I'm fine," he answered, but his voice sounded distant.

The waiter stood beside them, his pencil poised. Ryan glanced at the menu. The words blurred. "Anything," he said.

Andrea turned to the waiter. She ordered dinner for both of them. As the waiter left, Andrea reached across the table and touched Ryan's hand. "What's wrong, Ryan?" she asked.

"Nothing—everything," he said.

They lapsed into silence. As they waited for dinner, he agonized at the thought of putting her in constant jeopardy. She had been a surveillance assignment, a kill command, if necessary. From the moment he had first seen her, he wanted to protect her. She had been a pleasant interruption to his daily life in Paris, an exciting interlude, a leverage against Harland C. Smith. In these last few days, she had become infinitely more.

The waiter was back with their dinners. Mechanically Ryan moved the fork from the plate to his mouth and chewed, unaware of what he was chewing. Halfway through dinner, he realized that Andrea was speaking to him. He forced himself to listen.

"Ryan, I'm going to the American embassy in the morning to report my missing passport."

"You can't do that," he said, desperate to stop her.

She looked at him in surprise.

"Don't go alone, Andrea. Wait until I can take you. There were some bomb threats while you were away."

"Yes, Ryan, I know. The Louvre and the Metro were both

threatened." Her lip quivered. "If there had been a bombing at the museum, you might have been there."

I would have been there, he thought, *but not painting.* "Don't go to the embassy alone. Wait for me."

"I'll be safe. It's near your hotel."

"I know that, Andrea. It's just across the street, but please don't go until I can go with you."

Chapter 14

The Avenue Gabriel, cater-cornered from the Place de la Concorde, was a one-way street with the American embassy on the corner and the embassy annex farther away on the Rue Saint Florentine. Andrea expected to see American Marines in their dress blues standing guard. But except for the U.S. emblem over the door post and Old Glory flapping from the balcony, the building was plain, colorless, unimpressive.

Concrete barriers and a wrought-iron fence formed a bulwark between the tree-shaded street and the embassy. Security was tight with several armed French guards visible on either side of the fence. An unmarked command truck sat parked across the street, its high-wired antenna indicating a fully equipped radio transmitter.

She aimed her camera at Old Glory, wanting a picture of this part of America on foreign soil. As she focused, she felt a powerful grip on her shoulder.

"No pictures," a French guard thundered.

She stared at the gun pointed her way.

"No cameras. No pictures," he repeated.

As he urged her to leave, she tried to tell him about her passport. "Please," she begged, "I need to go in there."

He gave her a faint smile. His lips formed the word, "No."

His eyes seemed to say, "You're standing on French soil, outside the protection of the American embassy." He pointed toward the surveillance cameras mounted on the building.

A commotion at the embassy door startled them both. Two men engaged in a heated discussion emerged. The older one was a distinguished, gray-haired gentleman, stately in appearance, an attaché case in his hand. The six-footer beside him was dark, attractive even in his anger. A third man, his face hidden from Andrea's view, walked discreetly a few steps behind the others.

As they neared the sidewalk, Andrea recognized Sherman Prescott, the strapping, dashing American with raven black hair. She stepped forward, confident that he saw her.

"Please, may I bother you, sir?" she asked.

He brushed past her, his scowl holding her at a distance. She tried again, but it was useless as the three men cut across the Avenue Gabriel toward the park.

"The older man—who is he?" she asked the guard.

"That's the American ambassador."

"And the other two—do they work here?"

He shrugged.

She stared at their retreating forms as they passed the unmarked truck and disappeared into a hedge-lined park.

The ambassador, she mused. *Perhaps he would help me.*

Andrea dashed across the street, her eyes meeting the curious gaze of a guard standing by the truck. His face was somber as he watched her, his hands folded behind him. She nodded, her heart pounding as she passed him safely.

She entered the park, slowed her pace, and looked around. Only a few winter flowers glossed the park with cherry reds and a flaxen gold. An old man with his dog sought the seclusion of the trails. Mothers huddled on benches, their collars turned up. Children chased the dry leaves around an empty, circular pool. The ambassador and his companions had taken the walkway that curved toward a boulevard, heavy with noon-day traffic.

Andrea overtook them at the other end of the park. They had stopped short of the boulevard, their faces grim, their voices tight with anger. She walked past them, wondering how to approach the ambassador when he was arguing so heatedly.

Just ahead of her, she heard a sudden screeching of brakes. A Renault careened against the curb. Its passengers tumbled out—three swarthy men with automatic weapons in their hands.

Another man, fair-skinned and bearded, stared at her and then ducked back into the driver's seat. He jerked the Renault forward, scraping the curb. Seconds later he braked, bolted from the car, and darted across the sidewalk. Andrea watched him disappear behind some trees, something about his retreating form vaguely familiar.

The other three men charged in her direction. One halted stock-still, a yard from her, brandishing his weapon. Gunfire exploded. The ambassador cried in pain as he slumped to the ground. His two companions crouched beside him.

"Get down," Prescott shouted at Andrea.

She stood transfixed, her voice soundless, her throat dry. Her fingers were icy, numb.

"Get down," he yelled again, belly-crawling toward her.

Another spurt of gunfire sprayed the path before him, thwarting Prescott's efforts to reach her. More shots punctured the air around Andrea. People screamed. The wounded fell. The seconds ticked off in slow motion to the cries of the dying and the sobs of children. The sounds seemed unreal to her, like the hollow echoing of voices in a long, empty tunnel.

She tried to whisper, "Dear God. Katrina. Dad." But none of the words squeezed through her lips.

A block away Ryan Ebsworth whipped off his wig and false beard and stuffed them into his jacket pocket. He heard the rapid spurt of gunfire, the frightened screams of women and children. He agonized for Andrea caught in the cross-fire behind him. He fought for calm, meticulously wiping the stock of his Uzi clean before dropping it in the public waste container. He had run out, deserted the others, but it would be his word against Kusa's. He spun around and walked rapidly toward the boulevard, down the steps through the tunnel walkway that ran beneath the Place de la Concorde. He could hear the muffled sound of traffic above him, but he could not distinguish the police sirens that must surely be wailing by now.

He made his way up the steps on the other side into the brisk air and clear daylight. Andrea had disobeyed him and gone to the embassy against his warnings. His flame of anger intensified. He'd never known anyone like her. But did he dare risk going back to her? In the park their gaze had locked briefly, her delicate expression puzzled before he dashed away.

Gradually, his mind cleared. He must find out if Andrea had recognized him. He would head to her hotel. If she made it, if she were still alive, she would go back there. He would go to her. If she had seen through his disguise, she would not be able to hide it. He would never allow her to turn him in. But could he bring himself to destroy this lovely woman who had captured his heart? His gut wrenched.

The gunfire ceased. The welter of discordant sounds faded. Andrea remained paralyzed. One terrorist still stood an arm's length away, smug, his gaze riveted on her, his assault rifle braced against his chest.

She had an absurd sense of the man's face—hand-carved, sculptured from a singular mold. Its features were bold and distinct: a harsh, bony protrusion on his nose where the chisel had chipped unevenly; a small scar on his lower jaw. He inched closer, his mahogany eyes cold and calculating, full of hatred.

In a hairbreadth of eternity, five seconds at most, she heard him wheeze, watched him glare at her. He would blow her into immortality, but she was too panic-stricken to pray, her mouth too dry to form even a child's prayer. Her twenty-six years of running from God mocked her as the man centered his Uzi automatic and aimed it at her.

A cry boomeranged above the chaos, "Kusa. Kusa."

A flicker of indecision crossed his face, a barely discernible movement of his dark, brooding eyes. He whirled Andrea around with him, his fingers digging into her flesh, his automatic slamming against her breast.

"God help me," she cried.

Suddenly, Kusa released her and broke into a run. His two companions sprinted in different directions, escaping by foot. Gunfire split the air again. One of the terrorists dropped to the graveled pathway, his skull splintered and bleeding. The man called Kusa kept dodging bullets. As he reached the curb, a taxi slowed for him. He scrambled into the front seat. The taxi lurched forward and merged with the traffic.

Andrea turned to flee, slid in the gravel, and pitched forward beside the fallen ambassador, the fingers of her hands spread. Pebbles dug into her skin. She forced herself to look at the ambassador.

"Oh, my God," she cried. "Oh, dear God."

He lay on his back, his eyes glazed and lifeless, his hair snow white like her father's.

As she pushed herself to her feet, pain seared through her hands, the pebbles embedding deeper. She stumbled past the body, her stomach still churning at the sight of his blood-soaked shirt. Her camera case caught on a tree shrub and fell beside his outstretched hand. She made no attempt to retrieve it. Adrenalin pumped life back into her body as she broke into a run. She was fleeing to Ryan Ebsworth, her only friend in Paris.

As she fled, Sherman Prescott staggered to his feet, dazed, his scalp wound oozing. He started after her. Vic Wilson restrained him. "Let her go," he said, picking up her camera case. "She's not our problem, Prescott. We need to get you out of here. You're wounded."

Sherm shrugged off Wilson's grip and stooped down beside the ambassador. Blood seeped around his fingers as he checked for a pulse.

"He's dead," Sherm said, stumbling back to his feet.

Vic steadied him. "I know, Prescott. Come on. The safest place for us is the American embassy. You need medical attention."

Sherm snatched up the ambassador's attaché case.

"What about the meeting with Porter Deven?" he asked.

"I'll page him, Sherm. He can meet us at the embassy."

"If he had done that in the first place, the ambassador would still be alive."

"Don't blame him, Prescott. Deven knows what he's doing."

"Does he?" Sherm asked bitterly. "He's blocked me at every turn. Kept me from the answers I've sought. Why? All I want to know is how my wife died—to salvage her reputation."

"You're a fool, Prescott. What happened just now has nothing to do with Porter Deven. A terrorist has just blown the American ambassador away, and all you can think about is your wife's reputation."

Vic pushed ahead of Sherm, flashed his I.D. at an ashen-faced guard, and beckoned Sherm to follow him around the stone barriers and up the steps to the embassy.

Another guard stopped them, American military this time. "Sorry, sir. I've orders to stop anyone from entering."

"I'm Victor Wilson. You darn well better get us clearance. *Now*. We almost got our heads blown off over there."

The stony-faced Marine lifted his Walkman and patched Wilson's message through. "One's wounded," he added. "Looks like a bullet grazed his scalp."

Within moments they were admitted through the embassy door. Immediately the ambassador's chauffeur led them down the hall to a back exit.

"What's going on?" Wilson demanded. "This man is wounded."

"I see that, sir, but you're to take the ambassador's limousine and meet Porter Deven at the Neuilly office."

"The ambassador's car?" Sherm challenged.

Wilson gave him a tough glance. "He won't need it anymore, and we need a diplomatic exit. Right?"

The chauffeur nodded, urging them into the back seat. He glanced at Sherm. "You've lost a little blood, sir. But Mr. Deven will get you fixed up when you get to Neuilly."

The man climbed into the driver's seat and headed the limo down the driveway, a diplomatic flag flapping from the aerial. He careened right onto the Avenue Gabriel, accelerated, and headed full speed toward Neuilly.

"Why the quick exit?" Sherm asked, his head throbbing.

"Deven may want you out of Paris. He won't want the Agency's name linked with the ambassador's death nor linked with you."

"Was Melody's death that important?"

"Only to you, sir," Wilson said, not unkindly. "I don't know who you know in Washington, Prescott, nor how you got in to see the ambassador, *but you were out of line.*"

Sherm shrugged, a defeated gesture. He looked squarely at Wilson's narrow face, made more angular by a long nose and sharply pointed chin. He judged him to be in his late thirties, a young man with thick brown hair, gray-green eyes. *A pleasant face,* Sherm thought, *if he were ever free to smile.*

Sherm looked again, recognizing him now. Victor Wilson, Deven's watchdog at the InterContinental Hotel, the uniformed waiter who had rolled the breakfast tray into Sherm's room and handed him the cup of steaming coffee.

Irritated, he said, "Tell me, Vic, how big a tip did I pay you for my coffee?"

Vic's deep scowl eased. "A bit of change, that's all."

"*So we were both out of line,*" Sherm said evenly. He patted the attaché case. "There's no need for Deven to have me followed again nor to worry. The information on my wife—the papers that I duplicated for the ambassador are here, safe in this case, Vic. No one else at the embassy even knows about them."

Wilson remained rigid, his eyes on the traffic. "Porter Deven will want to keep it that way," he said.

Chapter 15

Ryan paced the lobby of the InterContinental Hotel, beating a path across the oriental rugs until Andrea burst through the doors. She ran straight to him, crumpled into his arms and wept.

"Terrorists just killed the American ambassador," she cried.

He attempted to comfort her. "There must be some mistake."

"No. I was in the embassy park. I saw it happen."

The ambassador dead. But what about Prescott? Ryan wanted to ask. *Kusa promised me that both of them would die.*

Andrea rambled on as he led her to a chair. "They were ruthless, Ryan. They just kept shooting into the crowd."

He brushed strands of hair from her tear-streaked face. She was terrified, but not of him. He was convinced of that.

"Andrea, why did you go to the embassy alone?"

The reason seemed to elude her. He tried to still the tremor in his own voice. "Can you identify the terrorists?"

She blinked against the memory. "They looked like foreigners."

Ryan laughed, the relief unbelievable. "Andrea, you're in France. Everyone here would be foreign to you."

She tried to smile back and failed miserably; there was no laughter in her. "The terrorist who shot the ambassador had Latin coloring, Indian features, brooding dark eyes."

Ryan knew immediately: Kusa. "Did he hurt you, Andrea?"

She reached involuntarily to her breast. "He was going to kill me; then suddenly he ran away and escaped in a taxi."

Ryan squeezed her shoulder. She was confirming the facts for him. Kusa and Francois Deborde were still alive, Kusa no doubt reporting to Harland Smith right now. Had Kusa seen him flee? He would have to take the risk, his word against Kusa's.

"How many terrorists were there?" he asked.

"Three—no, four. The driver ran away."

"The police will ask. What did he look like?"

"No police, Ryan. I'm too frightened."

"What did the driver look like?" he persisted.

"He was your build, Ryan. Tall. Thin. Agile."

The pit of Ryan's stomach dropped. *Don't, Andrea*, he thought. *Don't recognize me. I love you. Don't recognize me.*

"I only saw his face for a minute, but his hair was dark. I know that. Maybe he had glasses. I can't remember."

Would she remember when she calmed down? he wondered. *Would she recognize him then?* For his own protection, he had to get her out of Paris. "Andrea, I'm going to be gone for a while. I have to make some arrangements for your safety."

"My safety? I don't understand."

"You were in the park, Andrea. The police will want to question anyone who witnessed the assassination."

"But they'll want to see my passport."

"Yes, I'm afraid so."

"I don't have one. I'll have to go back to the embassy annex on Saint Florentine. Go with me, Ryan."

"Security makes that impossible. It would get long and involved—especially if they recognize you. No, Andrea. You won't be safe now, not if someone saw you running away."

"How would anyone know who I am? There was too much confusion."

"There are surveillance cameras at the embassy," he said.

She recoiled at the warning. "And there was that American with the ambassador. He saw me. He's a guest here at the hotel."

So Prescott had recognized Andrea? He had to check her

out of the hotel before Prescott came back. He signaled for the concierge. Claud Bodinat came at once.

"Miss York is ill. She needs help getting to her room."

Claud nodded. "Will she need a physician?"

"No," Andrea said urgently. "No doctor. Just some tea."

"Mr. Bodinat, I'll send a friend back to be with Miss York."

Claud snapped his fingers. "Micheline, see our guest to her room. Miss York is not feeling well. I'll order tea."

Micheline helped Andrea stand. "Have you heard the news—"

"Not now," Claud warned. "Our guest is ill."

Bodinat turned back to Ryan, wariness clouding his eyes. "Is there anything else, Mr. Ebsworth?"

So he knows me, Ryan thought. *By name.* "No. You've already been most helpful, Mr. Bodinat."

۞۞۞

As Ryan entered the Cafe Amitie, the stunned waiters stood in small groups discussing the massacre. Ryan avoided Jacques's eyes and stared at the television mounted above him. News. The same news over and over. The American ambassador—dead. A French guard—dead. One unidentified terrorist—dead. Two children—dead. Dozens injured. Kusa had left a bloody mess behind.

He made his way to Jacques's office and waited for Harland Smith's reprimand. By now Smith knew that the attempt on Sherm Prescott's life had failed. The political implications from the ambassador's death were already mushrooming. The call, when it came, almost blasted Ryan out of the chair. Smith's mood was savage, his voice stony as he spoke over the scrambler.

"You ran," he said. "You ran out on the others."

"The American was there. She could have identified me."

"You could have shot her then and there."

No, Ryan thought. *I want no part of that.*

"If you won't, Kusa will. The ambassador is dead." His voice hardened. "What about the Texas businessman?"

"He's not listed among the casualties, sir."

"As long as he is alive, he poses a threat to you, Ryan—to all of us. I've postponed our negotiations with Iraq."

Ryan kept silent. He would deal with Prescott later.

"Leave Paris immediately," Smith said.

Ryan stalled. "Leave? How?" he asked.

"That's up to you. Don't contact me. We'll be in touch."

If I live long enough to get out of town, Ryan thought.

"Sir," he said, "we can negotiate a different arms deal with other buyers. You could meet with them on my aunt's farm."

"In Canada?" Smith scoffed. "That's too far away."

"But safe. We've met there before."

"Yes. And you stayed conveniently away from the farm that day, too. Do you always run and hide, Mr. Ebsworth, and leave the entertaining to your aunt? She was a reluctant hostess."

"She won't be this time," Ryan promised. "I'll make certain."

"Then I'll consider it, Mr. Ebsworth."

"Sir, what about the American tourist?"

"The woman? Kusa will take care of her." Smith laughed, a cold, hard chuckle. "Unless you have a better plan, Ryan?"

Ryan bit his lip. He would take Andrea with him.

"Your accommodations at the de Crillon have been canceled, effective immediately, Ryan." A click and the line went dead.

Ryan drummed his fingers on Jacques's desk, contemplating ways to convince Andrea to flee the country with him. He needed her for his own survival. Harland C. Smith feared Andrea, yet he fearlessly cheated more than one buyer in the sale of weapons. Once Ryan reached Canada, he would threaten Smith with exposure. He would barter Andrea's life against the safety of Monique and her sons. Ryan lifted the phone and placed an anonymous tip to the editor at the *Le Monde*. He presented himself as an eyewitness to the ambush near the American embassy.

"There were five terrorists," he said. *One was a woman.*"

He sensed the spark of interest on the other end of the

line. He hedged on statistics, but gave height, weight, and hair coloring close enough to be Andrea York. Satisfied with his success, he called the *Herald Tribune*, the international press. This time he boldly described Andrea fleeing toward the embassy.

The editor stalled. Were they trying to tap into his line to trace him? *It's all yours, Jacques*, Ryan thought.

He recounted the massacre in detail and then risked adding, "The woman dropped her camera case by the ambassador's body."

The editor pressed for more. Ryan described Kusa. Vengeance almost choked him. Because of Kusa, he was on the way out. On the run.

Leave Paris immediately, Smith had said.

It was kill or be killed. Ryan said cunningly, "The woman works for an American businessman who frequents the Amitie."

He dropped the receiver in place, not willing to talk any longer. The possibilities delighted him. The news media would dig for answers. Like weasels, they would ferret out information about the Cafe, toppling Harland C. Smith and exposing Jacques for his cowardice.

❁❁❁

Ryan found Collette Rheims waiting for him in the late afternoon shadows outside of the Cafe Amitie. She stepped out as he came toward her, looking angry and uncertain. He smiled at her. He pulled her back against the safety of the building. "Collette, I need your help."

"No, I won't have any part of it. People died in the park, even the American ambassador. Why, Ryan?"

He pressed his shoulder against hers, pinning her to the wall. "I wasn't there, Collette. Believe me."

"Kusa said you were involved."

"No, Collette. Kusa wants you to believe that."

She touched his hand. "You didn't hurt anyone?"

"I swear I wasn't there." He eased the pressure on her shoulder. "A friend, the American woman, is ill."

"Kusa told me she was with the ambassador when he died."

"But she didn't kill him," Ryan said calmly. "She was caught in the cross-fire, right beside the terrorists with people dying all around her. But no one will believe her. The gendarmes are looking for her now. I want you to go to the InterContinental. Help Andrea York pack."

Collette shrank back. "I can't."

"Use the service entry. Take her luggage to your place. Francois Deborde will bring Andrea later." He ignored her mounting defiance. "She'll need to stay with you a day or two. Then she'll be gone, out of the country."

"For good?" Collette asked. "She won't be back?"

Nor will I, he thought.

She hesitated, agitating him even more. He smiled, the corners of his lips twisting. "As soon as she's safely out of France, we will be together again, Collette, eh?"

Hope sprang in her face. He knew that when he betrayed her, she would go straight to the gendarmes and talk. He touched her cheek. She had tried to be his friend, had been his lover. She had served her purpose.

Lovely, lovely Collette, he thought. *I am so sorry. But I cannot let you and Kusa interfere.*

He leaned down, kissed her, and felt her body yielding as his lips lingered on hers. He knew now that she would do his bidding.

As he released her, the color drained from her face. She chin-pointed across the street. Was it possible? Kusa there in the crowd spying on them! Ryan's mouth went dry. He cut across the boulevard toward him, but Kusa slipped through the throng and disappeared before Ryan could reach him. When he looked again, Collette no longer stood in front of the cafe.

He quickened his pace and headed back to the de Crillon. The attention of the hotel staff was riveted on the carnage off the Place de la Concorde. They barely noticed Ryan as he mounted the decorative stairs to his hotel suite.

Ryan packed his luggage, leaving out a clean set of clothing, a gray wig, and fancy cane. He stowed the locked suit-

cases behind an eighteenth-century chair for Francois
Deborde to pick up. Then he showered in the luxury of the
marble bathroom for the last time, angered that he was
leaving this imposing opulence.

No more gourmet French cuisine on Baccarat crystal, he
mused as he stood before the mirror and adjusted the gray
wig. As an afterthought he attached a handlebar moustache, twitched it, and smiled sardonically.

Minutes later, disguised as a hunched old man with a
gold cane, he limped across the Sienna and Portor marble
lobby. He had nothing more than his briefcase in his other
hand, a camel topcoat over his arm, his padded money belt
tied securely around his waist, and Andrea York's passport
tucked safely in his pocket.

He passed Francois Deborde on the way out without even
a flicker of recognition from Francois. Safely outside the
hotel, Ryan lifted his cane, hailed a taxi, and drove away.

Chapter 16

Andrea sat on top of the quilted bedspread, the food cart with tea and open-faced sandwiches in front of her. She pushed the sandwiches away, nausea and fear coming at her in new waves. She was fresh from the shower, her soft blue robe wrapped loosely around her, but nothing washed away the memory of the embassy park.

She looked up and caught her own reflection in the mirrored sliding doors—an unsmiling, frightened face, her eyes wide and listless. Without makeup, her ribbon of freckles stood out like tiny blotches. In the open neckline of her robe, a deep, purple discoloration ran parallel with her birthmark, its imprint shaped by the butt of the Uzi.

Across the room the French girl was pulling the clothes from the closet. Andrea watched her absently. They were her clothes—Andrea's marvelous, well-kept garments being yanked from their hangers and tossed into the empty suitcases. She found her voice and said, "What are you doing, Collette?"

The girl paused defiantly. "I'm packing."

She was a slender young woman in a low-cut blouse and a leather miniskirt. The skirt and boots emphasized her long, coltish legs. Worry lines tightened the corners of her mouth. She turned and shoved another dress into the suitcase.

"Leave my things alone and come over here," Andrea

said. She winced in pain as she lifted the urn and poured two cups of tea. "Come, Collette. Stop this foolishness. Have some tea with me."

Collette hesitated and then dropped the clothes hanger on a chair and moved toward Andrea with quick, efficient steps.

"We must leave," she urged, sitting down and facing Andrea.

"I have no reason to run, Collette. I haven't done anything."

Another jolt of pain shot through Andrea's breast as she handed the cup of almond tea to the girl.

Collette frowned. "You're hurt?"

"I'm bruised where the terrorist hit me with his rifle."

"You were with them and they hurt you?"

"I wasn't with *them*, Collette."

"But Ryan—" As she sipped the tea, Collette's eyes tiptoed through the luxurious suite. Then her gaze settled back on Andrea. "Ryan said the gendarmes are looking for you."

"That's ridiculous. Why?" Andrea's words were hot, angry.

The thin shoulders shrugged. "Andrea, you followed the ambassador from the embassy into the park. You stood with the terrorists while people died all around you. Just stood there."

"I couldn't move. I was terrified, Collette."

"Ryan said that no one will believe you. He's right. You are a foreigner in my country. You would be detained— maybe even imprisoned for months—while they sorted out the truth."

Collette picked up a sandwich and chewed it thoughtfully. "Ryan and I are trying to help you get safely out of Paris."

Andrea fought a sudden weakness. "I'm not going."

"*I am.* As soon as I know that you are safe, Andrea, I'm going to leave Paris myself. I'm going to travel south to Lyons and home to Thoissey. Nobody will find me. I don't ever want to see Ryan or Kusa again."

"Kusa?" Andrea asked.

She wavered. "Isn't that what you said someone called the terrorist?"

"Yes, it was a name something like that."

"I fear for you. They will link you with him—an American journalist imprisoned with a terrorist. Is that what you want?"

Alarm pricked Andrea's spine. Her career was at stake. Even an hour in a French police station could ruin her career. Collette was right. She had to get out of Paris.

ⓦ ⓦ ⓦ

Porter Deven sat at his desk in the office in Neuilly. His official quarters were in the American embassy under the guise of working for the State Department, but he conducted much of his business here in this granite and steel complex. Porter jabbed an emery board over his thumbnail. He had a boorish, bulldog expression on his face, his crystal blue eyes fiery, as Victor Wilson and Sherm took their seats across from him.

Sherm met Porter's contemptuous gaze. He made no effort to speak or shake hands, but slowly allowed his eyes to center on the polka dots on Porter's tie.

"Wilson, what happened to the ambassador?" Porter asked.

"A quick ambush, Porter. Mac never knew what hit him."

"That was merciful. Mac and I go back a long way."

"I know," Wilson said. "I'm sorry. In spite of all your warnings, the ambassador cut through the park often."

"Mac was a fool to cut through the park at all, but he was destined for a bullet the way he spoke out against terrorism."

"The park was his way of saying, 'I'm a free man.'"

"A dead man, Vic," Porter answered bitterly.

Sherm lifted his gaze from the design on Porter's tie as a fourth person entered the room, a squat man built like Porter. He began cleansing Sherm's head wound efficiently.

"Thanks, Doc," Sherm said when he finished.

The man grinned. "Thank my brother, Porter. I'm Zach

Deven—just an old army medic. You'll have to get your follow-up elsewhere."

"I will through the Kippen office here in Paris." To Zach Deven's raised brows, he added. "Off the record, of course."

The interruption had left Porter motionless, his head bent forward. Mac's death hung like an albatross around Sherm's neck, too. "Look, Deven, the whole mess is my fault," Sherm said. "If I hadn't persuaded the ambassador to help me—"

Porter's lips barely moved. "I don't like you, Prescott. But no one could predict the ambassador's location at that precise hour without an informant. What about it?" he asked. "Who knew that you had an appointment with the ambassador?"

"My father-in-law in Texas. The Kippen office in Paris."

Victor Wilson tossed a camera case on Porter's desk.

"The beautiful woman who dropped this and ran away may have signaled for the ambush as we left the embassy," he said.

"Vic, you know that's crazy," Sherm protested.

Porter's eyes were cold. "Beautiful like your wife, Mr. Prescott? Are you a sucker for a pretty face?"

Sherm shot out of his chair. Wilson yanked him back, saying, "She and the guard may have set us up, Prescott."

Porter scrutinized the camera case. "No name. Just numbers. How are we to identify her, Vic?"

"Check with the embassy. If they caught her on one of the surveillance cameras, we can get a blowup."

The possibility revitalized Deven. He was on the scrambler at once, calling Drew Gregory, demanding a photo.

"Deven, her name's Andrea," Sherm said. "Andrea York. She's a guest at the InterContinental Hotel."

Porter's grip on the phone tightened. "York? *You know her*? The same young woman who has been dating Ryan Ebsworth?"

There was no time for Sherm to answer. Porter was back on the phone. "Sorry, Drew. I was distracted. You've heard the news, I'm sure. Yeah . . . Mac bit the dust. No, we have to keep the Agency's name out of it."

He paused. "Mac's wife? If she's anywhere in Paris, she must know by now. Look, Drew, go by. Express our condolences. I need to keep a low profile. She'll understand."

Suddenly, Porter's fist came down hard on the desk, a 7.0 on the Richter scale, his face blotching in his fury. "The surveillance team lost Ebsworth again? How, Drew?"

Porter sent a scathing glance Wilson's way, the scarlet blotches on his face deepening. He covered the mouthpiece and said, "They saw Ebsworth at the Amitie with *that* waitress Collette. Then they followed him to the de Crillon and lost him."

Porter's utter contempt replaced reason. He doubled his fist again. There was another high on the Richter scale. "Drew, get over to the Amitie first and track down that waitress. I want to know where Ebsworth was all day right on up to the minute he left her. Particularly where he was when Mac was killed."

Porter rubbed his chest with the palm of his hand, as though by the intense rubbing the pain would ease.

"After that, Drew, go over and see Mac's wife."

He rang off and glared at the camera case. "Andrea York and Ryan Ebsworth," he mused. "Vic, send someone over to the InterContinental and pick that woman up. Get her out of the country on the first flight out of Paris. If the French find her, they'd have Ebsworth, too. *Ebsworth is my spoil.* Remember that."

His gaze strayed back to Sherm. "You were convincing, Prescott. The ambassador believed you. If he had made it here today, you would have ruined everything I've strived for."

"It wouldn't have mattered, would it, sir?" Sherm asked. "The ambassador would have sided with National Security."

"But you would have known exactly how your wife died."

Sherm's sense of injustice sharpened. He eyed the ambassador's attaché case, stood, and picked it up. "Do you mind, Deven? What's inside wouldn't be of interest to you."

◉◉◉

Porter glared as the door closed behind Prescott, but Vic gave him his tongue-in-cheek grin. "Don't worry, Porter. Prescott will find an empty case when he gets back to the privacy of his room. I emptied it before we left the embassy with the ambassador."

"So what was Mac so fired up about?"

"Mostly Mac was carrying reports related to Prescott's wife. But there was one detailed memo on the Agency's blunders in Canada that linked us to Mrs. Prescott's death. I don't know where Prescott got that information. Accurate guesses, perhaps. But Mac could have hung us with that one. I asked the secretary to shred it."

He flashed another devilish grin. "If Prescott gives you any trouble, you can ask French Security to arrest him for carrying the American ambassador's missing briefcase."

❦ ❦ ❦

The day after Mac's death, Drew stood by the windows at the Neuilly office. "Porter, have they located Ebsworth yet?"

Porter exhaled, the smoke rings swirling into the air. "Ebsworth and the American fashion journalist are both missing."

Drew turned and leaned against the window casing. "Gone?"

"The concierge at the InterContinental saw them together shortly after the assassination. The woman was ill. This morning the de Crillon and the InterContinental Hotels reported what we already had discovered: Ebsworth and Andrea York's rooms were empty."

"*Andrea York*," Drew repeated. Another smoke ring drifted toward him. He slid a telex across Porter's desk.

"What's this?" Porter asked, scanning it.

"A message Andrea York sent to me in London."

Porter exploded. "The same woman? You know her, too?"

"I served under her grandfather in Normandy."

Porter snuffed out his cigarette. "She's Ebsworth's friend?"

Drew shrugged. "It looks that way. You should have

accepted my resignation long ago. I don't want to deal with Captain York's granddaughter. Not if she's teamed up with Ebsworth."

"Retire?" Porter scoffed. "Where? To the old family farm in upstate New York? You'd die of boredom."

"I've still got friends at Langley, Porter, but I'm more apt to head to the Scottish Highlands."

"The bleakness of their winters fits your personality."

As Porter lit another cigarette, Sherm Prescott stormed into the office and slammed an attaché case on Porter's desk.

"Deven, where's Wilson?" Prescott demanded. "You both knew that the ambassador's case was empty. You set me up."

Porter scraped back his chair and stood. "You wanted the ambassador's case. You got it." He pointed toward the door. "Now get out."

"Not until I know what really happened to my wife." He whipped his wallet open and held it close to Porter's face. "That's my wife, Deven. She didn't drown, so don't ram any more excuses about National Security down my throat."

Drew studied Prescott. The man wasn't going to budge from the office without answers. As Drew crossed the room, he caught only a flicker of surprise in Prescott's eyes.

"I'm Drew Gregory," he said. "We met in the lounge at the InterContinental. I know how you feel, Prescott. I lost my wife, too, years ago. But not in the same way."

He didn't clarify that it had happened in a divorce court. For Drew it had been as final as a cemetery. Losing Miriam had left him empty, alone, totally angry. He understood Prescott's pain. He had vented his own rage boxing shadows for years, hating Miriam for leaving him, loving her in spite of himself.

Prescott's handclasp was firm.

In an even, unemotional tone, Drew said, "You're right about your wife, Prescott. She didn't drown."

He saw relief in Sherm, disbelief and fury in Porter. Porter slumped into his chair, his neck veins bulging. "The woman's dead, Gregory. It doesn't matter how she died."

"It does to this gentleman, Porter. He wants the truth."

He faced Sherm. "Twenty-eight months ago your wife walked in on an illegal arms transaction. We don't know the particulars. But whatever information she had, she died for it."

"Dear God!" Sherm cried. "Then my wife was murdered. Poor Melody. And I let her go swimming alone that day. She begged me—"

Drew put a hand on Prescott's shoulder to steady him.

Sherm shrugged off the restraint. "This doesn't add up, Gregory. According to the police records and autopsy report, there were no marks on my wife's body to indicate foul play."

Drew nodded. "But the real records are sealed. Her death was not accidental. It was a forced drowning."

Prescott's voice was flat when he asked, "Was it Ebsworth?"

"No official charges were filed."

"Nor even permitted?" he asked.

Porter quickly said, "It's who Ebsworth works for that's important to us. We believe his contact is here in Paris."

"Is that why you need Ebsworth?"

Prescott seemed to be layering the facts in a mental computer, his dispassionate response more troubling than if he had detonated at the thought of his wife's murder.

Drew exchanged glances with Porter and then said, "We believe there's an arms deal in progress in Paris right now—the sale of illegal weapons to a Third World country. We have reason to believe that the recent acts of terrorism and the arms deal are linked to the same organization." He hesitated. "Your presence in Paris, Prescott, may threaten their whole operation."

"I don't see myself as a significant player."

Again Drew looked to Porter before saying, "You've been tracking Ryan Ebsworth. Those he works for may think that you know what Melody knew. That risks your safety. They may even think you're working with us. Should I go on?"

Prescott's gaze sharpened. "Yes, tell me, what did my wife know? We were vacationing in Canada. We knew the same people. How did she get involved?"

Drew leaned forward. "We may never have the full details. Right now your safety is our concern. We believe Ebsworth was in the park yesterday to identify you. Possibly to assassinate you."

"For information I don't even have?" Sherm turned to Porter. "I'm really to back off this time?"

"Unless you want to work with us," Porter suggested.

Life sprang back into Sherm's expression. "Then you'd feed me just enough information so I'd trust you."

Porter ignored the remark. "Ebsworth may be heading back to Harrison Lake. You visit there frequently. Your presence there wouldn't arouse any suspicion—"

"Sorry, Mr. Deven. I always go in September."

"Ryan Ebsworth won't know that."

"Porter, I still work for Kippen Investments, remember?"

"All the better, Prescott. No tie-in. We'd put you in touch with Canadian intelligence. You could report to them."

"Not to the Devenshire Corporation in Canada?"

"We're only based in Europe."

"What's in it for me, Deven?" Prescott challenged.

"You could tighten the web around Ebsworth."

"I'm not certain I want vengeance anymore."

Porter plunged on. "You'd keep a watch on Ebsworth and the American woman if she goes there. You'd check out Ebsworth's aunt and report any clandestine meetings going on at her farm."

"And reduce myself to the level of a rat fink, Deven?"

"A temporary operative."

Deven spread some surveillance photographs in front of Prescott. "The woman in the park and the lady Ebsworth has been seeing—it's the same woman."

Sherm met Porter's caustic gaze. "I told you that yesterday. She's Andrea York. I've been trying to call her room."

"Don't bother," Porter said. "She was out of there before Wilson reached the hotel. It's reasonable to conclude that she's with Ebsworth, willingly or unwillingly." He handed a thin file to Sherm. "This is all we have on Miss York. Nothing spectacular."

Prescott scanned it. Andrea York—born in Index,

Washington. No siblings. Middle class family. University of
Washington graduate: majored in business with a minor in
political science. Postgraduate studies: fashion design.
Resides: Westwood, California. Unmarried. No criminal
record. No traffic violations. Votes Republican. Employed by
Style Magazine: on assignment in Paris. Keeps company
with Ryan Ebsworth, known subversive. Hotel room search:
negative. Her social security and passport numbers were
listed. Sherm skimmed the detailed list of fashion houses
and tourist sites visited with date and time. There was a
notation in the margin that her passport number matched
numbers found in her camera case.

Prescott slapped the folder on the desk. "This file says
nothing about Miss York's political views."

"The company she keeps does," Drew said. "I served with
her grandfather in World War II. Conrad York was a great
man. But political views often change from generation to
generation." He ran his hand through his hair and then
smiled at Prescott.

"Porter says you're a religious man, a Christ-follower.
Captain York was, too."

"Was he? What about you, Gregory?"

"Impossible! God and intelligence work are at odds."

"Then, I couldn't possibly work with you, could I?"

The stress lines on Prescott's face tightened. He stood and
shoved the attaché case toward Drew. "I wonder if the
ambassador knew it was empty?" he asked.

"I'm not in on that one, but give me a few moments with
Porter and I'll give you a ride back to your hotel."

"I'd appreciate that. But—tell me one more thing, Drew.
Do you think Melody suffered long?"

"I don't think so, Prescott. It's likely they used a hypo-
dermic. That's why there was no evidence of her struggling
when she drowned."

Prescott's brave facade crumbled. "I keep wondering
whether my wife knew what was happening, whether she
cried out for help?"

From where he was standing at the time of her death,
Drew had heard one piercing scream. And then silence, not

even the sound of the splash as Melody fell into the water. He and Benj Reever had cut out on a fast run, but Melody Prescott was dead before they reached her.

Melody's widower still waited for his answer.

"No one could have reached your wife in time, Prescott."

Prescott's shoulders convulsed, his emotions no longer detached. Drew turned away, allowing him the sanctity of his grief.

◉◉◉

Sherm waited in the back room, sipping yesterday's rank coffee, his head throbbing. It struck him—now that he'd met Zach Deven—that the Devenshire Corporation was a legitimate business under government contract. But Porter was merely a figurehead. Zach controlled the business, offering a perfect cover for Porter's work with the C.I.A.! Somehow Porter was linked with Melody's death in an official capacity.

As Sherm stood there, squinting against the sun, he relived his last morning with Melody.

"Come on, Sherm," she had begged, slipping out of bed and dropping her nightgown on the floor. "Go with me."

"I don't swim in the morning," he had grumbled.

She picked up her nightgown and tossed it at him. "But I really need you to go with me."

He had watched her slip into her Body-Glove swimsuit and toss a towel around her neck. At the door she turned and came back to sit on the edge of the bed beside him.

"I love you, Sherm Prescott. You know that, don't you?"

His hand rested on her thigh. "It's what motivates me."

"Then honestly, Sherm, get up and go with me."

He had teased her then, splitting the sheet, inviting her back into bed with him.

"After I go swimming," she promised. "I'll be back."

"I'll keep a spot warm for you."

She leaned down and kissed him. "I love you, Sherm."

"No more than I love you." He pulled her down against

his chest, holding her, not wanting to let her go. "You'll be careful? Swim in the pool, not the lake."

That was his usual warning, and she responded with her usual bubbly laugh as she pushed away from him. "I never swim alone. You know that. It's not safe. I meet the regulars at the pool everyday. Don't worry. I'll be okay."

At the door she turned to him once more and blew him a kiss. Alone, he punched his pillow, stretched on his side, and fell asleep smiling. He slept while his wife was murdered.

He had awakened with a start, instinctively knowing that Melody had called his name, that she needed him. He had yanked on his trousers, slipped his bare feet into loafers, and grabbed a pullover sweater. Not waiting for the elevator, he ran down the stairwell to the hotel pool, then outside. He ran along the lake calling her name.

He found her face down in the water in a little eddy a quarter of a mile from the hotel. Lifting her in his arms, he had carried her limp body back to the hotel, grief-stricken, hating himself for not going with her. Even then as he stared down at Melody's colorless, water-logged cheeks and those vacant eyes, he knew intuitively that she had not drowned.

In the silence of the Devenshire kitchenette, Sherm's mind cleared. He thought of Drew saying, "You're a Christ-follower."

Coffee cup in hand, Sherm settled the score. God hadn't pushed Melody into the lake. Once again he confessed his guilt, his rage, and poured out his grief.

"Oh God, forgive me," he cried out. "Forgive me for blaming You. Help me, Lord, to be the godly man You meant me to be . . . help me."

For the first time since her death, peace really washed over him. Sherm was free to let Melody go. He would go back to the Harrison in Canada and spread another dozen roses on the lake in a final tribute to her.

Suddenly, he realized he wanted to help Porter and Drew. He'd leave Paris this afternoon and head to the Kippen offices in Geneva, then cut north to Munich. From there he'd fly to England. He'd call Buzz Kippen from the London office and ask for some vacation days.

He rinsed his cup and hung it back on the rack. Meomnts later as he shook hands with Porter, he said, "I'm accepting your offer. I'll be in Harrison Hot Springs on Wednesday."

"Sooner," Porter urged.

"Wednesday or not at all, Porter."

Chapter 17

On Friday the embassy flag still flew at half-mast as Drew took a taxi back to Neuilly for a meeting with Porter Deven. The ambassador's body was en route to the Dover Air Force Mortuary, his final port-of-call. Already Mac was being inched out of the news, the choice for his replacement taking priority.

A rotten way to end a long diplomatic career, Drew thought. Now at the end life was summed up in a flag-draped coffin and Old Glory lowered on the flag pole. As a former navy pilot, Mac's final destination was Arlington. He'd have the solemnity and honor of a horse-drawn caisson and the woeful dirge of taps, a comforting final chapter for Mac's wife and family. Little else.

Drew wondered where Mac might be now. He credited these brooding emotions to Prescott, the Christ-follower. For all of his anger, Prescott had a strong grip on what had happened to his wife the moment after she died. With Mac, Drew couldn't be certain. He and Mac had never verbalized what lay beyond dying. Mac, a good father and husband, was the kind of guy who always toasted the unending tomorrows.

Something else ate at Drew's gut. The glaring headlines of the *Le Monde* lying on the taxi seat beside him: "WOMAN FLEES SCENE OF AMBASSADOR'S ASSASSINATION."

He folded the paper with the headlines turned in. Why an anonymous phone tip to the *Le Monde*, he wondered. Now all of Paris was looking for the granddaughter of Conrad York. Had this been Porter's way of forcing her to leave Paris?

At Neuilly Drew managed a cheerful greeting, but Porter squelched it, saying, "There's been an explosion near the Basilica of the Sacred Heart. A Bohemian artist blew sky high."

"Why this sudden interest in a street artist, Porter?"

"They found bomb fragments attached to Ebsworth's easel."

"Ryan Ebsworth dead in a bombing? That's not his style."

"I'm telling you, Drew, French Security thinks the man is dead."

"No, that's what Ebsworth wants us to think. So he's still in Paris? We've sent Prescott to Canada on a wild goose chase."

Porter held out the charred corner of a passport. "There's an American woman dead, too. Check the name."

"*York.*" Shock replaced Drew's indifference. "They think the woman is Conrad York's granddaughter?"

Porter thrust a surveillance photo into Drew's hand.

"Security showed this to the waiters in a nearby cafe. They identified Ryan as the artist. He'd been in for coffee earlier. But they weren't positive that Andrea York was the young woman at Ryan's side moments before the explosion."

Drew studied the blowup. "She looks like her grandfather."

"Looked like him," Porter corrected. "They had to sweep her off the sidewalk. The State Department asked France to release any fragments for immediate transfer to Dover. If anyone can come up with a positive I.D., those boys at Dover can."

"That's our second Dover shipment in forty-eight hours."

They brooded for several minutes. Then Drew spread the *Le Monde* newspaper open on Porter's desk. "I thought this was your way of forcing Miss York to run."

Porter thumped the paper. "I had nothing to do with this. Yesterday I wanted her out of the country. This morning I was on the horn with Langley. *They gave orders to get her out.*

And then suddenly this explosion—"

"Why this interest from Washington?"

"The pressure is on from this end, too. The French don't know about Ebsworth's involvement, but they think they've traced those recent acts of terrorism to a prominent figure here in Paris. An American. For political reasons they're keeping a lid on it."

"Do you know who it is?" Drew asked.

"I'm not privy to that. And Washington won't settle for not knowing. Ebsworth was my chance for answers, but with him dead—"

Porter leaned back in his chair, his expression splenetic, morose. He folded his hands and stared into space. "I was so close. I was closing in on the top man, and now the French will nail him first." He shrugged. "It reminds me of my toy pagoda, Drew. My father kicked the gut out of it when I was a boy."

"What's a toy pagoda got to do with this?"

Porter formed a pyramid with his hands and thumped the tips of his fingers angrily. "I was almost to the top. The man I'm looking for has friends in high places. I can't get to him."

"You mean Ebsworth's boss! Porter, you know who he is!"

Porter lifted his brows quizzically, the effort almost exhausting him. "There's a wall of secrecy around him. He's terrorizing Paris, but it's politically convenient to take him quietly. We won't even know." Porter's hands went limp, his pyramid crumbling like his toy pagoda. "I'll never know who it was—for certain."

"Porter, you didn't answer me. Do you think you *know* the man at the top of your pyramid?"

"Yes, I may have dined with him at the Cafe Amitie."

Scorn marked Drew's question. "Did you drink with him, too?"

Porter's shoulders sagged even more. "One drinks with friends. Besides, wine goes with my meals."

"Then you talked too much and sold yourself straight down the Seine. The man must have been laughing at you behind his champagne—thinking about you looking for him and Ebsworth."

"I took his counsel as a friend," Porter said.

"Is that what happened to the Canadian operation twenty-eight months ago? You told a *friend* about it?"

Porter nodded. "I'm sorry, Drew. The top man may have been a dining companion. I'll never know—not with Ebsworth dead." He tried to focus back on Drew. "My past is catching up with me."

Drew shocked Porter from his lethargy, saying, "Porter, what if Ebsworth is still alive? What if he planned the explosion? Maybe he arranged for someone to take his place at the easel for the sake of a picture? Five hundred French francs to pretend to be an artist and his girlfriend—someone who owed Ebsworth a favor. The minute the man picked up the paintbrush to pose for the camera shot—swoosh!"

Drew ran his hand over the fragmented edges of the passport. "Maybe he burned this part with a cigarette lighter, then dropped it, and kept the rest of the passport. He wanted us to find Andrea York's name."

"Then we'd be the only ones who think they're still alive."

"Good, Porter. No one else will be looking for them at the airports. Keep the surveillance on Ebsworth in full force."

"You don't keep searching for a dead man, Drew."

"Ryan likes his own handiwork. He'll mull through the wreckage and rise out of the ashes *and take the York woman with him*."

"He can't afford that error in judgment."

Drew stalked to the wall map. "Our opposition would just kill her. They wouldn't place an ad in the paper. So Ebsworth must be the one who wants York to leave the country. Think like Ebsworth, Porter. Where would he go?"

"I'm not a terrorist."

Drew ignored Porter's remark and ran his finger from Paris across the channel to England. "London," he mused. "No, that's not his style either. He's traveling with a beautiful woman. Maybe a romantic setting like Switzerland or Austria."

"Until the explosion, we were checking airports and border crossings. A united Europe makes crossings easy these days."

Drew kept his eyes on the map. "Ryan's counting on us to pull off surveillance. Maybe he's trying to convince his contact here in Paris that he's dead. Then none of us will look for him."

Porter was functioning again. He walked over beside Drew, chose a red tack marker and flagged British Columbia. "I'm thinking like Ebsworth now, and if I were alive, I'd high-tail it home to Canada. Maybe his aunt has a summer place where he can hide out."

Drew hit the map with his fist.

"Sometimes, Drew, I think you hate the work you're in."

"It cost me my family. Miriam despised intelligence work. Uncovering enemy agents isn't a glory road any longer, Porter."

"It never was." Porter sighed, belly deep. "You're not the kind of man who would be satisfied with a pipe and a fireplace."

"That was a controversy with Miriam. I got restless when the home fires were burning."

"Is that why you divorced her, Drew?"

"Miriam divorced me." He stabbed Harrison Lake with a green marker. "Porter, I'd like to book a flight to Canada."

"I'll ask Tony Brackmeyer to keep checking leads at Charles de Gaulle. If Ebsworth and York show up, he'll make certain they get out of Paris safely—while French intelligence isn't looking."

"Porter, you're crazy like Ebsworth. But tell Tony I'd like to catch the same flight if possible. What about York's family?"

"State Department will notify them that she's missing. They will wait for the Dover report before suggesting anything worse."

Drew hesitated at the door, his hand on the knob. "Keep your eye on the Cafe Amitie while I'm gone."

"You're still chasing your missiles at the cafe?"

"Vic and I put surveillance equipment in Jacques's office."

"You'll have French Security down my neck, Drew."

"I met with Stephan Marseilles at his chateau south of Vendome on Sunday. I cleared it with him."

"It'll blow up in your face, Drew."

"Or in yours, Porter." Drew opened the door. "I'll need some backup in Canada, *not counting Prescott*."

"I'll send Victor Wilson and Jeff Akers in a day or two. You do your job, Drew. I'll take care of Prescott."

As Drew left, Porter slammed the desk and swore. "Drew Gregory, darn if I don't think you still want my job."

❂❂❂

Andrea turned as Ryan came into the room and dropped a newspaper on the chair. "I wish I knew more French," she said.

"Why? I know enough for both of us."

She pointed toward the television. "The terrorists struck again. Look, Ryan. It's in the Montmartre district—right near that cathedral where you paint."

He crossed the room in swift strides and snapped off the picture. "We've seen enough of terror and killing. Leave it off."

She glared back at him. "I know enough French to know that an American tourist and a young artist were blown up by a bomb."

He went to her and took her hands. She tensed as he gripped her fingers. "I'm sorry, Andrea. I just don't want anything to frighten you. I went by the American embassy," he said. "Security is very tight. There's no way we can see about your passport."

She pulled free. "Collette will go there with me."

She saw the surprise on his face.

"I don't think she's coming back tonight. She's working late." He shrugged. "She doesn't always sleep here, you know."

No, Andrea thought. *She's been at the de Crillon with you at times.* "Then I won't stay here alone with you."

His eyes narrowed. "Don't be prudish, Andrea. But don't worry either. Collette's bedroom has a lock on the door. You'll be safe."

He stomped off toward the kitchen and then turned back waving a passport at her. "It's Canadian," he said. "You fly to Vancouver tomorrow as Jane Arlington. You're traveling as my sister. Once we're there, I'll try to clear up this mess and get you home."

"Ryan, is Francois Deborde driving us to the airport?"

"He won't be able to, Andrea."

"I still *need* to call the American embassy, Ryan."

"You can't. There's no phone in this apartment."

She looked around, startled. "There was yesterday."

His expression twisted. "Was there?" he asked.

He nodded to the paper he had tossed on the chair. "You made headlines, Andrea. 'WOMAN FLEES SCENE OF AMBASSADOR'S ASSASSINATION.' That's you! I've sacrificed to protect you. Forget about turning yourself in. You'd threaten my safety as well."

Andrea fled into Collette's bedroom. Locking the door, she leaned against it. She heard Ryan cross the room again, saw the knob rotate, heard him breathing hard on the other side. The opportunity to turn herself in had vanished. *But if I had ended up in a French prison, Katrina might die before I could see her again. I must go to Canada.*

She removed her dangling earrings, crossed the room to Collette's dresser, and glanced in the mirror. The frightened face that stared back was hardly her own—except for the splash of freckles. Her eyes seemed wide, pale; her lips taut. As she put her earrings down, Andrea saw Ryan's signet ring lying beside a snapshot of Ryan and Collette wrapped in each other's arms. Andrea recoiled, knowing that Ryan had rendezvoused with Collette in this room, probably in the very bed where Andrea planned to rest.

She sat down and considered her situation, viewing it like a management meeting at *Style Magazine.* Her immediate short-term goal was survival; her options out of Paris, limited. Step one: she would fly out with Ryan tomorrow. Step two: once she was safely in Vancouver, she would arrange for legal counsel. Then she would go home to her parents and to her dying grandmother.

۞ ۞ ۞

At Charles de Gaulle International, Drew functioned on intuition, convinced that Ebsworth would leave Paris before the dead tourist could be identified. He had watched five departures. Nothing. Now, banking on Brackmeyer's latest suggestion, Drew positioned himself near the British Airway check-in counter in a waiting room that was empty when he arrived, but crowded toward flight time. It was down to the boarding call when he spotted Ebsworth brazenly guiding Andrea past two gendarmes to the check-in desk.

At the desk Ryan said, "We're the Arlingtons. My sister isn't feeling well. Could we board early?"

"Yes, sir." The attendant pointed. "We're pre-boarding now."

Drew was on his feet, dashing in front of another passenger. He noted the attendant's name tag. "Aubrey, I need to take this flight."

"Sorry, sir. We have a full passenger load."

Drew nodded toward Tony Brackmeyer in an airline uniform. "Aubrey, ask your supervisor. I must catch this flight."

Brackmeyer stepped forward and checked the computer. "We have Monsieur Gregory booked on an aisle seat, two rows behind the Arlingtons who just checked in. Ticket him, Aubrey."

Aubrey stamped the ticket. Drew grabbed it and dashed for the boarding ramp, knowing that another passenger would soon find his seat no longer available. He handed his luggage to the flight attendant, saying apologetically, "I was standby."

He risked a glance at Ryan and Andrea as he passed them. Ebsworth was staring out the window. Andrea sat with her eyes closed, a drawn expression on her face. Once they were airborne, after the layover in Heathrow, Drew could sleep, too. Ebsworth wouldn't be going anywhere until they reached Vancouver.

As Drew buckled his seat belt, Brackmeyer ran down the aisle, a briefcase in his hand. "Sir, you forgot this."

Drew didn't argue. "Careless of me," he said.

He slipped his hand inside, blindly checking the contents. Drew felt a bulge and knew that his Beretta was safely on board. He wondered how Porter had managed that. So what about Canadian customs? Or did Porter have that one covered as well?

👁👁👁

Drew awakened three hours out of Vancouver. He stretched and walked, stopping at the kitchenette to ask the flight attendant for coffee. He took it down in quick gulps.

"How do you polish off that bitter stuff?" she asked.

He saluted her with his cup. "It's a good eye-opener."

As he drank a second cup, he studied Andrea. Drew judged her to be about his daughter's age. Even with her troubled expression, York was a golden-haired beauty. But she kept the wrong company.

Ebsworth looked unimpressive as he dozed in his seat, a spindly, raw-boned man with a veneer of boyishness. The Agency file had Ryan at twenty-four, wasted years as far as Drew was concerned. Too young for negotiating illegal arms to foreign countries.

Andrea looked at Drew as he made his way back to his seat. He smiled at her. She didn't respond, but he noticed the quick uptilt of the stubborn jaw so much like Conrad York's.

Memories rushed at him as though forty-odd years had never passed. June of '44 was like yesterday. Captain York had stood near him as their ship plowed a steady course on that rain-washed sea toward Normandy. Drew was a kid then. Scared, seasick, and still too young for the army. He had vomited into his helmet until his sallow color blended with the khaki green of his uniform. He crouched on the deck with other frightened, ill men. York bent down and took Drew's helmet. When he came back, it was washed clean.

"You'll need this," he said. "Put it on, son."

Drew offered his crumpled packet of Lucky Strikes to the captain. When York refused, Drew put a cigarette to his own lips, but nausea rolled over him again like the waves of the English Channel. He never smoked again.

The captain eased down beside him. "How old are you, son?"

"Almost seventeen, sir."

Shock silenced the captain for a moment. "You should have told me sooner, Gregory. It's too late for me to send you back."

"I'm old enough, sir. I'd disgrace myself going home."

"We'll talk about it again once we dig in." York kept his tone reassuring. "Do you have a family, son?" he asked.

Captain York was a young man himself, thirtyish, but the word *son* was comforting to Drew. "There's just my parents and my half-brother Aaron. Aaron's younger than I am. And if the war isn't over when he's old enough, he'll beat the draft."

"Maybe he'll enlist like you did," York said.

"No, sir. My stepdad says Aaron's smart enough for law school. He doesn't want him blown up over here. He told me if I'd been smart enough, I wouldn't be in this mess myself."

Drew sensed York smiling in the semidarkness.

"Captain, what happens if I freeze when we go ashore?"

York gripped Drew's shoulder. "Son, we're all afraid."

"But some of us aren't coming out of this alive, sir."

"Some of you will. You're going to make it, son."

York offered something more comforting, but Drew resisted as the captain read from his Bible, "The Lord is your Shepherd, son . . . even though you walk through the valley . . . "

Two hours later the captain was dead before he could scale the cliffs or reach the Germans' barb-wire barricade. Dead on the bloody beach. When he fell and died, Drew grew up. He was still a kid when they liberated Paris, not even eighteen when the war ended. But he had a ribbon or two. *For bravery*, the army told him. *For the captain*, he told himself.

He owed York a lot. He was about to repay it by tracking down the captain's granddaughter. The thought sickened him.

                    ۞۞۞

As the seat belt sign went on for landing in Vancouver, a flight attendant knelt beside Drew. "Mr. Gregory, when we land, you'll be deplaning first from the rear of the aircraft."

"What about my luggage?"

"The captain said we'll have it to you as quickly as we can. As soon as he brakes, come to the back before the aisles fill. Don't fall." She smiled as she stood. "Thank you for flying with us. I'm glad you enjoyed your flight."

The jet landed smoothly, and Gregory negotiated his exit from his aisle seat almost as swiftly. As he deplaned, he recognized Benj Reever waiting for him. They shook hands.

"Good to see you, Gregory. I think we worked together before."

"Yes, I remember. Twenty-eight months ago."

"We've a second chance. We won't blow her, eh?"

Reever served with Canadian intelligence. He was forty-ish, a British emigrant, a straightforward man with a bushy blond moustache—a pleasant chap, yet deadly serious about his work.

"We'll be through customs in a jiff and off to the Harrison," he told Drew.

"What about Ebsworth and the girl?" Drew asked. "They traveled into Canada as Keith and Jane Arlington."

"I have men on it. If their destination changes, we'll know at once. I've a transmitter-receiver in my car."

"Should I ask about my suitcase?"

"My boys will pick it up right off. Should be in the boot

of my car by the time we get to the parking lot." Benj Reever smiled, pleased with his own efficiency.

They cleared customs with merely a nod from Reever, the unregistered Beretta safe in Drew's briefcase. As they settled in the car, Reever said, "Porter Deven told us to expect three of you. I've booked you in a bungalow behind the hotel, less conspicuous for you there. Number 10 has two beds and a divan. Tried for number 7 for luck, your mother being Irish and all, but that was taken."

"Good memory," Drew said. "Remembering Mom was Irish."

"You had quite a bit to say about her your last time here."

"She was alive then. On my mind because I saw her so seldom."

"Tough on families, this work we've chosen."

"Any news for me from Porter?" Drew asked.

"He said to tell you *two checked in at Dover*. I told him things may be building up on this end, Gregory."

"Besides Ebsworth?"

"Including Ebsworth."

"They never settled that Prescott drowning, did they, Benj?"

"Dead ends. But the woman's husband hasn't put it to rest. He has a friend here in the area, a Jack Sedgwick. Sedgwick keeps things stirred up for Mr. Prescott."

"Prescott's heading this way. He's on our team this time."

Reever took his eyes from the road for a second. "Not good. You should have checked with me first. I don't like extra problems. Put Prescott in touch with me. Our blunders last time came from higher up. Was it your end of intelligence, Drew?"

Drew knew the truth now, but didn't dare admit it. He said, "Porter always points a finger at Canadian operatives."

"Hardly. Someone in Paris blew the whistle and ruined the whole operation. We run the show this time, Gregory. No interference from Paris. Are you with me?"

Drew agreed. "I hear you, Benj."

Reever's optimistic lilt was back. "We told Porter that if

Ebsworth makes one questionable move, we pick him up
this time. No more waiting."

"Did Porter swallow that?"

"About as well as he would an uncooked lobster."

Andrea felt Ryan's steadying hand on her elbow as they
walked into the terminal's crowded restaurant. Ryan chose
a table by the windows overlooking the runways; the drone
of jets drowned out the conversations at neighboring tables.

She sat listlessly as he ordered, neither of them speaking
until the waitress returned with their order. As he slid the
cream toward her, he said, "I'm leaving you for an hour,
Andrea."

She pushed her coffee away. "Why?" she whispered.

"We're being followed. I'll pick up the luggage at the baggage claim, yours and mine. And then get my car. They can't
follow us both. I'll lose them. I know Vancouver. Trust me.
In an hour go outside the terminal. Wait for me by the bus
stop."

"I'll be fine now, Ryan. I'm only a few hours from home."

He stood and gave her a searing grin. "You'd never get
there. You just flew from Paris to Canada under false identity. Don't endanger yourself or your family. Wait one hour,
Andrea."

He turned to the waitress. "Where's the men's room?"

For the next hour, the waitress's sympathy increased
with each coffee refill. Twice Andrea slipped away to place
a collect call to her parents' home in Index. As she came
back to the table the second time, the waitress said, "Still no
answer, dear?"

"No. I'm trying to reach my family, but no one's home."

"Perhaps they're on their way to meet you."

"No," Andrea said, "they don't even know where I am."

She paid the waitress, adding a sizable tip for the
woman's concern. As she stood, she asked, "Do you know
me?"

The waitress studied her. "No, dear. Should I?"

"I'm Andrea York." *Fugitive*, she wanted to add.

The waitress patted her hand. "I'm sorry, dear. I still don't know you. Can I help you in some way?"

"I guess all you can do for me is remember I was here."

The waitress frowned again and nodded. "I'll do that, dear."

As she left, Andrea glanced back at the waitress. Their gaze met. The woman smiled, lifted the desk phone, and dialed.

Ryan was waiting outside the terminal in his royal blue two-door, a speed-worthy vehicle. He said little as he maneuvered the car through the streets of Vancouver. A half-hour later, he turned east and headed toward Harrison Hot Springs.

As they drove up to the Harrison Hotel, Andrea broke their long silence. "I'm going to the Canadian authorities in the morning, Ryan, with or without your permission."

"I won't let you," he said, his tone chilling. "You're a fugitive. I helped you flee from Paris, remember? Canada would have to honor an extradition order and turn you over to France."

Ryan left his car in a no-parking zone and carried her luggage into the hotel. At the reception desk, he took a wad of bills from his wallet and registered her for a week.

"I can't stay that long," she protested.

"Then get a refund and risk the lives of your family."

He stormed off, travel-weary and impatient, the blueness of his eyes purpled like a shadowed mountain.

"Ryan Ebsworth, wasn't that?" the receptionist asked.

Andrea nodded.

"Thought so," Henny prattled on pleasantly. "He used to work here. Always having stormy fits even then. But he'd be back the next day all smiles and charm."

Henny handed the room key to Andrea. "Don't fret, Miss York. Once he gets some rest, he'll be himself again."

Himself again? Andrea mused as she followed the bellhop to the elevator. The ever-changing, ambivalent Ryan, as contradictory as the pictures he painted.

As she chained the door to her comfortable room on the

West Wing, she feared that Ryan was making no effort at all to get her safely back to America. She picked up the phone, determined to call home. The line was dead at the switchboard.

Chapter 18

Rand Jordan glanced up from his desk, his surprise changing to aggravation as a stranger pushed his way into the office.

"He wouldn't take no for an answer, Mr. Jordan," the secretary apologized. "He's F.B.I. or something."

Rand waved Cindy off as the stranger sat down.

"Who the devil are you?" he asked.

A fragmented hint of a smile crossed the stranger's narrow face. He flashed his I.D., his manner brusque, authoritative. "The name's Victor Wilson. We need to talk."

"Forget it. I'm running a magazine here."

"I'll be brief. We're looking for Andrea York."

"If it's a personal matter, take it up with her."

"We can't, Jordan. She's missing."

Rand glanced at his desk calendar. "She's due back to work tomorrow." He shuffled the papers on his desk. Andrea was a stickler on deadlines, on keeping appointments. Worry lines creased his brow. "So what's the problem, Wilson?"

"Miss York is missing, officially. Possibly dead."

Rand thought the walls of his plush office would cave in on him. "What happened?"

"She witnessed the assassination of the American ambassador in Paris. She hasn't been seen since."

"Abducted?" Rand's volume dropped a notch.

"We think she left Paris with one of the terrorists."

Rand thumbed through Andrea's articles and held out the St. Laurent interview. He had been making marginal notes when Wilson burst into the room. "She faxed this from Paris early Wednesday morning. She scribbled a note at the top about a missing passport, but she was flying home on time."

"Wednesday. The day of the assassination. The day she disappeared from the InterContinental Hotel."

"If York had been in trouble, she would have called me."

"Jordan, she may be in trouble without realizing it. We can trace the business end of her trip, but we're concerned about her social life. Her boyfriends. Her lovers."

Rand laughed. "You have the wrong woman, Wilson, or I'm a poor judge of Andrea's virtuous character." He knew from his own unsuccessful evening with her. "Outside of dinner dates or a stage show, she's too busy for serious dating."

"Did she have any friends in Paris?"

"It was her first trip abroad. A business associate of mine got in touch with her. Other than that, no one."

"She saw one young man in Paris frequently. They acted like old friends. She may have left Paris with him."

"Maybe an old acquaintance, a college friend?"

"No," Wilson said. "Ryan Ebsworth isn't a college man. He fancies himself an artist. We keep close tabs on him."

"Not close enough if Andrea is missing. And if she ran off with some young fool, it has nothing to do with *Style Magazine*. So how did you find me?"

"York's expense account at the hotel—under your name."

Rand reached for the phone, rage shooting through him.

"I wouldn't do that," Wilson warned. "More publicity will only endanger Miss York. We need your help."

Rand gestured toward his plush surroundings. "I may be a wealthy man, but I guard how I spend my money. So what do you want from me, Wilson?"

"Not your money. Your cooperation. We need to know everything about Andrea York. What she's like. What she likes to do in her spare time. Where she's apt to hide."

Rand rubbed his jaw thoughtfully. Andrea York was a

composite—a serious individual, an aggressive young designer climbing a success ladder. She was charming, creative—both useful to him. Yet she was stubborn, guarding her privacy and never trying to impress him by attending office parties or dining with him. She never dated any of the employees in spite of ample opportunities, but she liked museums and concerts, pretty clothes, and Dodger Stadium. She participated in annual walk marathons for charity purposes, always hitting him for a sponsorship. And she idolized her grandmother.

"Are you trying to come up with an answer?" Wilson asked.

Rand glared back. "Miss York is a dependable employee, a woman of integrity, a virtuous, attractive young woman."

"Very attractive," Wilson agreed.

"She has an excellent work record here. She's never late, never absent. Always productive. Often vocal."

"That doesn't say much about her life outside the office."

"We don't fraternize socially," Rand said. His tone turned more civil. "I'll do some checking, Wilson. If I learn anything—"

Wilson stood and handed his business card to Rand. "If you hear from her, get in touch with us right away. Whether she left Paris willingly or not, she is in danger."

"Wait, Wilson. This says Devenshire Corporation: Exports-Imports. I thought you were U.S. government."

"You can reach me through them," Wilson said.

❂❂❂

Pam Eden limped into the room seconds after Wilson left. Rand smiled. Pam was pushing forty-three, but her shapely figure and her stylish clothes shoved back the years.

"You've trashed the crutches, I see," he said pleasantly.

"Yes, yesterday. But who was that man, Rand?"

He read from the card. "It says Victor Wilson. Devenshire Corporation: Exports-Imports. A government company of some sort."

"Exports-imports? Jewelry?" Pam asked. "You're buying?"

"Not everything he said. But some of it. Pam, Andrea York missed her flight out of Paris."

"Yes, I called the airline. I'm worried about her, Rand."

"With good reason. She's disappeared from the face of Paris."

Pam gripped the chair back. "What happened to her?"

"No one knows. But the reputation of *Style Magazine* is at risk. If we get any calls regarding her, put them off."

"Andrea wouldn't do anything out of line. You know that."

"Something important enough to write about." He flicked his pen like a cigarette. "She disappeared after witnessing the assassination of the American ambassador in Paris."

Pam stared at Rand. "Andrea? How could she be involved?"

"I don't know, but whatever happened to her, the government is interested. That's bound to make good copy."

A crack split Pam's beauty mask. "You're going to publish something against Andrea?"

"Right now she's newsworthy. And that sells magazines."

"Is that all you care about, Rand?"

He tried to calm her with a smile. "Andrea was talking about traitors and spies before she left for France. Call the printer. Let's make some changes in our magazine issue."

"It's too late. They're running copy tomorrow."

He ignored her. "We'll just change my editorial."

"Your two-pager on the history of fashion in Paris?"

"Yes. Hold that one. Terrorism makes better copy."

"What about the 'People in Fashion' column? A lot of fans read that one. It's quick, concise, easier to change."

He considered Pam's suggestion. "Good. That should work."

"But, Rand, any changes will cost you a pretty penny."

"No," he said, his decision firm, "it will cost them. If I can't get the changes, we'll switch printers next issue."

He saw questions in Pam's scowl, her lips pursed to argue. He squelched her, saying, "We don't need bad publicity. I've got to prove *Style Magazine's* noninvolvement in the whole mess."

She nodded. "I'll call the printer."

As he walked her to the door, he said, "Have someone check out the recent terrorism in Paris."

"How much time do we have, Rand?"

He checked his watch. "Until three this afternoon. We'll hold a management meeting then. We'll need photos of Andrea."

"She's on the cover this issue—in one of her own designs."

"In the excitement, I'd almost forgotten," he said. "And, Pam, Andrea's grandfather is buried in Normandy. Find out about him. Traitors. Spies," he mused. "Maybe there's a link."

He sensed Pam revolting. "It's human interest, Pam. Call Pierre Deborde and Claud Bodinat in Paris. I'll talk to them once you get them on the line. I want to know everything that Andrea did on her trip, who she saw, where she spent her time."

He saw the loathing in Pam's face as he tipped her chin up. "I'm glad you're off the crutches, Pam. If we pull this one off, we can go dancing to celebrate."

"At three you said?"

"For dancing?" he asked.

"For the management meeting you've called."

Hours after leaving the office at *Style Magazine*, Vic Wilson arrived at Sea-Tac International, rented a car, and drove north to the York family home in Index, Washington. The quaintness of the tiny town mesmerized him. He stalled his car for a moment and studied the cloud-shrouded mountains jutting above Index. They loomed like an ominous warning, nudging him with uneasiness.

His visit at the York home did not go well. The Yorks and Sabrina Jensen were struggling with misinformation and wild rumors. Upon learning his identity, they confronted him two steps inside the front door.

"Look," he said finally. "You must face it. Your daughter left Paris with a young man with radical political views."

Will York grasped his wife's hand, his lips blue. "Perhaps you should go, sir, until you have something definite to tell us."

Vic handed Sabrina Jensen his card. She crumpled it. "My friend is not a terrorist," she said defiantly.

She urged him through the door and stepped out on the porch with him. "Our town has been invaded with news media, and my best friend's reputation slandered with lies."

He handed her another card. "Please, Miss Jensen, *when* you hear from Andrea, get in touch with us."

On his way back to the airport, Wilson stopped at the Bethann Manor. The older Mrs. York lay ashen-faced, listless, as he stood by her bedside. He didn't like the way she was breathing. He wouldn't put any odds on them finding Andrea York in time to see her grandmother again.

After that he sent a telex message to Porter Deven: "No recent word to family, friends, employer. Grandmother incapacitated, terminal. Lonely. Joining Criss on holiday. More later. Vic."

In Paris Porter Deven understood the message.

"No recent word": If she were still alive, Andrea York had not contacted her family, friends, or employer.

"Grandmother incapacitated, terminal": possibly dying.

"Lonely": Andrea a loner. Few close friends.

"Joining Criss": Heading to Canada to assist Drew Gregory.

"More later": Reports from there pending.

Porter's stomach knotted as he locked Wilson's message in the file. He had set Andrea up, risking another Melody Prescott on the Agency's conscience. There was no time to waste. He had a luncheon appointment with a man from French Security, someone from DGSE suddenly interested in discussing Andrea York and Ryan Ebsworth. *So they had a label on Ebsworth!* Or were they ready to point a finger at possible C.I.A. involvement in the bombings?

Porter tossed some antacid chewables into his mouth to ease his distress. It was too early to barter for an exchange of information. The French still insisted on withholding the identity of the American businessman involved in terrorism. Porter decided to bluff his way. He would deny know-

ing Ebsworth and York. He knew it wasn't acceptable to
deceive a host country, but it happened in this business. He
would take charge of the conversation, press for an account-
ing of the ambassador's death. He'd remind the man that
the American President was growing impatient, demanding answers.

Chapter 19

Tuesday. Mid-February. More than forty hours had passed since Andrea had checked in at the Harrison Hotel. She had slept on and off, a vulnerable fugitive dragging from jet lag and escaping into the safety of a deep sleep. Her sleep had fled now, leaving her captive to four walls and a locked door with a Do Not Disturb sign still on it.

She padded barefoot across the room and opened the drapes. The room flooded with light. Outside, wintery sun rays danced across Harrison Lake, spreading shades of Nile blue and deep purple over the mountain slopes. She pressed her hands against the sliding glass door, crisp and cold from the mountain air. Her parents' home in Index was like this—isolated and quiet with the craggy, snow-capped Cascades at their back door.

Defying Ryan's warnings, she turned to the room phone and tried again to call her parents. The line was dead at the switchboard, Ryan's precautions still in force.

In spite of her fears, she showered, dressed, and left the room. Down the corridor, hotel guests were vacating their suite, their English phrases magnifying her homesickness. She hesitated, then slipped into their empty room, and placed a collect call to her family home in Index.

Sabrina Jensen answered, "York residence."

The operator cut in. "Collect call from Andrea York."

Andrea cried out, "It's me, Sabrina. I'm at the Harrison—"

"Sorry," Sabrina said, a catch in her voice. "You have the wrong number. Perhaps you should try the Index elementary."

Andrea stared at the dead phone in a daze. Sabrina. It was definitely Sabrina sending her a message as they had done as kids. But why couldn't she accept the call? Was the phone line being monitored? At least she could call Sabrina later at the school where she taught.

ooo

Drew Gregory sat in the lobby, newspaper in hand. He glanced up from the business section, pleasantly surprised as Andrea York took the red-cushioned chair across from him.

"Good morning," he said, smiling at her. "Why a wrinkled brow on such a pretty day?"

"I frown when I'm thinking," she said, her scowl easing into a smile. "You look familiar. I think we traveled from London on the same plane."

"Did we?" he asked seriously.

"Didn't we? Are you British?"

"No, but I make my home in London."

"I'm from the States. My name—my name is Andrea."

Yes, the same handsome York features, he thought.

"I'm Criss, Criss with a double s. I've a daughter about your age."

"That's dangerous, guessing a woman's age."

"Well, yes. Robyn is twenty-six."

"Then you guessed right, huh, Criss. Is she here with you?"

"No, I'm here with friends. And you?" he asked pointedly.

"I'm alone."

She glanced out toward the mountain-rimmed lake, avoiding his gaze. "It's peaceful out there," she said wistfully.

"But Hell's Gate Canyon isn't far away."

Her head snapped, her eyes narrowing. "Sounds turbulent."

"It is. Don't tumble in. The sockeye salmon survive the

Fraser's narrow gorge, but it's a dangerous swim for humans."

"If that's a personal warning, I'll keep it in mind."

"You do that." Pleasant, he kept thinking. How could he line her up with terrorism? How could he avoid it? He wanted to say, *Go home, York. Stay clear of Ebsworth.*

Instead he asked, "Do you holiday here often?"

"I didn't even know the place existed until recently."

"It has for some time," he assured her. "At least it didn't take another Caribou Gold Rush to get you here."

She turned politely his way, her gaze curious.

"That was back in the 1800s," he said, "but the legendary Sasquatch were probably here before that. You know, those hairy creatures with big feet and wispy beards who roam the mountains."

"Oh, you don't believe that nonsense."

He warmed to her amused grin. "No, but then I never saw their sixteen-inch footprints."

"You know a lot about the place. Are you a history buff?"

"Of sorts," he admitted. "British history mostly."

She suddenly curbed her curiosity and stood, sadness tugging at her face. "Have you had breakfast, Criss?" she asked.

"Hours ago. I lingered over three cups of coffee."

"Then I'll eat alone."

As York's graceful granddaughter walked off toward the Lakeside Terrace Room, the cords of memory tightened around Drew. Her presence had entangled him in the Normandy web, forcing him to remember the men in his unit—especially the captain. Captain York was a man of honor, a godly man. Could his granddaughter really be clever and cunning like Ebsworth—one moment discussing the Sasquatch legend with a stranger, the next disbursing illegal arms throughout the world?

He picked up his newspaper again. She hadn't mentioned Ebsworth by name. He'd wait. Waiting was half his job. Drew sat rereading the sports page for the third time when Ryan Ebsworth entered the hotel and headed for the elevators on the West Wing. He was still there, newspaper in hand, when Andrea and Ryan left the hotel, Ryan's attention riveted on Andrea.

Drew tossed the paper on the chair and followed them as they cut west along the lakeshore toward the sulfur hot springs a quarter of a mile from the hotel. He lagged behind, his Beretta in his shoulder holster, his coat collar turned up against the chill breeze that rippled across the lake. The stirring of the water unleashed unwanted memories of Melody Prescott and the way she had died.

Back then, the phone lines at the hotel had crossed accidently at the switchboard, allowing Melody to pick up on fragments of his conversation with Benj Reever. "Enemy agents . . . secret documents . . . arms deal . . . the exchange of money into the millions."

"Wait," Reever had said. "Someone's on the line listening."

"Yes," Melody answered. "I'm calling the police."

She would have blown the whole operation. "Wait. Meet me in the Fireside Room," Drew urged. "I'll explain everything."

He was desperate to identify her. When they met, he had appealed to her patriotism. For twenty-four hours she had served as his agent. But the whistle had been blown in Paris, the enemy agents tipped off. Everything moved rapidly to a head the day Melody died. Drew hadn't counted on her going swimming that morning. He didn't know her habits, barely knew Melody.

He had inched his way toward the rendezvous point, Beretta in hand, Benj Reever yards behind him. When they heard Melody scream, they knew that she had come face to face with the foreign agents as secret documents and money changed hands.

A young man, Nordic and blond, twenty or so, stumbled over the rocks, scrambling from the shallow waters, Benj Reever in hot pursuit. Drew ran to Melody. She lay face down, dead in the lake, the strap of her bathing suit holding her to the shoreline.

Drew fired. The shots missed the two men who sped away in a motorboat in the direction of the helipad and a private jet. One man fired back—a man Drew's age with thick-rimmed glasses and coal black hair.

The whole operation had now exploded in their faces. The men they planned to apprehend were miles away, no longer across the lake hiding out in one of the summer homes, but airborne. Drew left Melody face down in the lake and went back to the hotel to pack. Benj Reever broke off his chase, allowing Ryan Ebsworth to seek refuge in the hotel. Neither Benj nor Drew dared risk public awareness of their presence in the area that morning. Not with an innocent hotel guest dead in the water.

Hours later Drew boarded a plane in Vancouver and flew out of Canada—an American agent crisscrossing international boundaries for a career, his mission foiled. Even now it grated on him that Ryan Ebsworth was still a free man. Porter Deven insisted that the Agency's purposes were best served by that temporary freedom.

As Drew neared the sulfur springs, he heard Ebsworth arguing heatedly with Andrea, his words indistinct. Drew ducked behind a stately evergreen, his hand on his Beretta.

Andrea stepped back as Ryan gripped her wrists with a violence that stunned her. "You can't leave," he said, his words garbled in his excitement. "I've risked everything to protect you."

"I don't want your protection, Ryan. I want to go home."

His grip tightened. "I can't let you do that."

"Ryan, you're hurting me," she cried, trying to pull free.

He drew her nearer to the boiling springs, a wild glint in his blue eyes. Hot steam vapors blew against her, the stench of the sulfur unbearable.

"Don't cross me. It isn't safe for either of us."

She heard desperation in his voice, saw fear in the madness that had overtaken him as he said, "You don't understand, do you, Andrea? We're still being followed. They play for keeps. I ran out on my job in Paris because of you. Maybe they'll give me another chance. But they'll kill me if you leave. They'll kill us both."

She broke free and ran, Ryan's footsteps close behind her.

"Andrea," he said, falling in step with her, "Rand Jordan didn't ask me to take care of you in Paris."

She stared hard at him. "Who then?" she asked.

"It doesn't matter. At first I didn't know why you were so important or what you had done. But from the moment I saw you, I didn't want anything to happen to you."

"Ryan, I haven't done anything."

"I know." He rubbed his fingers lightly over her cheek. "I want you to stay. Please, Andrea. Don't run out on me."

At the hotel entryway she turned to him. "Don't come in with me, Ryan. I need time to think."

He glanced around furtively. "I will be gone this weekend."

So will I, she thought.

It was as though he knew her thoughts. "Please, Andrea, my aunt is expecting us on Friday." He touched her bruised wrists. "Give me time to work it out. I'll try and get you both across the border. You'd take Kathryn with you, wouldn't you?"

"I don't know, Ryan. But whatever I decide, I'll need Collette's address in Paris."

"Collette? Why?" he demanded.

"You didn't let me wait to thank her for her kindness. She rushed off to meet you that morning in the Montmartre district. I never saw her again."

"I don't have her address."

"Don't you?" she challenged. "You were there often enough. You even left your ring on her dresser."

He stared at his ringless finger.

"You're wrong," he said, but she saw worry take over.

"Perhaps that's how they found out that we left Paris, Ryan. They traced us to Collette's apartment."

"Impossible," he said. "Impossible."

Late Wednesday afternoon Sherm Prescott arrived at

Harrison Lake. As he stepped from the helicopter, Jack Sedgwick greeted him above the roar of the whirling rotors.

Jack, a broad-shouldered banker, hefty from his wife's good cooking, was swift on his feet. He kept grinning, his handclasp as solid as his friendship.

"Are we on the Ebsworth trail again?" he asked.

"Not in the same way, Jack."

Jack grabbed Sherm's luggage and led the way from the helipad to his car. He tossed the cases in the back. "But your visit still relates to Ebsworth, doesn't it?"

Sherm hedged. "Ryan's in deeper than we thought. There's even concern about his aunt's involvement."

Jack slipped into the driver's seat and slammed the door. "I gather I'm not to ask questions, eh? I'll grant you that. But remember, Kathryn Culvert's a good woman."

The drive up Esplanade from the copter to the hotel was a short run. Jack whipped around the curved entryway and stopped, his car engine still running. He stared straight ahead for a moment. "Sherm, Kathryn Culvert and my wife are close friends. Someday they're both going to know how much I've helped you build a case against Ryan. Tina will understand because she loved Melody. But the truth may break Kathryn Culvert's heart."

"I'll try not to involve you anymore, Jack. I promise."

"Good. Now how about dinner after church on Sunday? That will give Tina time to plan your favorite meal."

Sherm was out of the car, the luggage on the sidewalk. He gripped Jack's hand firmly again. "You're a good friend. Thanks for standing with me since Melody's death."

"My pleasure. But be kind to Kathryn." He tipped his hat. "Sunday then. Before, if you can spare the time."

Sherm's mood crashed as he entered the lobby with its haunting memories. The receptionist arched her brows in surprise, then scanned the registry.

"Oh, Mr. Prescott, you don't have a reservation."

He said politely, "I know, Henny. I'm early this year. But if Andrea York is registered here this week, I'll take the room next to hers."

Henny's facial muscles slipped to neutral. "Andrea York?

Let me see. Here she is. She signed in days ago. Room 352 on the West Wing. But we're booked solid, sir."

"Please, check again, Henny. There's got to be something."

The new assistant manager turned to them. "What about the suite in the East Tower? There's been a cancellation there."

Henny added, "And that's it. Absolutely."

Sherm didn't asked the room rate. He never did anymore, not since his wife's death. He picked up the pen. Henny pushed the registration pad toward him. He scrawled his bold signature on the card. "I'll need the room for a week, Henny. Is it available that long?"

Henny smiled now, a relaxed friendly smile. "For a week then," she said as she handed him the the key-card.

He crushed a twenty-dollar bill into her hand. "Thanks, Henny. I'll see myself up to the room."

Just as he reached the stairwell, he paused to read the latest entertainment ads. Behind him he heard the assistant manager ask, "Henny, who is that handsome, sad-faced man?"

"Sherman Prescott," Henny said, her voice high-pitched. "He's a regular guest. But he's early this year. He always comes the first of September." He heard her sigh before she added, "He used to come with his wife to celebrate their wedding anniversary. Mrs. Prescott drowned in the lake a couple of years ago on their anniversary. Now he comes alone and puts flowers on the lake in her memory."

"How morbid."

"No," Henny defended. "He's lost without her."

Sherm stood motionless.

"Since his wife's death, Mr. Prescott travels in Europe a lot, but he always comes back in September. Interesting. He asked for the room beside the guest in 352—a beautiful woman."

The assistant manager chuckled softly. "*She* might be his reason for coming back early."

"I guess you're right," Henny yielded. "What else would have brought Mr. Prescott to the Harrison in the winter season without a reservation?"

Pain shot across Sherm's temple. He blinked against its intensity. He wanted to say, *You're wrong, Henny. I'm here on business. Strictly on business.*

He picked up his luggage again and climbed the stairs, his feet heavy, his steps echoing the words, *Andrea York. Andrea York. Andrea York.*

Chapter 20

That evening Andrea dressed for dinner and made her way to the Copper Room, praying that she would find someone who would risk driving her across the Canadian border to Index. Uncertainty swept over her as a waiter with gangly Ichabod Crane arms led her to a table for two and handed her the menu. He flicked his hair from his face with his pencil, peering at her through wide rimless glasses.

"Are you waiting for a guest?" he asked.

"No, I'm alone. I'll order now. The rack of lamb. House salad and dressing. Rice. Green vegetables."

He nodded, whisking away the extra place setting.

While she waited, she scanned her surroundings. Earthtone rugs and dimly lit gold chandeliers gave a coppery glow to the room. Her chair was cushioned in burnt orange, a singular bronzed carnation centered on the table. Strangers crowded the room, mostly couples, except for Criss two tables over. He met her gaze with the interest that diners afford one another, a brief, casual smile.

The waiter came back—Andrea's steaming platter of food in his hands. The aroma whetted her appetite. She lifted her fork and savored the first bite of mint-roasted lamb as the four-man orchestra played old-time favorites. She tapped her foot to the beat of "Singing the Blues" and "Kingston Town," her mood swinging with the melodies.

As she finished her meal, her eyes strayed back to Criss.

He lifted his wine glass to her, a concerned gleam in his eyes as though he were watching a fragile sand castle crumbling.

Embarrassed, she glanced across the room, past the dance floor. Sherm Prescott, the attractive stranger from the InterContinental Hotel in Paris, sat there dining alone. Her rack of lamb doubled inside her, tying her stomach into knots.

Sherm Prescott had watched the waiter remove the extra place setting from Andrea York's table. Her presence at the Harrison signaled only one thing—Ebsworth was still in town. Throughout dinner Sherm had studied Andrea's reflection in the gilt-edged mirror. A dozen scenarios played in his mind. Andrea York the journalist in pursuit of a story. Andrea York the terrorist finding refuge at the Harrison Hotel. Or had Ryan forced her to flee to Canada with him?

As Sherm twirled his water glass, he glanced her way and found himself amused at her foot tapping rhythmically with the music. As another love song ended, their eyes met, producing an electrifying jolt that caught him unaware. She was beautiful and alone as he was alone. He longed for companionship here where life had once been full of romance and joy.

Multicolored stage lights reflected off the drummer's shiny forehead. The small dance floor filled, blocking Sherm's view of Andrea. His desperate attempt to crawl to her during the terrorist attack had failed. He owed her an apology. He pushed back his chair and cut across the dance tiles, weaving among the couples.

Two tables from Andrea, he was startled to see Drew Gregory calmly sipping a glass of red wine. He started to speak, but the agent gave a curt warning signal.

When Sherm reached Andrea, he smiled. "I'm Sherman Prescott. May I join you? No one should dine alone at the Harrison. At least no one should have dessert alone."

"I'm not planning on dessert," she said as he sat down.

"But they have Yorkshire pudding." Her nose wrinkled in distaste. "Then a fruit plate and a cup of Earl Grey tea?"

She rewarded his effort with a faint smile. "The tea and fruit sound good, Mr. Prescott."

If she recognized him, she masked it, her blue eyes slightly cagey. "Tell me about yourself," he said. "Your name for instance?"

"I'm Andrea York. But I think you already knew that."

"But I don't know what you're doing at the Harrison."

"Hiding," she said as the waiter brought their tea and fruit. "But I think you knew that, too, Mr. Prescott."

He gambled a light response. "Hiding? Not from me, I hope."

Again she rewarded him with a faint smile. "From myself."

They were playing word games, Russian roulette with the little they knew about each other. "Is this your first time at the Harrison, Andrea?"

"Yes. It's lovely here, isn't it?"

"That's why I've come back every year for ten years."

"Alone, Mr. Prescott?"

"Call me Sherm, please. And, no. I didn't always come alone. My wife and I met here. We were married here. Honeymooned here. We spent every anniversary here."

She looked at his wedding band. "You're still married?"

He rubbed his thumb over the ring. "I'm widowed. My wife died here twenty-eight months ago on our seventh anniversary. I still come back every year to gather up my memories."

"I'm sorry about your wife." She kept her eyes on his ring. "Do you wear that to protect yourself from people like me?"

"I wear it so I'll remember how very much I loved her."

They fell silent, listening to the soloist croon the words of "Sentimental Journey": "counting every mile of railroad track that takes me back . . ."

"Do you dance?" she asked.

"No, but Melody dragged me out on the floor once a year

for the 'Anniversary Waltz.' I was always glad when the song ended so I could hide my two left feet under the table."

"You can't be all that bad."

"Well, I'm good at tennis, and I'm an expert on skis."

"Then you're quick on your feet sometimes," she quipped.

Their eyes met again briefly, her gaze gentle, concerned. *No*, he thought, *those are not the eyes of a terrorist.*

"Do you travel often in Europe, Andrea?"

"Not often. And you, Sherm?"

"I lived in Europe for three years, thanks to the army. More recently I was there on a business trip."

"With people in high places?"

Checkmate, he thought. *But neither of us is winning.* "It was personal business."

She eyed him curiously as she popped a grape into her mouth. "Do you work for the government, Sherm?"

He avoided mentioning his commitment to Porter Deven. "I'm an executive for the Kippen Corporation, a worldwide investment conglomerate headquartered in San Antonio."

"Investments?" she questioned.

"It started as a family business, my father-in-law's actually."

"That's how you met your wife?"

"Yes." He stirred his sugarless tea. "Andrea, I didn't come to your table to talk about my wife. I came to apologize to you. I tried to reach you in the park the day the ambassador was killed. I failed you then. But if you still need my help—"

Her teacup rattled as she put it down. For a moment her face seemed like a still-life painting. "Yes, you can help me. Can you get me across the border without my passport?"

"You don't need a passport at the Canadian border."

She frowned. "I'd forgotten that. I'll be visiting a friend's farm on Friday. After that while he's away this weekend, I want to go home."

You'll never make it alone, he thought. *Ebsworth will never let you go.* "I have friends in Harrison, Andrea. I'll try to borrow their car."

"You'll help me? You weren't sent here to hunt me down?"

"I told you. I come here all the time. I'll help you."

He stood and walked around to her side of the table and pulled back her chair. "Let me see you to your room."

She dropped her napkin beside the teacup and took the hand he offered to her. "That won't be necessary, Sherm," she said softly. "I can find my own way."

Sherm nodded, but followed politely a few steps behind her. As they left the dining room, they passed Drew Gregory's table. Drew's angry expression seemed to say, *You're a fool, Prescott. You'll blow everything.*

۞۞۞

Sherm sat up late, images of his hour with Andrea vivid. He knew so little about her; he wanted to know more. He tried to downplay the emotional tug, the incongruity of being charmed by a fugitive. Was it the familiar atmosphere? Or was it the remembered joys of being at Harrison Lake? Was he confusing the two—the Melody of yesterday with now, with Andrea?

At midnight he heard a persistent knock on his door. He swung it open to admit an angry Drew Gregory. Drew sputtered, "Prescott, what did you think you were doing, dining with that York woman?"

"She was good company."

"Ebsworth missed you at the embassy, but once he spots you here at the Harrison, you're a dead man."

"Not until Monday. He will be gone for the weekend. I'll keep a low profile until then."

"Prescott. I'm here in Canada now. We won't need you."

"Sorry, Gregory. My coming here was Porter's idea. Yours, too. But tell Porter I plan to get Andrea out of here."

"We need her here, Prescott, so Ebsworth won't run."

"That risks Andrea's life. I can't let you do that."

Drew snarled, "Your own life is still at risk, too, Prescott. Even more so if you line yourself up with York."

"Sorry," Sherm repeated stubbornly. "Don't threaten me."

"A man from Canadian intelligence sat at the table next

to mine. A short man with a bushy blond moustache. Brown tweed jacket. Your Canadian contact if I hadn't come."

"I didn't notice him, Drew," Sherm admitted.

"He has you pegged, Prescott. If you stay on at the hotel, you play along with us. For York's sake and your own."

Drew reached up and snapped off the room lights. Then he stepped back into the midnight stillness of the empty corridor, leaving Sherm alone in a room shrouded in darkness.

۞ ۞ ۞

On Friday as they drove to the farm, Andrea ran imaginary pictures against Ryan's silence—a stereotyped farm with chipped red paint on the silo and barn, a wood stove in the kitchen, and the stench of cows and chickens outside. She visualized Kathryn Culvert as a hefty woman in a cotton dress, her hair tied in a bun.

Twenty miles from the Harrison Hotel, Ryan cut from the highway, his tires squealing as his car roared up a tree-lined driveway. The Culvert farmhouse loomed in front of them, a modern, two-story structure with a steep blue roof. A well-kept yard offered a green pathway to the shiny red barn; a sturdy wire fence marked off the grazing area for a hundred head of cattle. On the back of the property a whitewashed cottage perched on a knobby hillock, the grounds sloping toward a creekbed and rising into a thick clump of trees.

As Andrea stepped from the car, Ryan grabbed her hand and raced her into the house where a petite woman waited for them. "Aunt Kathryn," he said, "*this is Andrea.*"

Kathryn stood by the glowing fireplace, her silvery white coiffure flawless, an onset of wrinkles lining her face. Bifocals dangled from a sterling chain around her neck. Her back was bent as though osteoporosis had ravaged her spine, but her expression was vibrant. She took Andrea's hands and smiled warmly.

Her manner was as genteel as the highly polished furnishings. An archway separated the living and dining rooms. Eight tapestried chairs surrounded the oak table on which two places were set for tea with delicate Dresden cups.

Crackling logs in the fireplace and wide windows made the living room cheerful. A Chippendale chair sat by one window, Kathryn's teaploy conveniently beside it. A family portrait hung above her grand piano, Ryan's fragile personality evident in the sad blue eyes that stared down at Andrea.

Her eyes swept the room again. "Kathryn, your place is so lovely and the grounds far larger than I anticipated. How—"

"How in the world do I manage? I sublet to the rancher's family in the cottage behind me. Ben's idea before he died. Philip Vaughan needed a job and a place to raise his children. Now the Vaughans seem like family to me. We share the profits."

Ryan's "tartan" mood sent scowl ridges along his forehead, darkening his eyes. "The Vaughans share too well."

She smiled patiently. "Andrea, my nephew rarely approves of my generosity, but it was his choice. I keep praying that someday Ryan will reconsider and work the farm with Philip."

Andrea noticed affection in Ryan's eyes as he glanced down at his aunt, but his words were harsh as he said, "Never. I'll leave the cows and manure for Philip Vaughan."

Kathryn placed a restraining hand on Ryan's arm. "Someday, dear! And now, why don't you leave Andrea and me alone, Ry, so we can get acquainted? Please, give us some time together."

As Ryan left, Kathryn said, "Some of Ry's friends are staying at the cottage. It's an imposition for the Vaughans, but Ryan insists on it. He expects more guests this weekend. I try to keep Ryan happy when he's here, always hoping, praying—"

Her troubled gaze settled on the family portrait.

"Ryan was twelve when we had that taken," she said.

"He's not smiling, Kathryn."

"He didn't smile much back then."

Nor now, Andrea thought as Kathryn led her into the dining room for tea. They sat around the table for hours, Kathryn reminiscing about Ryan's unhappy boyhood.

"I never had children of my own so Ryan filled a void for me." She spoke kindly of him, her voice edged with sadness, not just for his broken childhood, but for the choices he had made.

As the day wore on, Andrea was shocked when Kathryn said, "I would gladly welcome you into our family, but Ryan is wrong for you, Andrea. You know that?"

"Oh, Kathryn, we're just friends, nothing more."

"Strange. Ryan plans to marry you. He brought you here to get my approval. My blessing."

Andrea felt the color drain from her face. "That's ridiculous, Kathryn," she blurted. "Ryan knows that."

"Come," Kathryn said, leading Andrea to the sofa in the living room. "Tell me about your relationship in Paris."

Andrea confided everything—the missing passport, the tragedy at the embassy, her own fears, their escape.

"Ryan is so unsettled, Andrea, restless like his father."

"Then why do you send him to Europe so often?"

An obscure, polite smile crossed her face. "Is that what Ryan told you—that I was his benefactor?"

Andrea blushed. "Yes. I'm afraid so."

"Not anymore. I can no longer pay for Ryan's artistic dreams. He tries, but he doesn't have his father's talent. Robert L. Ebsworth is not an easy man to love. Ryan hates him, but Robert is a gifted artist."

Kathryn's hands clasped maintaining the tranquil facade. "Ryan speaks several languages, but Arabic and Russian won't make him a living. He just goes on dreaming about being better than his father." Her voice lowered. "But there was a certain madness in his father."

A chill ran the length of Andrea's spine, magnifying the nameless concerns about Ryan that had haunted her in Paris.

"For years my husband Ben tried to make me realize that Ryan had problems, too. I always made excuses for Ryan. I'd say things like, 'Ben, the child is my sister's boy.' As though being Kori's son would make a difference."

Her words flowed gently, as if by their softness she could ease her pain or erase Ryan's troubled childhood. "I don't want you hurt, Andrea. Ryan's unstable like his father. He's not capable of loving anyone for very long."

"He's very fond of you, Kathryn."

"Because I overlook his faults, praying that someday he will be at peace with himself and with God."

"Ryan thinks that you and I are in danger, Kathryn."

For a moment only the crackling sounds of dying embers in the fireplace broke their silence. Then Kathryn asked, "How was Ryan involved in the tragedies in Paris?"

"Just in helping me escape."

"Perhaps you were both running. I will speak to him. You may be in more danger than you realize."

"Kathryn, he would be furious."

"I'm used to his moods. Now let's have another cup of tea to warm you up. You're trembling."

As they stood, Ryan crept into the room, his face haggard as he added another log to the fire.

"You're early. Should I start dinner?" Kathryn asked.

"No. I have to pack. I'll be gone for a few days."

"Again? But what about Sunday, Ry? I thought you and Andrea would go to church with me."

He was grim as he came toward them. He reached out and brushed his aunt's cheek with his knuckles. "You never give up, do you, even when I'm hopeless?"

"Never," she said, her voice faltering.

He turned to Andrea. "I'll have answers for you when I get back. You will wait until then, won't you, eh?"

"I can't promise, Ryan."

He hugged her with a strange finality. Moments later the back door slammed shut behind him.

"Where is he going, Kathryn?"

"To the hayloft. Whenever he loses something, he goes back there." Kathryn seemed suddenly old as she faced Andrea. "He thought I would persuade you to stay on in Canada with us. Whatever his faults, he fancies himself in love with you."

"And I'm running out on him just when he needs me."

"Andrea, he needs God even more," she whispered.

She moved gracefully around the living room, drawing the thick velvet drapes. With her back to Andrea, she said, "I'll make a few phone calls while Ryan is gone. I'll try and find out what he's doing, what he's involved in. If there's anyway I can protect you, Andrea, I will."

Her voice tightened. "But I won't risk Ryan's safety, Andrea. I'm all that Ryan has. Please understand."

Chapter 21

Andrea awakened at dawn and strolled briskly along the lake shore, pacing herself to the hot springs, her hands thrust deep into her jacket pockets, her body energized by the February chill. As soon as Ryan left town, she would cross the border, flying over it by chartered flight out of Chilliwack Municipal or racing across the Sumas border by car. Sherman Prescott had promised to help her. But could she trust him?

As she stood at the bubbling mineral springs, hot steam vapors rose in vertical clouds; early morning sun rays glinted through them. Sulfuric fumes burned at her nostrils, the stench like the gnawing fear of incurring Ryan's wrath or his aunt's betrayal. Andrea's flight from Paris with Ryan had only added to Kathryn's burdens, forcing her blind maternal instincts to rise protectively in defense of her nephew.

Andrea stumbled back across the pebble-strewn path toward the hotel, nestled in the trees in its Swiss-like atmosphere, its lake rimmed with mist-capped mountains. She had just outdistanced the sulfur fumes when she saw Sherm crouched on the shore, his muscular frame braced against a tree trunk. His dark hair was disheveled by the wind that swept in from the lake, his skin ruddy from the mountain air. Crimson flowers floated on the water in front of him, drifting with the wind and current.

"Good morning, Sherm," she called.

He turned, his expression a mixture of toughness and tenderness. "You're up early," he said.

"I like to run in the morning."

"I jog best after work." He reached out to steady her as she sat on the log beside him. "Did you hurt your leg?"

"My ankle gives me static when I'm tired." She shivered as the lake winds whipped against her. "You'll freeze to death sitting out here, Sherm."

"I won't stay long," he promised.

She knew at once that she was intruding. She weighed her words. "Is this where you lost your wife?"

"Yes, only yards from the stinking smell of sulfur, but too far from the hotel for her to call for help."

"I didn't mean to intrude," Andrea said, trying to stand.

"Don't go. It's nice to have company."

"But isn't it painful to keep coming back? It's like—"

"A shrine?" he finished. "Not really. Melody loved roses." He studied the lake as though the memories buried there were slowly emerging as they talked. "My wife swam professionally. Sometimes when my job kept me from her swim meets, I'd wire roses."

He smiled as the wintery sun broke through the morning mist, casting sun-diamonds across the lake. "Melody and I guarded our times together. Once when she missed her plane, she wired roses to me. After that it was a special link between us. If you can't keep a promise, send roses."

Andrea tossed a pebble into the wind-rippled water. "Did you promise to send roses if she died?"

"No, but when we married, I vowed to protect her. I felt as if I broke that vow when she drowned."

"Her death wasn't your fault, Sherm."

"In a way it was. Melody asked me to swim with her that morning. I wouldn't even get out of bed."

He seemed a strange blend of pain and sorrow, of peace and calm. "She told me that she would ride over the clouds in a chariot one day. She caught her chariot here. That comforts me." Sherm faced Andrea, strength in his gaze. "I can't describe Heaven to you, but I know my wife is there."

"My grandmother talked confidently about Heaven, too."

"And you're not certain, Andrea?"

"I used to be. I believed all those things when I was a child." She paused, unwilling to share the memory. *I was eight then,* she thought. *Crying and kneeling at my grandmother's knee. Repeating Katrina's prayer, "Jesus, come into my heart."* "Yes," she said aloud again. "In the embassy park when I thought I was going to be killed, I thought about God and eternity, and I was terrified."

"I kept praying for you that day."

"*You* prayed for me, Sherm?"

"Yes. I couldn't reach you because of the gunfire, but I prayed that God would protect you even though I couldn't."

She managed to say, "*He* did." Embarrassed, she added, "My grandmother is ill and dying. And—and confused. But even now, church and God and prayer are still important to her."

Sherm stared at the roses on the water. Then he placed his strong hand on Andrea's. "Andrea, don't you think it's time you believed in all of those things again?"

She pulled free. "I have to work it out myself."

"It takes longer that way," he said kindly. "It seems like you've been running ever since Paris. Why?"

She flinched under his gaze. "Sherm, I was running long before Paris—running from God, running up the ladder of success."

"That's not fatal. God is on every rung."

She stared at him. "Then God knows that I'm in serious trouble. I'm a suspect in the ambassador's death in Paris."

"God knows and cares. But who told you that you're a suspect?"

"My friend Ryan."

"How would your friend know that?" he asked.

"From the *Le Monde* headlines."

Sherm stood and helped Andrea to her feet. "Your hands are like ice. We'll have coffee in my room."

She drew back. He smiled reassuringly. "Andrea, I'll leave the door open if you like, but we need to talk. You're in danger. I think you know that."

"It doesn't matter. I'm going home today."

"And you want to be gone before your friend comes back?"

"Yes," she whispered. "Home to Index."

Melody's roses had drifted far from the shoreline. Sherm forced himself to turn from them. He touched Andrea's elbow and guided her over the fallen logs back to the path. When they reached his room in the East Tower, he shut the door and led her to the easy chairs by the windows.

"Have you eaten?" he asked. "If not, I'll order breakfast."

While they waited for room service, he stretched his legs until his toes hit the glass-topped coffee table.

"The headlines were the result of an anonymous tip, Andrea. Someone wanted you frightened enough to run." He kept his voice calm. "Ryan urged you to leave the InterContinental—to run away with him when there was no need for you to run. Ryan is the one in serious trouble."

"Why? Ryan just wanted to protect me."

He suppressed the urge to tell her the truth about Ryan. "Perhaps Ryan needed you to protect himself. Actually it was the C.I.A. that allowed you to leave Paris with Ryan because it was convenient to them."

She frowned, perplexed. "Do you work for them?"

"I told you. I'm an investment executive. I was at the embassy that day on matters that concerned my wife."

"Sherm, you're wrong about Ryan."

"What about his aunt?"

"She's a godly woman, Sherm. Ryan's her whole life."

Her defense of Ryan and his aunt was cut short as the man from room service set their tray on the coffee table. Sherm signed for the meal without glancing at the tab. As soon as they were alone again, he poured their coffee.

"Andrea, stay over until tomorrow. Give it one more day. I want you to talk to a friend of mine here at the hotel. Drew can explain our concerns about Ryan." He pointed to the phone. "Call your family. Let them know I'll get you home soon."

"I've tried calling. I'm afraid of putting them in danger."

He handed her the phone. "Try them again."

She dialed, her hands trembling as she waited. And then, "Mother, this is Andrea. . . . I'm fine. . . . How're Dad and Katrina? No, I'm not in Europe. . . . Yes, someone is with me."

As she talked, her eyes sought Sherm's. "I'll be home in a day or two," she promised.

As she hung up the phone, Andrea said, "My grandmother is still alive, but, Sherm, the State Department told my parents that there was an explosion in Paris. That I—"

Sherm's anger soared, volcanic. "Yes, I know. They thought you and Ryan had both been killed."

"In that explosion in the Montmartre district?"

"Did you leave Paris before or after the explosion, Andrea?"

"We left Collette's place the day after that happened."

"Collette?" He leaned forward. "She may be important."

"Collette Rheims. She works at the Cafe Amitie. I think she was Ryan's girlfriend once, maybe even his lover."

"Until you arrived?"

He watched her turn painful shades of scarlet.

"If you drive me home today, what happens to Ryan?"

"He'll run and end up in more trouble."

"And if I stay until tomorrow, will it clear his name?"

Sherm knew, but he couldn't tell her.

She glanced at her wrists. "You're wrong about Ryan."

He detected uncertainty in her voice. "Talk to Drew first. If you still want to go home, I'll take you tomorrow."

He reached for his wallet. "I'll write Jack Sedgwick's number on the back of my card. Call me there."

She glanced at his open wallet, her eyes on a picture. "Is that your wife?"

"Yes, shortly before Melody died." It was his favorite one. She was alive, beautiful, her lips smiling, her eyes dancing.

"Sherm, I've seen that picture before. Recently."

He replaced his wallet. "Her death was well publicized."

"It was more recent than that. It'll come to me."

She seemed troubled. He touched her hand; she responded with a deepening fuchsia in her cheeks. Even then Andrea was beautiful. Not quite like Melody. Yet very much like her—graceful, sensitive. The same, yet different. Inside, something stirred, something more than the need to protect Andrea York.

His grip tightened. "Andrea, I'll ask Drew to meet you here in my room at one. But this evening perhaps you and I could have dinner together, just the two of us?"

Her eyes met his—wide ultramarine, a dark green-blue like the color of Harrison Lake. "But Melody—"

"Melody is gone," he said. "I'm asking *you* to have dinner with me in the Copper Room."

Her uncertainty turned to a smile. "I'd like that, Sherm."

"At eight then," he told her. "In the lobby."

᳄᳄᳄

Drew Gregory knocked on Sherm's door promptly at one. His knuckles had poised to rap again when Andrea opened the door.

"Hello, Miss York," he said. "I'm Drew Gregory."

He wanted to erase her stunned expression and step inside.

"The other day you called yourself Criss with a double s."

"A nickname. Please, may I come in?"

As she led him to the chairs by the windows, he was aware of the silk shine to her hair, the graceful motions of her body. His thoughts fled to his daughter, but Robyn's face faded as Andrea said, "I'll order coffee, but first I'll call Sherm at his friend's place to let him know you arrived, Criss."

He watched her smiling into the phone, her face animated.

"Criss," she said, "with a double s." Make that code name *Crisscross*, he thought, *a name that became history in the simple act of escaping Croatia and crossing the English Channel to a desk job at the State Department. Diplomatic Attaché.* That was Porter's way of controlling Drew, a strong deterrent to disloyalty to the Company.

Drew eased into the chair across from Andrea, thinking how the compromise of that name had put his whole career on the line. He had shaved his thirty-year moustache, switched his hair part to the left, battling its resultant cowlick, and was fitted by a London optical company for contact lenses that took some getting used to. He forced himself to erase football scores and players from his mind and turned instead to rugby and the study of British history. He took a flat on the outskirts of London, its spartan furnishings and barred windows ample for his needs. And more than once, he had tried to get in touch with Robyn and failed.

"Criss—Mr. Gregory, are you listening to me?"

"Sorry. You always remind me of my daughter Robyn."

The blush in her cheeks had faded now that the phone call was over, but she had forgotten, he noted, to order coffee.

"Do you see Robyn often?" she asked.

"Not since she was ten years old."

He felt as if the jury was in, the gavel in Andrea's hand. *Yes, I'm guilty as charged. Guilty of neglect of my ex-wife, neglect of my child. All for love of country.* He tried to explain. "Not seeing Robyn was one of the stipulations in my divorce."

"And you agreed to it?" Her accusation was searing.

"I was back in Europe by then. My brother handled the divorce arrangements for me. I told him I'd sign anything as long as Robyn and her mother were well provided for. Divorces can be nasty. I didn't want Robyn to remember me that way."

"I was lucky. My dad was always there for me."

"I wanted to be there for Robyn," Drew defended himself.

She nodded. "Maybe someday you'll see her again, Criss."

"Maybe you're right."

Then before she had time to raise her defenses, he said, "Sherm Prescott told you that we're willing to protect you in exchange for information on your friend Ryan Ebsworth."

Her brows sharply arched, but she let him go on.

"Your friend is in serious trouble. For one thing, we need to talk to him regarding a missing waitress in Paris."

"Collette?" She was visibly shaken. "I don't believe you."

He leaned forward. "You spent considerable time with

Mr. Ebsworth while you were in Paris. You left Paris with him. You've known him for a long time perhaps?"

"I met him in Paris at my breakfast table. I thought Rand Jordan, my employer, had sent him. I assumed he was my taxi driver."

"Shrewd."

She blushed again. "Charming, actually."

"Did he charm you into fleeing Paris with him?"

"No. Ryan and Collette terrified me into fleeing. I didn't want to go to prison in a foreign country on false charges and disgrace my family or ruin my career."

"Running was still wrong, Andrea."

"Yes, but I understand the C.I.A. allowed me to run."

"Did they?" he asked.

She ignored his denial. "Drew, I lost my passport. That's why I went to the embassy. After that massacre in the park, all I could think about was getting out of France safely."

Drew sat quietly, putting the pieces together: a stolen passport fragmented in a bombing, the twisted mind of a young artist. "Andrea, what made you spend so much time with Ebsworth?"

Andrea chewed her lower lip thoughtfully. "His love of art mostly. That part of him reminded me of my grandmother."

Yes, Drew thought, *that was one of the things Captain York always mentioned about his wife. That she was a gifted artist— that she had given up everything to marry him.*

"Ryan is charming," Andrea said. "And after the bombing at Charles de Gaulle, he was so protective. He lives for art, Criss. He has a great sense of color. He blends colors well. But—"

She gazed out the window and then turned back to Drew, her eyes honest and direct. "He's not an artist. He just makes shattered images on his canvas. Nothing concrete. Nothing real or lasting except for the colors."

She seemed to be struggling now for the right words. "My grandmother always said that anyone who truly loves art couldn't be all bad. She used to help young artists who came to Index, sometimes with just a cup of coffee or a free night's lodging."

"And you were trying to see Mr. Ebsworth's art from your grandmother's viewpoint?" he asked gently.

"Yes, I think you're right. Ryan was my self-appointed tour guide in Paris. I had decided not to see him again. He was possessive, moody. And then—" She paused. "Then I saw his futile attempts to be a painter and I pitied him. I felt as if my grandmother wouldn't let him down."

"You never wondered what he did, other than painting?"

"Paris was a working vacation, Criss. Beyond my three weeks in France, I never planned to see Ryan again."

"Andrea, the man you describe isn't the Ebsworth we know."

"He can't be as bad as you think either, Criss. I've been with him at the museums in Paris. Ryan comes alive there."

"Alive in a dead museum?"

"Don't you appreciate the great artists of the past?"

"In small doses," he admitted. "But what about Ryan's waitress friend, Collette Rheims? When did you see her last?"

"The morning before Ryan and I left Paris. She went out with Francois Deborde. When she didn't come back that night, I thought she had gone home to Thoissey without saying good-bye."

"She never made it to Thoissey, Andrea. She's missing."

He reached out to steady her. "It's possible that Collette died in the explosion with Francois Deborde."

"At Ryan's easel?"

"Yes. We'll have confirmation soon."

They talked through the afternoon, Drew's questions unhurried. Andrea seemed perplexed when she discussed Ryan, yet equally disquieted when she spoke of Sherm Prescott. She talked mostly of Ryan's moods, his kindnesses to her, his art work, his aunt, his hatred of his father. She struggled against betraying friends, particularly Ryan's aunt.

"Perhaps his aunt is involved?" Drew suggested.

She reacted vehemently. "No. You can fill me with doubts

about Ryan, but not about Kathryn Culvert. She's a good woman."

"'A godly woman,' Sherm quoted you as saying."

He saw mutiny in her eyes. "Did Sherm run a tape on our conversation? Is he one of you? Part of your elite Company?"

Drew made no effort to deny it. He saw himself as Miriam had seen him so long ago—fracturing friendships, even now planting doubt in Andrea York's mind about Sherm. Drew was, as Miriam had often said, "a man flawed by the art of deception."

"I'm going home, Criss. In the morning."

"Andrea, if you run, Ryan will too."

As he watched her, he saw a feminine replica of Captain York—the determined chin, the direct gaze. But did she have his sharp mind for detail? His insatiable curiosity? His daring? His integrity? If so, these strengths would be useful. Even against her utter distaste of betrayal, she would help them. He considered again how much to tell her. "Andrea, there's an illegal transfer of weapons going on in this area."

"Involving Ryan?"

"Yes. Possibly centered at the Culvert farm. You've been there. Was there anything unusual going on?"

She hesitated. "I didn't see them, but Ryan has several friends there, strangers that frighten his aunt."

"We want you to go back to the farm for us as our eyes and ears. Think about it, Andrea. We'll talk again."

He stood, shaking her hand. "You still look puzzled."

"I'm having trouble with you being Criss and also being Drew Gregory. It's as though I should know you."

"You do. You sent me a telex in London."

"About my grandfather? You're *that* Drew Gregory?"

He smiled. "Yes, I'm one of Captain York's men."

"Oh, Criss, were you with my grandfather when he died?"

"Smitty was with him when he was injured."

"Harland C. Smith?"

"Yes, that was his name. How did you know?"

"I tried to call him in Paris; he wouldn't return my calls."

"Smitty in Paris?"

"He lives there. He owns the Plastec Corporation."

She took snapshots from her purse and offered them to Drew. "These were my grandfather's army pictures."

Drew felt a trickle of a smile splinter his frown. "They're good of the captain. I'm the kid on the left."

His eyes strayed to Smitty. "Smitty came to the unit late. We lost some men on a training mission in England, a forerunner for Normandy. Smith was one of the replacements. He wasn't a friendly guy. We fought often. In fact, I did a nose job on him."

"You what?"

He grinned. "I flattened his nose. Fractured it actually."

"I wish Smith had returned my calls. It would help knowing that someone was with my grandad when he died."

Drew leaned forward. Gently, he said, "The bloody beach was filled with men, but for the most part, the dying died alone. The captain and Smitty went down the LST ramp ahead of me. I lost my foothold in the choppy waters just trying to get ashore."

He groaned, the memory bitter. "We were all running, crawling, stumbling over one another, crouching behind tanks and jeeps heading toward the German lines. When I reached the captain, Corporal Smith was kneeling beside him. Smitty told me to move on. But I froze. The captain lay face down, bleeding profusely from the back."

"Shot in the back, Criss? Was he shot by the Germans? Was he running away?"

Drew gave her an unbridled beating with his gaze. They sat in awkward silence, Drew wiping away the decades. In his memory he ran again over the Normandy beach and dropped beside the captain.

"Andrea, the captain was not running away."

"If he was shot in the back, he may have been killed by friendly fire. Isn't that what they call it these days?"

Drew closed his eyes against the possibility. He was certain that Smitty had been running directly behind the captain.

Andrea pulled an Elgin watch from her purse and handed it to Drew. "This belonged to my grandfather. As far back as I can remember, my grandmother talked about a traitor in Grandfather's unit. I wonder now how she thought up such a story. His letters were all censored. Even now in her illness, it still troubles her."

He noted that her lip was trembling, that her voice had dropped to a whisper. "Just before I left for Paris, my jeweler found a microfilm in my grandfather's watch. That's why I thought the unthinkable—that Grandpa was a coward or traitor."

Drew wedged the back of the watch open and stared at the film. "That type of code belongs to the archives," he said. "Would you like me to try and get it decoded?"

"What if the truth dishonors my grandfather?"

"What if Harland Smith intended for that to happen? He may have hidden something in your grandfather's watch deliberately."

"Why would you think that, Criss?" she asked.

"I'll tell you why. Harland knew watches. He grew up in his uncle's watch repair shop. Back in Normandy when I reached Captain York, Smitty was tugging at *this* watch. I still don't know whether he was trying to take it off or put it back on your grandfather's wrist. Then a medic came along and ordered Smith and me to move on."

Andrea swayed. "Trying to steal it from a dying man?"

"It wouldn't be the first time Smitty stole something."

Chapter 22

Late that evening Andrea sat with Sherm in a cozy fireside room. They faced the fire, its flames snapping and crackling at the pine-scented logs. Its flickering light danced over Sherm's strong profile. The scent of his Lagerfeld closed in on Andrea. As he turned her way, his expression reflective, a wisp of ebony hair fell across his forehead. She was tempted to reach up and push it back in place. Instead, she asked, "What are you thinking about, Sherm?"

"You and your career."

"Do you think I place too much importance on it?"

"Maybe you should slow your pace. Enjoy your career growth. You're running too hard for it. You're young. You've got time—"

"I didn't think so that day in the embassy park."

He patted her shoulder. "I know," he said.

"My grandmother gave up her career when she married. I don't want that to happen to me. That's one reason I left home."

"And the other reason?"

"Neal Bennett. Neal hailed from Galena, up the river. He was terribly handsome, muscular and brawny with thick-lashed gray eyes and little ambition except to rock climb and fish and drift. He swept me off my feet in high school and stayed around for years. So I moved away. I want to succeed, Sherm, in spite of setbacks, in spite of Neal and my family—"

"I thought your family was proud of you."

"They are, but they're worried, too. Dad thinks fashion is a cut-throat industry. And if Mom had her way, I'd spend the rest of my life in Index running a little dress shop just to be near them. You know, the old York traditions."

"A dress shop? Then she's interested in fashion."

"Mother is very attractive. She just thinks a fashion collection of my own is out of reach for a small-town girl."

"Is it?" he asked.

"No. I know I can make it, Sherm. I plan to be out of *Style Magazine* by the time I'm thirty, out on my own. My employer has used several of my sketches in his magazine."

"What about getting started with ski outfits, Andrea? Ski sweaters for kids, more glamorous outfits for women."

"Why start there?"

"I have a lot of contacts through Kippen Investments—in Europe, in the States. I'm well known at several of the ski resorts. Perhaps I could help you, *if you're good*."

"I am good."

They fell silent for a few moments. Then she said, "Sherm, forgive me. I've spent this whole evening telling you about my family and my fashion designs."

"And about the Wayside Chapel and the Bush House and your friend Sabrina," he teased. More seriously, he added, "But, Andrea, you've avoided talking about your time with Drew."

She traced the pattern on the sofa. "Drew thinks Ryan is involved in the sale of guns to foreign governments. He's sure they're using Kathryn's farm for the meeting place."

"And you don't believe it?"

"I don't want to believe it." Her eyes met Sherm's again. "Drew wants me to go back to the farm and mingle with Ryan's friends. I'm to listen and observe and report back to him."

Sherm tipped her chin, his hand gentle as he touched her. "It'll be over soon, but promise me that you'll be careful."

She was glad for the subdued lighting in the room, glad that he couldn't see her feelings riding on the surface.

"Drew won't let anything happen to me. I remind him of his daughter. But I still don't understand why you and Drew came halfway around the world chasing Ryan."

"I didn't come with Drew. Remember?"

"What about Drew then? He's using Ryan to bait others."

"You don't think much of the C.I.A., do you, Andrea?"

"I don't like what I hear—covert action, clandestine meetings, Molotov cocktails, and bullets that explode on contact."

"Don't underestimate Drew Gregory's job," Sherm warned. "Nor Ryan's involvement. If there's a sale of warheads at the farm, Drew needs to channel that information to the intelligence analysts in Washington. He needs your help."

"And what is your job with the government, Sherm?"

His wry chuckle caught her unaware. "Ten years ago I did a stint with the army. Now I work for Kippen Investments."

"Is that a front for the C.I.A.?"

"You still want my name, rank, and serial number?"

"Don't laugh at me, Sherm. I'm worried."

"Andrea, I am not with the C.I.A., believe me. After college I joined the army. I considered making it a career, but Melody's dad offered me an opportunity I couldn't resist. So I gave up my captain's commission and went to work for him."

Andrea reached out and ran her finger lightly over Sherm's wedding band. "And married the boss's daughter?"

"Not right away. Buzz kept insisting that I meet her. He's a giant of a man, big physically and generous with others— hardly the type for a matchmaker. You don't walk on him, but he's there for you. He's been my strength since Melody died."

He smiled. "I refused to meet her at first. I was meshing back into civilian life. I didn't need emotional entanglements."

"So when did you meet her?"

"Much later—on a trip to British Columbia. I was heading

here for a vacation. Melody was in the area for a swim meet. To push things along, Buzz told her to take a few days at the Harrison."

"So you really did meet here?"

"Actually, we met at the Vancouver airport. I'd just flown in from Dallas, disgruntled as I waited for my baggage to circle. When I reached for my case, I collided with a wide-brim lavender hat."

"Melody?" Andrea asked, laughing.

"Yes. My luggage wound around the conveyor again. I turned toward her. We were almost eye level. Here was this lavender hat with a fuchsia ribbon. The hat matched her suit, and her blouse matched the ribbon—a ridiculous, glamorous outfit.

"I asked her where she'd been all my life. She said, 'Swimming.' And then she grabbed her suitcase and slipped into the crowd while my own luggage made its way around the conveyor belt for the fourth time."

"You let her get away?" Andrea asked.

"I thought that was it, but moments later we were vying for the same taxi. I held the cab door open for her and then on impulse I leaped in beside her. 'Where to?' I asked.

"'To the Pan Pacific. *Alone*,' she told me.

"'But what are you doing tomorrow?'

"'Sorry. My father wants me to meet someone.'

"As she left the taxi, I asked, 'Is it someone important?'

"'I'll know tomorrow,' she said, walking out of my life."

A log in the fire split. Sherm gave it only a passing glance. "When the boss's daughter arrived at the Harrison the next day, I squared my shoulders for the obligatory meeting. And then in the lobby I saw Melody Kippen in that silly lavender hat."

Sherm fell silent, his expression suddenly melancholy.

Andrea's eyes locked with his. "What was Melody like?"

"Melody was a one-of-a-kind lady. She was everything Buzz had said—beautiful, popular, competitive, transparent. Melody believed in winning, winning for God, winning for herself. She chided herself when she didn't, but she respected her opponents."

He barely paused. "We surprised ourselves. We were married ten days later in the little Gospel Chapel not far from the hotel."

"Melody sounds so special, Sherm."

"She was. I really miss her."

It pleased Sherm when they fell into a comfortable silence. They watched the last of the dying embers in the fireplace and listened to the crackling of splintered logs. Except for the two of them, the room had emptied.

Andrea was good company. At first, all through dinner, she had wavered between wariness of him and a desperate longing to trust him. Now she seemed relaxed, happy.

There had been other dates since Melody's death. Well-meaning friends had thrust him with widows and unattached females, uncomfortable moments that made him withdraw. This evening with Andrea had been enjoyable. For the first time, he had talked freely of Melody, delighting in the memories, sharing her with Andrea as the joy of his past.

He broke their silence, saying, "Andrea, thank you for letting me tell you about my wife."

"I'm glad you did, Sherm. I know you better now."

He grinned. "You know that I'm impulsive and romantic?"

"And caring—a special person because Melody was special."

Andrea leaned toward him, and old desires welled inside of him. He glanced around the empty room, trying to think of ways to separate his past from this moment. "It's nice here," he said lamely, "like the fire rooms at the ski lodges where I stay."

"Did Melody ski?"

"No. She'd go with me sometimes, but she usually curled up with a good book. She wouldn't risk a broken leg or back injury. Skiing was strictly mine. It's exhilarating for me."

"Like rock climbing or Bungee jumping?"

He laughed at the comparisons. "Skiing is more graceful."

"I never had the nerve to try," Andrea admitted. "Heights frighten me. I'm always afraid of injuring my weak ankle."

Sherm gazed at her intensely. "When this is all over, when we leave here, perhaps—" he hesitated, "perhaps you should learn to ski."

"Is that what you were going to say, Sherm?"

"I was going to suggest that I teach you how to ski, but we don't exactly live next door."

Her cheeks glowed. "They have ski slopes in California."

"Then I'll fly out some weekend and we'll go skiing."

She smiled. He grinned back. "I usually ski in Europe on my trips there. So once you're good on the downhill, we'll try the European challenge. It's a great place to ski."

"No doubt on a long weekend," she teased. And then more wistfully, "*When this is all over*, of course."

He found himself unnerved that he had slipped so easily into future plans that included Andrea York. This girl was wrong for him. They were going in different directions. Yet he knew that she would be beautiful even on skis, snow flurries in her hair. He wondered whether Neal Bennett was still waiting for her back home.

"How serious was your affair with Neal Bennett?" he asked.

She did a double take, staring up at him, startled. Mutiny and amusement played games in her gaze. "*My affair?* What are you asking, Sherm? Whether I lived with Neal Bennett?"

"That came out wrong, didn't it?" he said. "But I guess that's what I was asking. You seem unhappy when you speak of him. Either you're still in love with him or he hurt you deeply."

She found her voice and said softly, "The latter. And you're right. He did want me to live with him, to share his bed, not his life." She glanced down. "I almost did, but people in a small town talk. No—not even that. It was against the way I was brought up, against everything my family believed in."

Sherm took her fingers and ran his thumb gently over them. "I'm glad you didn't live with Neal Bennett," he said.

"I think God preserved you for—for someone else. . . . Is Neal still important to you?"

"No. I don't think Neal will ever settle down and marry. If I wanted him—and once I thought I did—it had to be on his terms. He still calls me. And he still goes by and visits with my folks. I guess Neal was my first real love."

"And who was your second?"

"My career."

"No marriage or children in your future plans? Ever?"

The pencil-thin brows arched. "They're in my mother's plans, not mine." She kept her tone light. "At least not yet."

She traced the sofa pattern again with her fingernail, saying, "Sherm, Drew told me you don't believe your wife drowned in the lake."

"She didn't," Sherm said quietly. "Melody was a competent swimmer. An Olympic Gold medalist doesn't drown accidently in shallow water. Did Drew tell you that?" Abruptly, he was on his feet. "Andrea, would you like me to see you to your room?"

"No, I'll sit here for a little longer. By myself."

"You won't be alone for long. Drew Gregory just came in through the lobby door."

Andrea made no attempt to turn and greet Drew. She waited until he stood in front of her, his back to the fire, the flickering light shining against the cowlick in his hair. She welcomed him with a wary smile.

In the brief silence, she noted again his concerned gaze, his gentlemanly appearance—dark blue suit, striped shirt, bright tie. He had a strong face, a firm chin—no extra flab or dark circles under his eyes like her dad had, not even a ghost of a moustache. Nature had thinned Drew's hair, powdering it sparingly with gray, but she thought him an attractive man, older than her father, but not old. His height and build and expression exuded vitality, virility.

There was warning in his voice when he said, "You keep late hours, Andrea."

"It was a lovely evening."

"It could be explosive if Ryan sees you with Prescott."

"Ryan is away."

"No, he came back early."

She tensed. "What do Sherm and Ryan have in common?"

"Twenty-eight miserable months."

"You're talking in riddles."

"Am I? Come, Andrea, I'd feel better if you were safely in your room, not here by the fireside alone."

Her skin prickled. "You're here with me, Criss."

"Yes, Criss with the double s." He pulled her to her feet.

"Ryan won't hurt me." *Not again,* she thought.

"Not deliberately."

"And if he phones me, I'm still to go with him?"

"He'll call."

As they walked down the corridor, she asked, "Drew, what branch of army was Sherm with?"

"He didn't tell you?"

"Would I ask if he had? Tell me," she begged.

He brooded over her question. "Army intelligence."

"A good background for working with you."

"Sherm works for his father-in-law. For your own safety, keep away from him. I need that edge on Ryan Ebsworth. I can't risk Ryan seeing you with him."

As they reached her room in the West Wing, he held out his hand for the key. "Will you be all right?"

Her nod was more like a tremor. He tipped her chin up, his expression stoic, unsmiling. "When this is over—when you're home again—greet the captain's wife for me, won't you, Andrea?"

The prickling started at the base of her spine. "Yes, if Katrina lives until I get there."

He hung the Do Not Disturb sign on the doorknob and left, leaving her confined to four walls again. She paced the room, cutting a pathway between the locked door and windows. She heard every sound in the corridor and the endless flushing of toilets in the guest rooms beside her.

At three in the morning, in utter desperation, she lay down with the room lights still on. Sometime before dawn she dozed, awakening with a miserable headache and the sound of toilets flushing again. Over that came the muted ring of her room phone.

Ryan, she thought. *Ryan is calling.*

Back at the bungalow, Drew sat in the darkness watching a half-moon play silhouette games on the carpet. It was a compact room, comfortably furnished. A portable transmitter sat on an end table; an outside phone line with a secure key lay on the arm of the sofa. The bath and sleeping quarters for his men were down the hall. The bungalow was more to Drew's liking than a plush room at the hotel; it suited his needs and his hours.

He took Benj Reever's call shortly after reaching the room. "Benj, I need twenty-four-hour surveillance on York."

"A problem, eh?" Benj asked.

"I can't risk losing her."

"I'll have someone there within the hour, a midnight tourist demanding the West Wing. How's that?"

"You have the photos of Andrea? The room number?"

"Got it all. Even a report that just filtered in from Vancouver. An airport waitress reported the arrival of a couple that fit the description of Ebsworth and York. She said the girl was anxious to be recognized—as if she might be in real danger."

"She is. That's why she needs our protection."

"She's got it." Reever cut off without another word.

For the next forty minutes, Drew half-dozed on the narrow sofa that would make out for his bed before the night was over. He twisted and turned, his body drained, his mind still running on Parisian time. He only half-slept because of Normandy, his thoughts on a traitor in the unit. He fingered Captain York's watch, wondering whether to let dead heroes lie. He could let Porter deal with the problem. But would he like what Porter found?

He swore. Harland Smith had reappeared at an inconve-

ALWAYS IN SEPTEMBER   221

nient time in his life. Drew didn't need the added burden of a watch that had almost been stolen fifty years ago.

Drew gave in at last. Sitting back up, he switched on the lamp and placed a call to Porter Deven in Paris. His concise report updated Porter on Ebsworth and York and the build-up on the Culvert farm, twenty miles from the Harrison.

Finally, Drew said, "I caught the ambassador's funeral on the nightly news. Did you see it? An appropriate farewell, taps and all. Mac's widow held up well."

"Yes. The Vice-President was there. I should have been."

Then Drew asked for an Interpol check on Harland C. Smith, owner of the Plastec Corporation. He was certain that Porter sucked in his breath before he said, "I've met the man at embassy gatherings. He's all right. He's a personal friend of Mitterand and well accepted in Paris."

"Porter, just check it out for me, please. And I have something to be decoded, World War II vintage."

"Air express it to Langley or army intelligence," Porter told him. "By the way, Drew, we have a positive I.D. on those two who blew with Ebsworth's easel, Francois Deborde and Collette Rheims, the missing waitress from the Amitie."

"So the Amitie was tied in? How thoroughly?"

"Don't make me eat crow, Drew. French Security traced Kusa, one of the terrorists, to the Amitie. The cafe was definitely Ryan and Kusa's contact point."

"And Jacques Marseilles?"

"The maitre d' vanished. No trace of him."

"Porter, it's a case of the French taking care of the Frenchman. I'm guessing that Jacques is safely hiding out in a chateau a hundred kilometers from Paris. Unless he was personally involved in the terrorism, you might want to leave his discipline to a group of Resistance fighters."

To Porter's expletive he said, "Jacques missed the firing squad almost fifty years ago. Now he may be facing another one."

Before signing off, Drew asked, "Porter, do you have a lead on that American businessman yet, or has that blown over?"

"Negative, but I meet with French Security again tomorrow."

"Things are tight on this end, too. Benj Reever won't give it much longer. It's his operation, and he favors the safety of Kathryn Culvert and her rancher. I can only count on forty-eight hours."

Porter's voice boomed over the wires. "Then it's up to you to make certain that Reever doesn't do anything foolish. I want both Ebsworth and his contacts. And when you wrap it up there, we'll need Miss York back here in France to identify Kusa for us."

"She may not agree to come. Her grandmother is dying."

"Then pressure her. With the political uproar going on, we could lose Kusa. Tell Andrea French Security knows that she fled the country with Ebsworth. They want to question her."

Drew cradled the phone, snapped off the lights, and allowed himself to be swallowed up in darkness. He pulled the blankets up from behind the sofa where he had dropped them that morning. Then he slept exhaustedly in his clothes, Omaha Beach in Normandy and terrorism in Paris playing leapfrog in his dreams.

Chapter 23

Andrea's anxiety mounted as Ryan's royal blue two-door swept around the circular driveway to the hotel. Drew Gregory smiled reassuringly. "I have to go now, Andrea. You'll be fine. My men and I will have you covered every minute. Nothing will happen to you."

"How can you be so sure, Drew?" she called after him. "You just told me how the flight attendant at Charles de Gaulle and Francois Deborde and Collette Rheims died, needlessly, brutally, because of Ryan."

Dear, dear Collette who befriended me, she thought.

Drew paused long enough to put his finger to his lips. He smiled rakishly, and then with a quick, brisk wink he walked away. If he had intended to make her cautious with his warnings, he had failed. She felt grief-stricken over Collette and terrified as Ryan entered the lobby. She wanted to scream, "Lies. All lies." But her mouth felt dry, the air in her windpipe cut off.

Ryan came to her, his expression guileless, his smile quick and easy; but his eyes seemed glazed from lack of sleep. She pulled back as he kissed her on the cheek.

Once she stepped into his car, she felt committed, like a jetliner rolling down the tarmac for takeoff, disaster minutes away. As the car lurched past the East Tower, Andrea glanced up. Sherm Prescott stood by the window of his suite, Drew Gregory right beside him.

So you're watching, she thought, *but where's my body-*

guard, Drew? Your man Wilson is sitting there in his car, dozing behind a newspaper. No one is following us. She gripped the door handle with a clammy hand, angry with Drew.

"Ryan," she said, fighting for control as they rode toward Chilliwack, "you said you had news for me."

"I want to marry you," he announced.

"Be serious."

He kept his eyes on the road. "I am serious."

She struggled for words, trying not to antagonize him. Finally she said, "Ryan, I'm not in love with you."

"I know. It doesn't matter. Given time—"

"Someone else will come along someday."

He flinched. "Without you I may not have long."

His face, so attractive when she had met him, seemed thinner; his skin, which had a coppery glow three weeks ago, now seemed pale. A troubled face, a troubled man. She saw him now as Kathryn Culvert did—a certain madness in the father, a certain madness in the son.

"I'm going home. You know that, Ryan?"

He risked a glance her way. "Don't leave me."

She thought of him at the gardens at Giverny where the beauty awakened the gentleness in him, the part of Ryan that Kathryn Culvert wanted to salvage. The melody of a hymn tugged softly against the strings of Andrea's heart. If she could recall the words, they might comfort Ryan. She could almost hear her grandmother singing the song, something about fathomless billows of love, something about wonderful peace. Gradually, she remembered and began to hum. She sensed that peace as the song soothed her own fears. She wanted that peace to sweep over Ryan, too.

"You're humming," he said.

"Yes, a hymn my grandmother used to sing."

"My aunt sings that one, too."

He broke into a phrase, a rich tenor quality to his voice. "'Marching down the rough pathway of time' . . . It's too late for me, Andrea. I'm running out of time."

She stared at the traffic surging around them, Ryan's words chilling, eternal. The car beside them edged closer,

cutting across Ryan's path, close enough for Andrea to recognize Vic Wilson at the wheel as he sped past them.

"Fool," Ryan said, hitting the gas pedal. "The fool."

"Let them go, Ryan. Don't chase them."

His tires squealed as he turned into the Minter Gardens'
parking lot, riding over the gravel to the main gate.

"Ryan, the gardens are closed. We're the only ones here."

He gazed around the empty lot. "We could come back
some other day if you marry me. I'd run the farm for
Kathryn. She'd let me, Andrea. We'd be safe living there."

Andrea heard the childish whine in Ryan's voice, the
adult uncertainty. She pitied him for the futile promises
that he could never keep.

"Tell me something, Ryan. There really wasn't any reason for me to run away from Paris, was there?"

"I wanted to protect you, to protect us both."

"When I leave, will you be safe?"

His hands slipped from the steering wheel. "I'll know soon."

She gambled on her own safety, her voice taut. "Do you
remember the bombing at Charles de Gaulle International?"

"What made you think of that?" he asked.

"An American flight attendant was killed."

"Possibly. Two or three people, weren't there?"

"Ryan, were you there when it happened?"

His expression crumbled. "I was with you that day."

"You were gone for a while," she said evenly.

"Not long enough to get to the airport and back. What was
that all about, Andrea?" he asked, his eyes hard.

"I was curious, that's all."

"Andrea, I just wish you understood what I'm doing,
what I believe in. Your life depends on it."

His gaze strayed toward the SEED & SOIL truck that
raced across the parking lot, screeching to a halt not far
from them. The truck was a nondescript vehicle with
wooden panels across the back and thread-worn tires. A
workman in overalls swung a pick and shovel over one
shoulder and ambled their way.

Beads of perspiration dotted Ryan's upper lip as the gardener strolled in front of them, whistling. Ryan shoved his

door open and stepped from the car. "I need to talk to that man. Perhaps he can get us into the gardens."

He ran, rounding the path only steps behind the man until they were both out of Andrea's view. She looked around for Drew Gregory, but she saw only a lone jogger with a dog at the far corner of the lot. The brown-speckled pointer tugged at his leash, ears alert. As they ran past her toward the SEED & SOIL truck, the runner lifted her hand and waved at Andrea.

Andrea left Ryan's car and circled the truck. There were no sacks of soil, no smell of fertilizer, no license plate—only some scraps of trash in the bed of the truck and a Minter Gardens pamphlet on the dashboard. She allowed the question to surface: Why would Minter Gardens hire an outside gardener? She provided her own answer: They would have their own delivery service, their own supplies, their own garden staff.

She glanced around furtively as the jogger ran by her again. Then Andrea stumbled across the well-kept lawn toward the gardens, hoping to spot Ryan and the gardener.

Drew Gregory would ask her what the man looked like. Andrea remembered the work clothes, remembered that he turned his face when he passed her. The shovel and pick in his upraised arm had shielded his face.

She peered through the fence and hedge into the gardens. Two seasons lay within sight—the budding of an early spring, the dying of winter. Cedar trees and vine maples rose in their natural settings, shading the ferns and flower bulbs that would make the gardens come alive with color in the spring and summer months. Muted pinks and golden yellows touched the shrubs and trees with their promise of spring. Snow-capped Mt. Cheam towered high in the distance. But Ryan and the gardener were nowhere in sight.

Drew stationed himself in the wooded area, close enough to reach Andrea if she needed him. At the sound of crackling twigs he turned and saw Vic Wilson cutting cautiously toward him.

Vic waved. "Is York okay?"

"She's up by the fence looking over the gardens. But Ebsworth took off with the driver from that SEED & SOIL truck. My bet is on a planned rendezvous." He studied Wilson curiously. "I thought you were staying with the car."

"We just had a transmission from Benj Reever."

"Out with it, Vic."

"Benj has some names on the house guests out on the Culvert farm. There are a couple of South Americans, but the biggie seems to be an American businessman from Paris. Name's Harland C. Smith."

"Head of the Plastec Corporation on the Champs-Élysées."

"So you do know him?"

"Knew him. Mostly I know about his nose. I broke it for him once. We were in Normandy together. But Andrea York clued me into his present location. Imagine—the head of some fancy corporation! Old Harland has come up by his boot straps."

"And dirtied some waters along the way," Vic added. "French Security tipped Reever off. Seems like this Smith took off in his private jet while the French were looking for him."

"That sounds like his Machiavellian personality. He was as Janus-faced a man as I ever met."

"You really liked him, eh?"

"Yeah."

Drew adjusted the telephoto lens on his camera. "What have they got on Smith besides his home address?"

"Questions mostly. But Benj said to tell you that Smith was registered at the Harrison when Melody Prescott died."

"Somehow that doesn't surprise me." Drew squinted one eye as he rotated the camera over the parking lot.

"You don't think too much of Smith, do you? Especially if you relocated his nose."

"I did him a favor, Vic. It was his ticket out of the war zone. We were dug in one night in our march toward Paris.

And Smitty came at me with such vengeance that I lifted my rifle in self-defense and flattened his nose."

"You didn't get a court martial on that one?"

"No. There were others there when it happened. They just thought Smith had gone off the deep end. Battle fatigue. I don't think so. I think he knew exactly what he was doing. I remember something else about the guy. He had a slightly twisted thumb, a birth deformity. He used to tug at his ear with the knuckles of his fingers, that crazy thumb sticking straight out."

"That's weird. Why would you remember something like that?"

"The last time I saw Smith—and saw that thumb—Smitty was tearing a watch off the wrist of a dying man."

"Weird! Do you want me to head back to the car, Drew?"

"No, Vic. Stick with me for now." He squinted, his eye to the camera. "Here comes that jogger again. Must be Reever's man." Drew chuckled. "Change that to a lady runner. If Benj sent her, she's good."

He scanned the area, focusing the lens on Ebsworth and the gardener. "Ebsworth's meeting is heating up. They're arguing about something. His contact is a tall man. Broad-shouldered. Thick-rimmed glasses. A man about my age."

Drew snapped a roll of film in rapid succession, pictures of Ryan, of the gardener, of the two men together. "That fool runner is resting," he said. "Right within earshot."

"Maybe it's the dog's rest stop," Wilson suggested.

"But I don't like it. She's not safe there."

In case it wasn't Reever's agent, Drew took some close-ups. The runner had a strong face, athletic build, short-bobbed hair, and a tiny recorder clipped to her dark blue sweat suit. Drew judged her to be five-eight, a solid 130 pounds. The jogger moved on back toward Andrea.

Drew rotated the camera, focusing on Ryan again. The stranger had a firm clasp on Ryan's shoulder, a taut, disciplinary grip.

"What would a gardener want with Ryan Ebsworth?" he asked.

"That's what we're checking out," Vic said, pointing out

the obvious—a source of amusement to him, an annoyance to Drew.

The stranger's shoulder grip on Ryan slackened.

Drew bristled, his eyes on the stranger. "Vic, I've seen that man before. But I must be nuts. It can't be Smith. If Smith is a house guest at the Culvert farm, why would he meet Ebsworth here in the gardens?"

"What are you talking about?"

"Add forty years-plus and a gardener's suit, and we may come up with Corporal Harland C. Smith tugging his ear in the same old way. Here. See for yourself."

Wilson adjusted the camera lens. "You think it's the Paris connection—the one that Porter Deven's been tracking down? Wait, that's it," Vic said. "The meeting's over. Do we follow Ebsworth?"

Drew glanced around. "No, we'll leave that up to Reever's jogger. Head back to the car, Vic, and let Reever know what we're doing. Tell him we'll wait for the gardener. He should be along soon. If it's really Smith, I'd like to know his destination."

◉◉◉

Two hours later back at the Harrison, Drew placed another call to Porter Deven in Paris. "Did you get my information on Harland Smith?" he asked.

"Got it right here, Drew. Interpol ran analytical and punch-card checks for me. I did some checking on my own as well." Porter cleared his throat.

A deliberate delay? Drew wondered. "Come on, Deven. What did you find out?"

"Nothing that would make this man important to you, Drew."

Drew jotted notes as Porter spoke. "Harland Cornelius Smith: 68. Born in Brooklyn. No known aliases. No physical defects except a partially deformed left thumb. U.S. army veteran, World War II. Owner of the Plastec Corporation with offices throughout the European Community. Heavily invested: French, Swiss, and Spanish bank accounts. High school education. Married to French woman, Monique Dupree. Two sons, Anzel and Giles."

"Hope he made a better father than I did," Drew grumbled.

"Last known trip to States for mother's funeral, 1982. Periodically under surveillance for political views. No criminal record. Secretive appearance in Angola netted him Interpol's interest. Owns company jet. Presently vacationing in Canada. And, Drew, I know from personal experience that he is well received in embassy circles and at state functions." Porter hesitated, his pause so brief that his words slurred. "I've dined with the man myself, Drew."

"I can add to your portfolio, Porter. We spotted Smith right here in Harrison. I'm having some photos blown up, photos of Smith meeting with Ryan Ebsworth at the Minter Gardens."

He heard Porter Deven gargling his own saliva. *"Ebsworth's Parisian contact?"*

"Quite possible," Drew said. "Vic and I followed him from his rendezvous point with Ebsworth straight to the Culvert farm. Yes," Drew repeated, "it's possible that we've found Ebsworth's contact here in Harrison, half a world away from France."

"Wild!" Porter said. "I really have known the man all along."

"By the way, Porter, did the French give you a name on the American businessman yet, the one involved in terrorism?"

"No," Porter said. "I think you just gave it to me."

"Smith? You don't sound happy about it."

"I told you, *we're acquaintances–friends.*" Porter seemed to be choking on the words. "At least socially. He's a friend of the top brass here in Paris, too. No wonder they've kept a lid on his identity."

Chapter 24

Prescott's attention riveted on the Sedgwick phone. *Come on, Andrea,* he thought. *Call me. Let me know you're safe.* He swiveled the rocker and stared at Jack's wife.

"You're gloom itself, Sherm," Tina said. "We could have fed you crocodile steak and you would never have known it."

"It was lamb. And blackberry pie."

"Blueberry pie," she corrected. "The next time the phone rings, we'll let you answer it."

"No need, Tina. *She's* not going to call anyway."

The Sedgwicks exchanged glances. Tina asked, "Who is *she?*"

"Andrea York."

"That's all? *Just* Andrea York."

"She's a fashion journalist. A designer, too. I met her in Paris. We had dinner together last evening in the Copper Room."

"Someone important to you?" Tina asked.

"Someone who drove off with Ryan Ebsworth this morning."

"Then she doesn't keep good company," Jack growled, anger in his eyes. "There's something going on out at the farm. I don't like it, Sherm. Someone out there—someone using the name Keith Arlington—is playing games with

Kathryn's funds. Five hundred thousand dollars gone! Wiped clean with an unauthorized transaction to a bank in Zurich, Switzerland."

Sherm considered the amount and what little it could buy in arms procurement. "Is Ryan involved?" he asked.

Tina glanced at her husband. "Ryan knew Kathryn's account numbers. As bank manager, the blame falls on Jack."

Jack sported his perpetual frown. "Kathryn would rather sacrifice every dollar than risk Ryan's safety."

"What can I do about Andrea York's safety?" Sherm snapped.

Jack's burly figure inched forward. "Wait until dark, Sherm, and we'll go out to the farm and check it out."

Tina exploded. "No way. Let Sherm go alone. What would this town think if the local banker got caught trespassing?"

"We won't be caught, honey. We'll just look around."

"And get yourselves killed? I don't take lightly to being a widow, Jack Sedgwick. I love you, you big ox. If you want to know something, knock on Kathryn's door like gentlemen."

۞ ۞ ۞

Later Tina's face registered intense displeasure as Jack went out the front door.

"Honey, we'll be back by midnight," he told her.

"One second later and I call the RCMP and tell them to look for a couple of rogues trespassing on private property."

Sherm checked the hall mirror. *We look more like black ravens,* he thought. *Black hair. Navy jeans and pullover sweaters. Old skull caps in our hip pockets. And Tina's mascara smeared across our cheeks.* "We won't be gone long, Tina," Sherm promised.

Her anger peaked. "Just long enough to get Jack in trouble."

Jack's excitement mounted as they neared the Culvert farm.

"Sherm, there's a dirt path between the ranch and the neighboring farm that leads down to the creek. Keep a watch for it. We'll park down there and cut back to the house."

"Can we get on the Culvert property that way?"

"If we wade through the creek; it'll be cold after last week's rain and the melting snows, but we'll go in unnoticed."

"Are there any watch dogs?"

"Just Philip Vaughan's German shepherd."

"Hope they kennel him."

"Philip has kept himself scarce these last few days. He's usually visible and vocal. Even the children didn't show up for school Friday."

"There, Jack. I think that's the turnoff."

Jack made a sharp exit from the main road, tires squealing. He hit the lights. Blackness engulfed them. Branches scraped the sides of the car, one catching Sherm's cheek through the window.

"Careful, Jack, or we'll end up in the hedges."

"Better not. There's a barbed fence beyond them. Old Ben Culvert never wanted the cows to get out or strangers to get in."

The exhaust pipe hit a rock and broke free; the car rattled as Jack bounced blindly toward the creekbed.

🌣🌣🌣

Benj Reever and his men had waited in the woods for darkness to settle. Against Drew Gregory's arguments, Benj had ordered a night raid. The incoming traffic on the Culvert farm threatened the safety of the widow who lived there.

They advanced toward the back of the house, keeping cover in the shadows as they passed the barn. A spattering of stars set a dimly lit stage, more light than Benj had counted on. He stopped his men and checked his luminous watch. In two minutes Gregory, Wilson, and young Jeff Akers would cut over the knobby hillock and approach the main house from the side.

He spoke into his walkie-talkie. "Benj here," he said.

Drew Gregory's static response came at once. "Okay so far. *Wait*. We've got trouble. Two runners. Both doing a marathon."

"What? Drew!" Benj shook his receiver. No answer.

⚭⚭⚭

Sherm Prescott jogged steadily behind Jack, darting among the trees. Suddenly, he caught the shadow of a man leveling a karate chop that missed its mark; it winged Sherm's neck and crashed into his shoulder blade. He dropped to the ground, the sleeve of his sweater tearing free.

He felt the cold steel of a Beretta against his jugular. A knee jabbed into his shoulder, pinning him to the ground and rubbing the gravel into his skin. He sucked in his breath, stunned. Then he heard the man hiss, "Prescott, what are you doing here?"

"Drew Gregory?" he asked. "Are you trying to kill me?"

"I could have," Drew said, dragging Sherm to his feet.

"Look, Drew. My friend's out there. Jack Sedgwick."

"And you're out of here. My men and I will handle it."

Vic Wilson inched forward as the door to the cottage opened, sending shafts of light across the yard. The beam of light caught Jack Sedgwick's bulky frame. Shots riddled the night. Jack reeled and fell. Shadowy figures barreled out the door. A German shepherd snarled behind them as they dragged Jack into the cottage.

"Drew," Sherm gasped, "Jack's been hit."

"We'll get him. Now get out the same way you came in."

Sherm balked. "It's not just Jack. Andrea's here, too."

"According to Reever," Drew said, "Ebsworth came back alone."

Drew contacted Reever. "Hold your positions, Benj. We've got problems at the cottage . . . A possible injury . . . No, if we go in now, it might cost the man his life . . . Yeah, I've got an I.D. on him; Prescott here tells me he's Jack Sedgwick, the local banker. No, Benj," Drew said irritably, "we didn't fire the shots. But some fool didn't have a silencer."

He turned and shoved Sherm toward Jeff Akers. "Get Prescott out of here while I still have a mind to let him go."

The pain in Sherm's shoulder burned now. He shrugged off Akers's grip. "I'll find my own way back," he said.

Akers stayed on his heels. Twice Sherm tried to slip back. Twice Akers blocked him. Sherm staggered against a tree, his shoulder throbbing. "Go on, Jeff, I'll stay out of the way."

"Where's your car, Prescott?"

"On the other side of the fence. Down by the creek."

"Go back to it. I'll let you know about your friend."

Akers ran back toward the cottage. Without a weapon, it was useless for Sherm to follow. Slowly, his eyes adjusted to the darkness until a sliver of moon ran the length of the shifting stratus clouds. It cast an eerie path on the creekbed. He stepped from the shadows and ran a zigzag course to the water, but stopped abruptly. He could not, would not risk leaving Andrea behind.

◈◈◈

Inside the main house a fire crackled in the fireplace. Kathryn Culvert sat on the piano bench; Ryan stood behind her. "Why didn't you bring Andrea home for the evening?" she asked.

"I didn't feel like inviting her."

She thumbed through a hymnbook. "Mr. Smith says that you're engaged now. It isn't true, is it, Ryan?"

"Only until this weekend; it's safer that way for Andrea."

"And after that?" Her fingers moved lightly over the keys.

"She's free to go home. That's what she wants."

At the sound of gunfire, Kathryn froze. "Those were gun shots, Ryan. Did your friends take Ben's hunting rifles?"

"I don't know. Keep playing. Play the one on peace."

"Peace?" she asked, her voice trembling.

His fingers dug into her shoulders. "We're safe here."

In response to the urgency in his voice, she played; the music came out jerky, discordant. She longed to swing around and confront Ryan with his need for peace, his desperate need for God. She kept her back to him.

"I want your friends out of this house," she said.

"Just seventy-two more hours, Aunt Kathryn. We're expecting one more important guest tomorrow. After that, we'll all be gone."

"I'm frightened for you, Ryan. I've heard your friends talking about the sale of weapons to Iraq."

"Iraq. Cuba. Africa. What does it matter?" he asked.

As she played "Peace, peace, wonderful peace," the words comforted her, distancing her from her nephew. She sang, "'Sweep over my spirit forever I pray' . . ." For a phrase or two, Ryan blended his rich tenor with her soprano.

When the song ended, she asked, "Who is Keith Arlington?"

"How would I know, Aunt Kathryn?"

"Some of my bank funds have been transferred to a Keith Arlington account in Zurich, Switzerland."

"Why did you do that?" he asked, his voice even.

She turned and caressed the hand that still rested on her shoulder. "Are *you* using the name Keith Arlington, Ryan?"

His fingers dug deeper into her flesh.

"Why, Ryan? It would have all been yours in the end." Softly, she added, "I love you no matter what happens."

"Very touching, Mrs. Culvert."

Harland Smith's mocking voice boomed across the room as he entered and sat down in her Chippendale chair. His large frame filled it. He wiped his glasses, his black eyes cold as he studied her. "Very touching," he repeated.

"I want you out of my home immediately," she told him.

"I'll be gone by the end of the week."

"Now," she demanded, strengthened with the decision.

His glasses were back on, magnifying the intense anger in his eyes. "Have you forgotten your nephew works for me? I need your nephew one more time, Mrs. Culvert. And after that—"

"And after that you'll let him go free?"

His beastly smile broadened. "Of course."

Kathryn reached for her phone.

"Don't, Aunt Kathryn," Ryan begged. "Do what Smith says."

"And if I don't?"

Smith answered, "My men in Paris have located the older Ebsworth, the painter. If anything goes wrong here, they have my orders to crush the man's hands."

"My father means nothing to me," Ryan said, but Kathryn heard the agony in his voice.

"Then *your fiancee's* safety is at stake," he challenged. "I should have killed her at the Minter Gardens. Then obedience would not be so difficult for you, Mr. Ebsworth."

Kathryn gripped Ryan's icy hand. "Andrea's safe at the hotel, isn't she?"

Ryan shook his head. "No, she's being watched all the time."

"By some of my men," Harland gloated. "Excellent shots."

His words startled her. "The gunfire moments ago?"

"An intruder perhaps. Would you be so good, Mrs. Culvert, to accompany me to the cottage just to be certain?"

At the kitchen door she said, "Wait here, Ryan."

She flipped on the floodlight. Smith snapped it off.

"That won't be needed," he said.

They walked to the Vaughans in the glow of his flashlight, Kathryn's heart pounding.

֍֍֍

As soon as Jeff Akers was out of sight, Sherm back-tracked through the woods, making his way cautiously toward the main house. A lone dry twig crackled under his weight. Ahead of him, he heard voices in the darkness. He stayed in the shadow of the trees as Kathryn Culvert came by. The tall man at her side kept a grip on her elbow.

As they disappeared, Sherm sprinted across the lawn toward the house, his injured shoulder throbbing. When he opened the back door, a crack of light beamed across the porch. He stepped inside and stole through the house into the living room.

"Don't go another step," a man threatened.

Ryan Ebsworth stood yards from him, their gaze meeting. Ebsworth brandished a two-prong fire poker in one hand.

"Prescott! What the devil are you doing here?" Ryan asked.

"I came for Andrea York."

Ryan's grip on the iron poker tightened. "She's not here."

Twenty-eight months of rage rose in Sherm. "You're a liar, Ebsworth." He stepped forward.

"No closer. I've a good aim. I'll pierce you with this."

In his anger over Melody, Sherm risked it all. He ducked, sidestepping the Chippendale chair, and lunged toward Ryan. Ryan swung the poker. It grazed Sherm's injured shoulder and slid off, crashing into the teaploy. Sherm winced as he dove toward Ryan again, propelling them both to the floor. They grappled and rolled toward the intense heat in the fireplace. The flames singed the hair on the back of Sherm's hand. He gripped Ryan's wrist and slammed it against the bricks, wrenching the poker free as they pitched back toward the middle of the room.

Sherm stood over Ebsworth now, the poker aimed at Ryan's chest. The agonized glint in Ryan's eyes, hell itself, stopped him.

"You're not worth it, Ebsworth," he said tossing the poker back toward the fireplace. It skidded across the dusty rose carpet, leaving a soot-covered trail behind it.

"Now where is she, Ebsworth? Where's Andrea?"

Sherm stalked through the living room into the empty den. He was climbing the curved stairwell when Ryan gasped, "Andrea's not here, Prescott. She's back at the hotel. She's safe for now."

Sherm turned.

Ryan stood by the piano, the poker back in his hand. A trickle of blood ran from his right nostril. "I didn't let Andrea come, Prescott. Now get out before I change my mind and kill you. I won't miss this time," he warned.

Sherm went slowly down the steps. He stopped and faced Ryan. "If you lay one hand on Andrea York like you did my wife, I'll see you hung for it if I have to hang you myself."

Ryan's tone was scornful when he answered, "Prescott, you should know that vengeance belongs to a higher power. Now get out before my house guests find you here."

Sherm retraced his steps to the back door, straightening the Chippendale chair en route. Another searing pain tore through his shoulder. He leaned against the porch railing, cradled his arm and gazed at Ebsworth standing in the doorway.

"Look, Ebsworth," Sherm said, "Jack Sedgwick is being held hostage down at the cottage. He's injured. He needs your help."

"Shot?" Ryan asked, his tone bland. He hesitated, then said, "My aunt is clever, convincing. She'll get Sedgwick out of there."

۞۞۞

As Kathryn Culvert entered the crowded cottage, her gaze settled on Jack Sedgwick lying on the floor. Philip Vaughan knelt beside him, bathing Jack's swollen face. She swallowed her shock. Her banker looked like a hobo. "Who is this man, Philip?" she asked, her voice surprisingly calm.

She saw relief in Sedgwick's face as Philip answered, "The town tramp, Mrs. Culvert. He's been roughed up a bit. And shot, but it's just a flesh wound."

"What was he doing trespassing on my property, Philip?"

"He meant to set a beaver trap down by the creek."

"This is private property," she said, her eyes meeting Jack's.

"I meant no harm." His words slurred through cracked lips.

She turned to Harland. "Mr. Smith, this man is nothing but a vagrant, the town drunk, but his wife loves the old fool. She never rests until he's home. We should let him go."

"No, we can't do that, Mrs. Culvert."

"Why not?" she snapped. "Oh, go ahead. Hold him if you want. If his wife knows he's out this way, she'll find him. If she's a sensible woman, *she won't come alone.*"

She eyed Smith contemptuously. "We're expecting more company. Tomorrow, wasn't it? This man has been injured on my property. He could bring charges against me, but I think he'd settle for his freedom. But do as you wish, Mr. Smith."

At the door, she looked across the room to the Vaughan children huddled in the corner. "Philip, bring your family up to the house in an hour. I'll make them a batch of cookies."

The boys glanced at Smith, their eyes pleading.

"Yes," Smith grumbled. "I have boys of my own." He kicked at Sedgwick. "And this man, get him out of here, too."

A brawny guard followed Sedgwick, his revolver nudging Jack to the fence. Jack limped the remaining yards to his car alone, his head splitting. As he dragged into the driver's side, he saw Sherm crouched beside him.

"Keep down, Sherm, or that man will blow your head off," he said as he backed the car wildly out the dirt road.

"Looks like Kathryn's got real problems, Jack."

"So do I with this face of mine," Jack answered. "And what happened to you back there when I needed you?"

Sherm eased to a sitting position. "I got hit and hit hard. The entire place is under surveillance. We almost blew Drew Gregory's whole operation."

Jack touched his battered lip. "Don't repeat the man's name. I can't keep secrets from Tina. It'll take me the rest of the night just to explain this face of mine."

"That bad?" Sherm asked. "How'd you get out of there?"

"Not with the help of the men you're talking about. If they're there, they kept out of sight. Mrs. Culvert came to my rescue. I'm her banker, but she told them I'm the town vagrant. She let me know that they're expecting important company tomorrow."

"I'll pass that word on to Drew—"

"No names, please. Tina—remember. What time is it?"

"Almost midnight. Is Mrs. Culvert holding together?"

Jack canceled his effort to smile. "She's calm enough to bake cookies for the Vaughan children."

He turned onto the main road, switched on the headlights, and accelerated for home, his foot to the floorboard.

He was racing against time, trying to beat his wife's midnight curfew.

◉◉◉

All evening Andrea sat in the Fireside Room, sketching designs and glancing around, searching for Sherm in the crowd. He was on the stairwell when she finally saw him, a black skull cap in his hand. "Sherm," she called, hurrying toward him. "Wait."

He flinched in pain as he turned to her.

"You're hurt, Sherm. What happened?"

"I ran into some opposition. A fire poker for one."

He touched her cheek. "Don't worry, Andrea. I'm all right."

"You're not all right. Look at you."

He glanced down at his torn jeans and bruised hands.

"Your face looks worse," she said.

"I thought you were at the farm. I was worried about you."

"You went out *there*? To Ryan's. You saw him?"

He tapped his shoulder. "He convinced me you weren't there."

"I've been here at the hotel all evening, sketching." She held up her sketch book.

"I'm glad you're safe," he said.

"But you weren't. Sherm, let me look at that shoulder."

He grinned. "Here on the stairwell?"

She flushed. "In your room, if you don't mind."

He offered her his hand. She took it and walked with him to his suite on the third floor, slowing her steps to match his painful ones. In the room he sat down on the edge of the bed and glanced at the framed photo of his wife on the bedside table.

Andrea put her sketch pad beside it and began to work the blood-stained shirt away from Sherm's body. "Cuts and abrasions mostly," she told him. "But the wound is caked in soot and gravel. Come to the bathroom. I'll cleanse it the best I can."

He looked embarrassed. "I could shower."

"Good. I'll go down to my room for my antibiotic cream. I always carry some." She turned his chin and inspected his facial wound. "We'll bathe your shoulder and cheek with the antibiotic when I get back."

He stood, grimacing. "I feel like a locomotive hit me."

"You look like it, too, Sherm. Make it a quick shower. I'll leave your room door ajar and come right back."

He was sitting on the bed in his pajama bottoms when she returned. His dark hair was tousled from the shower, his muscular chest bare, his injured shoulder reddened. Her sketch book was in his hands. "These are ski designs," he said, sounding pleased.

"You suggested them, Sherm. Remember?"

"I like the crop turtleneck tops, especially the pink ones."

"Designers are thinking pink this year, but they're into ethnic animal prints, too. Check my next page. It's my casual evening wear to be worn at the lodge after a day on the ski run."

"More pink and very feminine. They're good, Andrea."

"I told you I was good."

"You'll be on the runways in Europe one day."

"I plan to be there," she said as she focused the lamp on his shoulder. Soot was still ingrained in the wound. She went immediately to the steamy bathroom for a clean towel. The room was as Sherm had left it—a pile of dirty clothes on the floor, his bath towel draped over the shower door, his tooth paste lid off. Sooty water and soap were splashed around the sink.

Human. Approachable. Not perfect. The thought amused her.

He smiled as she came toward him carrying the ice bucket for a basin. "It looks like you've cleaned wounds before."

"I have. Neal Bennett did a lot of rock climbing and white river rafting. He was against doctors so I mothered him. "

Sherm gritted his teeth as she scrubbed deep into his wound. "You're not angry that I went out to the farm, are you, Andrea?"

"No. You had your reasons. I won't question them. But I've told you, Sherm—I've told Drew—Ryan won't hurt me."

She covered his wounds with ointment, then placed a clean towel over the pillow. "Now get to bed, Sherm, and get some rest."

"Yes, ma'am," he teased, but his voice sounded weary.

He swung his angular bronzed body into bed.

Andrea brushed back an unruly lock of hair from his forehead, then pulled back in embarrassment. "I'll leave the medicine here," she said, but her voice sounded unnatural in her ears. "Put some more on in the morning after you shower."

As he fell asleep, Andrea went back to the bathroom, straightened up the mess, turned out the lights, and left him.

Chapter 25

In the bungalow behind the hotel, Drew Gregory came awake with a start, one arm swinging, his head pounding from exhaustion. Vic Wilson pinned him to the sofa with a firm grip on his shoulder.

"Take it easy, Drew. You were going wild in your sleep. I had to wake you before the neighbors came calling."

Drew blinked against the grogginess. "What time is it?"

"A bit past six in the morning."

"Three hours of sleep?"

"If you want to call it that," Wilson said cheerfully.

"What's happening at the Culvert farm?"

"Jeff reports constant arrivals. And according to Jeff, Benj called off the raid, *for now*. He wants to know what's going on before he goes in. Sounds a bit hairy to me."

"He's in charge."

"That's what makes me nervous," Vic said, his cocky grin spreading. "He's asked us to take the next twenty-four hours. Surveillance boys, that's us." He poked Drew on the shoulder. "Why don't you shower, Drew, to clear your mind? I'll head out to the farm to relieve Jeff Akers. I've got the coffee pot plugged in. Are you okay now?"

Drew leaned forward, bracing his head in his hands. "I'll be fine, Vic. Go on. I'll join you there later."

Drew moaned as Wilson squealed off on threadbare tires. His nightmare still clung to his consciousness. He had been racing to the lake shore to rescue Melody Prescott. In his sleep, he had seen her again, floating face down in her Body-Glove swimsuit. He turned her over, but the face in his nightmare did not belong to Melody Prescott. Andrea York had stared up at him, her blue eyes vacant, a bath towel swung jauntily around her neck.

Odd, he thought now. *Melody's bath towel was never recovered, only her limp, lifeless body.*

He didn't want the same thing to happen to Andrea York. Andrea needed to go home to safety, but if she left, would she be safe from those who had gathered at the Culvert farm?

The minutes ticked away, slipping quietly into an hour. Still he sat there, arguing with himself about Andrea's safety. As he sipped his third cup of coffee, he did something totally out of character. Putting caution aside, he placed a person-to-person call to Katrina York at the Bethann Manor.

As the distant ringing stopped, the administrator came on the line. "I'm sorry, operator," she said firmly. "We can't call a resident to the phone at this hour."

"It's an emergency," Drew said, cutting in.

"Perhaps you should speak to Mrs. York's family then."

He could picture her drumming her fingers, peering over half-moon glasses. He challenged her authority. "Madam, I'm with the U.S. government. I must speak with Mrs. York on grave matters."

"An emergency you say?" She kept her impatience in check. "Sir, I didn't get your name."

"The name's Criss. I'm an old friend of the family."

"Criss, Mrs. York is incapacitated. I can't guarantee that she will be able to talk with you." He heard pity creep into the voice of authority. "Mrs. York rarely speaks now, but when she talks, it is only of the past, of years gone by."

"That's what I want to talk to Katrina about, the years gone by. Please," he said, in the same strained voice that he had used so many years ago, *Please, Captain, don't die.*

She yielded. "One moment, sir."

Over the phone wires, Drew heard the administrator put the receiver on the desk. He imagined her walking a lengthy corridor to Katrina's room, a buxom woman moving rapidly. And then, as though time stood still, he heard Katrina York's frail, soft voice saying, "Conrad, is that you?"

"No, Katrina, I'm a friend of Captain York's . . . Yes, I knew the captain well . . . Yes, Captain York was a wonderful man. I was with him in Normandy."

He could tell by the sound of her voice that Katrina York felt young again, revived, her wispy voice rising with hope. As they talked, he remembered landing on Omaha Beach and the hell of crawling over the sands of Normandy. "The Captain prayed for us before we went ashore," he said. "We were on board, waiting for the landing craft to lower, to belch us out on the beach, and the captain read something from the Bible, something about the Lord being our Shepherd."

Katrina picked from memory the words about green pastures and quiet waters, her voice confident as she spoke of Conrad dwelling in the house of the Lord forever.

"That's the one. He prayed for us with his eyes open."

She chuckled. "Conrad didn't dare close his eyes if you were going into battle."

Confused? Drew asked himself. Katrina's answer had been appropriate. "Katrina, the captain prayed that if someone died—that it wouldn't be any of his men."

"Did Conrad die?" she asked. "Did he suffer?"

He said yes to both questions, but spared her the details. "Did you know there was a traitor in Conrad's unit?"

"Yes, I know that now, Mrs. York."

"I worry for Conrad." Her voice faded.

"Katrina, we found the traitor."

She caught her breath. "Was it one of Conrad's friends?"

"No, Katrina, not a friend—someone who was trying to pass the invasion plans to the enemy, but he failed." Drew pictured her frail hands clasped around the phone. "Mrs. York, the captain wouldn't want you to worry about the traitor."

"Oh, I won't. As long as Conrad knows."

"He knows," Drew said. "I'm sure he knows."

"What is your name again, young man?"

He laughed, feeling old at the moment. "I'm Criss."

"I don't remember that name, but I'm getting forgetful." Her words trailed, the voice growing faint. "The only person who doesn't think so is my granddaughter, but she went away."

They talked about Andrea, and Katrina's pride was obvious. She told him that Andrea was so much like the captain, a special child, still a child in Katrina's mind. But Katrina York's love and faith broke through her confusion, cutting across the phone wires and landing on the soft spot of Drew's agnostic heart.

As Katrina said good-bye, her voice faded again, but he caught the words, "Young man, give my love to Conrad."

The administrator was on the line at once, her tone exuberant. "It's amazing," she told Drew. "Mrs. York has been so ill, yearning for her granddaughter. And now she's beaming and crying all at once. Criss, I have Mrs. York's son on another line. He wants to talk to you."

Drew cradled the phone, severing the connection. He sat in the bungalow another twenty minutes, bone-weary, lonely. It was one thing to risk his own life in this cat-and-mouse business; it was wrong to put someone else in jeopardy, a girl so much like his daughter Robyn. As soon as this case was over, he'd retire in Scotland. *And, God, whoever You are, wherever You are*, he thought, *help me get Andrea York home in time to see her grandmother again.*

As he showered and dressed, Drew decided to send Andrea home at once before Ryan or Sherm or Benj Reever were aware of her absence. He left the bungalow and entered the hotel through a back entry, going at once to Andrea's room on the West Wing. He expected her to be wide-eyed and anxious when she opened her door, but there was a calm to her expression.

"Criss, come in. I just tried to call you."

As he sat down across from her, she frowned. "Are you all right, Criss? You look like you haven't slept much."

"I didn't," he answered. "We were busy last night."

"Should I ask? Were you with Sherm?"

"Andrea, it would be better if you didn't know."

"I know enough to be worried. Sherm came sneaking back to the hotel in tattered clothes, his face bruised and dirty, his hair messed up. He was in pain from an injured shoulder. He was a wreck—hardly my image of the Kippen executive."

She couldn't let it go. "Ryan? Sherm? Which one, Drew?"

Drew squeezed her hand. "You'll know soon, Andrea."

"Will I, Criss? Or will I wake up one morning and both Ryan and Sherm will be gone? You'll pack the truth in your luggage, reports in triplicate, and fly back to Paris. And I'll never know which one I betrayed."

He wanted to tell her that Sherm was above suspicion. It was too soon. He knuckled her chin, tilting it up. "I'm sending you home, Andrea, as soon as you can pack."

She smiled unexpectedly. "You waited too long. I have a date with Sherm tonight. An appointment with Ryan now—"

"Break them."

"No, Criss, I'm on to something."

Drew watched the York jaw clamp tight, her mind set in cement like the captain's.

👁👁👁

After leaving Sherm's room the night before, distorted images had invaded Andrea's mind for hours. Brooding melancholy. Ugly thoughts. Over and over she asked herself: *Could the picture in Ryan's wallet be Melody Prescott?* If her suspicions proved true, then Kathryn was right. There was a certain madness in Ryan's father, a certain madness in the son. And Kathryn, no matter how much she loved her nephew, was in grave danger.

But now Andrea wondered what Ryan would say about Sherm being at the farm last evening. Ryan was so convincing, so persuasive. His words could twist her thinking. Would Ryan tell her that he had witnessed Melody Prescott's death? That for twenty-eight months he had feared for his own safety? That he had stood at the sulfur hot springs and watched Sherm bending over his wife in the shallow waters of Harrison Lake—drowning her?

She felt Drew studying her intently. She didn't mention her fears about Melody. Instead, she pointed to her grand-father's snapshots spread out on the coffee table.

"I've been fitting the pieces together," she said.

"And?" he asked, handing the Elgin wristwatch to her.

She smiled faintly, wrapping her fingers lightly around it. "One more puzzle piece. Thank you, Criss."

"Andrea, did the army return your grandfather's watch with the rest of his personal effects? Or was it mailed to your grandmother at a later time?"

"I'd have no way of knowing. I wasn't born yet. Why?"

"We know now that the message in Captain York's watch was intended for the German High Command. It contained last minute details on the Normandy Invasion and libera-tion of Paris."

"So Katrina was right all along. But whatever the message said, it doesn't matter any longer. It's fifty years too late."

"No, Andrea, your grandfather circled the face of the same man in each snapshot. That may be as important as the message in the watch."

"Yes," she agreed. "But, Criss, whatever my grandfather was trying to tell us died with him."

"No, it came alive when you discovered that cryptic film." He tapped the snapshots. "Andrea, the circled face in each of these pictures is Harland C. Smith."

"I decided as much. Does that make him the traitor?"

"He transferred from Eisenhower's staff to our unit."

"Why didn't he flush the message down the toilet, Drew?"

"Perhaps he still hoped to deliver it to a courier."

"Obviously, he didn't, so why didn't he toss it away? Why would he plant the film on my grandfather?"

Drew forced her to face him, his hands resting gently on her shoulders. "The captain kept close tabs on Smith. He never really trusted Smitty. If Harland wanted to get even, the Elgin was a perfect hiding place, a dead man the perfect target."

"What are you suggesting, Criss?"

"I told you. Smitty knew the watch repair business. He could have hidden the film in the Elgin. I remember that he tried to repair the captain's watch just before Normandy. It's supposition, of course, but if I can prove that Harland Smith's pattern of deception and treason dates back to Normandy, I may be able to link him to recent acts of terrorism."

She pulled back abruptly. "And you believe that Ryan works for Harland Smith now?"

He nodded.

"Criss, there's much more involved, isn't there? More than the death of Melody Prescott. Even more than the ambassador's assassination. Otherwise, you wouldn't be here."

"Yes, and Ryan is involved in all of it. What's important is whether he's involved in the sale of arms to other countries."

"I'm sorry, Criss. What's important to me right now is the death of Melody Prescott. I have to know the truth about Ryan and Sherm and Melody."

She gathered her grandfather's pictures up and put them in her purse. "Ryan agreed to pick me up and take me back to the farm this morning. Perhaps he'll tell me everything."

She reached out and shook Drew's hand. "While I'm finding my own answers, Drew, I'll try and find out what's going on at the farm, too."

"You won't go home? Jeff Akers could drive you."

"Tomorrow, Drew. Tomorrow I'll go."

"Andrea, you're buying time for all of us. Be careful." He cupped her chin, fatherly fashion. "If you were my daughter, I'd be very proud of you. In fact, I am proud of you."

Chapter 26

Three hours later, Ryan's Chevy pulled into the hotel driveway. Andrea hurried outdoors and was climbing into the passenger side before she realized the driver wasn't Ryan.

"Who are you?" she demanded. "Where's Ryan?"

"I'm Philip Vaughan, Mrs. Culvert's rancher."

He glanced her way again as he started the car, the lines on his weathered face older than his forty years. "Mrs. Culvert sent me, Miss York. She wants you to get Ryan out of the house until Mr. Smith and the others leave."

"I'm to whisk in there and rescue him, Philip? I'm a fashion designer, a journalist, not a miracle worker."

"Mrs. Culvert says you can pull it off. The house guests think you're Ryan's fiancee. They'll accept your presence."

"We're not engaged." Andrea's hands felt icy, her throat parched. "Philip, why don't you call the police?"

"And risk bloodshed and the safety of my children?"

"What about my safety, Mr. Vaughan?"

He looked as though she had wrenched his arm as he said, "God helping me, I don't want anything to happen to you. We're counting on Ryan loving you enough to let you go. We left Kathryn's car at the neighbor's farm. The keys are in it."

A tic ran the length of his jaw. "Another guest arrived at the farm this morning, but Mr. Smith is the man in charge.

Right now they are meeting in the library with their South American contacts—planning the sale of weapons worldwide."

"How does Kathryn know that?"

"Years ago Ben installed a listening device between their bedroom and the library. He was a wealthy man, security conscious. Kathryn used it to listen in on these meetings. She heard enough to know that Ryan is deeply involved."

"And she still wants Ryan to escape?" Andrea asked.

"Yes, *from Smith*. Ryan will catch the Canadian Pacific on the lower terminal at Hell's Gate Canyon. The train slows around that curve. He'll hop on while the train's in motion. Maybe he'll get himself killed. That would be merciful."

Andrea gasped at his bitter words. "And me?"

"Refuse to go. He'll only have seconds to go without you."

"This lower terminal—how do I get out of there?"

Vaughan signaled for a turn. "The airtram is down for the season until mid-April. The fishery trucks use the suspension bridge. You'll have to walk across it back to the highway."

"No. I hate heights. I hate the insanity of what you're asking me to do. It's all wrong. Take me back to the hotel."

"I can't, Miss York," he said, pulling to a stop in front of the house. "I can't risk bloodshed here at the farm. My boys are only seven and nine. You've got to help us."

He urged her from the car and up the porch steps.

"If you can, Miss York, persuade Ryan to turn himself in. Kathryn just wants him to go on living, hoping that as long as he's alive, maybe he'll find God."

"She'd risk her own life for that?"

"She's risking all of us," Vaughan said as he left her.

Andrea found Kathryn standing by the kitchen window, her smile reticent. "My dear," she said, pressing her wrinkled cheek to Andrea's. "Thank you for coming. I need your help."

"There must be another way, Kathryn—"

"No, I considered everything. When Ryan gets out of the meeting, leave with him. Go down to the creek. There's an old trail through the woods where Ryan played as a boy. It leads to the neighbor's farm. Keep running, Andrea. Don't even look back."

"Or we'll turn into pillars of salt?"

Kathryn's words were threadbare as she answered, "Just help him. The train will carry him a safe distance away; then he has airplane reservations out of the country on Friday."

"I won't go with him, Kathryn. You know that."

"He'll try to persuade you."

"Ryan will have to go alone. Will he have enough money?"

"Yes, Andrea. He'll have ample. He's stolen some of mine."

"Kathryn, as soon as we leave, call Sherm Prescott at the hotel. Tell Sherm I'm on my way to Hell's Gate with Ryan."

"The fewer who know," she protested, "the safer for Ryan."

"And it's safer for me if you notify Mr. Prescott. It's important that he knows that I didn't go away willingly—"

"Ryan never had a chance with you, did he?" Kathryn asked. She put her finger to her lips. "No more of this. Ryan is coming."

When Ryan reached them, he leaned down and hugged Kathryn. "I'm sorry, Aunt Kathryn," he said, "for everything."

She cupped his face. "I love you. Now go. I'll steep some tea while you're out for a walk," she said, loud enough for the others to hear her. "We'll have tea and crumpets when you get back. Give me fifteen minutes."

That's how long you're promising us, Andrea thought.

At the kitchen door, she turned to wave, but Kathryn was standing by the phone, her china teapot in one hand.

Benj Reever and his men watched as Ryan and Andrea crept by the barn and over the hillock to the creek. Moments later the back door burst open. Two Brazilians, .45-caliber guns in their hands, ran down the back steps. Reever recognized the Iraqi house guest behind them from a photograph made early that morning at the Vancouver airport. Kathryn Culvert ran on the Iraqi's heels, china teapot clutched in her hand. Reever fired warning shots.

The two men in front raced through the cow pasture, yards from where Ryan and Andrea had disappeared. Mrs. Culvert tugged savagely at the coat of the Iraqi, pounding his arm with her teapot. Suddenly, the tail of a cow swished backwards, catching the Iraqi off guard.

Reever fired his weapon, dropping the Iraqi with laser-scope accuracy; he fell, his body limp and twisted in manure.

"Get down, Mrs. Culvert," Reever shouted.

She ignored his warning and turned, the broken handle of her teapot still in her hand. She pointed toward the back porch. Harland Smith stood there, a stranglehold on a small boy, a .38 snub-nose pistol to the boy's temple. Reever and his operatives converged on the house, running in the open. Mrs. Culvert and Philip Vaughan ran behind them.

"Call them off, Vaughan," Harland yelled, backing toward the kitchen door. "Or your son's dead."

Vaughan froze. Benj stopped his men, his revolver pointed skyward. Harland leveled his gaze on Kathryn, his grip on the child tightening. "Where did your nephew go with Miss York?"

She glared back at him, crying, "To Hell's Gate Canyon. But you can never have him now, Mr. Smith. You can never have my nephew."

Harland yanked the child inside; the back door slammed behind them. Kathryn and the others waited, motionless, until they heard Smith's car roar away. They found the Vaughan child in the front yard, unhurt, crawling terrified into his mother's arms. Philip knelt beside them.

Reever whirled on Kathryn. "Get everyone in the house and stay there. Now." He ran toward the driveway. Victor Wilson was at the wheel of Reever's car, slowing long enough for Benj to pile into the passenger side before careening off toward the highway.

"You drive like a crazy American," Benj shouted. "This isn't the Indianapolis 500."

"I've got Smith's car in view. I'm not losing it."

"It won't matter, Wilson. We know where he's going."

As they swerved on the country road, Reever radioed Drew at the Harrison. "They're gone, Drew," he said. "Smith included. He's headed to Hell's Gate Canyon. The Iraqi is dead."

"That will create an international ruckus."

Reever braced as the kilometer needle rose. "The man was shot trespassing private property. No, Gregory, we're fine on this one. They wouldn't risk U.N. intervention. Not again."

He added, "Drew, you and Akers head down to the helicopter pad. One of my pilots will wing you out to Hell's Gate. It'll take us an hour by car, less at the rate Wilson drives."

"Will do," Drew told him, "but we can expect more company. Prescott had Andrea call her family from his room. The wires in Index were tapped. They traced the call to the Harrison. U.S. agents will flood this area. Two of Andrea's friends are already here making a lot of noise—Sabrina Jensen and Neal Bennett."

"Darn," Benj said. "We have less time than I thought. I'll get men over there right away. Now get going to Hell's Gate, but keep Prescott and Andrea's friends out of there."

"No problem with Prescott, Benj. He left the hotel moments ago in a borrowed car. Sightseeing, maybe."

🏵🏵🏵

Ryan kept his foot to the floorboard, the tires of his aunt's car burning the road as he swerved at the corner.

Andrea screamed. "Ryan, you'll get us killed."

"Then we'll die together."

"I don't want to die with you."

"You knew, didn't you?" His voice choked with rage. "You saw me in the park the day the ambassador died, didn't you?"

"You were the driver, the terrorist who ran away."

Her words infuriated him. "We meant to assassinate Prescott."

She gasped. "Because of Melody Prescott?"

"Yes. Yes." He seemed relieved to confess it.

She turned from him and stared out the window, salty tears blinding her as they roared down a two-lane highway. She felt anesthetized with the fear of dying, dying young. Through her tears, she saw the hillsides bathed in a patchwork of greens. Veiled sun rays reflected off the snowy mountains. A freight train snaked its way along the canyon on the rusty track beside them. Ryan skidded in gravel and took the first tunnel in the dark, his horn blaring.

Andrea prayed for a patrol car as they passed the town of Hope. She prayed that Sherm or Criss knew where she was. As she kept praying, they sped through Yale Tunnel, Saddle Rock, Sailor Bar, and on through the eerie darkness of the Hell's Gate Tunnel.

Finally Andrea asked, "Why do you carry Melody Prescott's picture in your wallet—the one I saw when we shopped in Paris?"

His face twisted. "She was my friend, Andrea. She tried to teach me to swim. I was always afraid of water."

"But you hurt her, Ryan."

"No. I wouldn't hurt her. The Parisian gave her the shot. I just lowered her into the water. She was so pretty. So pretty."

A childish quality crept into his confession. "You have to understand, Andrea. I didn't want to be a porter all my life. Melody tried to stop me from taking the Parisian across the lake. The man paid me well to interpret a big transaction for him. You do see, don't you, Andrea? Melody would have ruined everything."

"Does the same man pay you to sell arms to foreign countries?"

"You know that, too? You know about Mr. Smith?" he asked. "Then you do understand. Mr. Smith makes it all so profitable."

"That's all?" she said. "Profitable. Not destructive?"

She trembled convulsively as his foot hit the accelerator again. "Collette Rheims? Francois Deborde? Why? Why, Ryan?"

"They had to die. I had to get you out of Paris. Smith had to think you were dead, Andrea. I just wanted to protect you."

Fifty miles from the hotel, a quarter of a mile before the Hell's Gate airtram, he swerved left, taking a truck access road down toward the canyon. She saw the orange-red girders of the bridge and gripped the door handle, terrified that he would plunge them into the turbid Fraser River.

He jerked the car to a standstill, scraping it against a large boulder. Tossing the keys onto the dashboard, he pulled her from the car. Gusty winds howled through the canyon. The thick suspension cables squealed as the bridge swayed. Andrea stared down at the turbulent waters sweeping down the canyon.

"Go without me," she begged. "Catch your train."

"No, Andrea. I want you to go with me."

He forced her to step onto the bridge with him. The bridge swayed even more under their steady gait.

"Ryan, I'm terrified."

"Of me?" he asked, surprised.

"The bridge. The height. The open spaces."

He broke their gait, alternating their rapid speed with slow steps that eased the intense vibrations. Midway across, a car door slammed and a shout erupted behind them.

After receiving Kathryn Culvert's frantic phone call, Sherm Prescott borrowed Henny's car and raced alone toward the canyon, his injured shoulder temporarily forgotten.

From the hotel to Hell's Gate, he had twenty miles less distance to cover than Ryan and Andrea. Clocking his time, he checked his gas gauge and missed the turnoff to the bridge. He sped on to the vacant parking lot at the Hell's Gate airtram.

Minutes later Sherm stood alone, a solitary figure on a rocky precipice overlooking the foaming Fraser River. High cables stretched across the granite gorge, sloping down to the lower terminal. He shaded his eyes watching a helicopter sway in the gusty winds. The pilot hovered for split seconds over the canyon and then descended into the gorge and landed safely on the lower terminal. Two men climbed out, crouched low under the whirling blades and ran, disappearing around the empty airtram.

Sherm's gaze caught a man and a woman midway across the suspension bridge—Andrea, he was certain, and Ryan. A man ran on the iron girders behind them, his revolver glinting in the hazy sun. Sherm shouted a warning, his cry lost to the distance, mocked by the sound of the raging river. He raced back to his car, desperate to reach Andrea in time.

☙☙☙

Andrea froze. Behind her a man ran toward them. Ahead of her Drew Gregory stepped into view, brandishing a revolver.

"It's too late, Ryan," she cried. "Someone is waiting for you on both sides of this bridge."

Ryan scanned the shorelines, his gaze brittle. He grasped her wrist and raced a zigzag pattern, sprinting toward the lower terminal. "We're almost there," he said.

"Ryan, I won't go any farther with you."

In his fury he slammed her against the railing. "Don't you understand? I need you, Andrea."

"Understand what, Ryan? About terrorizing people?"

"You sound like my aunt," he scoffed.

"Your aunt loves you; she prays for you."

He stared at Andrea, infuriated. "The God routine? My aunt told me that one all my life."

"She loves you, Ryan."

"I have to grant her that. It's more than my parents did." His expression twisted to boyish despair. "God?" he asked. "Don't you see, Andrea? I've already made my choice."

Drew Gregory crouched, legs apart, a revolver gripped in both hands. He fired a warning shot above them and then lowered his aim at Ryan. "Let her go, Ebsworth."

At Drew's command, Harland halted, turned, and fled. The bridge swayed. Ryan fell backwards, cowering against the orange-red railing high above the swirling whitecaps. As Drew came toward him, Ryan swung his lithe body over the rail. For seconds his hands clung to it; his legs dangled free.

"I'm invincible, Andrea," he cried, "I'll swim to safety."

"No, Ryan," Andrea begged, grabbing for him.

His narrow face went ashen as he lost his grip.

Andrea's terrified scream and Ryan's final piercing cry blended as one as his body spun through space. He smashed against the rocks below and slid lifelessly into the swirling Fraser River. Andrea stumbled into Drew's outstretched arms.

"Criss, help Ryan," she cried, her words muffled.

"It's too late, Andrea. He was dead on impact."

Drew held up his transmitter, Andrea still leaning against him. "Reever," he said, "where the devil are you?"

"A mile from Hell's Gate with a blowout. How's your end?"

"Ryan is dead, Benj. He was swept away in the river. Can you notify the proper authorities to look for his body?"

"Yes, but what about Smith?"

Across the bridge, Harland's car squeezed past a fishery truck leaving a dust trail on the access road. "He's heading for the highway, Benj. We'll try and spot him from the air."

Andrea trembled as Drew glanced down at her. "York is safe."

Reever whistled. "I'll need you both out of Canada fast."

"Then we'll be in touch again someday," Drew told him. "Where's the helicopter, Gregory?"

"On the lower terminal."

"You're on private property, Drew. Get out of there before every fishery truck driver in town crosses the bridge to try to stop you."

Drew squeezed Andrea's shoulder. "We're on our way. We'll pack up our things as soon as we get back to the Harrison."

"I've got a couple of people out there. We'll have the bungalow and York's room cleared out by the time you get there."

"So we head right back to Paris?"

"Yes, I'll call Vancouver and make some reservations."

"Private jet, Reever?"

"No," Benj said. "Commercial if I can line up a flight."

"Then I'll see you around the world some place, Benj."

"In a couple of years maybe, eh?" Reever's voice was upbeat, full of hope. "I'll notify French Security that Smith slipped away. At least for our purposes, we don't need him. The French can pick him up when he lands in Paris."

"I'll still see if we can spot him once we're airborne."

"With Ebsworth out of the way, Smith is all yours," Reever said. "I'm washing my hands of the whole mess. Some of my men straightened up the Culvert farm before the Royal Mounties rode in." He chuckled at his own joke. "Apparently, Mrs. Culvert was in such a state by then that she couldn't remember York's last name. She told RCMP that the girl came *from* Paris with Ryan."

"Deliberately?"

"No. She wasn't thinking clearly. It's to our advantage though. It looks like we'll be able to keep York's name out of this. Yours, too, Drew. I'll file a report with RCMP later—after I go back to the farm and tell Mrs. Culvert that Ryan is dead."

"I don't envy you your task."

"She's a *grande dame*—she'll come through all right."

Drew was ready to race to the helicopter. "Gotta go, Benj."

"Yeah, Drew. Thanks for keeping Prescott out of this one."

"Sorry, Benj. You're wrong. He's coming our way right now."

Sherm Prescott stepped from the fishery truck on the opposite end of the bridge. He cupped his hands, his call as piercing as Ryan's final cry. "Andrea. Andrea, wait for me."

Drew tightened his arm around her shoulders. "You heard Reever, Andrea. I need to get you out of here."

Sherm ran toward them. Drew waved him off. "Go back, Prescott. We won't need your services any longer."

Sherm had almost reached Andrea. She recoiled, glaring

in disbelief at him. "You were with the Agency. You lied to me, Sherm."

She turned from him and raced with Drew toward the copter. A cloud cover rolled in as the helicopter lifted and circled the area for several minutes. Andrea pressed her face to the window pane, but Ryan's body had washed from sight.

Drew touched her hand. "I'm sorry," he said, "about Ryan and Sherm." He paused. "Sherm was only helping us."

"But on the bridge you said he worked with you—"

"It was the only way I could get you to leave. You can work it out with Prescott some other day."

Above the roar of whirling blades, she said, "I feel like I've lost them both. Have we lost Smith, too?"

He nodded, his mood somber. "It happens that way sometimes."

She gazed down on the rugged terrain with him, knowing by Drew's taut expression that Smith had found a way of escape over those tree-lined slopes. As a Canadian Pacific train snaked its way along the Fraser Canyon, steaming toward Hell's Gate, Drew called off the search. The pilot acknowledged his order with a thumbs-up and a sympathetic smile at Andrea.

Chapter 27

Sherm pulled into the town of Hope to top his tank. As they serviced his car, he found a pay phone and called Andrea.

"Miss York? Oh, she checked out moments ago," Henny said. "She left by helicopter with Mr. Gregory, *but not very happily.*"

"Left?" Sherm repeated. "Where were they going?"

"Paris. Imagine! Miss York is to identify someone." To Sherm's silence she added, "Mr. Gregory left you a message. He said a Mr. Reever will be in touch and explain everything to you."

Her cheerfulness grated on Sherm as she prattled on. "Miss York has friends in the lobby—a young couple. They don't even know she's gone, and I'm not to tell them. But Mr. Bennett is stirring up quite a ruckus, annoying our hotel guests."

Sherm felt the onset of a throbbing headache. "Not Neal Bennett?" he asked.

"Yes, that's his name. But it's all right. Mr. Reever will speak to them, too, and send them home."

"I've lost Andrea in more ways than one then," Sherm said.

Henny cut in gently, "Did you know Miss York's friend Ryan Ebsworth drowned? Such a terrible tragedy. He was so young."

So was Melody, Sherm thought, *when she died.*

As he severed the call and fed in the coins for overtime, he brooded over the past. With Melody gone—with Andrea gone—he'd leave for San Antonio in the morning. If he hurried, he could reach The Flower Mill before closing time. Just once more he'd drop roses on the lake in a farewell tribute to his wife. He had kept his promise to Melody, but for security reasons her death would always be listed as a drowning.

As he neared the hotel, the red roses on the car seat beside him, he knew what he had to do. He drove the extra twenty miles to the farm, rehearsing what he would say to Ryan's aunt.

When he arrived, patrol cars were parked in the driveway. Light came from every window. RCMP officers stood on duty, but Kathryn opened the door herself. He was speechless as he looked at her. She was small of stature, like a young girl with an old, grief-stricken face. A harsh evening breeze tugged at wisps of her silvery hair and tore them from place in the same violent way that her nephew had just been torn from her. She lifted her ringed hand and tried to finger-comb them in place.

"Mrs. Culvert, I'm Sherman Prescott," he said.

She offered him a faltering smile. "Andrea's friend."

"I'm a friend of the Sedgwicks, too."

"Yes," she said, her voice fragile. "They just called."

"You already know about Ryan then?"

She nodded and led him into the living room. She sank wearily into her Chippendale chair as he sat facing her. Her crooked spine fit unevenly against the cushion; it pushed her forward as though she were deliberately leaning toward him.

Shock held her rigid, her face drained of color, lifeless. She twisted a handkerchief in one hand and outlined the dent in the teaploy with the other. Her raw grief seemed like a window to her soul, making her vulnerable in Sherm's presence.

Out of respect for her, he glanced away. His eyes settled on Ryan's portrait—an attractive, boyish Ryan.

"Sherm, thank you for coming. Did you come as Ryan's friend?"

He nodded vaguely, not wanting her to know that he came in an act of contrition, wanting to prove to himself that he had really forgiven Ryan for Melody's death. He prayed that Kathryn would be spared the truth about Melody, about the destructive path Ryan had followed.

The tilt of Kathryn's chin and the direct way she looked at him now suggested that she knew more than he wanted her to. He took her hands and held them briefly.

"Ryan told me that you visited here last evening."

"Yes," Sherm admitted. "We quarreled over Andrea York."

"And not over the death of your wife?" The corners of her mouth quivered. "Mr. Reever told me everything. I'm so sorry for you, Mr. Prescott. Can you ever forgive Ryan?"

He came to console; he was being consoled. "That's why I came here this evening—to make certain that I had forgiven him."

"Ryan robbed you of someone very special to you."

"Yes, my wife. My very life."

She shook her head sadly. "Young man, don't let the memory of what Ryan did rob you of Andrea York as well. It's over for Ryan and me. But not for you, Mr. Prescott. Not for Andrea."

He shifted uneasily. "How did you find out about Ryan?"

"Mr. Reever brought my car back. He was kind, kinder than his own men. He left two of them here to search Ryan's room. They left it in shambles, but they didn't find these." She tugged at some papers edged into the Chippendale cushion and handed them to Sherm.

"My rancher is wiser than I am. Philip never intended for Ryan to flee the country. He took the passports and plane reservation from Ryan's satchel and hid them in the hayloft."

Sherm examined Andrea's torn passport, frowning at the fragmented corner.

Kathryn Culvert shrugged, a gentle movement of her narrow shoulders. "My nephew had it all along. I'm sorry."

She pointed to the one reservation for Zurich. "Ryan's father lives in Paris, Mr. Prescott, but he keeps a studio in Zurich. Perhaps Ryan was trying to find his father, but he never intended for Andrea to go with him."

Her voice seemed stronger for a moment. "Mr. Reever promised to keep Andrea's name out of his reports. I told him that she didn't go with Ryan willingly. She thought that Ryan's running away was all wrong, that I was wrong to let him go. Mr. Prescott, what *your* Andrea did, she did for me—to protect me, to protect the Vaughan children."

Sherm tried vainly to comfort her. "Ryan loved you."

She smiled faintly. "I was his harbor. His escape. For whatever he was to everyone else, he was dear to me. I loved him, Mr. Prescott, but I will never see him again. Never."

Sherm groped for the right words. "The sovereignty of God—"

She leaned forward and patted his hand. "My pain is unbearable. I prayed for Ryan over and over. I don't know where I went wrong nor why he made the choices he did." The tremor in her voice increased. "But I won't turn my back on a loving God."

She pushed back a strand of hair. "Sherm, I've cried all afternoon about my broken china teapot—about that horrible man in the pasture. But I can't seem to cry for Ryan."

Not yet, he thought. *But you're in shock, blocking out death and Hell and the everlasting lostness Ryan faces even now.*

He took her hands again. "Will you be all right?" he asked.

"The Vaughans will stay on with me. My husband Ben never quite trusted what I might do, not where Ryan was concerned. He made certain that I'd never lose the house or farm."

She lifted her gaze to his. "Mr. Reever called back just before you arrived, Mr. Prescott. Some hikers found Ryan's body crushed against the rocks."

Finality, Sherm thought. He should feel some justice to Ryan's dying face down in the water, the way Melody had died. He felt only pity.

"May I send flowers for the funeral, Mrs. Culvert?"

Her tears spilt then.

"There'll be no funeral. It's the way Ryan would want it."

"Will you let his father know?" Sherm asked.

She reflected for a moment. "I have no way of knowing where Robert is. He was in Paris the last we heard."

"I have friends in Paris. Perhaps they could locate him."

Kathryn dabbed at her eyes. "My sister Kori loved Ryan's father. For Kori's memory—and for Ryan's—perhaps it would be best to let Robert know that his son is dead."

"He wouldn't have to know the details, Kathryn."

She nodded gratefully as they stood. "And Andrea?" she asked. "Mr. Reever said she was safe."

"Andrea tried to stop Ryan from jumping."

"Dear God." She gripped Sherm's injured arm to steady herself. "Mr. Reever didn't tell me that. Is she—"

"I don't know. Andrea left the hotel for Paris."

"Europe?" she frowned. "Not home to her grandmother?"

"Paris first. The C.I.A. didn't ask my opinion."

"Go after her," Kathryn said as they walked out to his car. "If you don't want to lose Andrea York, follow her to Paris."

He shook his head. "Mrs. Culvert, Andrea's old boyfriend is at the hotel. He came to take her home and missed her."

"It's good that he missed her."

Sherm gave Kathryn a quick hug and then slid into the car.

She rested her hands on the window, tears in her eyes. "When Andrea was frightened, Sherm, you were on her mind. Not Neal Bennett. Oh, yes. She told me about Neal. But she wanted *you*. It's all right for you to fall in love again, you know."

He reached across the car seat for the bouquet of tribute roses and thrust them into Kathryn's arms.

She protested. "Andrea said you get these for the lake."

"For you this time," he told her firmly.

The flood gates opened. Kathryn stepped back from the car and buried her tear-streaked face in the fragile fragrance of memories.

Harland C. Smith's car roared up the truck access road and swerved left onto the highway. A mile later his driver pulled into a wooded picnic area, roughshodding over the twigs and gravel into nature's camouflage. As their car jerked to a stop, Harland ordered, "Attempt radio contact with my pilot in Vancouver."

"Someone could pick up our transmission, sir."

"Chance it," he snarled. "We need a way out of here."

He paced beside the car, his mind sifting through ways to salvage the operation. His losses had been small—three men, including Ryan and the Iraqi. Shipment of arms out of Seattle or Vancouver was out. He would make other arrangements.

His anger at Andrea York smoldered. He tore a strip of bark from a tree, shredding it in his fury. He should have killed her in the Colleville Cemetery or the Minter Gardens. Ryan Ebsworth's promises that she would join with them had been empty from the beginning.

At ten an unmarked moving van pulled off the highway, its emergency blinkers flashing. The driver glared down at Harland.

"Hurry up, Smith. Either leave it or help your man load it," he said, pointing to Harland's car. "I'm staying with my wheels. Any patrol car and I'm off."

The driver dropped a work uniform into Harland's arms. "Put that on," he said. "Anyone stops us en route to Vancouver and you're my relief driver. Got that, Mr. Smith? Your driver rides in the back."

Harland cursed as he hustled his man into the van and chained the door behind him. He took his place beside the driver, the man's defiance increasing as they drove along.

"The evening news is thick, Smith," he said. "They're looking for you for selling arms to foreign governments."

"Rubbish," Harland snapped.

The driver turned the radio dial. "Listen for yourself."

Harland's hand came down hard on the man's wrist. "Enough insubordination. Where's my jet?"

The man mellowed. "At a private airstrip outside of Vancouver. She's being serviced for a midnight departure."

Not safe, Harland thought. *French Security will pick me up in Paris the minute we touch down.*

"We're about the same size," he said to the driver.

"About that," the man agreed. "Give an inch or so."

"Have you ever been to Paris?" Harland asked.

"Never could afford it."

"Would you like a trip to Paris on me?" Harland asked, his dislike of the man increasing as they spoke.

"What's the gimmick?"

"When you leave Canada, you leave as me. In my clothes. When you arrive, you tell them you are a sales representative for Plastec Corporation authorized to use the company jet."

"And you come into Paris some other way?"

"In from Normandy where I holiday with my family."

Simple, Harland thought as he planned it. His pilot could chart a flight over the northern route. He'd send this driver on board carrying an attaché case with a bomb inside—a bomb timed to go off before the refueling station. It would be costly—the company jet, the pilot, and the man in the back.

"I'd like you to take off before dawn," Harland said.

"You're serious? All I have to do is impersonate you on leaving. Will that give you the time you need?" he asked.

Harland smiled into the darkness. "Ample time," he said.

Ample time, he thought. He would wait out the storm in his Swiss chalet, for months if need be, until he could safely send for Monique and the children.

🌀🌀🌀

When Sherm reached the hotel, he found Jack Sedgwick in his room. Jack looked like a war zone—both eyes bruised; red, raw abrasions down one cheek; stitches above his upper lip.

"You're looking great," Sherm said.

"That's not what Tina thinks." He tried to grin, the stitches twisting into a sneer. "Sherm, I came as soon as I heard about Ryan. What about Andrea?"

"She's en route to Paris to identify a terrorist."

"You let her go? Just like that?"

"No. I'm going to call Porter Deven in Paris and tell him to expect me on the first available flight."

"Jack, Andrea is wavering—afraid to believe again. These last few weeks have been devastating for her. I won't push her. But—"

"You won't marry her either?"

"No, not unless she's at peace with God again."

"It won't be easy for you, Sherm."

"Loving someone never is."

"How can I help? What about a nonstop to Paris first class?"

"Good. And, Jack, call Andrea's parents for me. Tell them I'll get her home safely." Sherm grinned. "But I'll have to call my father-in-law. He'll have my head or my job."

"Look, let me call Buzz Kippen for you once you're airborne. You've got leeway there, you know. You're part owner. Now pack and shower. I'll call the airlines. I'll phone Tina, too, and tell her we're driving you to Vancouver."

"No need."

"Not a need, friend, a pleasure. We can explain everything to Tina on the way—about Ryan and Melody, eh?"

Sherm was already stripping down when Jack said, "Tina sent her copy of *Style Magazine*. You can read it in flight."

Sherm was at the bathroom door. "What?"

Jack held up the magazine, his bruised face and perpetual frown easing carefully into a smile. "It's a nice picture of Andrea, but the article paints her as a fashion journalist wrapped up in spydom. Everything legal, of course. Tina wrote a scathing letter to the publisher."

Sherm turned the shower water on, then reappeared.

"I'll read the article, but, Jack, look in on Kathryn Culvert for me, often. She's going to bear the burden of who Ryan really was for a long time."

"You've come a long way, Sherm," Jack said.

Five minutes later Sherm came back from the shower, a towel wrapped around his waist, his chest bare and bronzed.

Jack handed him the phone. "I've got your friend

Porter Deven on the line. Seems like he doesn't like being awakened."

Sherm grabbed for the phone, dripping a trail of water across the rug. He cut short the greetings. "Porter, expect me in Paris within the next twenty-four hours."

Ignoring Deven's loud protests, he said, "Porter, tell Andrea York I'm coming. And make certain she gets my message."

Chapter 28

On Thursday Sherm and Andrea taxied a zigzag pattern through Paris. Leaving the wide boulevards, they cruised up and down narrow streets, finally reaching the Right Bank, north of the Seine, an hour after beginning their journey.

Sherm peered out the rear window once more. Confident that no one had followed them, he ordered the driver to stop in front of an impressive sixteenth-century stone structure with symmetrical arcades and a steep slate roof. An ominous high iron gate secured the unmarked facility.

Andrea frowned up at Sherm, the creases marring her delicate features. "We're only blocks from our hotel, Sherm. Was all that precaution necessary?"

He smiled reassuringly as he helped her from the cab. "It was Porter's idea. And his idea to meet here rather than at the police station. Once you identify Kusa, it'll all be over."

She brushed nervously at her sun-golden hair.

"You look lovely, Andrea. Stunning, in fact."

She nodded, vulnerable, the sparkle in her eyes gone.

"We could make another appointment," he offered.

"No. I'm flying home to my family tomorrow evening."

He squeezed her hand. "Then let's get this over with."

They met Porter and Drew in an office on the third floor. The uniformed commandant with them was a polite, articulate man with a handlebar moustache that looked like a whiskery ruffle on his upper lip. It twitched as he gave

Andrea a quick appraisal. He turned and pointed to the photographs spread on his desk. "You met this man, Miss York, yes?" he asked.

Sherm held her hand as they studied the pictures of a man Drew's age. The features were razor-sharp—snappy black eyes with baggy circles beneath; a wide, crooked nose; a cocky expression; thick glasses; dark hair, and sideburns.

"Sir, the terrorist was a younger man," Andrea said.

The commandant smiled patiently. "You sent this man a telex before you came to Paris, yes?"

She shot a worried glance Drew's way. "Harland C. Smith?"

"Yes, Andrea. Can you identify him?" Drew asked.

Sherm felt her hand tremble as she said, "He could be the stranger who followed me to the cemetery in Normandy."

Porter ran an emery board over his thumbnail. "What about the man at the Culvert farm or the Minter Gardens?"

"I didn't see the man's face at either place, Mr. Deven."

Porter's eyes narrowed to a frosty blue. "And now you never will. Mr. Smith's jet exploded en route back to Paris. But Drew Gregory *here* doesn't think Smith was on board."

"I'd gamble my life on it, Porter," Drew said.

The commandant twisted the tip of his moustache. "Mr. Gregory, we found Smith's Plastec Corporation ledgers all in order—as I would expect from one who traveled in embassy circles and dined with President Mitterand."

"What about the Plastec warehouses?" Drew protested. "Seal the shipments, Porter. Open some crates—"

"They'd be packed with medical parts and computer chips."

"The top layers would match the shipping manifests," Drew conceded. "But somewhere in those shipments we'd find weapons."

Sherm glared at Porter. "Deven, you wanted Ryan Ebsworth's contact here in Paris. It looks like you've found him. And you're going to sweep it away as though it never happened?"

Porter looked as if rigor mortis had set in; his body went rigid, his gaze stony, his lips lifeless. Finally, he admitted,

"Smith and I were *friends*. But for France, it's a matter of national pride and honor. Smith's plane crash is convenient to all of us. There's no need for scandalous headlines now."

"So you're going to cover it up—whitewash everything?"

"French Security will handle it." Porter nodded toward the commandant. "Thankfully, the decision is not mine."

The commandant palmed his hands, shrugging. His gaze included Sherm when he said, "We believe Mr. Smith gave the orders. Kusa and Ebsworth carried out the acts of terrorism against my country. With Mr. Smith's untimely death, we will not go public."

"Then I can't be much help to you, can I?" Andrea asked.

"Ah, Yes. You are here to identify Kusa," he reminded her.

As the door opened, Andrea's gasp echoed in the room. Kusa stood inches from her, his arms cuffed to two guards, his brooding eyes still full of hatred as he looked at her. She imagined the automatic Uzi in his hand and trembled at the image.

"You," she whispered. "You were in the park."

Sherm gripped her arm. "Sir, get him out of here."

The commandant remained stoic. "Miss York, is this the man who killed the American ambassador?"

"Yes. Yes, sir. He almost killed me, too."

Kusa's marbled expression turned scornful. He pursed his thick lips, a projectiled wad of spit splattering on Andrea in button-sized blotches.

The commandant snapped his fingers, shouting orders in rapid French. Kusa was ushered from the room, bullish and belligerent. Then the commandant turned to Andrea. "Pardon, pardon, Mademoiselle. Sit down, please," he offered.

She leaned against Sherm. "Get me out of here, please."

"It's over, Andrea," Drew Gregory said kindly as he walked them outside past the formidable security gate.

"Is it?" she asked. "Then how can Porter Deven and the commandant pretend that Harland Smith never happened?"

"They have to save face, Andrea. Smith traveled in high places among officials from several governments. There will be an investigation, superficial perhaps. Smith's operation will be closed down, at least in Paris, and the files sealed."

He waved his hand toward space. "He's out there. I have a score to settle with him on Normandy. I'll find him someday."

"And Kusa?" Sherm asked, his jaw clenched.

"Sentencing will drag. There'll be an exchange of political prisoners in the future and Kusa will go free."

Andrea shuddered. "I'm leaving Paris tomorrow, Drew. I'm resigning my job and going home to Index. I'll be safe there."

Doubt clouded Drew's gaze. "We'll arrange with Rand Jordan to seal your personnel file, to channel all references and questions about you through us."

"For the rest of my life?"

"At least for a while."

Impulsively, she reached up and hugged Drew. "Thanks for clearing my grandfather's name—for making me proud of him."

"You were already proud of Captain York."

"I'd like to do something for you, Drew. Would you let me look up your daughter while I'm in Los Angeles?"

"No," he said firmly. "Robyn would want to know how we met. I want to spare her who I am, what I do."

"But, Drew, families were meant to be together."

"Even mine?" he asked.

He smiled down at Andrea, shook hands with Sherm, and then turned and walked briskly back into the old stone building.

🌀🌀🌀

Friday, Andrea's last day in Paris. She locked her suitcase and then called home again with her flight number.

"We'll meet you," her dad promised, his voice throbbing. "No matter what hour you get in, Mother and I will be there."

When she met Sherm in the hotel lobby, he took her hands and said, "I'd like to think that smile is for me."

"Partly," she answered. "I just talked with my father. He prayed for me over the phone." Shyly she added, "We prayed together."

His smile widened. "I'm glad. Andrea, you won't forget the things we talked about—about God and you believing in Him again?"

"I won't forget. My parents and Katrina—"

"I'll be praying for you. And your grandmother—how is she?"

"Katrina is waiting for me to come back to Index to live. I never wanted to do that, but it's all I can think about now."

"So you're really leaving your job at *Style Magazine?*"

"Yes, but my goals haven't changed—just my attitude about them. I'll keep working on a fashion collection of my own. I have plenty of time, Sherm. Katrina doesn't."

"Don't forget that ski collection for Kippen Investments."

"You're serious, Sherm?"

"It has possibilities. Buzz has numerous projects. He's heavily invested. He might back you. It would be the York Design, but it would have to come under the Kippen Foundation label."

"I'll think about it."

She blushed as he tucked her arm in his.

"Andrea, I've been on the phone all morning trying to contact Pierre Deborde and Robert L. Ebsworth. Pierre is in seclusion, confined to an infirmary in the French Alps."

"Then I must stay over and try and see him."

"No. Some men need to face their grief alone. Respect Pierre for that." She sensed Sherm hesitating before he said, "Ryan's father agreed to see us at two. After that, we'll go out to the airport in plenty of time for your flight."

And after that, she thought, *I'll never see you again.*

"Do I take your silence as approval?"

"Yes. Sherm, you've been so nice. I'll miss your kindness."

"And I'll miss you."

She glanced up, but read only politeness in his expression.

᭺᭺᭺

They found Robert L. Ebsworth's elegant pink town-house in the Latin Quarter of the city, off from the well-traveled boulevards. Ebsworth, a long-legged man with narrow hips and gray unruly hair, led them into a sitting room that smelled of turpentine. His own paintings covered the walls. The place was spartan—four chairs, a partially stocked bar, a cluttered coffee table. Three easels held unfinished works, as though Robert swept from canvas to canvas with his changing moods.

"The bar's open," he said, brushing books off a chair and sitting across from them. "My guests freelance."

"Nothing," Sherm said for both of them.

"Then state your business, and then I can get back to my work. It's about my son you told me on the phone."

"Your son Ryan is dead," Sherm said. "A drowning."

Ebsworth drained his drink, an unnatural luster in his eyes. "The boy was always afraid of water."

"Your son wanted to paint as well as you do," Andrea said.

Bold blue eyes like Ryan's focused on her. "Did he?"

She glanced at the pictures on the wall. "He tried."

"He'd have been twenty-four. Right, Miss York?"

"Almost twenty-five."

"I only remember him as a six year old."

"Do you have any message for his aunt?" Sherm asked.

"Kathryn Culvert? We never had messages for each other."

"We'll go then," Sherm told him, standing.

They had reached the tiled courtyard when Robert plodded barefoot after them, a fresh drink in his hand. "Wait," he called.

They waited hand in hand, facing him.

"Kathryn was a good woman, always talking about God and peace." His words slurred. "She'd make certain my boy'd be okay."

"Ryan had no peace at all, sir," Andrea whispered.

Robert brushed against the tears that coursed over his bony cheeks. He saluted them with his glass.

"Tell Kathryn I'm sorry about my son."

🌀🌀🌀

As they stood in the Charles de Gaulle air terminal, Andrea glanced at her watch again. *Only thirty minutes before takeoff,* she thought. *Thirty minutes before Sherm walks out of my life forever.*

"Are you that anxious to leave me?" he teased.

"No, I just hate saying good-bye to you, Sherm."

"Me, too," he said, taking her hands. "But, Andrea, someone is waiting for you on the other end."

She caught his wistfulness.

"I'm glad your business brought you to Paris while I was here. I needed you. Are you staying on in Paris long?" she asked.

"Without you? No, you were my reason for coming back."

He tipped her chin until her eyes met his dark, intense gaze. "I came back to Paris because I didn't want to lose you. I think I'm in love with you, Andrea, but I need a little time. I want us both to be certain."

"I want that, too," she said as the boarding call sounded.

"Then come to Texas in the springtime, Andrea."

She wavered, twisting her cameo necklace as she faced him.

"Is something wrong with Texas—or with me?"

She shook her head. "No, not with you."

Outside the terminal signs of an early spring were pushing the winter clouds away, but still she said, "Sherm, will it take that long for you to know for certain?"

He grinned. "In the spring the blue bonnets of Texas blanket the hillsides. We'd drive through the countryside. You'd fall in love with Texas and me and never want to leave."

The passenger line moved steadily. "Spring is beautiful in Index, too, Sherm. Come there. Meet my parents and Katrina."

A final boarding call threatened to tear them apart. He leaned down and gave her a gentle, lingering kiss. Warmth invaded her as she responded. He held her against him a second time.

"Until springtime in Index," he told her.

She ran. At the end of the on-ramp, she looked back. He cupped his hands. "I already know for certain," he called. "I love you, Andrea York."

She was exhilarated, flushed, her heart thumping wildly as she blew him a kiss, a kiss that promised, *springtime in Index will surely come early this year.*

Epilogue

Mother's Day. Early spring showers had bathed Index with their freshness. Now melting snows cascaded down in glorious waterfalls, cutting a jagged path over the craggy peaks. At Andrea's home, the screen windows were in and the yard scented with new-mown grass. Crocuses sprouted along the walkway, early roses clung to the trellis, and Wini's fuchsia baskets swayed gently on the front porch.

The security of Index engulfed Andrea. She had slipped into a comfortable routine—jogging early in the morning with Sabrina, fishing on Saturdays on the Skykomish River with her dad, and sharing hours each day with Katrina at the nursing home. She spent most evenings with her parents in the family room and her midnight hours sketching fashion designs and writing to Sherm.

She stood on the porch now, running her fingers over the railing. In the three months since Paris, Sherm's work load had doubled with several trips back to the Kippen offices in Europe and long hours planning expansion programs for the company. It was as though he had called off any serious commitment. He never mentioned coming to Index to visit, never mentioned marriage, never explained why.

Yet his warm, friendly letters from Texas and the Kippen offices abroad always ended, "I love you, Andrea, but I'm giving you time to decide."

To decide what? she wondered. *I already know I love you.*

As the Yorks hurried out the door, her dad asked, "You won't go to church with us, Andrea, not even on Mother's Day?"

"Maybe next Sunday, Dad. I have plans for today."

Will frowned. "You're not going to visit Katrina?"

"Yes. Sabrina is going with me."

As soon as Will rounded the corner, Andrea was in her own car, racing the two blocks to Sabrina's house.

"I'm crazy," Sabrina said as she slipped into the car. "Your parents will have my scalp if anything goes wrong today."

"Nothing will go wrong. It's Katrina's *last* Mother's Day."

"They still won't let her come home to live?" Sabrina asked.

"I'm tired of trying to convince my parents that Katrina needs to be with us, that she's still part of the family."

Sabrina stole a side glance. "You look rested today."

"I'm sleeping better these last few days."

Only Sabrina knew that Andrea's first weeks at home had been nightmarish. Over and over Andrea had dreamed of the glazed, lifeless eyes of the ambassador or of Ryan toppling to his death near the tramway, sockeye salmon swimming away from him. There were other frantic dreams of roses floating on the shallow end of the lake or Sherm running through fields of Texas blue bonnets into Melody's arms.

This morning Andrea had awakened from a pleasant dream of a deer, with tree-branched antlers, running over the craggy cliffs behind her home. She could almost picture it again—pausing and lapping thirstily at a brook. She tried to explain to Sabrina, saying, "Since Paris I've been like the deer in the Psalm that Katrina quotes so often, my soul thirsting for the living God."

Sabrina squirmed. "I feel that way when I'm with Katrina."

The minute they walked into the nursing home, Katrina said, "Andrea, tell me about your visit with Conrad again."

"We're in a hurry this morning, Grandma."

"Tell me anyway," Katrina begged as they stuffed her arms into the sleeves of a pink sweater.

"He's in a quiet, peaceful place, Grandma."

She clapped her hands, mittened by sweater sleeves. "That's just what Conrad likes. He's not alone, is he?" she asked as her fingers popped free.

Andrea's eyes met Sabrina's. "There are hundreds of men there with him, and there's a chapel close by."

As they eased Katrina into the wheelchair, she fretted, "When is it that Conrad's coming to see me? He promised to come back. He asked me to wait for him."

"He knows that you are waiting, Grandmother."

As they reached the warm sunshine, Katrina tugged at Andrea's hand, asking conspiratorially, "Am I escaping?"

"For a few hours. Then you'll have to come back here."

"I have to come back? Have you asked Will?"

"I'll ask him again, Grandma. I promise."

Katrina dozed, her pink silk hat dipping precariously, while they rode through the backwoods to the whitewashed church Andrea and Sabrina had attended as children. The congregation sang as Andrea pushed the wheelchair down the center aisle to the pew where her parents sat. The familiar words caught in her own throat, nudging her gently—a song of praise and submission. Her own plans and ambitions had been swept away, toppled temporarily for Katrina. But in doing it for Katrina, she had done it for the Shepherd as well.

Will York's eyes misted when he saw his mother. He slid to the aisle seat beside her and held her hand. Wini reached over and squeezed Katrina's arm, her own expression a mixture of anger and embarrassment.

Katrina's friends mobbed her after the service, the choir director saying, "Winifred, what a pleasant surprise. Why didn't you tell us Katrina was coming?"

"It was a surprise for all of us," Wini said, her eyes meeting Andrea's. "Are you and Sabrina coming home for lunch?"

"Mother, we're spending the day with Katrina. We want you and Dad to join us. I made reservations for—"

"Not this time, dear." Wini's control was flawless, her smile obscured except for a flick of warmth toward Sabrina.

282 DORIS ELAINE FELL

She nodded at Andrea and then placed her cheek briefly against Katrina's. "It was good to see you this morning, Mother York," she said. "Happy Mother's Day."

She linked arms with her husband. Will's steps were labored as they walked away from his mother.

"We survived that one," Sabrina said. "I have my scalp and I'm hungry. Let's head for the Country Inn."

As they pushed Katrina into the crowded restaurant, her eyes sparkled with recognition. "Is Conrad meeting us here, dear," she asked as they settled at their table.

"No. He's waiting for you, but not here at the Inn."

"Is he waiting in Heaven?" Katrina asked softly.

"Yes, Grandmother. It won't be long until you see him."

Katrina smiled as Andrea patiently tried to feed her. Finally, she pushed the spoon away, her smile radiant.

"I'm not afraid, Andrea. You know that, don't you?"

"I know. But I am. I'm afraid of losing you."

The gnarled, vein-riddled hand rested on Andrea. "Dear child," Katrina said, "Don't hold me back. I have such a wonderful journey ahead." Her grandmother's hand was shaking now, but her eyes were bright and alert, beyond confusion. "Jesus loves you, child."

Andrea nodded, tears streaming down her face in tiny rivulets. "I love you Grandma."

"Not half as much as Jesus loves you. You know that, don't you?"

Sabrina sniffed and turned away. Andrea didn't care. She leaned closer to her grandmother. "I prayed by your bedside the other day."

The mist cloud of memory veiled Katrina's eyes again. "When you were a little girl?"

"Then, yes. But again the other day at Bethann Nursing Home. In your room. You prayed with me."

Katrina was gazing far off now, closer to Conrad than she had ever been. But it didn't matter. Andrea was at peace, remembering her prayer of repentance, her simple commitment to the Shepherd. Jesus had come alive for her again.

When Andrea reached home, Winifred was sitting by the kitchen window close to her potted violets.

"I called the nursing home, Andrea. Katrina is exhausted."

"She had a good time. I made reservations for you and Dad, too. It was my Mother's Day surprise."

Wini's brows puckered. "I wanted us to have dinner at the nursing home with Katrina. I had gifts and flowers for her."

"You never said."

"Nor did you, Andrea."

"I thought you didn't like her anymore."

"Andrea, Katrina hand-picked me for Will, mothered me all these years. Made me laugh and feel welcome. Doted on you, my child. How could I help but love her?"

An uneven stream of tears made their way down Wini's cheeks. "We're both so stubborn. Tell me, Andrea dear, when was it that we allowed Katrina to come between us?"

"I didn't mean for that to happen, Mother."

Winifred's long graceful fingers tapped anxiously on the windowsill. "If Katrina lives until her birthday next week, we'll celebrate by bringing her home again."

"You're bartering," Andrea warned.

"For something we both want—to be a family again."

"But you said—"

"I know what I said. I was only fooling myself that we couldn't take care of her. I realized at church this morning that you and your father need her here, but it won't be for long."

"Katrina doesn't have long, Mother."

"We know where she's going to be, don't we?"

Andrea met her mother's direct gaze. "Katrina spoke of Heaven at the restaurant. She's sick and confused, but not inside. She's clear as a bell there."

Wini bit her lower lip. "Oh, Andrea, I can't bear to think of Heaven without you there. Your father and I have prayed for so long . . ."

Andrea stumbled over her words. "It's okay, Mom. I will be there. The other day at the nursing home, Katrina kept telling me to just let the Shepherd be my Savior, to just take His hand, to trust Him. And I did, Mom. The other day."

Joy spread over her mother's face. "No wonder you're so much more at peace. Oh, Andrea, we've got to tell your father. He'll be home soon. He'll be so happy—"

"Mom, I'm at peace except for Sherm. Maybe he can't forget Melody."

Wini touched the petal of one of her delicate African violets. "She'll always be part of his life, but he can still love someone else. Why don't you call Sherm? Ask him what his intentions are."

"MOTHER! I can't do that."

"Why not?" A smile played at the corners of Wini's mouth. "That's what Katrina and I did."

"You? And my grandmother? You never told me that."

"The subject never came up."

"It's true. Believe me," Will York said from the doorway.

❀❀❀

For the first ten days, Katrina seemed stronger in her familiar surroundings—Conrad's picture beside her, the cameo necklace around her neck. Her canopy bed and rocker filled the family room—both positioned so she could see the mountains.

Will sat in his leather chair, peering at her over the top of his newspaper as she rested against her pillows. He winked. She smiled back, lacing her fingers with Andrea's. Illness had weakened Katrina, but her gaze strayed from her son's face to Andrea's as a car door slammed and footsteps pounded across the front porch.

"Right on time," Will said, glancing at his shiny old-fashioned Elgin. His eyes twinkled as the door chime rang.

"I'll get it," Wini called. Then, her voice full of laughter, she announced, "Andrea, it's for you."

Sherm stood in the entryway beside Wini, grinning.

Andrea struggled from the rocker, toppling her sketch pad to the floor. "Sherm, you didn't answer my last letter."

"The one with your good news about the Shepherd—the

news I've been waiting for? Your mother called and invited me to come in person instead."

"*She didn't!*"

"*She did!*"

His deep, rich voice rippled with laughter. "She asked me what my intentions were. I told her I intended to marry you."

He opened his arms wide and waited, his left hand ring-less. Andrea started toward him, running. He met her halfway and swept her off her feet.

"I love you, Andrea."

"I think I loved you in Paris when I first saw you."

"I think I knew back in the Fireside Room at the Harrison," he said quietly.

"Why didn't you let me know you were coming?"

"Your parents knew. We agreed to surprise you. Kippen Investments just transferred me to Bellingham."

"Bellingham? That's just north of here. Not Europe?"

He glanced at Katrina. "Switzerland in a year perhaps."

"Does Melody's dad know about us?"

"That's why he asked me to open the Northwest office. Buzz is a practical man, Andrea. I have his blessing, but he thought my leaving Texas would be best for both of us."

"Sherm, I could have met you at the airport."

"I have my car. I made a couple of stops en route. The Wayside Chapel for one," he teased. "It's small, but I like it. And then I stopped and rented a room at the Bush House."

"But you can stay with us. Can't he, Mother?"

"Andrea, I rented the end room, number 7, for next week-end." His eyes radiated merriment. "Actually, I rented all the rooms on the second floor for privacy. Number 7 has a quaint four-poster bed just like you said."

"Sherm, that's the room my grandparents rented more than fifty years ago."

"Yes, I remembered." He tilted her chin up. "I love you, Andrea York. I want to marry you."

His lips found hers, gently at first, then impassioned, inti-mate; hers yielding, tender.

When he released her, they walked to Katrina's bedside.

"I thought you were Conrad," Katrina said, wistfully.

"No, I'm Sherm, Sherm Prescott. But I know about Conrad."

"Do you?" She cupped Sherm's hand in her vein-riddled ones. "You're tall like he was."

She closed her eyes as though the words had exhausted her. "Why have you come?" she asked, opening them again.

"I've come to take you to a wedding. I want to marry your granddaughter. I'll carry you into the chapel and carry Andrea out. Would that be all right, Katrina?"

A single tear fell. "Will you take her away then?"

"No, as long as you need us, we'll both be here." He glanced at Will and Wini. "We'll all be here for you."

Katrina's lips moved, but they couldn't hear her words.

"Grandmother, what did you say?" Andrea asked.

Her words were audible this time. "Where will you honeymoon?"

Sherm bent down and brushed her ear with a whisper. A distinct chuckle escaped Katrina's lips, her sapphire eyes sparkling. "The Bush House? Room 7?" she repeated. "That's where Conrad and I went. It's a lovely, old-fashioned place to honeymoon."

16
17